SAVED IN THE CITY

JACQUELIN THOMAS

SAVED IN THE CITY

BET Publications, LLC
http://www.bet.com

NEW SPIRIT BOOKS are published by

BET Publications, LLC
c/o BET BOOKS
One BET Plaza
1900 W Place NE
Washington, DC 20018-1211

All Kensington Titles, Imprints, and Distributed Lines are available at special quantity discounts for bulk purchases for sales promotions, premiums, fund-raising, and educational or institutional use. Special book excerpts or customized printings can also be created to fit specific needs. For details, write or phone the office of the Kensington Special Sales Manager: Attn: Special Sales Department, Kensington Publishing Corp., 850 Third Avenue, New York, NY 10022, Phone: 1-800-221-2647.

Library of Congress Card Catalogue Number: 2004110647
ISBN: 1-58314-444-7

First Printing: May 2005
10 9 8 7 6 5 4 3 2 1

Printed in the United States of America

This book is dedicated to my daughters Bevin & Lauren:
May you continue to forge ahead toward your dreams
without fear or regret.
Live your life as it was meant to be lived—
filled with love, laughter, joy
and the freedom to become whomever you choose.
We all strive for perfect peace and happiness—
I found mine in you.

ACKNOWLEDGMENTS

Bernard
It goes without saying how much I love you. Thank you as always for your never-ending support, your love and your friendship.

My darling son
Like your sisters, you are some of my best work ever! I love you more than you'll ever know and I thank God for bringing you into my life. Never give up on your dreams.

Maxine Billings
I'm so very proud of you and all you've accomplished. Thank you for being not only family, but for being a friend as well. You are so special to me and I love you dearly.

Lisa Nelson
You were one of my biggest supporters from the beginning. Thanks so much, cousin. I love you and I promise to be better about keeping in touch.

Janet and Linda Saxon
I am convinced God brought you two into my life for a reason, and I'm so thankful to have such dear and wonderful friends. You will always have a special place in my heart.

There are no words to fully express my gratitude, but I would like to give thanks for the many book clubs across the country and for the readers who never fail to run out and purchase my books—you are all blessings to me. Writing has been a lifelong dream of mine and I'm thrilled to be living that dream, but the letters and wonderful words of encouragement that I've received from all of you—I cherish the most.

Chapter 1

Macy

As Macy Baldwin strolled through the stunning marble and mirrored lobby of the Le Galleria Luxury Apartments in Murray Hill, waving at the concierge as she sashayed toward the elevators, her shoes made a soft clicking sound.

She pressed the "up" button with a fuchsia-colored fingernail. She tapped her right foot impatiently against the Italian marble floors while waiting for the elevator to arrive. Out of the corner of her eye, Macy noticed the way one of the women standing nearby was staring at her Darius Cordell gown and whispering to her companion.

Most women would've been uncomfortable wearing the strapless black dress and matching tulle wrap at eight o'clock in the morning, but not Macy. It didn't bother her that her clothing announced to the world she'd spent the night someplace other than her own home.

With a subtle lifting of her chin, Macy gave the woman a haughty look. She was a grown woman and didn't have to answer to anyone. Nor did she give a flip what the woman thought.

The elevator arrived, bringing with it a sigh of gratitude from Macy.

She was the first one on and the first one off when the doors opened on the eighth floor.

Macy was tired, having spent most of the night in the arms of

William Michaels, a popular actor—only to have him run out on her as soon as she hopped into the shower. He'd come to New York to promote his latest movie on a couple of talk shows. Macy and William had been involved in an on-and-off-again long-distance relationship for the past year or so.

She had hopes that he would finally get around to proposing. Instead, this morning he'd broken up with her—only he didn't have the guts to do it himself. The jerk had sent his agent to do it.

Just thinking about William's rude treatment of her made Macy grow hot with anger. It wasn't like she was really in love with him or anything. Her ego was bruised. She would've preferred being the one to do the dumping, instead of the one being dumped.

Who did he think he was? It's not like he was a good actor anyway, Macy fumed in silence. He'd only gotten the part in the first place as a special favor from her godfather, one of Hollywood's more successful African American directors.

While thinking of ways to ruin William's budding career, Macy fumbled through her purse to find her keys as she strolled down the hall to her apartment.

She smiled at her neighbor, Austin, as she passed him in the hall.

"Good morning, girlfriend," he greeted. "Looks like you had a wonderful time last night."

"I did. This morning was different, though. The great William Michaels turned out to be a jerk." Macy didn't care that only a few days ago, she'd been singing William's praises to Austin in this very same hallway.

Austin frowned and huffed, "Men. You can't live with 'em and you can't live without 'em." Straightening his jacket, he said, "Well, sorry to hear that you and William are over—he sure is gorgeous."

"A gorgeous jerk," Macy mumbled as she unlocked her front door and stepped into her apartment. The last thing she expected to hear was an angry baritone voice asking, "Where have you been, young lady?"

Startled, Macy jumped and whirled around at the sound of her father's voice. She laid her purse down on the sofa table and placed a shaky hand to her chest to calm her rapidly beating heart. "You nearly scared the life out of me. What are you doing here?"

Macy regretted giving her parents a key to her apartment.

Then, Macy glanced around, fully expecting to find her mother. She wasn't disappointed.

Rhetta Larson-Baldwin walked out of Macy's bedroom.

"What were you doing in my room?"

Her mother didn't respond. Instead, she moved to stand beside her husband, wearing a judgmental furrow above her brow, her face as pale as the cream-colored Chanel suit she wore.

They were united, and their unity meant bad news for Macy. She was sure of it.

"Your mother and I want to talk to you." Maynard Baldwin's eyes scanned Macy's clothing with disdain.

"I spent the night with a friend," she stammered while pulling at the wrap. He was still an intimidating force in her life. Macy stood a few feet away from him, her face pale but proud.

"I gathered as much," he responded in a dry tone.

Inside Macy was bristling. *He's got some nerve. I'm grown. I can do whatever I want to do*, she wanted to say. She moved out of her parents' house two years ago and had since been living on her own.

"Father . . ." Macy began.

Maynard held up his hand as if to say he didn't want to hear whatever lie she'd managed to come up with.

"Why didn't you pack an overnight bag or something?" Rhetta inquired. "I would think that you'd prefer not to give your neighbors anything to gossip about. You really should be more discreet, dear."

"I don't worry about my neighbors, Mother," Macy shot back. "I'm not like you. I don't care what other people think. Besides, they're just jealous."

Her father glared at her, his mouth taking on an unpleasant twist. "When did you intend to tell us that you weren't graduating next week?"

"We've been telling everyone that you were graduating, Macy," Rhetta interjected. "What am I going to tell everyone now?"

"You don't have to tell them anything—it's not their business what I'm doing. But if you want to tell your friends something, just tell them I'm taking a few more classes."

Maynard uttered, "Macy, you can't stay in college forever."

"I'm not trying to," she countered. "Professor Greenley refused to let me take my final exam and then failed me. It's not my fault." Macy was unable to meet his gaze.

This time it was her mother interrogating her. "Why couldn't you take the exam?"

"I was five minutes late for class and he wouldn't let me in. I'd overslept because I'd been up all night studying for the test," Macy lied. Her mind was working overtime to appease her father.

Her father's expression indicated that he clearly didn't believe her.

Wispy bangs fell across her forehead. Frustrated, Macy pushed them out of the way. "I was only five minutes late. *It's the truth.*"

Like her parents, Macy knew that when she proclaimed something to be the truth, she was definitely lying.

"So, what happened with your other classes?" Maynard questioned. "Why are you failing them?"

It was becoming increasingly clear that her father wasn't going to let up on her. "My professors hate me," Macy whined. "Can't you see that? It's a conspiracy—they are just looking for reasons to fail me. They don't like the fact that I come from money. They have the mentality that we are trying to be like white people. They say that about anyone who refuses to walk around wearing African clothing, big Afros, and speaking Ebonics, especially Professor Mankuma. I've told you how he treats me."

"Surely you don't believe that, Macy." Rhetta asked. Shaking her head, she added, "I can't believe this is the best excuse you could come up with. When are you going to take responsibility for your actions?"

Pointedly ignoring her mother, Macy said, "Father, I've decided that maybe I should change my major. I really don't like African American studies. I was thinking that maybe I could switch to fashion design. You know how much I like—"

"What good would it do?" Maynard interjected. "Let's be honest here. Macy, the truth is that you have no interest in anything outside of shopping."

She gave her father a wounded look, her eyes filling with tears.

"I am very disappointed in you," Maynard began. "Your mother and I have paid good money to put you through the last five years of college, Macy. You've done nothing but mess around—most people would love to have the advantages you've been awarded."

"Father . . ."

His mouth dipped into an even deeper frown. "*I'm talking.*"

Macy was silenced by the tone of Maynard's voice and his dark, angry expression. She looked to her mother for help, but Rhetta just dropped her gaze. Her mother would not go against her husband. That was usually the case, Macy acknowledged and sighed in resignation.

Macy reluctantly returned her gaze to her father. She hated the stern expression he wore on his face. This time she was in hot water with him. She watched him as he took a seat on the leather sofa.

In a show of solidarity, Rhetta moved to join her husband. Maynard gestured for Macy to take a seat as well.

In her own apartment, she'd allowed herself to be reduced to a child again. Macy sat down on the club chair, waiting. For what, she wasn't sure. She just knew she wasn't going to like it.

Her father seemed to be searching for the right words. After a moment, he took Rhetta's hand and said, "Your mother and I have made a decision. First of all, I want you to know that this wasn't easy for us, but we have to do what we think is best."

Macy didn't like the vibe she was getting from her parents. She knew instinctively that what they were about to say was going to upset her. Her hands trembling, she pulled the folds of her wrap together to cover her cleavage out of respect for her parents.

"We've decided to make some changes," he said.

In a defensive gesture, Macy folded her arms across her chest as a wave of dread spread over her body. "What type of changes?"

"We're no longer going to support you, Macy."

It took her a moment to really comprehend what he was telling her. Surely he didn't mean it. He couldn't mean he was taking away her funds. Macy could endure almost anything but that. She unconsciously twisted her slender hands together.

"Father, just let me drop out of college. I really don't know what I want to do anyway. Maybe I can just take a year off and then go back."

Stroking his chin, Maynard regarded his daughter carefully. "I'm in agreement with you leaving college. You're not doing anything there but wasting time and money. Your mother and I give up."

His next words shocked her to the core. "You're going to have to get a job, Macy."

Patterson

"Start spreadin' . . . the news. . . . I'm leaving today. . . ." Patterson Haney sang under her breath as she stepped out of the black Lincoln Continental that was her father's pride and joy.

"Wait, chile. . . . I got sumpthin' fer you."

The sound of her mother's trembling voice made Patterson fall back into the car. "Mama, you doan have to give me nothing," she began. "I have my savings to get me by until I find a job in New York."

Her mother's bottom lip quivered and her eyes were wet from unshed tears—true testaments that she was having a hard time with Patterson's leaving.

Patterson made one last attempt to reassure her mother. "I'ma be fine, Mama. *I will.* You doan have to worry."

Pushing a fat envelope into Patterson's empty hand, Lema insisted, "Now I wont you to put this away for a rainy day. The church took up a couple of collections fer you. I got you one of those MasterCards, too. Just remember that every time you use it, you spending money you doan have, so only use it for emergencies. If you do use it, then try to pay your bill at the end of every month. Doan do those installment payments—theys the ones that git you in trouble. Your credit and your reputation, that's all you have in this world, Patterson. Now listen to me 'cause I'm not gon' lead you astray. My folks, they didn't tell me none of this stuff when I was growing up. I had to learn the hard way. I wont to make it a li'l bit easier on you."

Patterson leaned forward to plant a kiss on her mother's cheek before murmuring, "Thank you, Mama. I really appreciate this."

"You my baby girl. I doan wont nuthin' to happen to you in that crazy city. I heard all about the way people carry on in New York. I'm just praying that the Lawd will keep his angels standing guard over you." Lema blinked rapidly, then looked away.

Patterson placed a hand gently on her mother's shoulder, "I love you, Mama. I'ma miss you so much." Tears choked her voice. She had hoped they could make it through the farewells without shedding tears.

Lema grasped at the hand on her shoulder, holding on tightly. "Patterson, you doan have to go. You could stay right heh in Three Oak and work at the Wal-Mart like you been doin', or you could get a job in Atlanta and just drive back and forth."

"But Mama, I really wont to do this. It's been a dream of mine forever. Ever since I was little, I've wontned to be a model and live in New York. It's all I ever talked about." Patterson stole a peek at her watch before looking out the window for her father. It was ten after seven. Her train would be leaving at eight o'clock in the evening.

"Gwine let the girl go, Lema," Zeke Haney implored from outside the car. "There ain't nothin' heh in Three Oak for Patterson. We always said we wonted better fer our daughter. Well, this heh's her big chance. We sent her to that fancy college in Buckhead just so she could learn modeling."

"I know," Lema admitted. "But it doan make it any easier on me. It kills me to think of my baby all alone in New York. Patterson, there's no denying that you easy on the eyes. It's true, you a pretty girl and some people will try to take advannage. Look at all those girls who end up naked and on the computer."

"Mama, I'ma be just fine," Patterson assured her. "Emerald Model Management is one of the top modeling agencies in the world. Besides, God is always with me, so I'm never alone. That's what you always tell me."

Lema nodded, her lips turning upward into a sad smile.

"It's time fer you to go inside, Patterson Lynne," her father announced. "We don't wont you to miss that train."

This time when Patterson got out, she and her father stood for a moment just staring at each other before a last embrace. "I love you, Daddy," Patterson whispered. She breathed deeply, inhaling the spicy scent of the Stetson cologne her father was so fond of wearing.

Staring down lovingly at his daughter, Zeke replied, "I love you too, honey. Now you gwine have a good life in New York. I feel it in my spirit."

He bent his tall slender frame to pick up her suitcase. Patterson followed him into the station.

Half an hour later, Patterson was seated in the car behind the one designated as the café. She exhaled a long sigh of contentment when the train started sluggishly along the track before breaking into full speed. Then she placed her headphones over her ears and settled back against the seats with her eyes closed and crossed her legs.

Listening to jazz would help pass the time during her eighteen-hour journey.

Six hours later, they pulled into a small town in North Carolina. Having sat for so long, Patterson needed to get up and stretch once the train stopped. She went to the bathroom to freshen up and stopped to peruse the menu in the dining car before returning to her seat.

Patterson was grateful that she didn't have to sit with another passenger. She didn't feel much like making small talk—she wanted to spend time reveling in the prospect of her new life.

"Thank you, Jesus," she murmured. "Heavenly Father, I just thank you so much for getting me out of Three Oak. I thank you for allowing me to live out my dream as a model. I am truly blessed."

She exhaled a long sigh of contentment.

Patterson used to stare at the models in fashion magazines for hours. She would fantasize about the day her face would grace one of the covers. She loved clothes, shoes, and make-up.

Most of her teenage years were spent dreaming of posing for print ads and magazines, traveling to exotic locations for photo shoots, and strutting down runways in New York, Paris, and Milan during Fashion Week. Patterson closed her eyes, caught up in the fantasy of being a top supermodel.

LaRue

Since the death of her husband, LaRue Arnette-Hawkins had no words for God.

Until now.

"Dear Lord, I ask that you grant me a safe journey to New York. . . ." she prayed as the plane rolled along the tarmac, preparing for take-off. A sensation of nausea swept through her, forcing LaRue to place a trembling hand to her stomach. Since the 9-11 attacks, she wasn't comfortable with flying.

After her prayer, she settled back in her seat to read the *Vogue* magazine she'd purchased at one of the many newsstands located throughout the Los Angeles airport.

As the airplane soared toward the heavens, LaRue released a soft sigh of relief. She was on her way to the Big Apple to try for a chance at a modeling career. Becoming a professional model had not really been a dream of LaRue's, but it was a way to leave the streets of Compton behind, along with her unfulfilling job as a social worker.

Los Angeles held a lot of happy memories for LaRue, but there were some sad ones, too. Losing her husband not even a year ago, then her best friend, Janine, just one month ago, she was ready to start over.

Before her husband died, they'd talked about moving to the Big Apple. Now that he was gone, LaRue decided to keep that dream alive.

Because of LaRue's six-foot-two-inch height, her sense of fashion and her strong Afrocentric features, everyone often mistook her for a model. Although her parents were against her modeling, she wanted to give it a shot. What could it hurt?

It wasn't until she saw the information on Emerald Model Management's Web site that LaRue decided to audition. Her parents were so upset over her decision to move to New York that they refused to see her off this morning.

"Been to New York before?" the woman sitting beside her asked, cutting into her thoughts.

LaRue gave a forced smile and a tense nod of consent. "Yeah. A couple of times in the past, but it's been a couple of years since my last visit." She failed to mention that the last time she was there, she was on her honeymoon.

"I love New York," the woman continued. "I plan on living there. Just have to find a job first."

"Do you have any interviews lined up?"

She nodded. "I have one scheduled for tomorrow morning. What about you?"

"I'm strongly considering it," LaRue answered. "Like you, it'll depend on my getting a job."

"You really should try your hand at modeling," the woman suggested. "You look like one."

LaRue gave the woman a slight smile. Her comment was the confirmation she needed. "Thank you for saying that."

"I'm serious. You'd make a beautiful model."

"Good luck with your job interview." She turned her attention to the flight attendant who was about to give them an overview of emergency procedures.

LaRue listened to the instructions on how to inflate the life vests. She pushed an irritating long braid away from her face. The microbraids weighed heavily on her neck, making her wish she'd just pulled her hair into a ponytail.

Chapter 2

Macy

"You're going to have to get a job. . . ."

Macy couldn't believe that she'd heard correctly. "*Excuse me?*"

"You heard me, Macy," Maynard stated flatly. "I'm not going to give you a penny more. From this point on, you will have to be responsible for your own finances."

Macy began pleading with her mother, saying, "You can't let him do this to me. Mother . . . how am I supposed to live?"

Rhetta smiled benignly, as if dealing with a temperamental child. "Your father is right, dear. We've carried you much too long. You're almost twenty-five years old, yet you still act like a spoiled child. As painful as this is, this is the best scenario for you."

"You're my parents," Macy whined. "You're *supposed* to help me."

Maynard shook his head no. "We're supposed to teach you to be self-sufficient—this is where we failed you." He held out his hands, offering an apology.

Tears gathered in Macy's eyes. "No. You can't do this to me."

"Yes, we can," her father countered. "Macy, this is not our way of punishing you. We're simply trying to help you become the woman we know you can be."

"You *are* punishing me," she snapped. Shaking her head in dismay, Macy stood up and paced the floor. She paused to look up at the huge portrait of herself hanging above the fireplace.

Turning around, she asked, "What exactly am I supposed to do? I can't lose my apartment. . . ."

"You will have to get a job," Rhetta gently reminded her.

"I've never held down a job before. Who's going to hire me?"

A thought entered her mind, prompting Macy to turn to her father and say, "You can make me a vice president at Baldwin Pharmaceuticals."

Maynard dashed her hopes with a firm shake of his head. "You're not qualified to handle a position like that. The best I can do is give you a position as a receptionist."

"You've got to be kidding!" How could he insult her like this? She was too good to be a receptionist—even for her own father's company. She could hear her friends now. They would find this hysterical.

"It's a job, Macy."

"It won't pay for this place."

"Then find another apartment—one you can afford." Maynard glanced around. "I never really cared for this place anyway."

"Father . . . don't do this to me. Please don't be this way," Macy begged. She loved her apartment—her lifestyle. . . . She wasn't willing to give up any part of it.

"I'm so sorry, precious," her mother stated. "We made a big mistake spoiling you. We shouldn't have given you so much."

Macy felt as if she were going to faint and sat down, leaning back against the cushions of the leather club chair for support. She sat like that for a moment with her eyes closed, trying to digest all her parents had said. "I don't believe this. A lot of people drop out of college and their parents don't treat them like this. You might as well just disown me."

"You're overreacting, dear."

Macy's brows drew together in an agonized expression. She repeated over and over, "I don't believe this." Her throat tightened, her chest constricted, and she could hardly breathe. The palms of her hands felt damp. Macy closed her eyes once more to ward off the dizziness she was experiencing.

"Honey, the person you are—it's because of us. . . ." Rhetta tried to explain.

"Then why are you punishing me like this?" Macy questioned. "You've already admitted that this is your fault. It's too late to try to change things now."

"It's never too late, Macy."

Opening her eyes she glared at her father. "*You hate me.*"

"No, I don't, sweetheart. It's because I love you so much that I'm doing this. If you won't help yourself stay afloat, then I'm going to have to let you sink. It's my prayer that you'll find your way."

Macy knew the situation was futile. Her parents would never change their minds, but maybe they could reach a compromise of some sort. "I'm not going to be able to pay for anything right away. Will you at least give me six months to find a job?"

Her father shook his head.

"What about three months?"

"I can't do that, Macy. You're going to have to figure this out on your own."

She refused to resign herself to the fact that she would not be getting her way this time. Macy stated, "I am going to need money for next month's rent at least. It's due in three weeks."

"Then I suggest you start praying, Macy."

Here he goes with his "prayer works" speech, she thought silently. Macy hated when her father got on his religious high horse. At this point, she turned a deaf ear to his lecture. If God wasn't going to get her out of this mess, then Macy wasn't interested.

Macy removed her Jimmy Choo satin shoes when her parents left, leaving them lying on the living room floor while she went into her bedroom and undressed.

She padded naked into the bathroom and climbed into the shower. While the soapy water calmed her nerves, Macy's mind was busy trying to come up with a way to change her father's mind.

The last thing she wanted to do was get a job.

All I've ever wanted to do is design clothes, she thought. *If I can't do that, then modeling is my only other option.*

Running her fingers through store-bought, honey-colored hair that nearly reached her waist, Macy admired herself in the mirror. Her smooth skin had a tawny tint to it and was the perfect accent to her warm almond-shaped hazel eyes, thanks to the contact lenses she wore. Although slender, she'd been blessed with a curvaceous body and kept it toned and firmed with daily exercise. Her personal trainer, Emma, came three days a week to give Macy a thorough work-out.

"If I can make it as a famous supermodel, my parents will have a change of heart. Then they'll be willing to give me anything I want," she whispered aloud. "This will all work out."

The telephone rang.

"Hello."

"I miss you." Her caller's voice sent a delicious tremor down her spine.

She'd forgotten Frederick was coming into town this week. The handsome heir to the African American Cable Channel dynasty would definitely take her mind off her problems.

"I miss you, too," Macy responded back. She liked him, but loved the fact that he came with a huge inheritance.

"What's wrong? You don't sound like yourself."

"My parents were here when I arrived. They're upset about my not graduating this year. I told them I want to drop out because I'm sick of school. Things would be different if I could study fashion design. That's all I'm really interested in."

"I'm sure they didn't take the news too well."

"Not at all. In fact, they've practically disowned me. Frederick, my mother looked like she was about to faint. Boy, she is such a drama queen."

He chuckled.

"What's so funny?"

"You are. The queen of drama . . ."

Frederick had a way of seeing right through her. That was the one quality she didn't like about him. "Anyway, I don't want to talk about this anymore. I need to have some fun. Why don't you meet me in about an hour? I want to get out of the apartment for a while."

"I was kind of hoping that we could stay in," Frederick hinted. "I'm sure we could find something to take your mind off your problems. It'll relax you. . . ."

Macy's mouth turned downward. "I don't want to stay home today. Let's go to Connecticut or something. I need to get out of the city for a while."

It took more cajoling on Macy's part to get Frederick to finally relent. She hung up the phone and strolled into her walk-in closet, looking for something to wear. She wanted to look her best for Frederick, because she was counting on his generosity.

Patterson

The train arrived in New York at two o'clock the following afternoon.

Mesmerized, Patterson stepped outside of the building that housed the New York-Penn Station in the heart of Manhattan. She weaved in and out of the swift flood of human bodies on a journey to parts unknown. People were everywhere—more people than she'd seen in her entire town of Three Oak. Patterson wondered if anyone worked on Friday, as there were so many people strolling about. She stretched her slender neck to stare upward at the monstrous buildings, her honey-colored skin prickling in excitement.

This broader picture encompassed so much more than the one-dimensional scenes on the postcards Patterson had received from a cousin who'd visited the Big Apple a few years back.

The vibrant pictures were of the towering Chrysler and Empire State buildings, museums, theaters, and a vivid panorama of skyscrapers. Gone now were the twin towers of the World Trade Center that loomed gloriously toward the heavens before that fateful day of September 11. Patterson regretted not being able to view the majestic works of art in person, but they were forever memorialized in the postcards she carried.

Included in the intriguing collage of postcards were photos of Niagara Falls, the Statue of Liberty, and Central Park—all tantalizing images that made New York so appetizing and such a hotbed for tourism. Along with the postcards, Patterson had held on to the "I Love New York" bumper sticker her cousin sent her, the one with the red heart in the place of the word *love*.

She'd kept the life-changing mementos in the bottom of her jewelry box and even now carried them in her purse, because it had always been her dream to live in New York.

"Wow," Patterson exclaimed with intense pleasure, her eyes bouncing everywhere, attempting to take in everything, including the man selling hot dogs on the corner.

Being bumped on the arm by someone brushing past her in a rush caused Patterson to tighten the hold on her purse. She'd heard about all the mugging that went on in big cities such as New York and Chicago.

She wasn't really worried, though. She had forty dollars in twenties, two five-dollar bills and ten ones in a zippered compartment inside her purse. Patterson had hidden five one-hundred-dollar bills in her bra, and the rest of her money, in traveler's checks, was tucked safely away in the money belt around her waist.

Patterson watched a man standing nearby hail a taxi, and she imitated his actions. The bright yellow automobile breezed to a quick stop, but before she could wheel her suitcase toward the car, someone rushed past her and jumped inside.

The cab sped off.

"Hey!" Patterson couldn't believe what had just happened. Jutting her chin out, with her fingers curled into a fist, she hailed another cab.

She warded off another attempt with her suitcase as she strode briskly to the car. "Don't even try it! This cab is mine!" she yelled. This time the person backed off.

Patterson quickly climbed inside. "I need to go to 850 West End Avenue." She felt a small measure of pride in snaring this taxi. She was quickly becoming a New Yorker.

Looking out of the window from the back seat, Patterson continued to absorb every inch of her surroundings, sucking up the astounding views of impressive tall structures. Words like *biggest, best,* and *enormous* came to mind as she eyed the architectural masterpieces. The bustling crowds, the shopping, and the hurried pace of life in the Big Apple all drew Patterson like a magnet.

Her eyes landed on a couple of teens walking down Thirty-third Street and wearing spiked hair in shades of red and blue—and leather that looked like it was held together by safety pins.

"Well, I'll be . . ." Patterson muttered in bewilderment. *Even the people look different,* she thought. She'd never seen anyone dressed like that back in Three Oak. Searching her memory, Patterson couldn't recall seeing anything like that in Atlanta either. She'd attended Bauder College and had lived on campus. Beyond the two years at school, Patterson hadn't spent much time outside her small town. She liked Atlanta a lot, but her heart belonged to New York.

Patterson returned her attention to the scenery outside the confines of the taxi.

When the driver pulled into the entrance of the hotel, she paid him, then jumped out of the car, dragging her luggage with her.

"Let me carry this for you," a young man standing nearby offered.

"No, thank you," Patterson responded all the while giving him a quick once-over. He didn't look as if he worked at the West End Studios Hotel. "I got it. I'm fine."

She stood a solid five feet eleven inches and weighed one hundred twenty pounds. Patterson was slender but she was used to lifting loads up to seventy pounds. She often helped her father with chores around their farm, and she could even chop wood better than her two male cousins who lived on the neighboring farm.

Walking briskly, Patterson made her way to the registration desk. Smiling, she announced, "I'd like to check in, please."

"What is your name?"

"It's Patterson Haney." Her voice, tinged with a deep Southern accent, sounded out of place, even to her. She cleared her throat softly.

Ten minutes later, Patterson was all checked in and walking toward the elevators. Her room was on the second floor.

Inside, Patterson parked her suitcase near the closet, took off her shoes, and danced a tiny jig.

"I wont to be a part of it . . . New York, New York," she sang.

Giddy with happiness, Patterson plopped down on the king-sized bed after her soulful rendition of "New York, New York." Back home, her room had been too small for a bed this size. So, when she decided to come to New York, she determined never to sleep in another twin bed.

"So this is what a European hotel looks like," Patterson murmured softly. Her room was complete with cable TV, maid service, and air conditioning—everything except a private bathroom. She'd gotten a discounted rate of fifty-nine dollars per night on the Internet, so Patterson wasn't about to complain. She felt blissfully happy, fully alive, and wrapped in a silken cocoon of euphoria.

Staring heavenward, Patterson began to pray. "Heavenly Father, I just wont to take this time to say thank you. Thank you for your love and for all the blessings bestowed upon me. Thank you for allowing me to reach my destination safely and just for this opportunity. You are so loving and so wonderful, dear Lord." Her eyes filled with unshed tears. "Thank you so much fer your mercy. I love you so much. . . .

Oh, Father God, I just love you." Patterson paused for a moment before adding, "I wont to honor you, heavenly Father. Guide me and give me wisdom as I take this journey. This request I ask of you in Jesus' name. Amen."

After her prayer, Patterson felt a bottomless peace and satisfaction. Before she did anything else, she picked up the telephone to call her parents. They would become worried if they didn't hear from her soon.

"Hey Mama. It's me. I wontned to let y'all know that I made it to New York okay. I'm heh in my hotel. Mama, it's great."

"I'm glad to hear that, baby."

"Mama . . . I wont to ask you something. You okay with me gone? I mean, are you okay with me living in New York?"

"I miss you, chile. You my baby, but I do unnerstand that you got to live your own life. There's a part of me that wontned you to stay here in Three Oak. Young people today more advent'rous than in my time, I guess."

"I miss you and Daddy, too."

"So you really think you gon' like this New York?"

Patterson felt a warm glow through her. "I do, Mama. I've only been heh for a few hours and I love it already. It's filled with a whole lot of excitement—the air almost feels electrified. I can't really explain it."

"I'm real happy for you, Patterson. Now I wont you to remember that you have to keep God first in all you do. If you do that, then you can't fail."

"I know."

They talked for a few minutes more before Patterson inquired, "Is Daddy home?"

"He's heh. You wanna talk to 'im?"

"Yes, ma'am. Mama, I love you."

"I love you, too."

Patterson's eyes filled with tears. The only shadow across her heart was leaving her mother because they had always been close. As much as she loved being in New York, Patterson knew she would miss her dearly. It nearly broke her heart to hear the pain in her mother's voice.

"Hey, honey," her father's voice came through the receiver. "You made it safe and sound to New York, I see."

"Yes, sir."

"I wont you to know that I'm real proud of you, girl. Now you do us proud back heh in Three Oak."

"Daddy, I'ma give it my best shot. Modeling is all I've ever wontned to do. That and living in New York, of course."

Zeke chuckled. "It's sure all you ever talked 'bout. I don't know what you see in a city filled with tall buildings—no trees or grass and all those folks. Give me good farmland any day of the week."

"Oh, Daddy. I still love Three Oak and I'm gon' miss my family and friends, but this is where my heart has called me. It may not make sense to you, Daddy, but I know I'm supposed to be here. It's like how you feel 'bout Hawaii. You been dreaming 'bout taking Mama there since I was little. Don't give up on that dream, Daddy."

"You young folks are filled with big ideas," Zeke responded. "It's not a bad thing, I'm saying. Ain't bad at all. But sometimes you have to be realistic. Your mama and I probably ain't never gonna get to Hawaiyah, and we fine with what God has given us. Times are different than when I was growing up. One thing remains the same. You have to keep God first no matter what you do."

Patterson smiled because her mother had just said the exact same thing to her. "I won't forget, Daddy."

They talked for a few minutes more before saying good-bye.

Patterson was near tears when she hung up, already feeling the ache that came with missing her parents.

Patterson pulled her hair free from the scrunchy.

She stood up and navigated to the mirror.

It's too dark, she decided as she eyed her hair, a mass of curling tresses that ran just past her shoulders. The jet-black color did nothing for her complexion. Patterson played with the idea of dying her hair a warm brown hue.

Gazing at her reflection, Patterson continued to scrutinize her appearance. The more she stared, the more she became convinced that she should lighten her hair. A softer color would enhance her complexion and complement her dark brown eyes.

"Why didn't I think of this before?" she wondered aloud.

Patterson knew the answer. Her parents would've thrown a hissy fit if she'd changed her hair color. They still weren't crazy over the idea of her getting her hair permed.

"Well I'm twenty-one years old and living on my own in New York. I can do whatever I wont."

Her heart cautioned her to be careful.

LaRue

Six hours later, LaRue staggered wearily off the plane. She hadn't slept well the night before and then had to be at the airport early for a six A.M. flight.

Now that she'd landed safely in New York, LaRue was looking forward to getting settled into her hotel room and climbing into bed to relax. She didn't care much for flying and always felt nauseated afterward.

After securing her luggage, LaRue hailed a taxi. On the way to the hotel, she absorbed as much of the view as she could. It didn't matter to her that New York had one of the highest traffic densities in the nation or that the city was congested with people from all walks of life. She'd always dreamed of living in the Big Apple.

LaGuardia Airport was about twenty minutes away from the Ramada Plaza Hotel on Eighth Street. A couple of times during the ride, LaRue felt her eyelids closing and fought to stay awake.

The taxi driver dropped her off and LaRue pulled money out of her wallet to pay him. She then made her way through the lobby toward the registration desk.

After a short process, she had keys in hand and was on her way to her room.

LaRue immediately unpacked her clothes, taking time to iron out the wrinkles and hang them neatly in the closet. She grew wearier by the moment, but LaRue didn't stop until she'd hung up the last piece.

Satisfied, she lay down on the bed.

Although she intended to lie down only for a few minutes, her lids dropped over her eyes in surrender to sleep.

While LaRue slumbered, an image formed in her dream. A woman dressed in a long black robe walked up to an altar and opened the huge Bible lying on the podium. She lifted her face, but before she could utter a word, LaRue jolted up, shaken.

"No," LaRue moaned. "Not me, Lord. Not me. I don't know what I'm supposed to do, but I know that I don't want to be a minister. I can't do that, Lord. Please stop tormenting me with these dreams. After what you did to me—I don't want to do anything for you."

She sat for a moment as if waiting for an answer to drift from the heavens. Her eyes bounced around the room, looking at nothing in particular, until they landed on the mirror. LaRue climbed out of the bed and crossed the room in quick strides.

With a hand placed to her face, LaRue inched as close as she could to the mirror. She was extremely proud of her smooth skin. She had gotten her rich, dark complexion and full lips from her mother. From her father, she'd inherited his sculpted cheekbones, naturally arched brows, and almost black eye color. She'd also inherited his height. LaRue didn't feel awkward standing a couple of inches over six feet tall.

In high school and college she played basketball until she injured herself during the fourth game of the season. After that, her dreams to play professional women's basketball were over.

It still bothered LaRue that she couldn't play basketball, but she had always known deep down that her calling was elsewhere.

She continued to stare at her reflection in the mirror.

"I'm still angry with you, God. I don't want nothing to do with being a minister. What can I say to anyone? I don't have any faith in you. Not anymore." LaRue placed both hands to her face. "I'm not the one."

Memories from long ago rushed to the forefront.

During her freshman year in college, LaRue's father had a visiting pastor preaching at their church revival.

LaRue was late getting to the church and slipped into the building shortly after prayer. The visiting minister and her father had their backs to the congregation. Then they stood up and turned to face the audience.

"I have a message for someone here tonight," the visiting preacher began.

The hair on the back of LaRue's neck stood up.

"There is someone here wearing a red sweater and black pants. I need this person to come up to the front."

LaRue felt a shiver race down her back. She was the person wearing red and black. Slowly, she made her way down the aisle.

She stood there with fear in her eyes, looking at this man standing beside her father.

He laid a calming hand on her shoulder and said, "God has a message for you, young lady. He has given you a talent . . . a gift. You will minister to the heartbroken and the wounded in spirit. You will . . ."

His words died as LaRue focused on one word: *minister*. Even now she could recall the way she felt as panic rose within her. She didn't feel qualified to be a minister. She felt unworthy of such a calling.

But that night, her life changed. It was heading in a direction that LaRue had no intention of going; however, she would not deny God.

When Tom died, though, her feelings changed, and she decided to rebel. Maybe if God had answered her prayers and had healed her husband, she would feel differently. But He hadn't spared her husband, so LaRue saw no need to answer God's call on her heart.

Chapter 3

Patterson

It was now a reality. Patterson had successfully made her escape from the dusty farming town of Three Oak.

Cuddled on a plush window seat, Patterson stared out the window, watching young couples walking along West End Avenue. Some appeared to be in heavy conversation, some were laughing, and others were holding hands. They seemed so happy and carefree. She began to feel the familiar ache in her heart. Her heart's desire was to have good friends, a modeling career, and a man to love . . .

"That's the life I want, Heavenly Father. This is the desire of my heart. This and to serve you. Thank you for giving me the chance. I won't let you down, Lord. I'm gon' make you real proud of me."

She thought about Vincent and how much he'd hurt her.

Up until a few months ago, Patterson thought she and Vincent Atkinson Jr. would eventually marry. After she had constantly denied him sex, Vincent finally gave up and broke off the relationship, but not before Patterson found out about the woman he'd been seeing throughout the last two years of their courtship.

Although she knew Vincent wasn't the man for her, it didn't lessen her pain. She loved him still. In time, Patterson knew her feelings would die—at least she hoped they would. A man like Vincent certainly didn't deserve her heart.

Patterson wanted a circle of girlfriends. She'd grown up mostly around a group of men: her father, her uncles, and her male cousins. There weren't many girls her age left in the farming community. After high school, they either went to college or got married and moved away. Patterson wanted someone she could laugh with or confide in.

It was shortly after sunset before Patterson was able to pull herself away from the window. Her stomach protested loudly, a reminder that she hadn't eaten in a while. It was time to leave the security of her hotel room in search of something for dinner.

Patterson stopped briefly at the front desk to inquire about restaurants. She chose to pick up a turkey sandwich, soda, and potato chips from the deli that was located on the next block. As she walked back to the hotel, Patterson took in her surroundings.

It had been a perfect sunny day. Not too hot. She loved spring days like this. Patterson enjoyed being outdoors. She used to look forward to the annual summer vacations in July to St. Simon's Island during her childhood.

Her uncle Malachi Haney lived in Darien, Georgia, and they visited him and his family once a year. Part of that vacation was spent on St. Simon's.

Patterson and her cousins would spend their days either frolicking on the sandy beaches or playing in the Atlantic Ocean. The lamps in her bedroom back home still held the seashells she'd collected over the years.

Her mother's birthday was coming up in seven weeks. Since her mother was born on the Fourth of July, they often celebrated on the island by having a picnic followed by a fireworks display. This was the first time Patterson wouldn't be present. "I'ma buy you something really nice and pretty, Mama," she promised. "Or maybe I'll be able to pay for you and Daddy to finally make that trip to Hawaii."

Patterson entertained the idea that she might not make it as a model, but not for long. She truly believed that this dream would one day come true.

She had mustard-seed faith.

Macy

Later that evening, Macy stomped into her apartment, seething. All Frederick wanted was sex, totally dismissing all she'd confided to him. The last thing on her troubled mind at the moment was rubbing bodies together.

Macy had other worries—like how was she going to pay for her apartment or even the utilities. She had some money in her checking account, but it wouldn't last long, and maybe a couple hundred dollars left in her savings.

I could try begging Daddy again, she thought. *No way would that work. He's too mad and too stubborn to listen. It's just a ploy to get me to move back home with them.* Her mother never wanted Macy to move out in the first place.

Macy uttered a curse. "Why is this happening to me? What did I do to deserve this? Why won't you help me, God? Please make them change their mind. Please."

She picked up a newspaper and opened it to the classifieds. "Let's see if there's anything new today. . . ."

"Hmmm . . . video models needed. . . . " Macy continued to read. "Females needed for photo shoot. I bet." The last time she'd gone to one of those, the photographer wanted to shoot her with her clothes off. Her eyes traveled to a large ad.

" 'Top New York Modeling Agency Holds Open Call for New Faces.' *Yes!* This just might be the chance I'm looking for. I'm gorgeous enough to be a model."

Macy picked up a pair of scissors that had been lying nearby and cut out the advertisement. She went back over the ads listed under the models section of the classifieds. " 'Female Models Wanted: $1,000–1,500 per day.' " She noted the number and wrote it down. Macy planned to give them a call first thing in the morning—or early afternoon. She was not a morning person and usually didn't stray from her bed until well after ten.

The open call was going to be held at ten A.M., but Macy decided it was worth the effort to get up earlier. Emerald Model Management was one of the top agencies in the country. Although she'd gone to many of the open calls held all over New York, she felt good about this one. "I can feel it. I'm going to make it this time."

Macy read over the ad again, noting the part about late arrivals not being seen. "Guess I better go to bed early tomorrow night," she mumbled. *This is my chance to get back at Mother and Father. Success is the best revenge, and I'm going to be one of the most sought-after models in the world. I'm another Tyra Banks—everybody says so. Some people even think we look alike. My skin is just lighter.*

Macy got up and navigated to her room to shower and prepare for bed. Afterward, she sat on the boudoir bench, thumbing through her portfolio. Her headshot, the photos of her in a swimsuit, and the others were perfection as far as Macy was concerned.

Shortly after midnight, Macy climbed into her king-sized bed. After settling back against the stack of pillows, she admired her photographs, studying every angle. She ran her fingers lovingly through her long honey-blond tresses, wishing that the hair wasn't bonded strand by strand. Macy paid over twelve hundred dollars to make sure her hair looked as natural as possible. She could've gotten it sewn in or glued for a lot less, but Macy wanted long hair more than anything else in life—outside of money.

Outside of the weave and contact lenses, Macy decided that she was perfection. She just had to be picked up. She would be twenty-four years old in October, and there were only a few years left for modeling.

Deep down, Macy didn't really want to model, but it was the next best choice. Her passion was for designing clothing. That's where her heart truly was, but she was forced to keep it a secret. Her parents would never approve of her becoming a fashion designer—haute couture or otherwise. It did not fit the mold of what they had in mind for her.

LaRue

The next morning, LaRue was back in front of the full-length mirror that hung beside the bathroom door. She held up her long braids, posed, then released them and struck another pose, this time pursing her lips.

She broke into laughter at her reflection. "What am I doing here? Who am I trying to kid? I'm no model."

LaRue pulled the braids up into a ponytail. Peering closer, she examined her eyes, her lips, and her facial structure. *Not too bad*, she thought. She was happy with her physical attributes.

"This is going to turn out okay. I didn't just move here for modeling. That's just one avenue. If it works out, fine—if not, then that's okay, too."

She tried to convince herself that she felt less anxious about the open call than she truly did. LaRue picked up the magazine she'd brought with her and studied the woman gracing the cover, while trying to imagine her face on the cover.

After a moment, LaRue laid the magazine back down on the dresser and strode over to her suitcase. She pulled out a bottle of water and a banana-nut muffin for breakfast. Last night she decided to treat herself by ordering room service.

Dropping down onto the desk chair, she picked up a neatly folded piece of paper off the oak desk. Biting into the muffin, LaRue read the ad again.

"I can't believe that I'm actually doing this," she whispered.

LaRue placed the ad back on the desk, trading it for the telephone. She called her mother for the second time since her arrival.

While she waited for her mother to answer, LaRue checked her watch. It was ten-thirty on the East Coast, which meant her mother had been up for at least a couple of hours. Her father would be taking his morning walk. LaRue wanted to catch her mother alone.

"Hi . . ." LaRue mumbled.

"So you ready for this open call tomorrow?" Ruby asked without any enthusiasm.

"I read up about open calls on the Internet, and it says that I'm not supposed to wear make-up, and I don't need any fancy pictures, just regular photos, so I got all that. I'm ready."

Ruby released a long sigh. "Why are you doing this?"

"Because I want to, Mom." LaRue paused a moment before saying, "You know what? I won't bring it up again."

"Modeling is just not something I thought you'd do. Strutting around half-naked on a stage somewhere—it's sinful."

"*It's a job*, Mom. Why can't you and Dad see that? It's just a job."

They were both quiet for a moment.

Ruby broke the silence by asking, "You talk to your Daddy yet?"

LaRue shook her head. "No, and I'm not planning to. He's being so unreasonable about this whole move to New York."

"Hon, your father is just worried about you. He's spent a lot of time counseling models, actors, and athletes. He knows all about the evils in the fashion industry. There are people out there who'll take advantage."

"Mom, I'm twenty-six. I can handle myself."

"I'm sure you believe that you can."

"You and Dad have to let me grow up. I've been married and widowed. I lost my best friend. Mom, I can handle just about anything after going through that."

"Your dad and I just don't believe this is what God has for you, baby. I know you don't want to hear this right now, but the Lord dropped in my spirit that He has called you for great things."

"Mom, don't . . ."

"You remember that revival, LaRue?"

"I'm gonna be a model. It's what I want to do."

Ruby sighed.

"Why don't we change the subject, Mom," LaRue suggested. Her mother had a great sense of humor and LaRue enjoyed talking to her, and was filled with sadness when the time came to end the conversation.

"I'll call you tomorrow after the open call to let you know what happened. I love you, Mom."

LaRue hung up, her eyes damp. She wished her parents could be happy for her. Her father, the great Reverend Larry Arnette, was barely speaking to her since her decision to leave Los Angeles.

Although Ruby traveled with her husband, she also presented empowering seminars to women across the country and even volunteered some of her free time with Habitat for Humanity.

She eyed the woman gracing the cover of the magazine again. LaRue forced away her insecurities surrounding the modeling; instead, she considered her other options. She had experience in teaching elementary school and as a social worker.

Enough of this. LaRue decided it was time to get dressed and forge ahead to her future. Los Angeles was now her past, but it would always be home despite the fact that it had become a place filled with tragic memories.

She'd lost the love of her life to brain cancer and then, just a month ago, LaRue and her best friend had been involved in a car accident which left Janine dead. She needed to get away from Los Angeles before she lost her mind.

When LaRue went downstairs, she stopped at the front desk to inquire about the subway system. She planned to spend her day sightseeing and becoming familiar with the area.

The first on her list was Harlem, the black mecca of the world.

LaRue wanted a firsthand look at the original location of the Cotton Club, the Savoy Ballroom, and the Schomburg Center for Research in Black Culture. She took a taxi to 116th Street and Malcolm X Boulevard where she spied a young woman wearing a red hat and holding up a sign that read HARLEM HERITAGE TOURS.

She smiled and waved a greeting as she walked toward the tour guide. They made small talk as they waited for more tourists to join them.

Ten minutes later, the small group began walking.

The tour took place on foot and featured churches, jazz clubs, institutions of art and culture, and the Langston Hughes House, among several other famous residences and eateries.

LaRue took pictures of the Abyssinian Baptist Church, which was founded in 1808 and was the first African American Baptist Church in New York.

At the end of the tour, LaRue found that her thirst for knowledge had been only partially quenched. She still hungered for more. She loved history and was an avid collector of African American history books.

LaRue returned to the hotel shortly after six. She removed her clothes, carefully folded them, and placed them in the laundry bag she'd brought with her. Then she took a shower and put on a pair of pajamas.

Sitting cross-legged in the middle of her bed, LaRue stared at the Bible that her mother had discreetly placed in her suitcase. She wasted her time doing so, she decided. LaRue had no intention of reading it.

LaRue reached for the remote control. She surfed through several channels, stopping only when she saw her father's smiling face.

"Jesus describes four types of people who respond to the Word," Pastor Larry Arnette was saying. He then went on to describe them.

"The first group can hear with the physical ear, but that is the extent of their hearing. Satan takes away the Word so that they may not believe and be saved. The second group refers to those who are illustrated by the seeds falling on shallow ground. The seeds sprout quickly but don't put down strong roots." He paused a moment to let his words sink in. "The third group refers to those illustrated by the seeds falling among thorns. People like this hear the Word and give the appearance that everything is great, but in a short time are distracted by worldly things. And the fourth group refers to those who are illustrated by the seeds falling on good soil. People in this group hear the Word, retain it, and, by persevering, produce a crop. Jesus wants the Word to fall on this kind of soil."

LaRue picked up the remote and changed the channel.

She tried to focus her attention on the sitcom she was watching, but her father's sermon kept coming to mind.

Chapter 4

Patterson

She was ready to take on the world of fashion.
Patterson skipped breakfast and used her time to study her Bible before leaving. Nimble fingers gently brushed across each word as she absorbed every verse of the first chapter of Genesis. She referenced her notes from the sermon her pastor at home preached.

Pastor Franklin had spoken on the subject of relationships designed by God. One of the things he'd said stayed with Patterson. *Love keeps no record of wrongs.* He'd gone on to explain what a friend is supposed to be.

She glanced down at what she'd written:

> *F—A friend is Forgiving*
> *R—A friend is Real*
> *I—A friend Imparts Truth*
> *E—A friend is Embracing*
> *N—A friend is Not Selfish*
> *D—A friend is Dedicated*

This was another aspect of her life that Patterson would miss. She had a wonderful rapport with her pastor and felt comfortable seeking him out whenever she needed spiritual counseling. Now she would have to find a new church home. Patterson prayed for guidance in locating one with a pastor who didn't just preach—she wanted to be taught.

In the silence of the small room, Patterson could hear the soft ticking of the clock on the bedside table. She would have to leave in an hour, so closing her Bible, she rose to her feet.

Tiny taps clicked across the tiled floor in the bathroom as Patterson moved about, applying her make-up. All the hours spent at the department store's cosmetics counter in Atlanta and in her make-up class at Bauder were paying off, she decided as she scrutinized her reflection.

She'd read somewhere that you shouldn't wear make-up to an open call. Patterson quickly washed her face and began again. This time she applied a thin layer of face powder and a hint of clear gloss to her lips.

Fifteen minutes before Patterson was scheduled to leave, she changed into a sleek black pantsuit. She paused long enough to peek at her reflection one final time before grabbing her portfolio and heading out the door. One of her graduation projects at Bauder Fashion College had been to build a modeling portfolio. Patterson felt calm and assured. There was no doubt in her mind that she would be one of the lucky women selected. She could already envision her future with Emerald Model Management.

After a ten-minute taxi ride to Lexington Avenue, Patterson was one of the first persons to arrive for the open call. Holding her leather portfolio close to her heart, she whispered a silent prayer.

"Name?" a voice intoned from across a table, snapping Patterson out of her praying.

"I'm sorry. It's Patterson . . ."

The woman smiled. "You can have a seat over there. We'll be getting started soon."

Patterson listened to the sound of her heels tapping a continuous rhythm across the floor as she went to join two other women seated in an area adjacent to the reception area.

She was joined a few minutes later by a tall, slender, dark-skinned woman with waist-length braids. Patterson greeted her with a friendly smile.

"Do you mind if I sit next to you?"

Patterson was thrilled to have someone to talk to. She'd never felt
so alone until the moment she entered through the agency doors.
"Not at all."

Holding out her hand, she introduced herself. "My name is Patterson Haney."

Shaking Patterson's hand, the woman responded, "I'm LaRue
Arnette-Hawkins. It's real nice to meet you. I love your accent. I didn't
really want to sit by myself. I'm so nervous." Lowering her voice a
notch, she added, "You have a friendly face. That's why I came over
here."

Patterson leaned over to whisper, "I understand. Nobody seems
friendly in heh." She paused a moment before asking, "I don't sound
too country, do I?"

"I don't think so. You just sound Southern to me."

"Where are you from, LaRue?"

"Los Angeles. I'm here to see if I can make this modeling thing
work for me. But even if it doesn't, I'm planning to stay in New York.
I've always wanted to live here."

"Me, too," Patterson announced. "I'm not going back to Georgia . . ."
Her voice died when she spotted a representative coming into the
waiting area. "I guess they're getting ready to get started."

"I'd like to welcome all of you to Emerald Model Management. My
name is Constance Fairchild, and I am the agent for the women's di-
vision. . . ."

The noise of a door slamming and the defiant clicking of high-
heeled sandals drew Patterson's attention from Constance to the
beautiful late arrival. She recalled the warning in bold print that
stated late arrivals would not be seen and felt badly for her.

Macy

She loved attention.

Macy was well aware that all eyes were on her, but instead of feeling
embarrassed, it delighted her. Walking slowly across the room, with
hips swaying, Macy took her time. She was enjoying all the attention
she was getting.

Tossing her honey-blond tresses across her shoulders, Macy gave the receptionist a big smile, although the woman sat glaring at her. "Good morning. My name is Macy Baldwin."

"You're late," she stated. "We won't—"

"Traffic was awful this morning," Macy interrupted. "There was an accident. Something I had absolutely no control over. Besides, I'm not really late. It's two minutes to ten. Your clock is fast." Holding up her left arm, she went on to say, "I have an atomic digital watch and it keeps absolute time. You may want to consider getting one for the office, especially if you're going to penalize late arrivals."

Unabashed, she headed over to where the other girls were seated without waiting for a response.

Macy met the gaze of another model hopeful and granted her a sympathetic smile. In Macy's opinion, the girl was pretty enough, with long dark hair and a honey complexion free of blemishes, but she would never survive the modeling world. She didn't have that aggressive look about her that was needed to make it in the fashion industry.

Macy slipped into the chair in front of her and sat her portfolio down on the floor beside her. A few seconds passed before she realized that everyone was waiting on her to get settled before they continued.

"Once again, my name is Constance Fairchild. . . ."

Macy knew the reintroduction was for her benefit and gave Constance a nonchalant stare. Things like this didn't bother her. She was used to women being mean to her out of pure jealousy. Average-looking women were almost always jealous of the beautiful ones. *No point in being mad at me. Take it up with God. He made me this way.*

Constance looked as if she could read Macy's thoughts. Her expression changed and her eyes left Macy, who bit her lip to stifle a grin. Not really listening to Constance, she lowered her eyes and admired her manicured fingernails.

The agent quickly retreated into her corner office after her brief speech.

Macy's eyes swept through the sea of women—all from different walks of life, all with dreams of gracing runways and covers of fashion magazines. Most would never make it.

"Hey," a voice said from behind her. Macy swung her head around. "Are you talking to me?"

"Yeah. I wontned to introduce myself. I'm Patterson Haney. Folks don't seem too friendly round here."

Macy twisted her face in a frown and asked, "Where in the world are you from?"

"Three Oak, Georgia." Patterson got up suddenly and came around to sit down in the empty chair beside Macy, surprising her.

"I've never heard of it. . . . What did you call it?"

"Three Oak."

"Oh."

While Patterson rattled on, Macy assessed her competition.

This Southern belle was a couple of inches shorter than her own five eleven height, was slender with soft curves, and had a wealth of dark hair that reached past her shoulders. Macy searched for telltale signs of the curly mass being a weave, but found much to her disappointment, that it was real.

Miss Patterson Haney possessed the one thing Macy wanted most in the world—long luxurious hair. She hated traveling to Brooklyn to have extensions added to her own hair. Because Macy wanted the hair to look as natural as possible, she had searched high and low to find the right beautician to do the job.

Patterson was still talking. ". . . Three Oak. Everybody knows about Atlanta, but there's a lot more to Georgia than that. Lots of wonderful small towns and such."

"I'm sure," Macy replied offhandedly.

Patterson reacted as if she'd just remembered something. Leaning forward, she said, "Listen to me just running off at the mouth. I'm talkin' so much, I didn't get your name."

"My name is Macy."

"Really? Like the big fancy department store?"

Giving her a bored look, Macy nodded. "I was born in the lingerie department of Macy's."

"What a great story." Patterson turned around and gestured to a tall dark-skinned woman sitting behind them. "Come up heh, LaRue."

Macy glanced over her shoulder. The woman looked as if she were debating whether or not to join them. Macy secretly preferred that this LaRue person stay right where she was. She didn't relish the idea of meeting anyone—especially women. She felt that there was something about her that just didn't seem to sit right with other females.

Macy was polite through the introductions but remained silent during their conversation. She turned her nose upward at the sight of the long braids hanging down LaRue's back.

Macy pulled out her cell phone and checked her messages during the wait. She overheard snatches of Patterson's conversation with LaRue. *You two don't have a chance,* she wanted to tell them. *So you might as well pack your bags and go back to Tree Oak . . . Three Oak . . . wherever, Georgia.*

Once they got a good look at her, most of the hopefuls in the room would be out of the running, Macy told herself. She'd won a couple of beauty pageants as a teen and had been signed to a small modeling agency, but they could only book her for local assignments.

Macy was ready for something more. She would take over the fashion world.

LaRue

LaRue decided she didn't stand a chance. She glanced over at the exit doors, suddenly anxious to escape.

In spite of the fact that she didn't look her age, LaRue had a feeling being twenty-six years old would hinder her from getting selected. Most of the women in the room all appeared to be between the ages of fifteen and twenty.

She glanced down at the snapshots in her hands, resisting the urge to hide them in her purse. *What was I thinking?* she wondered. *I know this isn't for me, so I don't know why I allowed myself to believe I could actually have a chance. Me, a model.* The whole idea of it now seemed crazy.

LaRue sat in the chair, her thin fingers tensed in her lap. Every now and then she would steal a peek over at the woman sitting on the other side of Patterson. Although Macy had an ear glued to her cellular phone, LaRue felt she was actually paying more attention to her conversation with Patterson.

When Macy put her phone away, Patterson stated, "I was just telling LaRue that this is the first time I've ever been to an open call. This is her first time too. How 'bout you? This your first time?"

"I've been to a few of them before," Macy replied while slipping her phone back into her purse. Glancing over at LaRue, she asked, "Did you bring any pictures?"

"I have some snapshots. Nothing professionally done like you and Patterson. On the Web site, they said to bring candid photos."

Macy responded with a polite smile and settled back in her chair.

LaRue knew instinctively that she and Macy didn't click. It didn't matter to her anyway, because she wasn't looking for friendship from Macy.

They had absolutely nothing in common.

Chapter 5

LaRue

What she thought would happen—did.

LaRue was dismissed almost the moment she'd walked into the office. She was grateful, however, that the agent had not been rude. In a way, she felt relieved. She'd given it a shot, so now she knew. She couldn't cut it as a model. She wouldn't have to go through life wondering.

Holding her head up high, LaRue strolled out of the office, pausing long enough to say good-bye to Macy and Patterson.

"It was nice meeting you ladies. Good luck." She put up a brave front, even though her heart was heavy.

"You're still planning on stayin' in New York, right?" Patterson questioned.

"Only if I can find a job," LaRue replied. "I really don't think I'll have any problems doing that. But if I'm wrong, then I guess I'll head back to Los Angeles."

It was Macy's turn. She picked up her portfolio when they called her name and walked away without a word, slinging her hair one way and her hips the other.

LaRue shook her head in disgust. "That girl just thinks she's the *bomb*, as the kids say."

Patterson chuckled. "She does seem a little full of herself, but I like her."

LaRue shot her a twisted smile. "You've only talked with her a few minutes, Patterson. How do you know?"

"It's a feeling I have deep inside. I've got a strong feeling that she can be a challenge, but I also feel that she's in need of some good friends." Patterson broke into a grin. "Call me crazy, but I really feel it in my spirit."

"I'm not gonna call you crazy." Her arms folded across her chest, LaRue leaned back against the wall, sizing her up. "Patterson, you're the kind of person who only sees the good in people, huh?"

"I *do* believe there's good in everybody."

LaRue shrugged matter-of-factly. "I guess I'm more of a realist."

"Last Sunday, my pastor was saying that God does not intend for man to be alone; we are made to be in relationship with one another. Ecclesiastes 4:9 and 10 says, '*Two are better than one, because they have a good return for their work: If one falls down, his friend can help him up. But pity the man who falls and has no one to help him up.*' "

LaRue played with the straps of her purse. "Well, I'd better get out of here." She didn't want to hear anything about God.

"I'm on my way out, too." Patterson picked up her portfolio case and rose to her feet. "I hope we both get picked up by the agency."

"I won't be. I'm too old."

Patterson stopped and asked, "Did they tell you that?"

Shaking her head no, LaRue responded, "Not really, but I could tell just from the way they were talking. She went through the statistics and age range for most models."

"How old are you?" Patterson inquired.

"I'm twenty-six."

"Well, there still may be a chance that they'll choose you."

LaRue smile at Patterson's optimism. "They won't, but it's okay. I intend to try and find a job."

"You okay if you don't get a callback?"

LaRue nodded. "I'll have to be. There's nothing I can do about it."

After a moment, Patterson inquired, "Do you really want to model, LaRue?"

"Yeah, I do," she admitted. "I guess I didn't realize just how much until now."

"Then I doan think you should give up so easily. I'm not."

"You're going to check out other agencies?"

Patterson nodded. "What about you? Are you gon' try another agency, too?"

"I don't know, Patterson. I'll have to think about it."

"Well, I really hope you will. You have that look about you. You'd be a real good model, LaRue. You look just like you hightailed it off a magazine."

LaRue burst into laughter. "You're funny."

"I'm serious. If I didn't just meet you, I woulda thought you was one of those high-fashion models."

"Patterson, you've really made me feel a whole lot better. Thank you."

Macy

Patterson and LaRue were still standing out in the hallway, having a conversation, when Macy stormed out of the office.

"I already know that I'm not going to get anywhere with that woman," she complained. "I didn't care for her attitude at all. She's the kind of person that you have to cuss out now and repent later."

LaRue and Patterson burst into laughter. The tension left in Macy's body dissipated as she began to laugh with them.

While they stood there waiting on the elevator, Patterson said, "You may still get a callback, Macy. You look like you just stepped out of a magazine. You too, LaRue."

Macy grunted while LaRue gave her a grateful smile.

"LaRue, did they say why they rejected you?" Macy asked.

"They didn't reject me. I just think I'm too old."

"I thought you were older," Macy stated as she admired herself in the mirrored doors of the elevator.

LaRue's eyes were sharp and assessing. "Excuse me? You don't look much younger."

Macy glanced over her shoulder and said, "Don't get me wrong. You look real good for your age. You're just not model material. It's your eyes. You look young, but when people look into your eyes, there's years of experience . . . ." She paused for a second before adding, "And wisdom. Wisdom ages you, wouldn't you agree?"

Instead of answering Macy's question, LaRue posed one of her own. "I suppose you think you're model material then?"

Macy tossed her hair over her shoulder. "Yes, I do. I used to model when I was younger. Mostly local stuff, but it was modeling. I've even won a few beauty pageants as well. I love clothes, shoes, make-up—everything about fashion."

"How old are you?" LaRue asked.

"I'm twenty-four."

The doors to the elevator opened. Before Macy stepped out, she turned to LaRue and Patterson saying, "It was nice meeting you both. Take care."

"Wait, Macy. Don't leave. Why don't we have lunch together?" Patterson suggested. "I don't know 'bout y'all, but I'm starving and I hate eating by myself. I'd really like some company."

"Sounds good to me," LaRue chimed in. "I *am* hungry."

Both women looked at Macy.

"I . . ." When she couldn't think of an excuse, Macy nodded after a moment. "Sure. Why not? What types of foods do you ladies like?"

LaRue was the first to respond. "I like Italian, Chinese, Thai, Jamaican, and just plain soul food."

"I like all of those except Jamaican, but that's only cause I ain't never had any," Patterson stated. "Italian's my favorite, though."

"I know someplace I think you'd both enjoy. It's not too far from here." Macy led Patterson and LaRue out of the building. "We're going to Becco's for lunch. They have the Symphony de Pasta. It's a bottomless dish of three daily pastas. You're simply going to love it."

"I already love it," LaRue replied. "And we haven't even seen the place."

"Me, too," Patterson agreed with a laugh.

Walking ahead of them, Macy rolled her eyes heavenward. *This is going to be horrible. . . .* She released a soft sigh and held up her hand to signal a taxi.

The restaurant, located between Eighth and Ninth avenues, was busy when they arrived. After a short wait, the three women were seated.

Patterson's eyes bounced around the room, taking in everything. Macy couldn't help but wonder if she'd ever been inside of anything other than a roadside diner. "This is a nice place, Macy. Thanks for bringing us here."

"You're quite welcome, Patterson."

"I have a good feeling about today. I feel like we're going to see each other again."

"You really have to have a love and passion for modeling," Macy was saying. "That's the only way to really be successful. It's not as glamorous or as easy as you may think. It's really hard work."

Patterson replied, "I know. For me, this isn't a passing fling or something. It's all I've ever wontned to do. I doan wont to do nothing else."

"I hope you get a callback, Patterson. You too, Macy." LaRue pulled out her address book and pen. "Even though I may not be modeling, let's try to keep in touch."

"I'd love that," Patterson replied. "Give me yours, 'cause right now I'm staying in a hotel. I have to find a place to live."

"So you're definitely planning to stay in New York, then?" LaRue inquired.

Patterson nodded. "I'm planning on getting me a cell phone."

"That's great. I'm getting one, too. We have to keep in touch then. Especially since we're both so new to the area. We can look out for each other."

"This is going to be so much fun," Patterson exclaimed. "I'm so glad I met you two."

Macy wanted to ask, "Why?" She couldn't figure out why the girl was so excited. Biting her bottom lip, she kept her mouth shut. Macy couldn't believe she was actually sitting in a restaurant with two women who didn't seem to know when to stop talking. In the short period of one hour, she'd learned all about Three Oak, Georgia, and Compton, California. More than she ever cared to know.

"You sure are quiet, Macy," Patterson observed.

"I'm not really." She returned her attention to her plate, wishing Patterson would just shut up. Macy played around with the lettuce on her plate.

"How long have you lived here?" LaRue asked.

"All of my life. I can't imagine living anywhere else."

"I've always dreamed of living here in New York," Patterson confessed. "Even if I don't make it as a model, I'm still going to stay here. I'll find a job doing something, I'm sure."

Macy wasn't sure how much more she could endure. She hoped they weren't looking for her to befriend them. She didn't want or need any friends. "It's very expensive to live here. I don't know if you know that."

"*We do,*" LaRue interjected. "We've already done our research."

Macy turned her attention to LaRue. "Why don't you want to go back to Los Angeles? I can certainly understand why Patterson would want to leave that small town in Georgia, but not L.A."

"Because, like Patterson, I've always wanted to live here. It's always been a dream of mine."

"Have you been here before?"

LaRue's gaze never wavered. "A couple of times," she responded. "I love New York."

Macy laughed. "You sound like a commercial."

"I have an idea," Patterson began. "LaRue, you and I could become roommates. We can find an apartment together and share the expenses, if that's okay with you."

"I was just about to make that same suggestion."

Out of boredom, Macy inquired, "So where are you two going to live until you find jobs? Are you going to stay in a hotel together?"

"I hadn't thought of that, but it's not a bad idea, I guess." Patterson appeared to be giving the suggestion some serious thought. "I don't think we'll have to stay in a hotel too long, though. I have some money with me. It's enough to get me through the next three or four months if I'm careful and budget wisely."

"Same here," LaRue stated. "I have about six months' worth in my savings, two emergency credit cards, and some money in my checking."

Smiling, Patterson said, "We're so much alike. I have an emergency credit card, too, plus the money they took up for me at church. See, I just know everything is gonna work out."

Macy had completely underestimated the two women sitting in this booth with her. They were totally prepared—more so than her. Her parents' faces loomed in her mind, and the memory of their threat burned on her brain—and then she got an idea.

Macy spoke up before she could change her mind.

"I don't know how you two will feel about this, but I just might have a solution. I have a three-bedroom apartment. You can rent rooms from me, if you like."

Patterson was elated. "Really? You wouldn't mind?"

"Why would you want to do that?" LaRue questioned. "You don't know us from a man in the moon."

Macy had a strong feeling that she and LaRue wouldn't mesh. Yet, she couldn't afford to alienate her at the moment. "You two don't know each other, yet you're willing to be roommates," she pointed out. "Well, this is no different."

LaRue was still suspicious. "We'll need to see your place before we decide."

Macy nodded. "How about tomorrow around noon?" That would give her enough time to have it cleaned. She made a mental note to give her housekeeper a call as soon as she got home.

While Patterson and LaRue rattled on about sharing the apartment, Macy silently congratulated herself on coming up with the idea of having roommates. Until her parents returned to their senses, she would be able to meet her expenses. *Almost.* But, she reminded herself that she still had the shares of stock that her grandparents had given her. She would sell off some of the shares if needed.

Macy decided she wouldn't worry about it for the moment.

There would be plenty of time for worry later.

Patterson

Patterson let out a whoop as soon as she walked into her hotel room. "Yes!"

She picked up her suitcase and laid it open on her bed. "I know this is you, Lord," Patterson whispered. "This ain't nobody but you."

She was thrilled to have found a roommate so quickly. Patterson had a feeling that she and LaRue would get along well. To top that, they might be sharing an apartment with Macy; the idea thrilled her. She thought Macy Baldwin was a class act.

Patterson was in awe of Macy. She loved hearing her New York accent. She observed Macy all throughout lunch, noting the way she held her hands when she talked and how she nibbled her food.

She pulled some dresses out of the closet and packed them neatly into the suitcase, humming softly as she worked.

"I hope Macy's apartment works," Patterson voiced aloud. "It'll be a lot of fun. I just know it."

Just as she was almost finished, her mother called.

"Hey Mama. . . ."

"How did it go?"

"I think it went okay. They are going to post the names of the ones who get a callback. I wont to be one of them."

"We'll be praying for you, Patterson. If God say so, you'll get it."

Patterson nodded. "I know. I believe it, Mama. I just believe that I'm gon' be a real model." Patterson's eyes traveled to where her suitcase lay on the bed. "Oh, Mama . . . I have to tell you. I got a roommate. Her name is LaRue and she's one of the girls that I met at the open call. She's real nice."

"Where she from?"

"Los Angeles," Patterson answered. "I met another girl—named Macy like the big department store. She was born there."

"Born where?"

"In Macy's department store. That's where she was born. Anyway, she has an apartment and she's looking for roommates—we're meeting with her tomorrow to actually see the place."

"Just be careful now. Doan go jumpin' in stuff."

"I'ma be careful, Mama."

They talked for another ten minutes before Patterson hung up to finish her packing. The idea of sharing an apartment with LaRue and Macy made her smile. She really liked them and looked forward to getting to know them better.

LaRue

The idea of sharing an apartment with Patterson didn't seem so bad, but Macy . . .

LaRue had a feeling that she and that self-absorbed princess would constantly be at odds with each other. Secretly, she hoped that Macy's apartment would be all wrong for them.

I'll go see it tomorrow, but then I'm leaving, she thought to herself. She hoped that she and Patterson were in agreement when it came to selecting the perfect apartment for them and would not just jump at Macy's offer.

Her telephone rang.

"Hello."

"Hey, LaRue. I just called to make sure you made it back to your hotel safe."

She smiled at Patterson's concern.

"I'm so excited about us becoming roommates. Won't it be nice to live with Macy? I bet she has some real fancy apartment. She looks like she's stepping in high cotton."

LaRue made a face. "I guess."

"What's wrong? You doan sound like you really wanna move there."

"Patterson, we haven't even seen it yet. We may not like it, you know."

"I can see God's hand in all this, LaRue. I believe we s'posed to be livin' together."

What does God have to do with this? LaRue wanted to ask, but didn't. Instead, she said, "I think we should try and see a few other apartments before making a decision."

"I guess you're right, LaRue. We'll look at some other ones before we decide."

Satisfied, she said, "I'm going to check the newspaper tonight for apartments that we might be interested in."

"I'll get a paper and look, too. We can compare our findings tomorrow when we meet."

"Sounds good."

"Well, I won't keep you," Patterson began. "I'ma run out to the deli and grab a sandwich for dinner. I hope we do decide to move in with Macy. I'm pining for a real home-cooked meal."

"I'll see you tomorrow, Patterson."

"Okay. Talk to you then."

LaRue hung up her phone.

Ten minutes later, she left the room in search of a newspaper. She had some apartment hunting to do. Deep down she hoped they wouldn't have to end up living with Macy.

Patterson believed if given the chance, the three of them would become great friends, but LaRue wasn't quite convinced. . . . She didn't think she and Macy would ever be friends.

Chapter 6

Macy

She walked through her apartment, going from one room to the other. This place had always been her sanctuary, and she resented having to share her precious space with a couple of gabbing women.

"How am I going to get through this?" she asked out loud. "Three women living in this apartment? It's going to be crazy."

Her telephone rang, cutting into her thoughts.

She went to answer the phone, until Macy recognized her mother's cellular number. She rolled her eyes heavenward and walked away, ignoring the shrill ringing.

Macy had an appointment with her trainer, so she went into her room to change her clothes. She settled down a few minutes to return a few phone calls.

Macy checked her voice mail, erasing the one from her mother before moving on to the next one. She had no intentions of speaking to her parents until she was good and ready. This was always her way of letting them know she was furious with them. In the past, Macy had gone without talking to them for months at a time.

Her physical trainer arrived two hours later.

Macy enjoyed working out because she found the rigorous exercises relaxing and therapeutic.

Standing in the hallway, Macy and Emma made small talk as they stepped onto the elevator and headed down to the fitness center.

She began her workout by warming up and stretching.

"Good. Now let's do some leg extensions," Emma instructed.

Macy took a seat in the leg curl machine, locking her ankles behind the pads.

"Extend your legs. . . ."

Macy did as she was told, being careful not to use her hands on the supports to help lift the weight.

She did twenty repetitions before switching to leg curls.

After her workout, Macy met a friend for dinner. Although he showered her with attention, Macy wasn't really in the mood for company. She was irritated with both William and Frederick, so right now men were not on her *A* list. Citing a migraine headache, Macy ended the date early.

She spent the rest of her evening at home, basking in solitude.

Tomorrow would bring about changes—changes Macy didn't want to make, but had no other choice. It was a matter of survival. But until then, she had this one night, and she didn't want to share it with anyone.

LaRue

The next day, she met up with Patterson on Second Avenue. Together they walked to East Thirty-second Street where Macy's apartment was located.

LaRue's eyes grew wide with surprise when they arrived at the modern luxury high-rise building. She figured Macy would live in a nice area, but she hadn't expected something this nice. "Wow. The sistah is livin' large."

"Oh, my goodness," Patterson muttered. "Look at this place. I doan know if we're gonna be able to afford staying heh."

"I know I can't." LaRue stood frozen in one place. "Gurl, I can look at it and tell that this is too rich for me. We're wasting our time here." She turned to hail a taxi. "Let's check out the one that's ten blocks away from here."

Patterson stopped her by saying, "We're heh now, so I guess we should at least look at the apartment. We told Macy we would come by and look at the place."

Deep down, LaRue figured it was a big waste of time, but reluctantly agreed. "You're right. We'll look at her apartment, then turn Macy down. When we leave here, we'll look at some other places to live."

They greeted the smiling doorman holding the door open for them. Macy was standing in the lobby area.

She gave them a warm smile. "I'm glad you two made it here without any trouble."

"It was pretty easy," Patterson confirmed. "Macy, this place is real nice," she murmured as her eyes bounced around their luxurious surroundings, not wanting to miss anything.

"Let's head upstairs." Macy led them to the elevators. "All the bedrooms have walk-in closets; we have a laundry room in the apartment. Most don't. The fitness center is on the first floor and the business center is downstairs."

The apartment was a spacious convertible three-bedroom with a terrace, a large living room with built-in bookcases, high ceilings, hardwood floors, and lots of windows.

To LaRue, the beautifully decorated apartment could've graced the cover of *Home* magazine. She carefully inspected every room, while Patterson sat in the living room talking with Macy. She joined them after checking the third bedroom a second time.

Her eyes traveled to the huge painting of Macy that hung over the fireplace. There were photos of Macy all over the apartment. *Why am I am not surprised? The woman can't get over herself.*

"So what do you think?" Macy inquired.

"The rooms are larger than I expected—much larger," LaRue responded. "The apartment is gorgeous. I like a lot of windows."

"It sure is pretty," Patterson contributed. "I just doan know that we'd be able to afford something like this on our own. Gosh, Macy, you must be rich in order to live in a place like this."

LaRue agreed. She sat down beside Patterson on the sofa and leaned forward, saying, "Okay, let's talk money. What are you asking?"

Macy paused a moment before she replied, "Well, the mortgage payment is three thousand a month. I was thinking we could just split it three ways. Does this sound fair to you both? To be honest, you're not going to find much out there below two grand a month, and they certainly won't be as nice as this place."

LaRue regarded Macy with somber curiosity. "I want to know why you're so agreeable to us moving in? I got the impression yesterday that you were merely tolerating us, so what's really going on here?"

"LaRue . . ." Patterson began. She didn't want to get off on the wrong foot with Macy.

LaRue's eyes had a sheen of purpose. "I just want to know the real reason behind this gesture. I have a strong feeling that there's more to this story. It wasn't until we mentioned that we had some money saved that you invited us to live here. Are you in danger of losing this place or something?"

"No," Macy answered a little too quickly.

"I don't believe you," LaRue shot back. She had a strong feeling that Macy was hiding something.

"LaRue . . ."

She ignored Patterson's plea. "Macy, if you want us to be room-mates, then we have to be honest with each other."

Macy cleared her throat. "Well . . . um . . . this is so embarrassing. My parents are in a little tiff with me right now, and so they've cut me off. They were helping me pay for the apartment."

"I knew there was something behind your generosity," LaRue stated. "So what happens when you make up with your parents? Do you kick me and Patterson out on our tails?" She had a feeling that this uppity woman could not be trusted.

"I wouldn't do that."

LaRue gazed at Macy trying to gauge her sincerity. "I don't know about Patterson, but I'd feel better if we had a lease or something."

Macy glanced over at Patterson. "What about you? Would you pre-fer something on paper also?"

Patterson

Patterson didn't want to offend Macy, but she agreed with LaRue. "I think it's the proper thing to do. Macy, it's not that we don't trust you, but we wont to make sure all parties are protected. You can un-derstand that, can't you?"

"Okay. I'll have something drawn up immediately. In the mean-time, you ladies are free to move in any time."

"Do you wont a deposit or anything?" Patterson inquired.

"Just a five-hundred-dollar cleaning deposit," Macy responded.

"You can split it between the two of you. And since we're all just getting to know each other, I'm going to have the lease made out for six months. That way if this doesn't work out, we can go our separate ways without waiting an entire year."

Patterson smiled in appreciation. She had a feeling that this arrangement was not a coincidence. For whatever reason, the three women were brought together. She was confident that God would reveal the reason when He was ready.

Patterson and LaRue dug into their purses and withdrew money. They both handed Macy two hundred and fifty dollars.

"Thanks," Macy murmured. "I'll have the papers ready for you by the end of the day."

"We'll move in tomorrow then, if it's all right with you," Patterson announced. "I don't want to incur more hotel charges, if I don't have to."

Nodding, Macy responded, "That's fine. I'll have your rooms ready. Feel free to decorate your rooms to your taste as long as it's not too wild. You know . . . black lights, black walls—that kind of thing."

"I like what you've done," LaRue stated. "I do want to change the bedding, though. I'm afraid to have all that white on the bed. It looks so pristine and well . . . white. Did I say white? Gurl, I just want to be comfortable enough to just fall back and relax without worrying about messing up the bed."

Macy laughed. "I know what you mean. That's why it's in the guest room and not in mine."

"I agree with LaRue. I like what you've done with the rooms. I especially like the floral theme in my bedroom."

"I knew you'd like all those flowers," Macy stated. "That's why I showed it to you first, Patterson."

"Macy, tell me something," LaRue began. "Where in the world did you find that crystal telephone in my room? Does it actually work?"

"I bought it when I went to England last year with my parents. And, yes, it really does work."

"It's so beautiful. . . . I'm not sure I'll use it. I don't want to break it."

Macy chuckled. "LaRue, you won't break it. It's a telephone. *Just use it.* If you and Patterson want to get separate lines, that's fine, too."

"I think that'll be best," LaRue agreed. "What do you think, Patterson?"

"I agree. We should all have our own phone lines. It'll keep confusion down." She could still recall all the bickering between her college roommate over telephone calls.

"Speaking of keeping confusion down, let's discuss some ground rules," LaRue suggested.

Patterson was glad that LaRue brought up the subject of rules. It was next on her agenda.

"Ground rules," Macy repeated. "Hmmm. Well . . . let me just tell you both now that I'm not a morning person. I'm a bear until I've had my coffee. I don't mind sharing, but I don't want to run out. I drink French roast. The Starbuck's brand. They sell it in the market right on the corner."

"Fair enough," LaRue mumbled. "A pet peeve of mine is picking up after grown folk. I hate it. I'm sure we can share the cleaning of common areas. I don't have a problem with that."

"Well, I have a housekeeper who takes care of all the cleaning. Her name is Lupe. She comes every week and cleans everything. She even does the laundry and changes the linen. Don't worry—she speaks English pretty well."

"You have a maid?" Patterson asked.

"*We* have a maid," Macy corrected. "Let's discuss men. We're all single women, so I assume we'll have dates at some point. How do you feel about overnight guests?"

"You mean like a man staying over?" Patterson shook her head adamantly. "Oh, no, I definitely won't ever be having a man spending the night. *Ever.*"

"Are you a lesbian, Patterson?"

"Huh?" She swallowed hard.

"It's a free country and all. Might be a little uncomfortable . . ."

"I'm not a lesbian. I like men. I just won't be having any staying over."

LaRue chuckled. "You should see your face, Patterson. You're red— even your ears."

Patterson was perplexed. She couldn't imagine why Macy thought she was gay. "Why would you think that about me, Macy?"

"I didn't mean anything by it," Macy answered nonchalantly. "You just were so adamant about no men—I just wondered."

"I'm abstaining from sex until I get married," Patterson explained. "I like men a lot."

Macy burst into laughter. "You're kidding about the sex, right?"

When Patterson's expression didn't change, she said, "You can't be serious."

"I am."

Macy still couldn't believe it. "Really?"

Patterson nodded.

"Why? I love sex."

LaRue cleared her throat. "I probably won't be having overnight guests either. If something happens, it'll be over at his place."

"What if he has roommates or lives with his mother?" Patterson asked.

"If he is still living with Mom, then he definitely won't be seeing me."

They all burst into laughter.

"Well, lately I've been running into all these people who want to save themselves for something that may never happen. Not everyone is going to be lucky enough to get married." Running her fingers through her long hair, Macy stated, "Patterson, you're a better woman than me. I want to know what I'll be getting. I don't want to wait and find out after the wedding that he's lousy in bed."

"With AIDS and all the other diseases floating out there, you should be very careful, though," Patterson pointed out.

Macy announced, "I always use protection. I don't sleep with every man I meet. But when I do, I'm always safe."

"But the only sure way to not get anything is to abstain," Patterson pointed out.

Macy shook her head. "I'm just not sure I can give up sex. I love it too much."

"Maybe you should pray and ask God to help you."

She dismissed Patterson's comment with a slight wave of her hand.

"Really, you should, Macy. He'll do it."

Her eyes met Patterson's gaze. "You're really serious, huh?"

She nodded. "Aren't you?"

"You're a church girl. I should've known."

"I'm a Christian, if that's what you mean."

Macy turned to LaRue. "You a church girl, too?"

"As for my being a Christian, well, right now, that's the million dollar question," LaRue stated without emotion. "I grew up in the church, but me and God—we're not on speaking terms right now."

Patterson posed a question to Macy. "What about you? Do you know the Lord?"

"I was raised in church, but it's been a while since I've been inside one. I'm not perfect or anything like that, but I am a good person. I go to church sometimes and I give to charities—you know what I mean. The thing is, I like to have a good time and I enjoy having sex." Macy frowned. "Maybe this is not going to work out after all. I don't want to feel like I'm being judged in my own house."

"I wouldn't do that, Macy," Patterson quickly stated. "I am in no position to look down on anyone. I'm sure I can speak for LaRue when I say we're not without the blemish of sin. We all have sinned and will continue to sin."

"But you probably think I'm a bad person." Macy cast a glance in LaRue's direction. "Although God and I still talk every now and then."

"No, I doan. I do think it's important that as roommates we be honest with each other. Your life is your own, but if you ever want to be free of sexual sin, I'm here to help you."

Macy burst into laughter. "So you want to save me?"

"Only you can do that, Macy," Patterson responded.

"Let's say I bring someone home with me. A man. How will you feel about that?"

"To be honest, I would be a bit uncomfortable," Patterson answered. "It would be so awkward to walk in and find some man standing in the livin' room. This has nothing to do with my being a Christian. I believe I'd feel this way regardless. Like if you suddenly got married and we were all livin' together I—"

Macy cut her off. "That'll never happen."

"I'm just usin' the scenario as an example."

"Don't worry. I'd feel kind of awkward having someone over with you two in the house anyway."

LaRue gave her a grateful smile. "Thank you, Macy. I really appreciate your willingness to do this. Especially since this is your apartment. I don't think I'd be comfortable bringing someone home, although right now I'm not even thinking along those lines."

Patterson met Macy's gaze and smiled. "I have a feeling that we're gon' get along fine. This is gon' be a wonderful experience for all of us."

Macy's smile was tight.

Chapter 7

LaRue

LaRue attended an open call from another modeling agency and was turned down. She had an appointment with another, but LaRue debated whether she was going to actually show up. She wasn't sure she could handle another rejection.

LaRue didn't believe she'd have any problems landing a job. She would start with the temporary employment agencies first thing in the morning.

Two days before, LaRue moved out of the hotel and into Macy's apartment. After dropping off her suitcase, LaRue went shopping to buy a comforter set for the queen-sized bed. She chose a jacquard set in a taupe color to match the luxurious accents. The damask pattern boasted a rich texture and a subtle sheen, which added to the richness of the bedroom. LaRue also purchased the matching curtains and valance.

With everything unpacked and neatly in place, LaRue was pleased. She and Patterson shared a bathroom, so she made sure to leave space for some of her personal items.

Patterson was in her room still unpacking and trying to get settled. LaRue really liked the Southern belle. They had a lot in common and seemed to get along well.

Earlier this afternoon, Macy surprised them with lunch—her way of welcoming them to the apartment.

"This is so sweet of you, Macy. You didn't have to go through so much trouble." Patterson grabbed her in a bear hug. "Thank you."

LaRue bit her bottom lip to keep from laughing at Macy's surprised expression. It was clear she wasn't used to being around affectionate people. Patterson was more like her, LaRue decided. A hugger.

"It wasn't any trouble," Macy mumbled. "I was starving and I figured you ladies might be hungry, too, so I went to the deli and picked up some sandwiches." Macy paused a moment before adding, "I forgot to tell you that I'm not a cook, so don't go expecting any meals out of me. I eat out all the time."

"Oh, I love to cook," Patterson gushed. "I don't mind cooking for us."

They both looked at LaRue, who said, "I can cook. It's not exactly one of my favorite things to do, but I manage okay."

LaRue wasn't one bit surprised that Macy couldn't cook. The Black American Princess standing among them didn't look as if she even dressed herself—she was so pampered.

As if Macy could read her mind, she said, "I know you probably think I'm spoiled and shallow—"

"You're saying you're not?" LaRue interjected.

"I wouldn't say spoiled exactly."

"What would you say?" It was Patterson who asked the question.

"I don't deny that I've had a privileged life, but it certainly doesn't make me a bad person."

"I'm not saying that you're a bad person, Macy," LaRue quickly stated. "I really don't know you well enough to say that."

Macy's eyes grew large. Suddenly she burst into laughter.

LaRue and Patterson joined her.

Later when she was alone, LaRue began to have second thoughts. *Macy is everything I dislike, and while I'm grateful for such a nice place to live, I just don't know. . . . Patterson's a sweetheart. Talkative, but a sweetie. I hope we are mature enough to accept each other's shortcomings and wise enough to find ways to compromise when necessary.*

Patterson

It was a great day to be alive.

Patterson hummed happily as she settled into her new room. She ran her fingers across the delicate etchings in the headboard of her bed. Macy had wonderful taste in selecting home furnishings.

There was nothing about the room that she wanted to change. Patterson loved the rich burgundy-colored chaise that sat near the window. It was the perfect place for her to study her Bible.

Patterson fell back on the bed, reveling in the luxurious feel of the floral-and-scroll damask comforter accented by burgundy and gold pillows with bullion-fringe trimming. She'd always dreamed of owning a four-poster bed. This one was just like the rich cherrywood beds in the Ethan Allen catalog.

Patterson guessed that this one probably cost just as much—if not more than—the one sold at Ethan Allen. Last night had been the best sleep she'd had in a while. She'd never slept on such soft sheets before.

"I love it here," she murmured softly. "And when I'm a big model, I'ma buy me a bed and some sheets like this." She'd been turned down by the same agency as LaRue, but Patterson had no intentions of giving up. If she had to, she would be seen by every agency in New York.

LaRue was looking into finding a job to tide her over, and Patterson considered doing the same thing. She didn't want to risk running out of money.

Turning to lay on her side, Patterson ran her fingers along the delicate stitching on the comforter.

Macy rapped softly on the door before sticking her head inside. "I just wanted to make sure you have everything you need. I'm going out and won't be back until late."

"I'm fine," Patterson answered as she sat up. "I was just enjoying the bed."

Macy wore a strange expression on her face, but it disappeared after a moment. "Okay. Well, I'll see you tomorrow then."

"Bye," she murmured.

Patterson was a little disappointed to find that Macy was leaving her and LaRue home alone. She'd hoped they could enjoy an evening together just talking and getting to know each other better.

Later, she found LaRue watching television in the living room.

Patterson sat down in the leather club chair and said, "I really love this apartment, doan you?"

"It's nice."

"I was hoping that Macy would watch a movie or somethin' with us tonight."

"Patterson, I think Macy probably just wants us to pay the rent and not expect too much else. It's not like we're all chummy. We're just roomies—that's all."

"You're saying she doan wont to be friends?"

"She may not," LaRue answered. "Patterson, you're gonna make some friends of your own. You don't have to try so hard."

"Do you feel the same way?"

LaRue glanced over at her. "No, I don't. I think we're on our way to becoming good friends. Eventually, Macy may warm up. I'm just saying don't push so hard. Let her come around in her own time."

"I didn't think I was pushin' anything. I just thought when you live together . . . I thought we could do some things like . . . you know. Going to the movies or having dinner. We had such a great time when we went to lunch the other day."

"Like I said, it may come in time. We just moved in."

Patterson considered LaRue's words. "Okay. I'll back off then."

She didn't want to do anything to make Macy feel uncomfortable.

Macy

Macy didn't have anywhere special to be. She just knew she didn't want to be home, so she decided to have dinner at Alfredo of Rome on West Forty-ninth Street.

While waiting to be seated, Macy ran into an old family acquaintance. She tried to avoid Meredith Baxter, but before she could get away, the young woman spotted her and came rushing over.

She kissed at the air by Macy's cheek. "It's good to see you." Meredith assessed her from head to toe, then uttered, "Wow, you look stunning."

"Meredith . . . hello," Macy greeted. "I haven't seen you since we went to Martha's Vineyard with our parents."

"I know. I've been living in France. I just recently moved back to New York."

Macy searched her memory. She'd heard that Meredith was in France. "Were you in school?"

Meredith nodded. "I just got my master's in human rights and de-mocratisation at the Université de Montpellier." Changing her Louis Vuitton handbag from one shoulder to the other, she inquired, "So, what are you doing? My parents mentioned a while back that you were still at New York University. Are you working on a second degree?"

Macy's cell phone rang. She glanced down at the caller ID, saying, "Oh, excuse me. I need to take this call. It's my agent."

"Your agen—"

Macy cut her off, leaving Meredith to draw her own conclusions. "Bye now." She placed her phone to her ear and pretended to be engrossed in a heavy conversation. The call was an automated one to remind her of her hair appointment tomorrow morning.

She waited until she was clear across the room before Macy put her phone away.

"Are you ready to be seated?" the maître d' inquired.

Macy nodded. She glanced around, looking for Meredith. She released a sigh of relief when she spotted her talking to a man and a woman. She hoped they were her dinner companions, because she didn't want Meredith joining her.

"I just got my master's in human rights and democratisation . . ." Macy mimicked as she studied her menu. *Who gives a flip?*

Her waitress arrived.

"Could you get me an apple martini please?"

"Yes, ma'am. I'll bring it to you right away."

Macy continued to pore over her menu, trying to decide on whether to have the Insalata Alfredo or the Carciofi Marinati.

The waitress returned a few minutes later with her apple martini, which Macy downed quickly. She signaled the waitress to order another.

Maybe if I get drunk I won't think about just how bad my life truly sucks, she decided silently.

Chapter 8

LaRue

She held up the back portion of Patterson's hair. "You sure you want to change the color of your hair?"

"Yeah. I think it'll look good a light brown. Right now I look so plain. If we change the color of my hair, I think it'll make me look kinda sexy. The modeling agencies don't wont that innocent look anymore. They wont more of an exotic look."

"Patterson, it's not gonna get that light," LaRue explained. "Your hair is too dark." She picked up the box and held it out for Patterson to see. "See? Look at the color chart on the back."

Shrugging, Patterson responded, "It won't be as light as I thought, but I still wont to do it. I'm even thinkin' I can have it professionally lightened. More of a blondish kind of look."

"Okaaay . . ." LaRue murmured. "Let's get started."

Two hours later, Patterson stood in the bathroom admiring LaRue's handiwork.

She ran her fingers through her hair that was now a warm brown color. "You did a good job, LaRue. I love it."

"Patterson, you have beautiful hair," she complimented. "It's very soft." LaRue gently fingered the curls. "It's lighter than I thought it would be."

The color matched Patterson's eyes. "I think I look more worldly. Don't you think so?"

LaRue eyed Patterson's reflection. "You look more . . . I guess I'd call it more mature. You don't look like such a little girl anymore."

When they finished styling Patterson's hair, LaRue washed her hands and went to watch some television in the living room.

Patterson joined her fifteen minutes later carrying a bowl of freshly popped popcorn.

LaRue accepted the napkin she offered. "Thanks."

"What are we watching?"

"What are you in the mood for? We have *Law & Order, CSI* and . . ." LaRue's eyes scanned the channel guide. "What do you know . . . More *Law & Order.*"

Laughing, Patterson responded, "How 'bout *Law & Order?*"

During the first commercial break, LaRue glanced over her shoulder. "Is Macy still home? Her room is awfully quiet. We usually hear her television or radio."

"I think she left."

Out of the blue, LaRue burst into laughter, surprising Patterson, who was sitting on the floor watching television in the living room.

"What's so funny?"

"I was just thinking about Macy asking if you were a lesbian. The look on your face was priceless." LaRue handed Patterson the large blue bowl containing popcorn still warm from the microwave. "It was hysterical."

Patterson giggled at the memory. "It was kinda funny. I just couldn't understand where she was coming from when she asked that question."

"Well, I don't think it was an accusation—just a simple inquiry."

"I got that later." Patterson glanced over at LaRue. "Your braids are beautiful. How long did it take?"

"About eight hours. There were two people working on my head."

"I had my hair braided once, but I looked like a skint-headed chicken when it was done." Patterson shook her head at the memory.

"A what?"

"A skint-headed chicken. LaRue, my hair was so tight that my eyes were slanted." Pulling at her tresses, Patterson stated, "See, my hair is on the thin side. Braids don't work for me."

Fingering a braid, LaRue stated, "I love my braids. I've had them for so long, I'm not sure if I even have much of my own hair left on my head." She laughed at the expression on Patterson's face. "Gurl, I'm only kidding."

"I knew that."

"Yeah, right." LaRue held out her hands. "Pass the popcorn, please."

"What are you doing for the Memorial Day holiday?" Patterson inquired.

Shrugging, LaRue responded, "I don't know. Are you going home?"

"Naw. I wont Mama and Daddy to get used to me being gone. I think they still havin' a hard time of it."

"I actually thought about going home, but it's too expensive." LaRue cracked a smile. "You know we're pathetic. We sound so homesick. Here we are in New York—we should do something here to celebrate. We can check around and see what type of events they hold on the holidays."

"We can also ask Macy."

LaRue agreed.

The sound of voices coming from within Macy's room caught their attention.

"Macy must be home," Patterson stated. "Her TV just came on."

"That or she's got a ghost or one of those timers."

"I almost forgot. I brought some new movies with me from back home. We can watch one of them." Patterson rose to her full height. "I'll be right back."

Macy

Macy could hear Patterson and LaRue talking and laughing in the living room. Not used to sharing her space, she'd fled to the quiet sanctuary of her bedroom after their return from having dinner at a nearby pizza parlor. She sat at the writing desk in the corner of her room working on a sketch of an elegant wedding dress.

Macy laid down her pencil and rubbed her forehead. "What was I thinking? I don't want roommates," she murmured as she fingered the black sheer voile fabric of the canopy draped around her bed.

Thinking about this impossible situation that her parents put her in raised Macy's ire. "This is your fault, Father."

A soft knock on the door caught her attention. "Yes. . . ."

Patterson stuck her head inside. "Why doan you come out and join us? We're getting ready to watch a movie."

Macy pasted on a smile. "I'll be out there in a moment."

"Okay."

"Heavenly Father, please help me . . ." Macy groaned. "Please make my father come to his senses. I don't know how long I can endure these people in my house." They'd only been there one week and she had to admit, everything had come together rather smoothly. Much more than Macy ever expected. *I just don't want roommates,* she cried silently.

A few minutes later, Patterson stood outside her door. "The movie's starting."

"I'll be right there," Macy responded. She stood up and glanced around her room. The black-and-white silk hand-stitched quilt covered a platinum-colored metal bed flanked by a canopy adorned with garlands of red roses. Her room also housed silk variations of tropical and exotic plants.

She picked up a matching toss pillow, holding it to her breast. "Lord, you've got to help me. I don't belong with these two people. I don't even like women. If you don't make my parents come to their senses—well, I'm going to have a nervous breakdown."

Macy sighed softly as she left her room to join her new roommates. *I mean it. They are going to drive me crazy.*

Patterson

Early morning sunlight filtered through the blinds in Patterson's bedroom.

She turned to her left side, as she pulled herself away from the clutches of sleep. Noting the time on the clock, Patterson bounced out of bed. Last night she'd had a good time talking and watching a romantic comedy with LaRue and Macy.

She and LaRue had made a conscious effort to include Macy in on their conversation. They didn't want her to feel left out.

Patterson was a little surprised to find that she was so quiet. The most Macy talked the entire evening was to tell them about several events coming up for the summer. She was intrigued by the Barbecue

Over Broadway. She'd never heard of having a picnic seven stories above the city.

"They also have the big Macy's Extravaganza . . ." Macy was saying. "That's if you love fireworks."

While the whole country watched the dazzling display on television, Patterson thrilled at the thought of having a firsthand view. Maybe she could talk her parents into breaking tradition and coming up to New York to celebrate her mother's birthday.

Bringing her thoughts back to the present, Patterson did her morning stretches, humming a soft melody while she exercised. When she was done, Patterson opened her blinds. The sun cast a glow throughout her room. "It's a beautiful day, New York," she whispered. "I love this city."

Although she didn't hear anyone moving about, she was sure Macy and LaRue were up. "They may be out and about already. I need to get moving."

She picked up her robe off the bench at the foot of the bed and slipped it over her nightgown. Patterson paused to get her toiletries before leaving her room—and sang while loosening her plaits.

Macy

The sound of someone singing jolted Macy out of a drug-induced deep slumber. She'd had trouble falling asleep last night, so she'd taken a sleep aid to help her.

"What the heck?" Macy pushed her hair away from her face. She jumped out of bed and rushed out of her bedroom, slamming into LaRue in the hallway.

"Was that you?" Macy demanded.

"Singing?" Shaking her head, LaRue replied, "No. Wasn't me."

Patterson stepped out of the bathroom fully dressed. "Good morning, roomies," she greeted brightly. "It's a glorious day, don't you think? I was just about to fix some breakfast. We can—"

Macy didn't bother to hide her irritation. "*Just shut up, will you?* Lord, you talk too dang much. Patterson, do you have a clue as to what time it is? What possessed you to wake us up with your rendition of 'I Can See Clearly Now'? You are not on Broadway."

Heat crept into Patterson's face. "I . . . I'm sorry, y'all. It's almost six, so I thought y'all were up already. I didn't mean to wake you."

"Who gets up this early?" Macy snapped. "Girl, you're not back home on the farm in Tree Trunk, Georgia. *This is New York.*"

Patterson's bottom lip trembled slightly. "It's Three Oak," she said quietly.

"I don't give a flip where you come from," Macy snapped.

She was near tears, but Macy didn't care.

"I'm so s-sorry, y'all," Patterson stammered. "I f-feel so bad."

Rolling her eyes and muttering a string of profanities under her breath, Macy turned on her heel and stomped back into her room, slamming the door.

She stood with her ear pressed to the door listening to them, because she knew they would be talking about her.

Macy heard Patterson ask, "What's wrong with Macy? She was kind of mean to me, don't you think? She didn't have to yell and cuss at me like that. If I wasn't Christian, I would've told her how the cows ate the corn."

"*The what?*" Macy heard LaRue ask. She had the same question.

"I don't cotton to people being rude to me like that. I said I was sorry. I didn't know y'all was still sleeping."

"It's okay, Patterson. Just remember that the walls are not sound-proof, so maybe you could keep it down a bit, please?"

Macy was so angry she could've strangled Patterson for waking her up.

"Would you like some breakfast?" she heard Patterson ask. "I was about to cook."

"Sure. Why not? I'm already up."

"Think Macy will want to eat?"

"I don't know. You'll have to ask her. Although if I were you, I'd leave Miss Baldwin alone. That's an evil child."

"Witch," Macy muttered. She didn't like LaRue at all. "I can't stand that jealous heifer."

A soft rap on her door caused Macy to jump. She heard Patterson's apology to her through the door, but didn't respond. Instead, she wandered over to her bed and climbed in, burying her head underneath the pillows.

She closed her eyes and tried to recapture her deep slumber, but the steady ticking of the clock on the bedside table kept her awake.

Muttering a curse, Macy sat up and rearranged her pillows, trying to find a comfortable position. She lay on her stomach for a few minutes, and then turned over, this time lying on her back.

Macy's day went from bad to worse.

In all her years, she'd never had to return anything to a department store. Furthermore, she didn't really want to return the clothes, but she needed the money.

When she'd purchased the items almost two weeks ago, the salesclerk had treated her as if she couldn't afford them in the first place. Her snobbish attitude inspired and motivated Macy to buy them, just to show the woman otherwise.

Now she had to skunk back to the expensive boutique and return them. She could only hope that the salesclerk she'd dealt with then was not working today.

Unfortunately, the witch was there. As soon as she spotted Macy, a big grin split across her face until she spied the packages in her hands.

"I need to return these," Macy stated flatly. "They don't fit."

"But you tried them on. They—"

Macy cut her off. "I said I'd like to return these. If this is too difficult a task for you, then please get your manager. I'm sure he or she can do this return."

The woman glared at her, but said nothing.

"Thank you."

The clerk proceeded to inspect every piece of clothing as if her life depended on it.

"I didn't wear them, if that's what you're trying to detect." Macy's anger got the best of her. "You want to know why I'm returning them?" she asked in a loud voice. "I couldn't get it out of my mind just how rude you were to me the other day, so I decided you don't deserve my business."

Macy was aware that the other customers had stopped shopping to listen, but she didn't care. "That's why I'm bringing them back."

Another woman rushed over to the counter. "Is there a problem?"

Pulling up to her full height, Macy gave the petite woman a haughty glare. "Who are you?"

"I'm the manager. Melinda Spielberg."

"I was just explaining to your employee how dissatisfied I was with her treatment of me when I was here the last time. I purchased all these items despite her rudeness, but once I got them home, I real-

ized that she'd upset me to the point where I would derive no enjoyment in wearing them." Macy paused for a brief second. "From the
moment I walked into the store, she rushed to judgment and decided
I couldn't afford to shop here."

"I'm so sorry, my dear. . . ."

"I don't want apologies. What I want is my money back." Pointing
to the clerk, she added, "And this witch fired. Until she's gone, I
won't ever shop here again."

Melinda sent a frustrated glance toward the stunned salesclerk. "I
am so sorry and I do apologize. What is your name?"

"Macy Baldwin. I'm Rhetta Baldwin's daughter. She's not going to
be very happy to hear how I was treated in your store."

Several apologies and a fifty-percent discount later, Macy felt much
better. There was hope for the rest of her day.

Patterson was home alone when she arrived. Still fuming over the
early morning event, Macy walked through her apartment making a
point to ignore her.

Macy was relieved she'd eaten dinner before coming home. She
didn't feel like socializing. She spent the rest of the evening in her
room sewing.

Designing clothes helped her to relax. Holding the fabric against
her body, Macy tried to imagine the vivid purple material transformed
into a blazer.

She smiled as she worked. This was her only happiness.

Chapter 9

LaRue

When Patterson came knocking on her door at seven-thirty the next morning, it took a moment before LaRue remembered that she'd agreed to work out with her in the fitness center.

She dragged herself out of bed and pulled on a pair of sweats and sneakers.

After a brief warm-up, both LaRue and Patterson started with the treadmill, walking slowly at first, then gradually increasing speed.

LaRue jogged for half an hour before working with weights.

One hour later, she did one last stretch before calling an end to her exercise regimen for the day. Watching Patterson finish her last sit-up, she patted her face and neck with a fluffy towel.

Patterson rose to her feet and reached for her own towel. "Let's do something fun tonight, like go see a movie," she suggested.

"That sounds like a good idea."

"Should we ask Macy to join us?"

LaRue chose her words carefully. She really didn't care to spend any more time with Macy than was absolutely necessary. "That's up to you, Patterson. You know she runs hot and cold. And after yesterday . . . I don't know." She felt Macy had overreacted some and had treated Patterson rudely.

"Oh, I'm sure she's in a better mood now."

"You really think so?" LaRue scanned Patterson's face to see if she was serious. "Gurl, she was nasty to you. She gave you the cold shoulder all day long."

"I know. I got mad at her, too, but today is another day. We have another day to get it right, as far as I'm concerned."

LaRue chuckled. "I must admit, Patterson, you have an interesting way of looking at things."

"I doan see much point in dwellin' on the negative."

"Remember, you're dealing with Macy. She's spoiled, uppity, and thinks the world revolves around her."

"She'll be all right, LaRue. I told her I was sorry, and I'll be more considerate the next time." Patterson threw her towel in the hamper. "You ready to go?"

They left the fitness center and took the elevator upstairs.

LaRue and Patterson weren't in the apartment five minutes before Macy walked out of her bedroom.

"I wondered where you two were," she mumbled by way of a greeting. LaRue gave Patterson a narrowed glinting glance, hoping she would keep her mouth shut. She wasn't in any mood to play referee.

Patterson opened her mouth to speak, but Macy raised her hand and said, "I don't want to hear anything from you."

LaRue was about to respond in defense of Patterson, but held her tongue. If Patterson intended to live here, she had to learn how to handle Macy on her own.

Patterson

With her back pressed against the doors of the double ovens, Patterson regarded Macy imperiously.

"I've apologized already," she stated calmly. "I can't undo what happened. All I can say is that I won't make the same mistake again."

Brushing away an unruly curl, Patterson continued, "Personally, I think you play your music much too loudly, but I don't go 'round here treating you like this. You've never heard me cuss at you, so I'd really appreciate it if you'd show me the same courtesy."

"Excuse me?" Macy strode into the kitchen. "In case you've forgotten, this is my house."

"I live here, too." Patterson's voice trembled. "Macy, if you don't want me stayin' here in this apartment, then you need to give me my money back and I'll be on my way right this minute. I'm not gon' let you treat me any kind of way."

"You are renting a room from me, and I won't have you trying to tell me what I can or cannot do in my own house, Patterson."

Patterson glanced over at LaRue, then back at Macy. "I didn't do that. All I'm sayin' is that if you want me to respect you by not singin' so loud in the morning, then you shouldn't play your music so loud."

"I'm gonna weigh in on this discussion," LaRue interjected. "Macy, we don't want you throwing up your ownership in our faces. We know you own this apartment and, yes, we are renting rooms from you, but you do owe us some respect."

Macy cut her eyes at LaRue. "So what is it that you're trying to tell me?"

"Perhaps you shouldn't be so hard on Patterson. We're all gonna make mistakes at some point. That's part of our getting to know one another. I agree with Patterson about the cussing. You need to do something about that."

"I think it'll be better if I move out," Patterson suggested. "I don't really see this workin'."

"Is that what you want, Macy?" LaRue demanded.

Macy sighed in resignation. "Before you moved in, I told you all that I was evil in the mornings. Especially before I have my coffee."

"I'm not saying that I'm not at fault," Patterson explained. "I do need to remember that just because I get up with the chickens, I can't expect everyone else to do it also. But Macy, if you doan want me here, I'll leave now."

"I never said anything about you leaving. You brought it up."

"I'm not gon' stay anywhere where people are gonna be nasty to me."

The room was silent.

"Is my music really that loud?" Macy blurted.

"Gurl, it's loud," LaRue responded with a laugh. "I don't even have to turn my radio on, because I can hear yours."

Patterson relaxed. She was grateful that she wouldn't have to move.

"I didn't know. I thought I had it down to a more conservative volume. I usually play it much louder."

LaRue shook her head in confusion. "I don't know how you can understand a word of what they're saying. I just can't get with hip-hop. I'm into old-school music. I love me some Earth, Wind & Fire, some Whispers, the Commodores, groups like that."

"My parents listen to all of them," Macy stated. "LaRue, you sound like an old twenty-six year old talking like that."

Patterson chuckled as she began taking dishes out of the dishwasher.

Eyeing her, LaRue posed the question, "What types of music do you listen to, Patterson? I'm almost afraid to ask, with you going around here singing Johnny Nash's 'I Can See Clearly Now.' "

"I like those same groups you mentioned. I also like Kenny Rogers, Dolly Parton, Garth Brooks, and Clint Black. I—"

"Whoa sistah," LaRue interjected. "Patterson, I know you from the South and all, but don't tell me you really listen to country music like that. *Dolly Parton?*"

"I like all types of music including country. I even listen to Yanni, Kenny G, and some rap."

"I have to say this is a first for me," Macy stated with a short laugh. "I've never met a sista who was into country & western music."

"Me neither," LaRue contributed.

Patterson broke into a wide grin. "This is so cool. We can learn so much from one another."

She finished wiping down the countertops, then crossed the room to join Macy and LaRue at the table. "We're gon' have so much fun together. Just y'all wait and see."

Macy shot an amused look towards LaRue.

"Patterson, why are you always so upbeat?" LaRue inquired. "Have you ever had a bad day in your life?"

"Yeah, but I try not to linger on it. I was taught that you should enjoy every minute of every day."

"Oh, Lord, we have Little Polly Sunshine living in here with us." Macy raised her eyes heavenward. "No wonder you wake up singing."

"I sing—you play music. What's the difference?"

Macy seemed to be considering Patterson's question.

LaRue checked her watch. "Are we still going to the movies?"

Patterson nodded. "If you're still wontin' to go. Macy, you interested in going with us?"

"Sure. My calendar's clear for this afternoon."

She was surprised that Macy had agreed to join them. Patterson fully expected her to refuse. "Well, if we're going to make the matinee, we should hurry."

Patterson truly believed that Macy was in need of a few good friends. LaRue thought that Macy was spoiled and self-absorbed, but she had a feeling there was much more buried underneath.

Patterson had a vision of the three of them becoming close and spending a lot of time together.

I am so grateful, Patterson thought. *LaRue and I really lucked out and probably saved some money.*

They never could've afforded a place as nice as this one on their own.

LaRue

While Patterson went to check out a couple of modeling agencies after Memorial Day, LaRue put in job applications all over Manhattan. She filled out the last one around noon. She had lunch before heading to her two o'clock interview.

"How did your interview go?" Patterson inquired when LaRue strode through the front door five minutes after five.

"It was fine. A lot of paperwork."

"What are you applying for?" Macy wanted to know. She sat in the living room polishing her nails.

"There's a new charter school opening in Harlem. I've applied to be a counselor."

Macy straightened. "I thought you were a social worker or something. Have you ever worked in a school?"

"Have you ever worked a job, period?" LaRue shot back.

"No. I never needed to work. *My parents are rich.*"

LaRue rubbed her temple with her fingertips, an action that had become a habit since her husband's death. "How fortunate for you, Macy. To answer your question, I was an elementary school teacher before I became a social worker."

"But don't you need some type of certification to work at a school in New York?"

"New York State has reciprocity agreements with more than thirty-five other states. California is one of them. I have other papers to fill out, but if I wanted to be a teacher, I could start teaching immediately."

"I'll be praying you get the job," Patterson interjected. "But I still hope you won't give up on the modeling."

Macy held out her right hand, admiring her handiwork. "I don't know why you'd want to work with kids. They're crazy these days."

"Not all of them, Macy," LaRue said softly, her eyes narrowing. "It's that type of attitude that breeds problems in schools."

"The last thing I'd want to do is work at a school." Macy closed up her nail polish and sat it on the marble-topped coffee table. "I'm having a hard enough time just trying to finish college."

"What do you want to do, Macy?" LaRue questioned, although she had a feeling she already knew the answer.

Macy carefully pulled her long hair out of the barrette that had been holding it back. "Fashion design would be nice. I love clothes and I've been designing my own for years."

"I've seen some of your drawings and they're real nice," Patterson interjected. "I think you should consider becoming a designer if modeling doesn't come through for you."

Macy shook her head, her curls going to and fro. "My father would have a stroke, Patterson. He wants me to get a 'real job,' as he puts it."

"Fashion design is a real job," LaRue pointed out. "I know how that feels. My parents aren't supportive of my modeling either."

"Why do y'all think your parents feel that way?" Patterson asked.

"My dad's a minister," LaRue explained. "He's the world-renowned Bishop Larry Arnette and he thinks that modeling is evil—women running around half-naked, having orgies, and doing drugs. That kind of thing."

"Bishop Arnette is your father?" Patterson asked in surprise. "LaRue, I watch your father all the time on television. I love to listen to him preach."

"Your father has that huge megachurch in Los Angeles . . . Compton or somewhere, right?" Macy inquired. "Didn't the congregation give him a Rolls Royce last year? I remember reading something like that."

"They bought him a Jaguar," LaRue corrected. "It was for his anniversary. He celebrated his twenty-fifth year."

"So you aren't the ghetto girl I thought you were."

LaRue sent a glare Macy's way. "Excuse me?"

"Don't be offended. I'm just saying that I thought you came from . . . well, I thought you were poor."

"I wouldn't say I was poor," Patterson tossed out. "But I do come from very modest means."

"What do your parents do?" LaRue inquired.

"They're farmers. We own the largest farm in Three Oak," Patterson said proudly.

LaRue folded her arms across her chest. "So, Macy, tell us what your parents do."

"My father is president and CEO of Baldwin Pharmaceuticals. That's where my parents want me—in corporate America. They don't consider working in the fashion industry prestigious enough."

Patterson gave them a sympathetic smile. "I'm glad my mama and daddy are supportive."

Macy shook her head, running her fingers through her flowing hair. "Well, I'm a grown woman. I don't care what mine think. It's not about them."

"I agree with you, Macy." LaRue played with one of her braids. "I don't care either."

Standing up, Macy announced, "I've got a date picking me up at seven, so I need to get ready."

"Have fun," LaRue called out as she headed to her bedroom.

"I intend to do just that." Macy paused long enough to add, "Oh, I'll be gone all weekend."

LaRue smiled at Patterson and said, "Well, it's just you and me, gurlfriend."

"You have anything in mind?"

Shaking her head, LaRue responded, "I think I'll do some reading and maybe watch some television. What about you?"

"I'ma do some Bible study. You're more than welcome to join me."

LaRue's eyes fell to the floor. "No, thanks."

"LaRue, can I ask you somethin'?"

"What is it?"

"Since your dad is Bishop Arnette. Are you . . . are you involved in church?"

"I haven't been in a while since I . . ." LaRue met Patterson's gaze. "Why?"

"I was just curious."

"God and I just aren't on speaking terms right now, Patterson. Now, I know you mean well, but I hope that you'll respect my wishes and not try to save me. I don't need saving. I don't need to be preached to either. Okay?"

Patterson nodded.

LaRue lay back on the couch, her eyes closed.

"What happened?"

"What are you talking about?"

"What made you lose your faith, LaRue?"

"I wouldn't say I lost my faith—no, that's not it. I'm angry, Patterson. Very angry. God wants me to do something for Him, but He didn't do anything for me. I was married to a wonderful man—he was my childhood sweetheart. God didn't save my husband when I begged and pleaded with Him to keep Tom alive."

"Did you ever consider . . ." Patterson paused.

LaRue sat up and leaned forward. "What were you gonna say?"

"I'm assuming you asked God to heal your husband. Right?" When LaRue nodded, she continued, "Well, did you consider that God takin' him to heaven is a healin'?"

"I wanted Tom with me," LaRue responded angrily. "I didn't want him to leave me alone."

"I understand that. Really I do. It's hard to lose someone you love."

A tear slipped down LaRue's cheek. "Tom and I had our whole lives planned. We wanted to have children. Then we found out that he had a brain tumor. Things just changed after that."

Patterson embraced her, saying, "I'm so sorry, LaRue."

"I know there's a God, Patterson. But He didn't listen to me. He didn't give me my heart's desire. God took my husband from me and I'm sorry, but I'm angry about it."

"Second Corinthians 5:8 tells us that *to be absent from the body is to be present with the Lord.* It's inevitable to feel loss because it's part of our life, but we should rejoice knowin' they went to be with the Lord."

"That's what it says, but my heart is still broken." LaRue rose to her feet. "I appreciate your words, Patterson, but I have to be honest with you. You can't change my mind. My Dad tried . . . my mom . . . I'm still mad at God and nothing's gonna change that for me. Maybe later, but not right now."

"LaRue . . ."

She held up her hand. "Don't push, Patterson. I mean it. I want nothing to do with God."

Patterson

Unshed tears glittered in Patterson's eyes.

She got up and made her way to her bedroom. She climbed into bed and reached for her Bible. Her heart was heavy from the pain weighing on LaRue's heart. She wanted to find a way to reach her friend.

"How can I help her?" she whispered as she thumbed through her Bible. LaRue was mourning, but Patterson sensed something more. She was in a rebellious stage, and it could lead her to trouble.

"Lord, please help LaRue move past her anger. She still loves you. I know she does. . . ."

Chapter 10

Macy

The cool air kissed the beads of perspiration on Macy's body, sending a chill through her. She opened her eyes and glanced around the room.

"Can you turn down the air conditioner? I'm getting cold."

Frederick pulled her lingerie-clad body closer to his. "I can warm you up," he murmured huskily.

Her lips puckered with annoyance. "I'm serious. You keep it too cold in here."

"Macy, must you complain so much?" He sat up, using the pillows as support against his back. "You didn't like the lobster, the wine was too dry. Why are you in such a strange mood?"

She didn't know what to tell him. All Macy knew was that she felt different.

"If you won't do it, I'll get up and do it myself." Macy swung her legs to the side of the bed and stood up. "You get on my nerves, Frederick."

He laughed in response.

Macy seethed. Money or no money, maybe she was getting bored with Frederick. She'd also heard he was seeing a young actress in Los Angeles. Maybe that's why she felt bad about having slept with Frederick. Her heart was telling her that she deserved so much more.

She was terribly unhappy, although she tried to keep that truth hidden from view. Macy was miserable in her life. She was lonely, unfulfilled, and now . . . she was poor. Hers was a wretched life.

Frederick's words cut into her thoughts. "Come back to bed, Macy."

Arms folded, she tossed a glance over her shoulder. "Why?"

Sitting up in bed, he surveyed Macy's face. "Okay, what have you heard this time?"

Her stare drilled into him. "You sound guilty of something, Frederick."

His gray eyes darkened as she held her gaze. "Macy, I know you. You're upset with me because you think I'm seeing someone else."

"Aren't you?"

"What about William?" Frederick asked. Noting the surprised expression on Macy's face, he said, "Yes, I know all about him. I've known for a while that you were involved with him."

"William and I are over."

Frederick got out of bed and walked over to where Macy was standing. "Honey, we've never talked about this thing we have. Maybe it's time. I want you to know that I care a great deal for you."

"Are you saying you want to have a monogamous relationship with me?"

Hopeful, Macy held her breath as she waited for his answer.

Patterson

She enjoyed taking evening strolls around her neighborhood in Murray Hill. This Saturday was no different. The pre-war apartments, brownstones, the walk-ups, and luxury condominium buildings held her attention while giving her a glimpse into the fascinating history the neighborhood possessed.

She was smitten by the nearness of the Pierpont Morgan Library, the Whitney Museum, and the Chrysler Building. The neighborhood was also filled with unique boutiques, trendy bars, and eclectic restaurants, so Patterson and her roommates never had to venture very far.

She felt truly blessed having run into Macy and ending up in a fancy apartment. Patterson especially loved her bedroom. Each room had its own unique personality, each one fit for a queen. The rich mahogany furnishings added to the aristocratic feel of the room.

Patterson made her way back to her apartment building. She arrived to find LaRue reading, curled up on the loveseat. She was home alone and seemed to be enjoying her solitude.

"Hey, you," Patterson greeted.

"Hey, yourself."

They hadn't seen Macy since she left the previous night. She spent most weekends away from the apartment, often coming home Sunday evenings to give them a review of the clubs she'd visited. Patterson wondered where she found the strength to party all the time. She also didn't miss the fact that Macy didn't seem to have any female friends. Most of her time was spent with various men, some more famous than others.

I just hope she's not sleeping with all of them. And if she was, Patterson hoped she used protection. There were too many sexually transmitted diseases in the world.

Although Macy didn't seem to mind sharing the details of her club-hopping, Patterson was acutely aware that she and LaRue were never invited to join her. She tried not to let it bother her, but Patterson couldn't deny that she was a little hurt. The three of them could be wonderful friends if only Macy would give the relationship a chance. They weren't exactly enemies, but they weren't friends either.

"Want to order a pizza?"

Patterson looked up from her task of scanning through a stack of mail that had been lying on the sofa table in the living room. "Sure. Can we do half pepperoni?"

LaRue nodded. "Fine by me. Do we have any coupons?"

"I don't," Patterson responded. "And I doubt if Macy does."

"Macy is definitely not the coupon type." LaRue got up and strode across the room toward the kitchen. She peeked into the drawers beneath the counter. "I don't see any."

"Vic knows us. Maybe he'll let us have the discount without a coupon."

Picking up the telephone, LaRue responded, "I'm gonna ask." She played with a long braid while waiting for someone to answer.

Patterson navigated to her room. Sitting on the edge of her bed, she picked up her phone and dialed.

She grinned at the sound of her mother's voice. "Hey, Mama. It's me, Patterson." Their conversation lasted until the pizza arrived. She made sure to call her mother regularly. Patterson didn't want her getting sick with worry.

LaRue

A large pepperoni pizza and a two-liter bottle of Pepsi—a single woman's date on a Saturday night. LaRue could tell that something was bothering Patterson. She wasn't her usual chatty self. Not that she was complaining. She liked Patterson a lot, but the girl could talk up a storm.

"You okay, Patterson?"

"Huh?"

She reacted as if she'd been caught daydreaming. LaRue repeated her question.

"I'm fine." Patterson reached for another slice of pizza. "Don't you find it kinda interesting that Macy usually comes home to tell us how much fun she has, but she never invites us to go out anywhere with her?"

"I'm not sure I want to hang out with Macy," LaRue responded. She bit into her slice and tried to keep the pepperoni from sliding off the melted cheese.

"It's not so much that I wont to go out with her. I just think it's rude she doesn't even bother to ask, that's all."

"Patterson, I know you really would like the three of us to become best friends, but, hon, it just may not happen. We are just roommates. You can't expect anymore than that."

"Maybe you're right," she whispered.

Patterson dropped her head to hide the tears in her eyes, but not before LaRue glimpsed them.

"Why is this so important to you?"

"I never had any real friends, LaRue. I'm in a new city and I have a new life. I want friends to share it with. I'm a Christian and I know you are, too, even though you seem to be running from it. You know what we have to deal with daily. I need someone who will hold me accountable, you know?"

LaRue was too stunned to respond.

"I know you gon' think I lost my mind, but LaRue, I wont to help Macy. She's in our lives for a reason. We got to help her."

"She doesn't want our help, Patterson. The same way I don't want you forcing God down my throat, Macy doesn't want us pressuring her for friendship."

"That's only because Macy doesn't realize that she needs us. Deep down under all that make-up and expensive clothes, is a lost little girl. Our job is to find a way to reach her."

LaRue didn't agree.

As far as she was concerned, Macy was a self-centered little witch with a false sense of superiority. She predicted that Macy's little nasty attitude would one day be her downfall.

Macy

She'd been dumped a second time within one month.

Macy ignored Frederick as she stumbled around the room, picking up her clothes. She muttered a curse when she couldn't find her bra. Finally, she just gave up.

Frederick held it in his hand. "Macy, you don't have to leave."

His expression bordered on mockery, which only infuriated Macy more. Snatching her bra, she stated, "I want to leave. All you want from me is sex. Well, I deserve much better, Frederick."

"Macy, you're trying to change the rules on me. When we started out, we were just two friends having sex."

She whirled around to stare at him, quick anger rising in her eyes. "I know all that." She slid into her underwear, then suddenly felt ashamed.

She unexpectedly recalled the story of Eve and the serpent in the Garden. *Strange that I would think about this now, but like Adam and Eve, my eyes are open.*

"What are you thinking about?"

Macy came out of her reverie. "Don't talk to me, Frederick. I'm very angry with you right now, so just leave me alone."

After she was clothed, Macy grabbed her overnight bag and walked with stiff dignity toward the door.

She wanted to put as much distance between her and Frederick as possible.

Standing on the other side of his door, Macy shed a few tears before making her way to the elevator. Her roommates would be surprised at her early return, but would not ask any questions.

Macy was thankful for that, at least. Partly because she had no answers. She wasn't exactly sure what had just happened.

Maybe this is my punishment for sexual sin.

"Where did that thought come from?" she whispered.

Macy told herself that God wasn't vengeful like that. He would not use loneliness as a punishment. He would not be so cruel.

Downstairs, she hailed a taxi.

Getting inside the vehicle, Macy instructed, "Take me to the nearest bar."

Chapter 11

Patterson

J ust waking up in such luxury brightened her day.
Patterson jumped out of bed humming softly. She was careful not to make too much noise for fear of disturbing LaRue and Macy.

Especially Macy. Patterson had heard noises around two in the morning. Concerned, she'd gotten up and crept to her door, carrying a baseball bat. She was about to confront what she suspected was a burglar.

Apparently, LaRue had the same idea, because she had some kind of stick in her hand.

They turned on the hall light nearly scaring Macy who was stumbling around in the dark. It was clear that she'd been drinking.

Without saying a word, she and LaRue returned to their own rooms.

Patterson had a strong feeling that Macy had been partying too much. She held her tongue because she knew that Macy really wouldn't be all that receptive right now to anything she had to say.

Before Patterson climbed out of bed the next morning, she lifted Macy in prayer.

Patterson was always anxious to start her day. After a quiet breakfast of bacon, scrambled eggs, and toast, Patterson returned to her bedroom to study her Bible. She and LaRue would be attending the eleven o'clock service held at a nearby church.

About an hour later, she heard someone in the hall. Patterson put away her Bible and peeked out her door. She found a pajama-clad La-Rue heading to the bathroom.

"Good morning . . ."

"Morning," LaRue mumbled. She paused a second and said, "I can't get that song out of my head now."

"What song?"

"That one you were singing the other day. 'I Can See Clearly Now.' "

Patterson grinned. "I love that song. I sing it every morning." Sending a look toward Macy's closed door, she added, "Well, I used to anyway."

LaRue grinned. "You're too funny."

"It's really a nice song."

"If you say so," LaRue responded. She pushed open the bathroom door. "I've gotta go. My bladder's full."

Patterson was in her bedroom singing softly with the door open when LaRue emerged. She stopped singing long enough to say, "I made some bacon, scrambled eggs, and toast. It's in the microwave," she announced.

"Thanks, gurl. I'm starving."

Chuckling, Patterson closed her door and got dressed. She thought about her parents and what they might be doing. Her daddy was most likely out doing chores around the farm and tending to the horses, while her mama was feeding the other animals. She would take the eggs and place them in cartons for her daddy to sell.

Patterson felt better having talked to them the night before. She tried to keep herself busy with job-hunting and getting to know Macy and LaRue. They had been checking Emerald Model Management's Web site daily, looking for the list of callbacks.

Although nothing yet, Patterson had a feeling it would be soon.

She and her roommates had sampled meals from most of the restaurants in the neighborhood, but Patterson had grown tired of eating out. She decided that she would make a stop at the corner market after church service to pick up a few items.

Tonight she was cooking dinner. Patterson wanted to make something special for LaRue and Macy.

"LaRue, would you like to go to church with me?"

"No, thank you," came her prompt reply.

Patterson let the subject drop. She wasn't going to push LaRue. "I'm gon' make dinner for us when I come home from church."

LaRue glanced up from her plate. "Really?"

"I'm tired of eating out. I want a home-cooked meal for a change."

"I know what you mean. I'll be more than happy to help you—just let me know."

Patterson nodded with a smile. "I will."

She headed to the front door. "I'll see y'all later. I gotta get out of here so that I won't be late for church."

Waving, LaRue returned her attention to her breakfast.

Patterson hummed as she took the elevator to the lobby.

Macy

"What's all that?" Macy questioned when Patterson, carrying an armload of bags, came through the front door. LaRue followed with a couple of grocery bags of her own.

"I'm making dinner for us tonight."

Macy looked surprised by Patterson's announcement. "Really? Why?"

"You've got to be tired of all that restaurant food. I know I am."

"Oh." Macy rose to her feet, saying, "Well, I'll be in my room. Call me when the food is ready."

Patterson hadn't expected an offer of help and wasn't disappointed.

She and LaRue burst into laughter behind Macy's hasty retreat.

"I'ma change my clothes," Patterson announced. "I'll be right back."

She strode to her bedroom, returning a few minutes later wearing a pair of denim overalls with a white T-shirt.

LaRue was putting away the last of the groceries.

After setting out everything she needed, Patterson wrapped an apron around her waist and set out her ingredients. A few minutes later, she was ready to create a delicious home-cooked meal.

"Girl, it's smelling good up in here," LaRue stated.

"Thanks. I just had to have a home-cooked meal today."

Lowering her voice to a whisper, LaRue said, "I don't know how Macy does it—eating out all the time. I'm with you. I want some real food." She leaned against the kitchen counter and asked, "Can I do something to help?"

Patterson glanced up from what she was doing. "Do you know how to make biscuits?"

"I sure do. My granny taught me. She was from Georgia and, gurl-friend, I'm here to tell ya, Granny could throw down on some home-made buttermilk biscuits."

Pointing, Patterson responded, "Great. All the ingredients are over there. Go for what cha know."

After a short burst of laughter, LaRue washed her hands. "Where is our dear Macy?" she inquired after a moment.

"In her room, I think. You know how much she likes to be alone. I was surprised to see her last night. And drunk—she's been doing a lot of drinking lately. I think something must have happened to set her off. Macy looks like she's been crying."

LaRue's expression was one of nonchalance.

"Sometimes I get the feeling that she doan really like me," Patterson said.

"I think Macy likes you a lot, Patterson. It's me she's not crazy about. Macy just strikes me as the type of person who is all about self. I try not to take it personally."

"We're roommates, the three of us. I just wont all of us to be good friends, that's all. *Why is that too much to ask?*"

LaRue gave a slight shrug. "Maybe she'll come around, Patterson. But if not, don't let it get to you. Women like Macy don't want many female friends."

Patterson continued cooking as she talked. "She's probably just afraid to let anyone get too close. You know, to see the real Macy. Something scares her, I think."

While stirring the mixture of shortening, self-rising flour, and milk, LaRue considered Patterson's words. "You may be right, but then again she just might be stuck-up and feels that we're not good enough for her. That's the impression I get."

"We have to keep her in prayer. For whatever reason, I believe deep in my heart that God placed us together for a reason. Maybe we're here to help each other through the storms of life. Wouldn't that be great? So many people suffer through trials alone and without a friend in the world. I don't wont to be that way." Patterson smiled in contentment. "I'm glad we found each other, LaRue."

"Me, too."

"I'm even glad we have Macy in our lives as well."

"Humph," LaRue responded. "I can't really say that."

"She's not that bad. Not really."

"No," LaRue admitted. "But she could be better."

"We all could," Patterson acknowledged. "I keep thinking about the last sermon I heard my pastor back home preach. He said that if we follow Jesus' example as the perfect friend, we can improve our relationships."

A wave of shame swept through LaRue, but she chose to ignore it. "Macy really taps on my nerves with those snobbish ways of hers. I'm tired of picking up after her, too. Last Friday, when I came home, I found her dirty dishes in the living room. *On the coffee table.*"

LaRue twisted her face into a frown. "I can't stand nastiness. She needs Lupe to come every day if she's not gonna even pick up after herself."

"We just have to be patient with her. We've been living heh for what? 'Bout three and a half weeks now?"

LaRue nodded. "Yeah. About that."

"As long as we're honest with each other and keep communicating, we'll be just fine. I really believe that."

"Forever the optimist, huh?"

Patterson began singing her favorite song as she cooked.

LaRue groaned. "Dear Lord, please help me. . . ."

Patterson doubled over in laughter.

Chuckling, LaRue stuck the biscuit dough in the oven.

LaRue

"Gurl, this fried chicken is good. You put your foot in it this time." LaRue reached for another wing.

Macy sat across from LaRue, watching her in silence. The woman had already eaten three pieces.

"You don't like chicken?" Patterson asked as she reached for her second piece. "I thought everybody ate fried chicken."

"I don't eat *fried* anything," Macy retorted. Folding her arms across her chest, she wished she were anyplace but home.

"Humph. More for us," LaRue stated before taking another bite of her chicken. After swallowing, she asked, "You one of those vegetarians, Macy? I don't ever see you eat anything but salads, pasta, and seafood."

"No. I eat fish and chicken, but only if it's grilled, roasted, or baked and without the skin."

Patterson wiped her mouth with the corner of her napkin. "I'm so sorry, Macy. I should've asked you."

"Well, it would've helped," Macy responded haughtily.

LaRue glared at her. "I think what Patterson did for us is very sweet and thoughtful. She didn't have to cook for us, you know."

"You're right. I didn't mean to be rude. Patterson, I've enjoyed everything else. Thanks for cooking dinner."

"You sure?"

Macy nodded. "You're a wonderful cook. I really enjoyed the biscuits."

"They were good, weren't they? I can't take credit for them, though. LaRue baked them."

She glanced over at LaRue. "You both are pretty good in the kitchen, I see."

"Thanks," LaRue responded. "And since we did the cooking . . ." She pointed at Macy with the fork. "You get to clean up behind us."

"Excuse me?"

"The dishes. You get to wash the dishes."

"Oh, no, I won't be doing any dishes. Lupe will be here tomorrow. That's part of her duties," Macy stated with a slight smile of defiance.

LaRue's eyebrows were knitted in surprise. "Macy, you mean to tell me that you can't wash a simple plate? Patterson washed up everything we cooked in except for these plates and the bowl holding the vegetables. It's not a lot, gurlfriend. *Certainly not enough to leave for Lupe.*"

"I don't do dishes."

LaRue merely stared, tongue-tied. When she finally spoke, she said, "You don't have to actually wash the dishes, Macy. You *do* have a dishwasher—just put them in there. I'm sure that's all Lupe will do." Rising to her feet, she muttered, "Oh, for goodness sakes. I'll do them. I've never heard such nonsense . . ."

Macy stood up as well. "Well, I'm sorry. I just don't see the need for doing something I can pay someone else to do. Besides, I don't do any cooking here. I don't usually have dirty dishes, but when I do, Lupe washes them. I don't know whether she uses the dishwasher or does them by hand. I really don't care."

"Whatever," LaRue muttered. "This is foolishness."

Macy's body stiffened in her seat. "Lots of people have maids. They need jobs like everybody else, you know."

"It's your money, Macy," LaRue shot back. "Do what you will."

Macy's lips twisted into a cynical smile. "Thanks for your permission."

"Come on, y'all. Let's not fight," Patterson pleaded. "We're having a nice evening."

"I'm done with it."

"Me, too," Macy stated. "Like LaRue said, it's my money to do with what I will."

"I made dessert," Patterson quickly tossed out. "I made a sweet potato pie and we have ice cream. Or whipped cream, if you like that. My cousin Brenda Lee, she always puts whipped cream on her pie. I tried it once, but I like ice cream better."

LaRue met Macy's gaze. "Would you like for me to cut you a slice?"

"No, I'm going to pass. Thank you anyway." Macy glanced over at Patterson. Her faint smile held a touch of sadness, making her change her mind.

"You know what? I think I will have a piece of pie. LaRue, you can cut a slice for me. I'll have just a dab of whipped cream on mine."

LaRue stuck her head out of the kitchen. "No problem, Miss Baldwin. Wouldn't want you to break a nail or anything."

Macy managed a tremulous smile. "Thank you, dahling. You are ever so thoughtful."

"Whatever . . ."

"You two are going to end up being the best of friends. Just wait and see."

Macy shot Patterson a crazed look. "What in the world are you drinking? Miss Arnette and I will never be friends."

"Mark my words, as my daddy would say."

Macy opened her mouth to speak, but LaRue was coming back. She entered the dining room carrying two dessert plates.

"Should I be worried about poison?"

LaRue released a sigh of frustration. "Can't you just say thank you?"

"Why, thank you, LaRue, honey."

"Don't you go thinking I'm gonna do this for you always, Macy. You better learn to get up off that pampered rump of yours."

Blowing a kiss toward LaRue, Macy uttered, "I love you, too."

"Humph."

Patterson eyed the two women before putting her hand to her mouth to hide her chuckles.

Macy

After dinner, Macy disappeared into her bedroom.

She turned up her television to drown out the sound of LaRue and Patterson laughing and talking. Macy had a feeling that she was the topic of their discussion, but she didn't care. It didn't bother her that they thought she was shallow and spoiled.

Her stomach rumbled and growled in protest. Macy was still hungry, having only eaten a small portion of vegetables, a biscuit, and then the pie. She got up and eased over to her door, pressing her ear against the wood. She didn't want to venture out with Patterson and LaRue in the living room.

Two hours later, Macy heard her roommates in the hallway.

"Oh, thank God. They are finally in their rooms. I'm starving," she mumbled.

Macy slipped out of her room as quietly as she could and tiptoed to the kitchen.

She eased open the refrigerator and peeked inside. In a clear plastic container, the chicken wings called to her. Patterson had skillfully deep fried them golden brown and crispy.

It couldn't hurt just to try one, she decided.

Unable to ignore the food beckoning her, Macy opened the container and took out a wing.

After putting the dish back into the fridge, Macy bit into the wing.

She closed her eyes, savoring the taste.

When she opened them up again, she found LaRue standing in the doorway, a big Cheshire-cat grin on her face.

"I knew you couldn't resist," she stated smugly. "I saw the way you were staring at that chicken earlier."

Chapter 12

Macy

She had been caught red-handed.

Macy muttered a curse and shut the door to the refrigerator with her right hand. In her left, she held the evidence, a piece of cold chicken. She itched to slap the smug expression off LaRue's face.

"Gurl, you need to wash your mouth out with soap. You cuss like a sailor."

Tossing her hair across her shoulder, Macy shrugged. "You should be happy. I thought about what you said earlier. Patterson went through so much trouble to make us a nice dinner and all, so I decided to give it a try."

"You're not fooling me. You were starving. I saw how much you ate. All you do is nibble on salad all the time. You got to be hungry."

Walking over to the glass breakfast table, Macy bit into the drumstick. "Mmmm, this is so good. I haven't had chicken like this in a long time."

Eyeing LaRue, she added, "There's more in the fridge. Patterson cooked enough for an army."

Laughing, LaRue made her way to the refrigerator and opened it. She reached in to retrieve some chicken for herself. "It's good all right. That Southern belle can cook like nobody's business."

"Are you two talking 'bout me?" Patterson asked from behind them.

She made her way over to the table. "I had a hankering for some fried chicken myself. Glad to see I'm not alone."

"Are the biscuits all gone?" Macy asked.

"There's no more biscuits." Walking over to the pantry, Patterson added, "We finished them at dinner. Just eat some some light bread. That's what I'm gon' have with my chicken."

"Light bread?" both Macy and LaRue questioned.

Patterson glanced over her shoulder. "Yeah. You know. Light bread . . ." She held up a bag of store-bought bread.

"Oh, you mean *white* bread," LaRue stated.

"Back home we call it light bread. I guess it's a Southern thang."

They all laughed.

Patterson brought the chicken and loaf of bread over to the table and sat down. The three women sat around the table talking as they ate their late-night snack.

After finishing her second piece of chicken, Macy announced, "Okay, now I'm ready for dessert. I think I'm going to have another tiny slice of pie."

LaRue and Patterson shared a laugh.

Bringing a knife and the pie over to the table with her, Macy announced, "I want you two to know that I'm way off my diet. Look what you've done to me."

LaRue's heavy lashes flew up. "Why in the world would you be on a diet, Macy? You're what? A size two?"

"I *want* to *stay* a size two," Macy answered. "This looks good on me. I don't want to be any bigger. Not a four or a six. I work out all the time because I want to maintain the weight I have."

"The weight you don't have, you mean. Right?"

"LaRue, you're not much bigger than me. What are you talking about?"

"I wouldn't mind being a little bit bigger. I'm so tall; I need a few more pounds just so I look healthy."

Macy eyed the large slice of pie Patterson heaped on her plate after eating two slices of bread and four chicken wings. Both she and LaRue had had tiny slivers of the dessert and two wings each—not that it was any better, eating this late at night. "How in the world can you eat like this, Patterson? How do you keep your weight down?"

"I exercise a lot and I'm very active. I guess that helps. Plus, I did a lot of the chores around my family's farm."

Macy got up and poured three glasses of iced tea. She handed one to Patterson and one to LaRue before carrying her own glass to the table.

"I've never met anyone who actually lived on a farm. Did you have chickens and cows?"

"We have chickens, two cows, and four horses. My dad sells the eggs to the grocery stores in the surrounding towns."

Macy wiped her mouth with a napkin. "Really?"

Patterson nodded.

"Is that how he makes money?"

"Some," Patterson responded. "He's also a mechanic. He works on all the cars in Three Oak. He's real good."

Macy reached for her glass. "What does your mother do?"

"She's a housewife. She helps around the farm, too."

"My mom travels with my dad mostly when she's not giving her own seminars," LaRue chimed in. "She also does a lot of charity work."

"My mother is my father's wife," Macy said. "That's what she does and who she is."

"You sound kinda bitter," Patterson stated.

"They just get on my nerves sometimes."

Patterson chuckled. "That's what parents do." She bit off a piece of her bread and chewed it slowly. After swallowing, she commented, "Your name is so unusual, LaRue."

"I was just about to ask if you had any idea of where your parents came up with the name." Macy grinned. "It's obvious where mine came from."

"I'm named after both my mom and my dad. Her name is Ruby and my dad's name is Larry. For a long time, I used to be so mad at them for giving me this name. I hated it as a child, but now I cherish it."

"I guess I'm just awful because I really hate being named after a department store. I don't know why Mother couldn't have been more original."

"Well, just think. You could've been born in Target or K-Mart."

Macy shook her head. "I don't think Mother has ever been in a Target or a K-Mart."

LaRue and Patterson burst into giggles.

Macy looked perplexed. "What's so funny?"

"It was only a joke. Goodness, Macy, you need to lighten up some. Nobody in their right mind would name their children 'K-Mart.' "

"You never know. Look at some of the names out there today. I guess my mother thought she was being chic or something."

"I think it's a wonderful tribute, Macy."

"Oh, please. It's so corny." Macy reached for her glass. "I'm getting some water. Either one of you want something else to drink?"

"No, thank you," they answered in unison.

Macy returned to the table and sat down with her ice water. "So, Patterson, did you leave some lovesick man behind? Or did you move up here to mend your broken heart?"

"I was planning to move up here no matter what. Vincent was gon' come with me, but . . . well, we broke up."

"How long ago did that happen?"

Patterson shrugged. "About five or six months ago. I try not to think 'bout it. I try not to even think 'bout him at all."

"You're still angry," Macy observed.

"I'm getting over him."

"I know what you mean. I've been dumped by two men in one month. I wonder if I've set a record of some sort."

"Did you love them?" LaRue questioned.

"One I thought I did. The other I cared a great deal for." Macy took a long sip of her water. "Neither one of them wanted to be in a committed relationship with me. Can you imagine that? I'm probably the best thing to happen to either of them."

"They just weren't the men for you, Macy."

"You're so sweet, Patterson. Don't you get sick of being so . . . so nice? It would drive me crazy."

LaRue broke into a short laugh.

"How old were you when you got married, LaRue?" Patterson inquired. "I know you mentioned that you and Tom were childhood sweethearts."

Macy's mouth dropped open in shock. "You were married before?"

LaRue nodded. "I got married when I was twenty-three and lost him eleven months ago."

"It must really be hard on you," Macy murmured. "Here I am whining about being rejected, and you've lost the most important man in your life. I'm very sorry for your loss, LaRue. Truly sorry."

"Tom Hawkins was the love of my life and my very best friend in the whole world. He was there for me when I really needed a friend. We'd been together since we were thirteen years old. He was a good man and I miss him."

Patterson gave LaRue a sympathetic smile. "You're very lucky to have loved and been loved in return."

LaRue pushed away from the table and stood up. "I have an idea. Why don't we go out tonight? I've been in New York for almost a month now and haven't been out on the town at all. We need to have some fun."

"It's late," Patterson stated. "We should get some sleep. Morning will be upon us before we know it."

Frowning, Macy asked, "Who are you? Mary Poppins?"

"I was just sayin' . . ."

"I know what you were saying, and you sound like an old woman, Patterson. I'm with LaRue on this. We should go out and have a good time. *This is New York.*"

LaRue spoke up. "Actually, I'm curious. Patterson, what did you do back home in Georgia? Didn't you ever go out and party?"

"I went to a few clubs in Atlanta, but I'm not a dancer, so I usually just sat around watching other people dance."

"What do you mean that you don't dance?" Macy inquired. "Ever?"

"I guess I should've said that I can't dance," Patterson explained. "I have no rhythm."

LaRue burst into laughter.

"Really, I can't."

"Have you ever tried?" Macy put a hand to her mouth to hide her amusement.

"Yeah, I've tried. I can't dance worth two cents."

"So, is this why you don't want to go out?"

"LaRue, I don't want to be a wet rag, but it's really late. We are not gon' want to get up in the morning."

"I'm an adult. I know what my limitations are, so you don't have to worry about me. I can handle one night of partying."

Macy ran her fingers through her hair. "If you don't want to come with us, you don't have to. We can go by ourselves. Right, LaRue?"

"Yeah, we can," she agreed. "I just thought it'd be more fun with the three of us."

"I'll go," Patterson interjected. "It's just one night. What can it hurt?"

LaRue

She checked her reflection in the mirror a third time. LaRue ran her fingers through her braids. She secured the upswept style with bobby pins.

LaRue glanced over her shoulder at the sound of someone knocking on her door.

"Come in . . ."

Patterson eased inside the room. "Does this look okay?"

She assessed her from head to toe. "That's what you're planning to wear?"

"I was," Patterson replied. "Why? Is something wrong with it?"

LaRue turned around. "It's a nice suit . . . but I think you should find something a little more fun."

"I don't think I have anything like that."

Macy entered the bedroom. Frowning, she asked, "Patterson, what in the world do you have on?"

"It's a suit. I don't have nothin' else to wear. All my stuff is real conservative."

"I have something that'll look great on you, Patterson." Macy eyed LaRue. "I have something for you, too."

LaRue glanced in the mirror. "What's wrong with what I have on?" She checked her reflection, studying the black jersey knit T-shirt and silk pants she was wearing.

Macy returned with a multicolored halter dress, which she handed to Patterson.

She gave LaRue a sheer black tank top. "This is a Dolce & Gabbana shirt and it'll look great with those pants. You'll need to wear a black bra, though."

"I have on a black bra."

"Good. Try on the shirt."

LaRue took off her top and slipped on the cotton top Macy gave her.

She broke into a big grin when she saw her reflection. "Yeah . . . this is sexy. . . ."

Patterson had gone to the bathroom to change her clothing. She came out, pulling on the fitted dress. "This dress looks like it was spray-painted on. You can see the lines of my underwear."

"You're not supposed to wear underwear. I usually can get away with it if I wear a thong. You got any?"

Frowning, Patterson shook her head. "I doan wear no thongs. Those things look like they'll hurt you."

LaRue cracked up. "Gurl, you crazy."

"Patterson, you have to take off the underwear."

"Macy, I ain't going nowhere with no drawers on. I'll just put my suit back on."

"Let me just find you something else."

Patterson surveyed the shirt LaRue was wearing. "LaRue, you gon' go out with your bra showin' through like that?"

"Yeah. This is the style now."

"I know. I've seen people doing that in the fashion magazines, but . . ." Patterson shook her head. "I couldn't be that bold."

"I'm still covered up."

"I guess I'm really old-fashioned."

"What are you gonna do when you're modeling? You may have to wear a shirt like this with no bra."

"I guess I'd have to really look at my career." Patterson ran her fingers through her curls. "I hope I don't ever have to go through somethin' like that."

LaRue put on her makeup. "I love this shirt."

She was ready to go out and party. LaRue needed to have a good time to take her mind off her troubles. She'd been thinking more and more about Tom lately. The one-year anniversary of his death was a few weeks away.

"You look great, LaRue," Macy complimented. "I told you that shirt was perfect with those pants."

Patterson examined the dress Macy placed in her hands. "I'ma try this one on, but if I have to lose my drawers—I'ma wear what I planned to wear in the first place. I can't be out there showing all my goods."

She left the room.

"I don't know how she plans to be a model if she's that shy about her body," Macy stated.

"She'll change."

"That shirt really looks wonderful on you, LaRue. You can keep it."

"Oh, no, Macy. I don't want to take your shirt."

Shaking her head, Macy responded, "Really, I don't mind. It's yours."

Patterson walked back into the room. "Okay, I like this dress—it's not so clingy."

LaRue assessed her and nodded her approval.

Macy grinned. "That's one of my designs. It looks wonderful on you."

Half an hour later, the trio took the elevator down to the lobby.

It didn't take long for a taxi to arrive.

"Where are we going?" LaRue wanted to know.

Macy responded, "Crash Mansion on Bowery between Spring St. and Rivington."

"What type of club is it?"

"You'll love it, Patterson. Tonight they're having a hip-hop showcase. Sometimes they have reggae music and jazz. It's the place to be seen for sure."

"I know the first thing I want is a drink," LaRue announced.

"You drink?"

LaRue shot a look Patterson's way. "Yeah. Sometimes. Why?"

"No reason," she mumbled in response.

LaRue knew she was being a little defensive. "Hey, I didn't mean nothing by that, Patterson."

"No problem."

Patterson was quiet the rest of the way to the club, making LaRue feel like a heel. She knew Patterson was sensitive and that she shouldn't have reacted so strongly.

When they arrived at the club, LaRue was in awe of the multilevel, multiroom, multibar complex. They entered the main floor where the bar seemed to go on and on.

"There are several party rooms upstairs," Macy pointed out. "They each have their own lighting and sound. So, if you're in the mood for hip-hop or if you just want to relax . . . you can find it all here."

"They serve food?" Patterson inquired.

"Yes. The food is superb."

"Patterson, you hungry?" LaRue asked.

"No, I just wondered—that's all."

Fifteen minutes later, with drink in hand, LaRue was on the dance floor, gyrating her body to the music.

Patterson

Patterson sat alone at the table Macy secured for them. Her eyes traveled across the crowded room as she tried to keep her gaze on LaRue and Macy. They were both on the dance floor laughing, dancing, and having a good time.

A man eased into the seat beside her. "Hello, beautiful."

"H-Hey . . ." Patterson looked away, praying that he would leave. She had never seen anyone up close with dreadlocks and decided she didn't like them.

"Would you like to dance?"

She gave him a polite smile. "No, thank you."

Muttering something under his breath, he got up quickly and stalked off.

I wish Macy or LaRue would hurry up and come back to the table. Patterson's eyes traveled back to the dance floor.

LaRue caught her gaze and excused herself when the song ended.

She walked over to the table saying, "Gurl, you look like you're scared to death."

"I'm not afraid of anything, LaRue. I just feel a teeny bit uncomfortable."

"Patterson . . . gurl, you got to relax and loosen up. We're in a club. Try to have a good time."

"I am." Patterson raised her voice over the music. "It's just that I'm not much of a dancer. It's not true what they say, you know. Not every black person can dance. I sure can't."

"Gurl, we gotta get you out more. Don't worry about it. I'll have you dancing in no time."

Another man walked up and asked LaRue to dance.

"I'll be right back," she told Patterson.

"I'ma be fine."

Macy strolled over to the table, looking wonderful in the strapless silk top and matching low-cut pants. Her midriff was bare, except for the tiny gold chain that dangled around her waist. The fuchsia color looked stunning on her.

Over the course of the evening, Macy and LaRue were both drinking heavily, only Macy seemed to be able to hold her liquor much better than LaRue.

Patterson was concerned for both of them. She knew Macy was a drinker because she'd smelled alcohol on her breath in the past. But this was a new side of LaRue she was seeing.

I hope you know what you're doing, LaRue.

Patterson had a feeling that LaRue was trying to run away from her pain, but this was not the way to do it. She prayed LaRue would come to her senses before she got into some serious trouble.

Chapter 13

LaRue

Friday morning arrived with a vengeance.

After her late-night binge with Patterson and Macy, it was a struggle for LaRue to pull herself out of bed. She swung her legs to the side and sat there for a moment, waiting for her head to clear.

She'd had two Long Island iced teas and a rum and Coke. Now she was paying for it. LaRue hadn't been out drinking like that in over five years. *What was I thinking about?* It wasn't like it made her feel any better. It didn't even provide her the temporary relief she sought.

When she walked out of her room, LaRue found Patterson in the kitchen cleaning up. "What time did you get up?"

"I'm running late today," Patterson responded. "I didn't get up until seven thirty-five. I don't have to be over at Bloomingdale's until eleven for my interview, but I wont to put in a few more applications before that in some of the little shops nearby."

"I'll be near the store around that time. Why don't we plan to meet afterward?"

Patterson left the kitchen and grabbed her purse off the sofa table in the living room. "Meet me on Third between eleven forty-five and noon. I should be done by then. Good luck, LaRue."

"You, too."

LaRue allowed herself two cups of coffee before leaving. She was going out much later than she'd planned to pound the pavement seeking employment. She preferred to be out by the time most companies opened their doors at eight.

She glanced over at the wall clock in the kitchen. "Fifteen minutes past nine . . . I need to get out of here."

LaRue wiped down the kitchen counter, made sure there was enough coffee left for Macy, and swept the floor.

The rest of her morning was spent filling out applications before heading to her eleven-fifteen appointment.

LaRue met up with Patterson on Third Avenue after her job interview with Bloomingdale's Department Store. LaRue had an appointment with another company in a nearby building.

"How did it go with Bloomies?" she asked Patterson.

"Okay, I think. Hopefully I won't have to actually get a job if we hear from the agency. But something like this will do until then. Gotta pay the bills, you know."

"Amen to that." LaRue glanced down at her watch. "Let's grab something to eat. My stomach was growling all through my interview." She broke into a short laugh. "I was so embarrassed."

"Fine by me," Patterson responded. "I haven't had anything to eat since breakfast."

"I've got a second interview at the Crisis Center at two-thirty," LaRue announced. "Maybe I'll get the job since they called me back."

"Are you givin' up on teaching?"

LaRue shook her head no. "Just trying to explore all my options."

"I understand that. I got a late interview myself. It's at four-thirty, so I'm not sure when I'll get home."

"I'm cooking tonight, so don't worry about that."

"Thank you," Patterson murmured. "I know I'm not gonna feel like cookin' anything by the time I get home. I'ma wonna kick off my shoes and just relax for a while. I'm so tired."

"You've been getting up early every morning and going to bed late at night. It's no wonder you're tired, Patterson. Tonight, why don't you take a nice hot bath and go to bed early?"

"That sounds like a wonderful idea. I think I will."

She and LaRue stopped at the first restaurant they came across. They were seated and served quickly.

While they waited for their food, Patterson sat across from LaRue, a big grin plastered on her face.

"Why are you wearing that silly grin?"

"We had fun last night. The three of us together."

Perplexed, LaRue asked, "And?"

"Well, I think that's a start."

LaRue was confused. "A start for what?"

"Friendship."

LaRue threw back her head, laughing. "You're not gonna give this up."

Shaking her head, Patterson responded, "Great friends are hard to find sometimes. You can't just trust your innermost feelings to just anyone. We all need someone we can go to for help, counsel, or just to be with, because we know they care and they know us well enough to be honest if we ask their opinion about somethin', don't you agree?"

When LaRue nodded, she continued, "I wont the kind of friend who'll laugh at my jokes, even if they aren't always funny. Well, maybe not, but they will tell you they're not funny in a nice way most of the time."

Their food arrived.

Picking up her turkey burger with both hands, LaRue took a bite. She smiled at Patterson as she chewed.

"I've never met anybody like you, Patterson. It's really nice to see someone who cares about people the way you do."

"You care just as much. LaRue, you act like you don't, but I can see right through you. You're a softie." Patterson picked up her pickle and bit into it.

LaRue shrugged nonchalantly. "I don't know what you're talking about."

"Take Macy for instance. You try to act like you can't stand her—"

"I can't," LaRue interjected. Pointing to her plate, she asked, "Do you want my pickle? I don't eat them."

Patterson reached over and took the pickle. "Thanks."

A tall woman walked by their table.

"Did you see who that was?" Patterson asked in an excited whisper.

LaRue glanced over her shoulder. "Who?"

"Charla Raye. She's in all the fashion magazines."

"Oh, yeah. I've seen her before." LaRue turned back around. "She's pretty."

"I can't wait for our day to come. We need to try Ford Models, doan you think?" Patterson picked up her menu.

LaRue took a sip of her water. "We've gone to two other agencies already. I don't think I can stand any more rejection. I'm giving up on being a model."

"Don't give up. You can't."

"I'm too old, Patterson." LaRue finished off her burger. "I think you'll have no problem making it, though. You and Macy both."

"I believe we all can make it as models, LaRue. We gotta keep tryin', though."

"You keep trying," she encouraged Patterson. "I'll find a job doing something—it just won't be modeling."

Patterson

Loud laughter from a nearby table caught Patterson's attention. One of the men sitting there gave her a wide smile and chastised his friends for being so loud.

She awarded the handsome man a grateful smile before returning her attention to LaRue.

Although Patterson tried to hide her interest, she found herself drawn to the young man. Each time she stole a peek at him, Patterson found him watching her as well.

"That guy sure can't take his eyes off you," LaRue observed. "He's watching you almost as hard as you're trying not to watch him."

Embarrassed, Patterson dropped her eyes.

LaRue laughed. "Gurl, it's okay. Don't be ashamed. You like the man."

Patterson hid her giggles behind her hand. "He is cute, don't you think?"

Frowning, LaRue responded, "He's all right. A little too yellow for my tastes."

"I don't care much 'bout skin color or physical looks. I just wont a man to be nice and treat me like I'm special. I wont a good man."

"I'm with you on that," LaRue agreed. "But now I have to be honest. I want a man that is dark—jet black with pretty white teeth and good skin. That's so sexy to me. I don't want him to be skinny either.

He don't have to be built like Mr. USA or anything, but I can't stomach a rail-thin man."

Patterson stole another look at the man.

LaRue hid her chuckles behind her hand.

"Doan laugh at me. I'm not good at stuff like this."

"Just be calm, Patterson. Stop acting like a nervous schoolgirl. Act like the self-assured and sophisticated woman that you are."

"Yeah, right . . . me . . . sophisticated? I'm a country girl." Patterson placed trembling hands around her glass of iced tea. She took several small sips.

"I can't believe you're so nervous."

"I told you. I'm not good at stuff like this." Patterson put a hand to her face. "I'm acting so stupid."

"No, you're not," LaRue assured her. It's okay. Just calm down."

She hid her amusement. LaRue didn't want to make Patterson feel bad. It was refreshing to find someone with such old-fashioned morals. Most women today would've already jumped all over the man.

LaRue

LaRue eyed Miller Baisden. After observing him discreetly, she found he didn't really impress her. In fact, she didn't trust him. It was something in his actions that bothered her. He reminded her of a man on the prowl—someone looking for innocent victims.

When they met her gaze, Miller's eyes were dark and insolent, which further convinced her that he was no good.

Every now and then, Patterson would cast a look his way. She broke into a sheepish grin when she caught LaRue watching her.

Her roommate's reaction amused LaRue. "Yeah, I saw you. I'm sure everybody in here can see that you're really attracted to that man."

"You think he feels that same way 'bout me?"

LaRue cast a quick glance Miller's way. "He's interested in something. I'm just not real sure what it is."

"What do you mean by that, LaRue?"

"I don't know if he really wants to get to know you or your body," LaRue admitted. "There is a difference, you know. He doesn't seem to have much manners. Talking all across the room like that."

Patterson leaned forward to make sure they weren't overheard. "Keep your voice down. He's just at the next table, LaRue."

"It's still rude to me."

Sighing softly, Patterson agreed. "You're probably right. Most likely, I'll never see him again anyway. It doesn't look like he's gonna come over here to talk to me. And I know I'm not going over there. I'm not fast."

"You really were sheltered, huh? Gurl, things have changed, even around Three Oak, I bet. Women are more aggressive these days."

"I guess I'm just so used to hearing my mama talk about fast women all the time—I don't wont to be one."

LaRue chuckled. "I don't think we have to worry about that at all, Patterson. You have sweet and innocent written all over you."

They finished their meal in silence.

Just as LaRue signaled for the check, she held her breath when Miller Baisden eased out of his chair. She had a feeling he was about to visit their table.

"Did you ladies enjoy your lunch?" he asked smoothly.

LaRue wiped her mouth with her napkin and replied, "Do you work here?"

"We did," Patterson answered quickly. "The food was delicious." She sent LaRue a pleading look before turning back to Miller and asking, "How 'bout you?"

He nodded. "The food is always good. This is one of my favorite places to eat."

LaRue rose to her feet. "If you two will excuse me, I need to visit the little girls' room before we leave." She had to get away from the slimy playboy wannabe. The man was up to no good. She could even see it on the faces of his friends. LaRue pretended not to notice the jabs they were giving each other as they spied on Miller and Patterson. She was disgusted by some of the childish games grown men still played.

LaRue returned to the table a few minutes later, grateful to find Miller and his friends gone.

"He asked for my phone number, LaRue," Patterson announced. "And he gave me his."

LaRue could hear the excitement in her voice. "I see," she responded as calmly as she could. "Did he give you his home number or his cellular?"

"His cell phone. He said he wonts me to be able to reach him at all times. Miller says he's hardly home because he works so much." She gazed at LaRue. "What's wrong?"

"Nothing," LaRue responded. "Actually, Patterson, I have to be honest with you. I know you're interested in this guy, but I didn't get a good feeling about Miller. I think you should just toss that napkin and stay away from that man."

Patterson looked disappointed. "He seemed so nice to me."

"I know, honey. I don't know why I feel this way, but I can't deny that I do. I know you don't want to hear this." LaRue picked up her fork and knife. "You're a grown woman, so it's really your call. I'll support you no matter what you decide."

Patterson smiled. "I appreciate your being so concerned 'bout me and all, but I'll be careful."

"I hope so. I've seen girls on their first time away from home fall into the clutches of some pretty ruthless men. These girls are not streetwise and the results are often disastrous."

"I'm not gonna do something I doan wont to do. I may not be too citified or sophisticated, but I'm not that naïve either. Vincent and I broke up because I wouldn't have sex with him. That and the fact that he'd been cheating on me for two years. Being Christian and single is hard work, you know. But I can do it. *I have done it.* Nobody, including this pretty man, Miller Baisden, is gonna change that."

"Just be careful, Patterson," LaRue warned. *He may look like a prize catch on the outside, but it's what's in his heart that determines if he's the real jewel.*

Macy

Macy was still in her pajamas when LaRue arrived home shortly after three. Her clothes from the night before were thrown on the floor, painting a path toward her bedroom.

LaRue struggled internally to keep from strangling Macy. She resisted the urge to pick up the clothing, choosing instead to walk past them. She chewed on her bottom lip a moment before saying, "I see you didn't bother to get dressed today."

Running her fingers through unkempt hair, Macy shrugged off

LaRue's comment. "I've only been up for about four hours. I had one too many apple martinis last night and passed out at my friend's house. I didn't get home until seven this morning. I had such a headache, so I took some pills that made me sleepy."

LaRue shook her head. "You couldn't change clothes in your bedroom?" Macy's eyes narrowed and her back became ramrod straight. "I could have. But since I—"

LaRue held up her hand, cutting Macy off. "Don't even go there with me. I'm not Patterson. I ain't gonna take no crap off you, gurlfriend. If you wanna dance, I'll be your partner. . . ."

"Must you sound so ghetto?"

"I'm just lettin' you know. I ain't scared of you, Miss Thang."

"Whatever . . ." Macy held out her hands to look at her nails. "I really need a manicure and a pedicure badly." She sighed in resignation and moved about the living room picking up her things. "I need money. There are so many things I need to do. I saw some dresses in Bloomingdale's that were gorgeous. They would look stunning on me, but I just can't buy them right now."

LaRue sat down on the sofa. Her dark eyes pierced the distance between them. "Have you considered looking for a job?"

"No," Macy answered quickly. "*Why should I?*"

LaRue knew that Macy fully expected to be one of the women called back to the modeling agency. Either that or the silent treatment she was giving her parents would convince them to rethink their position regarding her finances.

"I know that Patterson and I are paying you rent, but surely it doesn't cover all of your expenses. Or does it?"

"No, of course not."

LaRue watched Macy with a critical squint. "Then how are you paying your bills?"

"I've had some money saved," Macy replied, her eyes darting nervously back and forth.

"Uh-huh," LaRue uttered. She didn't believe a word coming out Macy's mouth, especially since Macy couldn't meet her steady gaze.

"Okay. I ran out of money a few weeks ago, so I borrowed some from a couple of friends," Macy confessed.

"How do you intend to pay them back?"

Macy didn't bother to hide her irritation. "Why are you grilling me? You act like my parents."

"Well?"

"I hadn't thought of it," Macy responded at last. "They have money. They won't miss it."

"Remind me never to lend you any."

"You know what I mean, LaRue. I just wasn't in any hurry to pay them back. I wouldn't do that to you."

"Why not?" LaRue wanted to know. "What makes me so special?"

Macy had the nerve to look offended. "Well, it's not like you have any real money. You'll need every single penny."

"Gurlfriend, you are in the same boat. In fact, the way I see it, you need money more than I do. Face it, Macy. You're just as poor as I am." LaRue broke into laughter. "Gurl, you something else."

She stood up.

"What are you getting ready to do?" Macy questioned.

"Cook dinner and don't worry. I'm not asking you to help. But there *is* one thing you can do for me."

Macy's expression became guarded. "What?"

"Go take a bath and brush your teeth. *You stink*. What did you do? Pour the martinis all over your body?"

Macy sniffed at her body. "I smell that bad?"

LaRue wrinkled her nose. "You'll feel better after a hot bath. Go on. Dinner will be ready in about half an hour." She made her way to the kitchen, pausing in the doorway long enough to say, "No bath. No dinner."

Macy sniffed at her body a second time and frowned. "You don't have to be so mean, you know."

"That girl . . ." LaRue muttered as she strolled into the kitchen.

Twenty minutes later, Macy walked into the kitchen wearing a white-colored wife beater and a pair of black denim shorts. She'd showered and pulled her hair into a ponytail.

LaRue glanced up from her cooking and nodded in approval. "You look much better."

"You were right. I feel much better." Macy sniffed the air. "What are you cooking?"

"I thought I'd make pork chops, rice, and gravy. I even made a nice spinach salad for you. I know how you are with your weight."

Her hands on her hips, Macy watched LaRue as she worked. "I know you don't think much of me, so why are you being so nice?"

"We're roommates," she responded. "Patterson's always saying that God brought us together for a reason. Who am I to question His will? Might as well make the best of our season together."

Bracing her body against the kitchen counter, Macy asked, "Do you really believe that God cared enough to bring three strangers together?"

"I haven't really given it any thought. Only time will tell, I guess."

"Patterson is so funny. Sometimes I feel like I have a saint for a roommate. I feel like such a heathen."

LaRue burst into laughter. "That makes two of us then. We'll be heathens together."

"I have some VIP passes to a party tonight. Want to join me?"

LaRue glanced up from her cooking. "What about Patterson?"

"She's probably not going to want to go. She didn't seem to have a good time when we went to Crash Mansion before."

"Maybe you should at least ask her if she wants to come. Let Patterson turn you down."

Macy shrugged in nonchalance. "I guess."

After dinner, Macy brought up the passes. "Would you like to come, Patterson?"

"Thanks for asking, but I think I'll say no tonight."

"If you're worried about dancing, I told you I'll show you some moves." LaRue stood up and began dancing in the middle of the living room.

Macy turned up the music, then joined her.

Patterson sat on the sofa moving from side to side. She laughed as she watched her roommates doing the bump.

"Okay, it's time for you to join us," LaRue announced. "C'mon gurl . . . do yo' thang. . . ."

Macy danced over and took Patterson by the hand. "We're going to teach you how to do the electric slide."

LaRue took on the role as instructor, guiding a clumsy Patterson through the dance moves.

Giggles erupted from Patterson as she tried to keep up with LaRue and Macy.

"You sure you still don't want to join us tonight?"

"Y'all go on. I'ma be fine stayin' home, Macy. Thanks for inviting me, though." Patterson pushed away an errant curl. "I'ma read my Bible for a little while, and then call it a night. I'm real tired."

LaRue ran her hands through her braids. "Well, I'm gonna go get ready. I'm in the mood for a party."

Chapter 14

Patterson

On Sunday morning, Patterson got up early and got ready for church.

She looked up, surprised when Macy sauntered into the room, her silk bathrobe waving all around her.

Patterson admired the turquoise color and the matching pajamas she wore. "Macy, you're up early. Did I wake you?"

"I was thinking we could go to Norma's for brunch. They have the most wonderful mango-papaya brown-butter cinnamon crepes; foie gras brioche; French toast; and a shrimp, tomato, and egg-white frittata big enough to feed the three of us. Afterward, we can do some shopping to work off all that food. What do you say? Sounds like a wonderful way to spend the afternoon, don't you think?"

"It does sound nice, Macy." Patterson paused a heartbeat before saying, "I don't know what LaRue has planned for the day, but I'm going to church. Why don't you join me? We can go to Norma's after that, if you wont."

"You go every Sunday almost. You can't miss this one Sunday? We should get to Norma's early. It can get pretty crowded. Especially since this is kind of a holiday weekend."

"I want to go to church. The pastor's planning on talking about a 'Thorn In the Flesh.' "

Macy yawned. "Oh. Well, wouldn't want to miss that. . . ."

"Actually, I don't. Macy, why don't you come go with me? It would be nice if you and LaRue would join me one Sunday."

She smiled. "Maybe next time."

LaRue staggered out of her room. She and Macy had gone out clubbing on both Friday and Saturday nights. Patterson was sure she had a hangover by the way she was clutching her head.

"Morning," she mumbled on her way to the bathroom.

Patterson waved at her.

"Have fun at church," Macy called out as she neared the door.

"I will," Patterson responded.

Outside, she had a thought.

Patterson pulled out her new cellular phone. "Hey, Macy. I was just thinkin' 'bout something. Why don't I meet you and LaRue at Norma's after church? Will that work for you?"

"Sure. I'll tell LaRue."

"Great. If there's a change, call me back on my cell."

Patterson hung up and stuck her phone back in her purse. She decided to leave it on until she reached the church.

She arrived five minutes before the pastor got up to speak. Patterson pulled out her pen and notebook.

"What's God's purpose for your life?" the pastor began. "Have you ever wondered about that? I'm not referring to questions like, what career should you follow . . . or whom should you marry . . . or how many kids should you have. . . . I'm talking about the big picture. What is God's overriding goal? His primary purpose for the lives of His people? What is He at work doing right now in your life and in mine? What is He trying to accomplish?"

Patterson considered each of his questions.

"We might come up with what may seem like a very obvious answer. God wants to make us happy. He wants to provide for our needs and take away our pain and sorrow. He wants to make our path smooth, and give us the good things we desire. We aren't talking about thorns, you see. We're talking about thrones. Turn in your Bibles to Second Corinthians, twelfth chapter, verses 7 to 10. . . ."

Patterson nodded in agreement along with several other members of the congregation as the pastor read the scripture.

Because of the surpassing greatness of the revelations, for this reason, to keep me from exalting myself, there was given me a thorn in the flesh, a messenger of Satan to torment me—to keep me from exalting myself. Concerning this I implored the Lord three times that it might leave me. And He has said to me, my grace is sufficient for you, for power is perfected in weakness. Most gladly, therefore, I will rather boast about my weaknesses, so that the power of Christ may dwell in me. Therefore, I am well content with weaknesses, with insults, with distresses, with persecutions, with difficulties, for Christ's sake; for when I am weak, then I am strong.

He paused for a moment to allow the scripture to sink in. "What a fantastic passage. . . . it's a hard one. Paul was given revelations from God, and he was afraid that it would go to his head . . . some translations say conceited. But you see . . . Paul was given a thorn in the flesh to torment him. He says that it was a messenger of Satan . . . but this messenger had a purpose for good. It was to keep Paul humble. . . ."

After the service, Patterson left to meet Macy and LaRue at Norma's. She hoped LaRue was feeling better. She debated whether or not to speak to her friend about her drinking, but decided against it. It wasn't like LaRue was doing it on a daily basis. Patterson didn't relish sticking her nose where it wasn't wanted, and she didn't want friction between her and LaRue.

Still, the deep sense of foreboding refused to leave her. Patterson wasn't sure if it concerned Macy or LaRue—maybe both of them. *They're grown women. I can't tell them what to do,* she argued with her conscience. *They ain't gon' listen to me.*

By the time she reached Norma's, Patterson found that both Macy and LaRue had already ordered drinks.

LaRue

"Patterson, what's wrong with you?"

"Nothin.'"

"You sure?" LaRue had a feeling that Patterson was troubled about something. "You can tell us."

"Well . . . it's just that . . . well this morning, you were . . ."

"Just spit it out," Macy uttered. "I'm starving. I don't have all day."

"Then why doan you go get yo'self somethin' to eat?" Patterson snapped. "I'm tryin' to talk to LaRue anyway. It doan have nothin' to do with you."

Macy was stunned for a moment. Picking up her Louis Vuitton purse, she muttered, "Whatever . . ." and stalked off, leaving Patterson alone with LaRue at their table.

"What's got into you?"

"She almost made me lose Jesus. . . ." Patterson shook her head in dismay. "I just left church, too."

LaRue leaned forward. "What is it that's bothering you? Why did you want to talk to me alone?"

"I doan wont to make you mad at me, but I feel I need to say somethin' to you."

"It's about my drinking?"

Patterson nodded. "I know you don't do it a lot, but I know what can happen. One of my uncles is an alcoholic, LaRue. It started off with him just drinkin' every now and then, and then it became more of a daily routine, you know."

LaRue held up her hand. "Patterson, it's not like that for me. I appreciate your concern, but you don't have to worry. I'm just having a good time."

"Okay. I won't press you. It was just in my spirit to say sumpthin' to you, that's all."

LaRue nodded. "Let's get some food. Okay?"

Smiling, Patterson rose up and followed her.

She wasn't upset, but it bothered LaRue that Patterson had even felt the need to try and talk to her about her drinking. She knew her roommate wouldn't have said anything if she had not been prompted by the Holy Spirit.

Nice try, Lord, but I'm not changing my mind.

LaRue glanced around for their waiter. Spotting him, she crossed the room and asked for another drink in defiance.

Macy

"What are you two doing for the Fourth of July?" Macy inquired while they were all seated in the living room polishing their nails.

"I wontned my parents to come up heh," Patterson answered. "It's my Mama's birthday. But they're not comin'. They doan wanna disappoint my uncle."

"Is your family having a party for your mother?"

"We usually have a big picnic for her on St. Simon's Island every year."

"That's what you're missing?" Puzzled, Macy made a face. "That doesn't sound like anything to miss. Bugs, dirt . . . not something I'd be missing."

She heard the irritation in Patterson's voice. "It's my family that I'm missin', Macy. And I miss being on the island, too. I love being near the ocean."

"Then why didn't you move there?"

Patterson rolled her eyes heavenward. "*B'cause*, Macy, I wont to be a model. I can't do that on St. Simon's."

"Hey, don't get frustrated with me. I was just asking some simple questions for clarity. I can't help it if your life is so boring. It's not my fault."

"Patterson, can you pass the polish remover?" LaRue interjected.

"Sure."

"LaRue, you didn't answer me. What are your plans?"

"I don't have any, Macy." LaRue's gaze met hers straight on. "Why? Are you taking us somewhere?"

"I have plans already," Macy shot back. "But I was going to tell you that there's a Circle Line Cruise that sails from five-thirty to eleven in the evening. You can see the fireworks as they light up the Statue of Liberty. They'll have a DJ, food, and drinks. I think the tickets are around sixty-five dollars."

"I think you told us something about it before." LaRue glanced over at Patterson. "It might be nice. You interested?"

Patterson nodded. "Sure. Sounds like fun."

Macy could tell that Patterson was still a little upset with her. She didn't care. The little country hick didn't do anything for her. She didn't know why she even bothered to look out for them at all. Macy didn't have to tell them about any of the events around the city for Independence Day, but did so out of the kindness of her heart.

LaRue admired her nails. "So Macy, what are you planning to do? You were all in our business."

"I'm going out with some friends, but if you want, we can go out afterward. We can go to Club Avalon."

"Sounds good to me. I'm always ready for a party."

Macy turned her attention to Patterson. "What about you, Miss Haney? You care to join us?"

"No, thank you."

"What are you going to do? Just sit in the house all the time?" Macy shook her head. "Girl, it won't hurt you, or stop you from going to heaven, if you go out and have a good time for a change."

Without responding, Patterson got up and stormed off to her room.

LaRue sent a sharp look Macy's way.

Feigning innocence, she asked, "What?"

"Why don't you stay off Patterson's back? She hasn't done anything to you, Macy."

"She gets on my nerves."

"And you get on mine, but you don't see me picking on you like that. Now leave her alone."

Macy muttered a curse. "It's my house. I can say what I want."

LaRue rolled her eyes. "One day, Patterson's gonna snap off on you."

"I doubt that," Macy uttered. "That little country mouse is scared of her own shadow."

The telephone rang.

"Want me to get it?" LaRue inquired.

"If it's my parents, just tell them I'm not here."

LaRue shook her head. "I'm not gonna lie to your parents."

"Then don't answer it." Macy concentrated on polishing her toes. "I don't know why they won't stop calling. I'm not talking to them."

"Do you really think this is the best way to get them to see your side of things, Macy?"

"It works for me."

LaRue laughed. "Really? Then why do you look so unhappy?"

Macy's head snapped up. "Excuse me?"

"It's as clear as that nose on your face. You're not very happy."

"Oh . . . and you are? I don't think so, dahling. You look just as unhappy as I am."

"I don't deny that," LaRue said quietly. "I'm grieving for Tom and for my friend, Janine. What's wrong with you?"

"Nothing's wrong with me. I just . . . I just want to be me. The real me. I love fashion. I want to be a designer, LaRue. That's who I really am."

"Then do it," she encouraged.

Macy picked up the nail polish and cotton balls. "And be more of a disappointment to my parents. You see what they've done to me. My father will cut me out of his will for sure."

"Life is too short, Macy. You have to make the best of it."

She pulled herself off the floor. "LaRue, I think you need to take your own advice."

LaRue rose to her feet. "I am. From now on, I'm gonna enjoy living. I'm going to make the best of what's left of my life. You can believe that."

Macy considered LaRue's words, but mostly she worried what was behind them. Something troubled her about the young widow.

LaRue

The Circle Line's Fourth of July fireworks cruise was the highlight of LaRue's day. The evening cruise sailed down the Hudson and up the East River—as she captured photographs of the Statue of Liberty and the Manhattan skyline at sunset.

As they sailed near the Brooklyn Bridge, Patterson tried to snap a photo of it. She turned and glimpsed LaRue watching her. Grinning, she placed the camera to her eye and clicked. "Got you."

Dangling her digital camera, LaRue stated, "I got one of those, too. I'll get you when you least expect it."

Patterson strode over to where she was standing. "You having a good time?"

"I am," LaRue confirmed. "What about you?"

"This is so much fun. I've really enjoyed myself." Patterson rubbed her belly. "I ate like a pig. I'ma really going to have to work out every day this week."

"I had two hot dogs," LaRue confessed. "I should've stuck with salad myself." She eyed the skyline and spread her arms wide. "I love this city. I don't know what it is about this place, but I just feel at home."

"It breeds excitement," Patterson interjected.

LaRue jumped at the sound of the fireworks display and broke into a short laugh. "I didn't quite expect that."

"It's beautiful. . . ." Patterson murmured. "I love watching fireworks. When I was little, I used to think that all the fireworks were for my mama's birthday. I remember thinking she must be really special 'cause we didn't have no fireworks for daddy or for me."

"Speaking of your mother—did you call and wish her a happy birthday?" LaRue had called her own parents to wish them a happy Independence Day. She and her father had been on the phone for a few seconds before they launched into a full-fledged argument.

Patterson was saying, "I reached her right before we left—at my uncle's house in Darien. They were just about to leave for St. Simon's. I sent her some flowers and candy. She cried when she got them." Patterson smiled. "It don't take much to make my mama smile."

"I can't wait to meet them. Are they coming to New York any time soon?"

"I think they're a little afraid of coming up heh. I'm gon' get them up heh, though. Sooner or later."

The fireworks ended promptly at eleven and they returned to shore.

LaRue and Patterson arrived home around midnight, with Macy arriving within fifteen minutes of them.

LaRue rushed into the shower.

Afterward, LaRue dried off and slipped on a strapless tube dress she had purchased just days before. The dress fit her like a glove and accentuated her hourglass figure. Even though she was slender, LaRue had a curvy shape.

Patterson was in the kitchen drinking a glass of water when LaRue came out.

"How do I look?" LaRue asked as she did a slow spin.

"You look sexy," Patterson murmured. "That dress really looks good on you. Those ankle-wrap shoes are perfect with it."

"I wouldn't wear red for a long time," LaRue admitted. "But I love this dress. I think I'll wear it a lot."

"It looks good on you."

Macy walked out of her room wearing a stunning see-through dress with lace insets covering her breasts and hips.

"Wow," LaRue murmured. "That's really something, Macy."

The dress looked stunning on Macy, but LaRue didn't think she would ever have enough nerve to wear something like that. It was too bold for her.

She was looking forward to partying this evening. She wanted something to take her mind off of the upcoming anniversary of Tom's death. Two days from now, she would have to endure the pain of her husband's leaving her to go live with Jesus.

"God, why did you have to take him away from me?" she whispered.

Patterson

Patterson thought Macy's dress was much too provocative, but kept it to herself. The last thing she wanted was to bicker with Macy.

She walked out of the kitchen and headed to her bedroom.

Patterson stayed in her room until Macy and LaRue were gone. She considered calling Miller Baisden, but couldn't summon the courage.

Patterson would've preferred Miller making the first move, but hadn't heard from him.

She spent the rest of her evening watching television until she drifted off to sleep on the sofa just before eleven.

Patterson was awakened shortly after three A.M. when Macy and LaRue entered the apartment.

As she neared them, Patterson could tell that both of them had been drinking again.

The way LaRue rushed into the apartment and stumbled toward the hall bathroom, Patterson knew she was having a hard time keeping the liquor down.

"The poor thing," she murmured almost to herself. "She's sick."

Macy nodded in agreement. "You should've seen the way she was tossing back those drinks. I've never seen LaRue like this. I think she really just wanted to get drunk. I tried to stop her, but she wouldn't listen to me."

As they neared their rooms, they could hear LaRue retching in the bathroom.

Patterson opened the bathroom door without preamble. She retrieved a clean washcloth from the linen closet and wet it.

She pressed the cool cloth to LaRue's forehead. "Here you are. This may give you some relief."

Patterson's eyes met Macy's. "Could you make some chamomile tea, please? And see if we have some saltine crackers?"

Macy nodded and disappeared down the hall.

Looking down at LaRue, she asked, "Why do you torture yourself like this?"

LaRue groaned in response. She tried to lift herself up, but stumbled.

Patterson helped her up, leaning LaRue against the wall. She turned on the water in the tub.

"I'm going to run you a bath. Once I get you in the tub, I'll get you some pajamas and your robe. Macy's making you some tea. It should make you feel better."

"I feel sick," LaRue mumbled. "Oooh, Lord. . . ."

After getting her settled in the tub, Patterson went into LaRue's bedroom to retrieve some clothing for her. When she returned, Macy was sitting on the edge of the tub, braiding LaRue's hair.

After her bath, LaRue had lost some of her ashen pallor. Wrapped in the luxury of her silk pajamas, matching robe, and slippers, she sat in the middle of her bed, sipping tea. She gave Patterson a sheepish smile. "Thank you."

"You okay?" Patterson inquired. "I know that we're not close friends or anything, but we *are* roommates. I care about you and . . ." She looked over at LaRue. "I'm really worried about your drinking."

"I don't drink a lot. I just . . ." LaRue shook her head. "I needed to find a way to escape. Just for a little while."

Patterson gave LaRue a puzzled look. "I . . . know you're in a lot of pain right now. I wish there was something I could do."

"You can't."

She glanced over at Macy, who said, "LaRue, we're here for you. I hope you know that. Just tell us what we can do."

"You can get me some Tylenol. My head is killing me."

Patterson's eyes filled with tears. "LaRue, please doan do this to yo'-self. This is not the answer."

"I'll be okay," LaRue assured her. "Tonight was a lesson for me. I won't overdo the drinking like this ever again. Right now I just want to go to bed." LaRue tried to stand up.

Patterson rushed to her side. "Let me help you."

She escorted LaRue to her bedroom and helped her get settled.

"You are such a sweet person, Patterson. Thanks so much for looking out for me."

Patterson gave LaRue a smile. "You're like a sister to me. I know we haven't known each other very long, but you're already in my heart."

She sat down on the edge of LaRue's bed. "I know what you're doin'. You tryin' to run away from God. It's not gon' work."

LaRue stared down at her hands. "I need to get some rest. We'll talk in the morning. Okay?"

Patterson nodded. "Rest well."

Macy was seated in the living room when she came out of LaRue's room.

"Tell me something, Patterson. Why do you do this? Why do you care so much?"

"Just because I do. There's no other reason."

Running her fingers through her hair, Macy uttered, "I've never been able to get along with women. I don't really like other females, except you and LaRue. You get on my last nerve most of the time, but deep down I know that you're okay."

Patterson grinned. "I feel the exact same way 'bout you."

Macy got up and followed Patterson into the kitchen. "Do you think LaRue will listen to you?" she asked.

Shrugging, Patterson responded, "I don't know. I can only hope so."

Chapter 15

LaRue

Tom died and left her exactly one year ago.

LaRue sat up in bed and swung her legs to the edge of the bed. She sat there for a moment, trying to summon the strength to see the rest of the day through.

She burst into tears.

There was a soft knock on the door.

LaRue wiped her eyes on the sleeve of her pajamas. "Come in."

Patterson walked into the room, followed by Macy.

"I made you some chocolate chip pancakes. They yo' favorite, I know," Patterson announced. "I even put some whipped cream on them just the way you like. Now mine might not be as good as the ones you get at IHOP, but I think you gon' like them just the same."

Macy sat down beside her. "I didn't cook anything because you know I can't cook. But I saw this while I was out shopping, and I thought it would be good for you." She held out a wrapped gift.

LaRue took the present and unwrapped it.

"It's a journal for you to write down all of your memories with Tom," Macy said. "That way you won't ever forget them. You can write down the way he smelled, what his favorite foods were—you know, that sort of thing."

LaRue was moved to tears. She wiped her eyes with a tissue Patterson handed her. "Thanks so much."

Patterson dropped down on the other side of her. "We love you, LaRue. When you're sad, we sad, too."

"The country girl is right," Macy began. "We care a lot for you. I have never lost anyone I loved, so I can't presume to know how that feels. Today, Tom has been gone for a year, but don't dwell on that. Keep your mind on all the happy times you shared with him. Remember the good times."

"I was thinking, we could do something together today," Patterson stated. "Unless you'd rather be alone?"

LaRue shook her head no. "I don't want to be alone."

"I'm glad you said that. I'd already canceled my spa appointment."

"Thanks, Macy. I guess I owe you, huh?"

"Yeah, and don't worry—I'm not going to let you forget it." Macy stood up. "Okay, now let's go eat before the food gets cold. But first . . ." She turned up her nose. "Brush your teeth."

LaRue put a hand to her mouth. Wagging her finger at Macy, she stood up and walked out of her room.

"Don't forget to use mouthwash," Macy yelled.

Laughing, Patterson walked to the door. "I'ma put the food on the table."

LaRue felt better after she washed her face and brushed her teeth. She strode out of the bathroom and went to join Macy and Patterson in the kitchen.

Over breakfast, they discussed their plans for the day.

"What did you and Tom do for fun?" Macy inquired.

"We used to go roller-blading a lot. It was something we loved."

Patterson poured LaRue a cup of coffee. "I've never been roller-blading. I know how to roller-skate, though."

"We can take LaRue to the Roxy Night Club," Macy suggested. "They have roller disco. It'll be fun."

LaRue broke into a tiny smile. "You'd do that for me?"

Macy nodded. "Now I have to confess that I've never been roller-skating or roller-blading, but I'm willing to try it this one time."

"I'm very fortunate to have you and Patterson in my life. With both Tom and Janine gone . . . I was feeling pretty lonely."

"Don't go getting used to this," Macy stated. "I don't get these kind of feelings very often. I'm all about self-gratification. It's all about me."

LaRue laughed. "Then this is all the more special."

Patterson

She was now an employed resident of New York. Patterson decided she would need to purchase a few new items to wear to work.

Patterson had been notified the day after she and Macy took LaRue to the Roxy Night Club. She smiled at the memory of watching Macy fall on her behind several times throughout the night.

Despite her clumsiness on skates, the princess seemed to have enjoyed skating. As soon as they returned to the apartment, Macy promptly went to soak in her bathtub.

After going shopping to buy some new clothes for work, Patterson strolled into the apartment whistling. Her spirits dropped at the sight of Macy's clothes strewn all over the living room. "Must have been some party," she murmured to herself, while bending to pick them up. Macy had gone out Sunday evening, but hadn't returned by the time Patterson left this morning.

"Gurl, let Macy or Lupe pick up that stuff," LaRue suggested. "You don't have to pick up after a grown woman."

A soft gasp escaped her. "I'm surprised to hear that coming from you. I know how much you like everything neat and clean."

"Oh, it's driving me crazy seeing stuff all over the floor like that, but I'm determined not to pick them up. Macy should be ashamed of herself. She's too old for this."

"I'm getting them," a voice said from behind them.

Macy strode over to Patterson and took her clothing from her. "Thanks."

"I know this is your house, Macy, but can you please undress in your bedroom?" Patterson requested.

Macy looked like she wanted to object, then changed her mind. "Fair enough," she responded. "I can do that."

"We would appreciate it," LaRue replied.

She did a double-take when she looked at Macy. LaRue wasn't aware she was staring, until Macy commented on it.

"Your eyes. They're darker."

"I took my contacts out," Macy stated. "You've seen me without them, haven't you?"

LaRue shook her head no. "This is the first time."

"I never knew you were wearing contacts," Patterson interjected. "I thought your eyes were really that hazel color."

"You two had not better ever tell a soul. I get compliments on my eyes all the time. It would devastate people to find out that this is not my natural eye color."

Shaking her head, LaRue laughed. "I hardly think anyone would be devastated."

Macy sent her a sharp look. "Don't you have something to do?"

"I hope everyone's hungry. Dinner is ready and waiting," LaRue announced.

Patterson clapped her hands. "Good. I'm starving."

Macy ran off to her room to put away her clothing. She returned a few minutes later.

They gathered around the dinner table.

After saying grace, Patterson tapped the side of her water glass with her fork. "Before we get started, I have an announcement to make."

"What is it?" LaRue and Macy asked in unison.

"I got a job. I'm now officially employed."

"That's wonderful," LaRue stated as she got up and moved around the table to give Patterson a hug. "Congratulations, sweetie."

"I'm happy for you," Macy chimed in. "Where and when do you start?"

"I got a job at Macy's. I'm a cosmetics beauty advisor, and I start my training tomorrow."

"So what exactly are you going to be doing?" Macy reached for her water glass and took a sip. "What do you know about giving out tips on beauty?"

"I know a lot. I took a whole course on make-up in college."

"In college? What kind of college did you go to?"

"Bauder Fashion College. Macy's is also sending me for advance training and make-up techniques. I'm gonna be doing make-overs on customers, working the cosmetics counter . . . that kind of thing."

"So, basically you're just a salesclerk then?"

"Yeah, I guess so. I'm going to be working the Chanel counter."

"I certainly hope they pay you well," Macy stated.

"Does any job pay well enough?" Patterson tossed out. "I don't think so, but this one will take care of what I need for now. Hopefully, my modeling career will take off and I can quit this job. But until then, I have to have a place to live and food to eat. Plus, I get a nice discount."

"Humph. I've never bought anything at discount," Macy said haughtily.

"Gurl, you missing out then," LaRue interjected. "Patterson, congratulations. I know you're glad to have a job. Can't wait to get one myself."

"I'm sure someone will be calling you any day now," Patterson encouraged. She enjoyed times like this—times when the three of them sat down to have dinner together. In a small way, it made them a family.

Stealing a peek over at Macy, she noted the dark circles underneath her eyes. Her lifestyle was going to catch up with Macy, if she weren't careful. You can't have friends if you're not willing to be one. One of Patterson's favorite verses was found in Psalm 27: *Do not forsake your friend and the friend of your father.*

Patterson's pastor back home had once explained in a sermon that the scripture cautioned us to not leave a friend when they need us, and also to be there for the friends of our parents.

She took that scripture to heart.

LaRue

"You look nice," Patterson complimented when LaRue walked out of her bedroom. "You must be going out."

"I'm going to a couture fashion show at Bruno's with this guy I met at Avalon."

Patterson was stunned. "Really?"

"We're just having dinner and going to the fashion show. He lost his fiancé in a car accident." LaRue peered into a nearby mirror. "It's not a date."

"Well, I hope you have a real nice time anyway."

LaRue glanced over at Patterson. "Have you heard from that guy yet? Miller . . . whatever his name is."

Patterson shook her head no. Swallowing her food, she wiped her mouth with the corner of her napkin. "I thought about callin' him, but I keep chickenin' out."

"I have to be honest. . . . I'm glad to hear it," LaRue admitted. "I—"

"What guy?" Macy interrupted. "Why am I just hearing about this? Patterson, you met someone?" She was full of questions.

"His name is Miller Baisden. I met him the other day while LaRue and I were having lunch."

Macy turned to Patterson and asked, "So why haven't you called him? Is he ugly or something?"

"I don't want to give him the wrong impression."

"Well, did you give him your number?"

"Yeah. He hasn't called me, though. I think if he was really interested, he would call me."

Gesturing with her fork, Macy advised, "Humph. If I were you, I wouldn't wait too long. He'll think that you're not interested and move on."

Patterson cast a look over at LaRue. "I hadn't considered that. Maybe I should give him a call."

LaRue stole another look in the mirror. "Well, I'm out. See y'all later."

"Have fun," Macy and Patterson chimed in unison.

LaRue stood outside the apartment, then headed toward the elevators. She wasn't as sure of herself now that she was actually on her way to meet Roger. She felt like she was cheating on Tom.

Chapter 16

Patterson

"Mmmm, this salmon is delicious."

Patterson smiled. "I'm glad you like it, Macy. This is only the second time I've ever cooked it."

"Well, you did a great job." Macy sliced off another piece. "Why is this your second time cooking it? Didn't you eat salmon when you were in Tree Trunk?"

"It's Three Oak and no, I didn't. I didn't have it until I moved heh to New York."

"Why is that?"

Patterson shrugged. "I doan really know. I guess it just wasn't sumpthin' my family ate. We grew most of our food and when we ate fish, my daddy caught it hisself."

"That sounds almost primitive." Macy shuddered. "Oh, my goodness. I could never live like that."

"You could—if it was the only life you knew."

"Humph. I bet you wouldn't go running back to that life now."

"I don't know, Macy. Depending on the reason I'm running, I might hightail it back home."

"Not after living here," Macy countered. "I don't believe it."

"This is just material stuff. I doan need any of it. I like it. I won't lie 'bout that. But I could walk away from all of it." Patterson took a sip of her iced tea.

Macy suddenly blurted, "You know what? I think we should do something to celebrate this momentous occasion."

"What are you talkin' 'bout?" Patterson asked. "What occasion?"

"You getting a job. I know just what to do. Why don't we go out this weekend? The three of us. There's this new jazz club in Manhattan. You'd love it." Macy stuck a forkful of salmon in her mouth and chewed.

Patterson broke into a happy grin. "Sure. Let's do it."

They spent the rest of their dinner talking about the modeling industry.

"Sometimes I think maybe I should give up on the idea of being a model. I've been to a couple of open calls and nothing."

"Sometimes it takes a while," Macy explained. "Me. I'm not giving up."

"I guess I didn't think it would take this long."

"You can't give up if you want to make it, Patterson."

After dinner, Patterson was mildly surprised when Macy helped her clean up the kitchen. She even spent the evening watching television with her. She actually seemed to be enjoying Patterson's company.

Yawning, Macy stretched. "Oh, excuse me. I'm tired."

Patterson stifled her yawn. "Me, too."

"I was trying to wait up to see how LaRue's date went."

"Macy, she said it wasn't a date. They are just comforting each other."

"Uh huh . . ."

Patterson rose to her feet. "I think I'ma call it a night. I can barely keep my eyes open any longer."

"There's another open call on Saturday," Macy announced. "I think we should go."

"Okay," Patterson uttered as she made her way to her room. "I'll see you tomorrow, Macy."

"Good night. I'm right behind you."

Patterson walked into her bedroom and removed her clothes. She slipped on a pair of pajamas and rolled her hair.

Right before crawling into bed, Patterson fell to her knees and said a prayer. She thanked God for her modeling career and added a request that God look out for LaRue and Macy, his lost children.

LaRue

She pretended not to notice Roger's lust-filled gaze.

"I won't lie to you. I'm a very lonely man, LaRue. I miss the companionship of a woman."

She nodded in understanding. "I know that feeling well. Usually, my best friend—her name was Janine—she would . . . she and I would sometimes stay up all night just reminiscing about my wedding . . . or the night Tom proposed . . . all the happy memories. When she died . . ." LaRue wiped at her eyes. "I was driving the night of the accident."

"What happened?"

"I guess I was driving too fast or I fell asleep. . . . I can't remember, but I believe that I fell asleep. We'd gone to San Diego and decided not to stay over. I wanted to come home. I told her that I'd drive. It was late."

Roger reached over and took her by the hand. "I'm sorry."

LaRue nodded. "I don't think I'll ever be able to forgive myself."

He handed her a tissue.

"Thanks," she murmured as she wiped her eyes.

"If you want, we can go back to my place," Roger suggested.

LaRue shook her head. "I'm not ready for anything like that."

"We can just talk."

"Not tonight. Thanks for taking me to the fashion show and for dinner, Roger. I had a good time with you."

"I hope that we can see each other again. I'd like to get to know you better."

Smiling, LaRue squeezed his hand. "I'd like that, too."

Thirty minutes later, a taxi dropped LaRue in front of her building. As soon as she stepped into the apartment, she heard a door open. It was Macy.

She surveyed LaRue from head to toe. "I just wanted to make sure you came home the same way you left."

LaRue laughed.

Patterson walked out of her room. "Hey. Did you have a good time?"

She nodded. "Roger's very sweet. And horny."

Macy burst into laughter while Patterson flushed red.

"He actually asked me to go back to his apartment with him, but I said no." LaRue walked to her bedroom. "We're gonna see each other again. So ladies, he passed."

Patterson embraced her. "Glad you enjoyed yourself. Good night."

"See you in the morning," Macy stated.

LaRue left her room to shower and change into her nightclothes. Before she went to bed, she thought about everything Patterson had said earlier about friendship. She was grateful to have two people who cared enough to make sure she came home safely.

Macy

Macy rolled her head to take the tightness out of her neck. A delicious weariness engulfed her. The evening had been good, satisfying.

Having roommates wasn't so bad, Macy acknowledged. She'd actually enjoyed spending time talking and watching a movie with them.

She was glad to see LaRue finally going out, instead of just sitting around the house. Macy wished Patterson would go out and meet someone, too especially since she wasn't interested in the other guy. She hadn't called him or anything. She'd never seen two more boring women. They were both beautiful . . . and alone.

Macy had to admit that she was just as bad. She knew she was stunning. She had men falling at her feet all around, but she just wasn't interested in any of them. She needed a certain type of man—rich.

Her eyes traveled to the telephone. Macy considered calling Frederick, but it was late. Her parents had called again, but she'd had Lupe tell them that she was away. She knew they might come up and try to get into the apartment, so she had the locks changed. Macy determined that her parents would pay for their treatment of her.

Macy pulled her tired shoulders up to ease the persistent ache in them. She glanced across the room to where her clock sat. Beside the clock was her Bible, new and unopened, despite the thick layer of dust settling on the top. "Lupe's not doing her job," she murmured to the empty room. "I'm going to have to get on her."

Yawning, Macy made her way over to her lingerie chest to retrieve a clean pair of tap pants and a camisole. She caught her reflection in the mirror hanging over her dresser and gasped. Her complexion looked washed out, and the dark circles beneath her eyes shocked her. She hadn't noticed them when she'd taken her shower earlier.

"Why didn't they tell me I looked so bad?"

Macy made a mental note to call for a spa appointment first thing in the morning.

She changed into her sleepwear and climbed in bed. Now that La-Rue was home safe, Macy was more than ready for a good night's sleep.

Patterson

She was jittery with excitement. Today was her first day of training.

Not wanting to risk being late, Patterson strolled briskly into the classroom setting in Macy's Department Store and took a seat. She sat in the third seat on the third row.

After everyone introduced themselves, the trainer gave a brief history of the company.

During the first break, a young man wearing glasses approached her. "My name is Jason Carter," he stated. "Welcome to the Big Apple."

Patterson chuckled. "I guess you could tell by my accent that I'm not from here."

He nodded. "You do have a strong Southern accent."

"Is that a very polite way of saying I talk country?"

Jason grinned. "Not at all."

They made small talk until it was time to return to the training room. They spent the early part of the morning working on store policies and procedures. Just before lunch, they'd started working on the cash registers.

Jason and Patterson had lunch together during the hour-long break.

"So what brought you to New York?"

Patterson added pepper to her chef's salad. "I wont to be a model."

"I had a feeling that was the case. Either modeling or acting. That's usually what girls that look like you come up here for."

"Thank you, I guess."

"I meant it as a compliment."

"Are you a native New Yorker?" Patterson inquired. "You don't sound like one." She stuck a forkful of lettuce into her mouth.

Jason shook his head. "I'm originally from Washington, D.C. I moved up here because I was following this girl. Things didn't quite go the way I expected so, she's now my ex-girlfriend."

"Oh, I'm sorry to hear that."

"Its fine," he assured her. "We're still friends—we just couldn't make it as a couple."

"My ex-boyfriend was planning to move here with me, but we broke up a few months before. Thank God, I guess."

"So have you gone to any of the modeling agencies?"

"I've gone to four so far. I really wont to be with Emerald Model Management. It's the biggest in New York. I figured if I don't make it there, I'll check out some others."

"Be careful. It's a lot of people out there manipulating young women into drugs, prostitution, and pornography."

"I know. That's why I'm not really interested in going with an unknown agency. I'm being extremely careful."

They finished their lunch and headed back to the store.

Looking up at the sky, Patterson stated, "It looks like it's gonna pour down. I hope I can make it home before it starts."

"The weatherman predicted rain for the rest of the week."

"I hope it's over by Friday night. My roommates and I are going out to celebrate my getting this job."

Chapter 17

Macy

W hen her nails were dry, Macy wrote out a check for payment. She
glanced out the storefront window, eyeing the dismal weather.
She hoped to make it home before it got any worse. Macy hated rainy
weather.

Handing the check over to the woman, she said, "Thanks so much,
Mimi. My nails look great as usual. I'll see you next Friday."

"You don't want your standing Wednesday appointment?"

"I have a hair appointment next Wednesday, so I need to switch it
to Friday. It's not a problem, is it?"

Mimi shook her head. "Not at all. I'll see you then. Eleven o'clock
okay?"

"Perfect."

As Macy walked along Lexington Avenue, she stopped in front of
the glass window of a little boutique. "What a beautiful dress," she
murmured. "This dress is perfect for the cocktail reception at the
Helen Yarmak Showroom tonight."

Momentarily forgetting the impending bad weather, Macy forged
into the shop on a mission.

When she strolled out of the boutique, Macy was four hundred dollars poorer. She wasn't even sure she had enough in the bank to cover the dress, but didn't care at the moment. If not, she'd just borrow it from someone.

Fredrick was coming back into town tomorrow, she recalled. He'd left a message on her voice mail requesting to see her. She'd originally planned to ignore his plea, but now changed her mind.

I'll just get the money from him. With that in mind, Macy decided that she would even splurge for the perfect pair of shoes. She intended to look her best when she attended the gala at the VIP showroom.

Macy knew this event would be attended by celebrities. Many of the Hollywood A-list were clients of Helen Yarmak's.

There was even a chance that her mother would be in attendance, but Macy didn't care. She would give her mother a cool reception.

Macy was looking forward to the event tonight. She loved Helen Yarmak's jewelry. She owned several gold pieces accessorized with topaz and diamonds. Frederick usually gifted her with one of the trinkets from the Yarmak collection when he came to town.

She muttered a curse. She'd left the last gift he'd given her, behind in anger. It would've been perfect with the dress she'd just purchased.

LaRue

The sky over New York City hung dark with clouds.

The soggy Wednesday morning was between showers at that moment. LaRue put away her umbrella as she neared the subway entrance. Hopefully she would be safe at home before it started raining again.

She didn't have long to wait. The train slowed to a sluggish stop and LaRue walked briskly, stepping inside. Seated near the back, LaRue pulled out a novel and began to read.

Twenty minutes later, LaRue walked up the steps and out onto the busy streets. Drops of rain were beginning to fall, softly at first, but then in full force. She opened up her umbrella. Her feet, covered in a pair of leather mules, moved at warp speed. The rain was coming down even harder.

She and Macy arrived home within seconds of each other.

"It's pouring out there," Macy stated. She shook the water off her shopping bags before setting them down on the floor near the sofa. Running her fingers through her hair, she sighed. "Now I'm going to have to get my hair done again before we go out Friday night."

"That's why I like having braids. I don't have to worry about it." LaRue placed her umbrella into the stand near the front door.

"They are pretty nice. I'd thought about getting some once, but when I mentioned it to my mother, she almost had a fit."

"Why?"

"Mother said it would make me look too ethnic."

LaRue burst into laughter.

"What's so funny?"

"You'd look about as ethnic as a white girl wearing braids."

Macy broke into a small laugh. "You're probably right."

A flash of lightning split the sky, followed by a loud clap of thunder.

LaRue noted the fear in Macy's eyes. "There's nothing to be afraid of. It's just some thunder."

Trembling, Macy nodded. "I know. It's just that it unnerves me."

"Why don't we just close the blinds and sit here and talk?" LaRue suggested.

"I'd like that."

LaRue made herself comfortable on the sofa, while Macy sat in the oversized chair nearby.

"What are you afraid of?" Macy asked.

Shrugging, LaRue answered, "A lot of things. Flying in airplanes makes me a little nervous these days. . . . I'm afraid of stepping too far out of my comfort zone. . . . And bugs—I'm deathly afraid of bugs and snakes."

"I'm afraid of dying and being forgotten. I'm afraid of thunder and lightning because it reminds me of the time I was lost in the woods. I was away at camp and I'd wandered off. It was dark and wet from the rain. The thunder . . . it was so loud. . . . A tree fell right in front of me."

"How old were you?" LaRue asked.

Macy's eyes were wet with tears. "I was six years old. Every time I went to camp, it rained. The last time I went, it flooded. I thought I was going to drown. I've always believed that the rain was after me somehow." She glanced over at LaRue. "Go on and laugh. I know you want to."

"Why? Because you think the rain is trying to kill you?" LaRue grinned. "You were a scared little girl."

"That's where you're wrong. I'm still scared."

LaRue knew that Macy's admission was a hard one for her to make. She cocked her head to the side, listening. "The rain is easing up."

She got up to open the blinds.

Macy joined her at the windows. "Thank you, Jesus." She turned to LaRue. "And thank you."

"For what?"

"For talking me through this. I usually just get in my bed and hide under the covers."

"I'm trying not to laugh at you, but if you tell me anymore, Macy, I'm gonna spill."

"If you tell Patterson about this, I'm going to deny it."

LaRue grew serious. "I won't," she promised. "I'm teasing you, but I saw how much the storm scared you." In her mind, she had to admit that Patterson had been right on the money.

Macy needed a good friend.

Macy

The rotten weather persisted on and off until Thursday afternoon, when the clouds finally dispersed.

Last night, Macy had a fantastic time drinking champagne and mingling with celebrities and luminaries from Russia and all over. She posed and smiled as members of the media snapped photographs of everyone in attendance.

She was pleasantly surprised to see Frederick. She hadn't known he was coming to New York. They made plans to see each other the next day. The only thorn in her side was the appearance of Charla Sheffield, her nemesis. Although once childhood friends, Macy now hated the sniveling witch. She knew Charla was after Frederick, but vowed she'd never get him.

The doorbell rang, bringing Macy out of her reverie.

She ran to answer the front door. It had to be Frederick. The doorman would never let just anyone come up without prior permission from the residents.

"It's so good to hold you in my arms again. I didn't like the way we ended things when I last saw you, sweetheart."

She looked up at Frederick, taking in his handsome smile, his smooth mocha-latte-colored complexion and dark hair that lay in tiny waves. He was extremely handsome and a wonderful lover, and Macy kept telling herself that their friendship was enough.

"Where are these infamous roommates you were telling me about? Do I get to meet them?"

"They're not home right now."

Frederick gave her a lustful look. "Really? So we're all alone?"

Macy stepped out of the reach of Frederick's arms. "Why is it every time you come to see me, you want to have sex? Why don't you ever want to spend an evening just hanging out together or talking like we used to do? After all, you just want us to remain friends. That is what you said, right?"

Patterson and LaRue were due home at any moment, but it was more than that. Macy was beginning to feel that Frederick was using her.

"You're not going to start that again, are you? Honey, this is who and what we are." Frederick rubbed the bare skin of her back and shoulders.

Macy straightened her halter top and stepped backwards. "I don't always want sex, Frederick. Sometimes I'd like to be romanced. You do know how to romance a woman, don't you?"

He seemed baffled by her attitude. "You've been hanging around your roommates too long. Where are they, by the way? I'd like to meet them."

"Patterson and LaRue have nothing to do with this, Frederick. This is just about you and me; so don't try to change the subject."

"Macy, if you don't want to make love, just say so. It's no big thing, believe me."

Her temper flared. "Excuse me?"

"Honey, all I'm trying to say is that we don't have to do anything if you don't want to. I missed you and just wanted to feel close to you, but if it's not what you want, we don't have to do anything."

"Good, because I don't want to have sex. Look, Frederick, I want something more out of life. I want a real relationship with a man. One that will actually lead to my walking down the aisle. You've already made it clear that I won't be doing that with you."

"I can't believe that you're suddenly getting serious on me, Macy."

"Believe it. I want more out of life."

"Since when?"

Macy glowered at him and turned away. Staring up at the huge portrait of herself, she mumbled, "Frederick, it doesn't matter. Not to you anyway."

He watched her in silence for a moment before saying, "I'm having dinner with my Aunt Jeanne at seven. Would you like to join us? She'd love to see you."

"Not tonight. Give your aunt my love."

Frederick nodded. "I'd better be on my way. Sure you don't want to come to Long Island with me?"

"Not tonight." Macy turned around to face him. "Frederick, I need a favor from you."

"What is it?"

"I need a tiny little loan."

"I thought your roommates were paying you rent. Why are you having such financial problems?"

Her lips thinned with anger. How dare he question her like that? He wasn't her husband or anything close to that. "Are you going to loan me the money or not?"

"I don't think I am. Macy, I don't know what's going on with you, but you've changed."

"I know what this is, Frederick. I won't sleep with you, so now you won't loan me any more money."

"I won't loan you money because you never pay it back," he replied sharply.

"I hate you, Frederick." Rancor sharpened Macy's voice as she glared at him.

His laugh irritated her. Reaching out, Frederick pulled her into his arms.

Macy pushed away from him. "I want you out of my apartment."

"Honey . . ."

"Don't 'honey' me," she snapped. "Just leave me alone. The next time you come to New York, do me a favor and don't call me. *Lose my number for good.*"

The next morning, Macy checked her checking account balance via telephone. She played the balance twice.

"That can't be right," she muttered.

She pressed *O* for the customer service representative and waited for a live voice to answer her call.

"First Bank of New York. This is Marcella. What can I do for you today?"

"You can tell me what's going on with my bank account," Macy snapped.

Chapter 18

LaRue

She walked past Macy's bedroom, slowing her steps to a halt when she heard the string of curses coming from within.

"Macy, I'm going to start charging you a quarter for every cuss word you say."

"Good morning to you, too." Macy sat at her desk thumbing through a stack of mail. "I can't believe I have so many bills."

LaRue knew Macy wasn't talking to her, so she didn't bother to respond.

"This is so crazy," she uttered.

"I'm surprised to find you up so early." Checking her watch, LaRue said, "It's only ten."

"I needed to take care of some things this morning. I was going to do some shopping, but now I can't. I think something's wrong with my bank account."

"What's the problem?"

"According to the automated phone system, I don't have any money. That can't be right. I made a deposit a week ago."

Macy tossed the bills onto the desk and sighed in frustration. "I'm getting a headache."

"I'm pretty good with money and balancing bank accounts," LaRue announced. "I can look at it, if you like."

"Sure. I have nothing to hide."

"Let's sit in the dining room. We'll have more space at the table."

Macy gathered up her bills and her checkbook, which she handed over to LaRue.

While she waited, Macy filed her nails.

"Where is your check register?" LaRue asked after a moment.

"Why?"

"Because I need it. I can't make heads or tails out of anything without the register."

"Oh. I don't use it."

"Excuse me?"

"I don't use the register. That's why I have the duplicate checks. I just check my account every day to see what's in there."

"Where's your last bank statement?"

"I don't know. I probably threw it away."

"How old are you, Macy?"

"Twenty-four. Why?"

"I can't imagine how you managed anything."

"My father put money in my account once a week. I just didn't worry about it."

"Do you know if your bank has online banking?"

"They do. I even signed up for it—just never used it."

LaRue stood up. "I'm getting my laptop. We're going to check out your financial situation and see if we can get this stuff straight."

Half an hour later, LaRue stated, "Macy, according to this, you're almost three hundred and fifty dollars in the hole. You don't have any money."

"That can't be right."

"We'll see. Give me your checkbook again."

While LaRue worked, Macy thumbed through the latest issue of *Glamour*.

"I hate to tell you this, Macy, but the truth is that you're broke," LaRue announced when she finished reconciling the account.

Macy held up several envelopes. "But I've got to pay these bills."

LaRue scanned through the stack of paper on the couch. "Overdue notices . . . Macy, how can we have late notices? What have you been doing with the money we give you?"

With her eyes darting around the room, Macy replied, "I've used it for bills and stuff."

"You're lying," LaRue accused. "You've been using our money to shop and party. Pretty soon we're gonna be homeless."

"I wouldn't let that happen."

"Just how do you intend to stop it?" In her mind, LaRue struggled between shaking Macy and just moving out. The woman was irresponsible. She sent up a quick prayer, asking God for the right words. She wanted her words to build Macy up and not destroy her spirit.

"I'm sorry, LaRue. What I've done is wrong. But you don't have to worry about being evicted. I've paid the rent. I'll pay everything else. I will. Please don't tell Patterson," Macy pleaded.

"I don't know if I can promise something like that."

"Please, just help me out this time. I promise I'll be better."

After giving it some thought, LaRue stated, "I'll do it, but on the following conditions. I will pay all of the bills from this moment forward and you agree to certain changes."

"Like what?"

"One of the first things I think we should do is get rid of the maid. That's an expense we really don't need right now."

She was in a panic. "We can't get rid of Lupe. I need her."

"Macy, we can't afford to keep her. *You* can't afford to keep her."

"Well, who's going to do the cleaning?"

"*We are.*"

Macy frowned and folded her arms across her chest. "I hate housework."

Glancing around the room, LaRue muttered, "I can tell."

"What else do I have to do?"

LaRue held up the checkbook. "Is this right? You pay fifteen hundred dollars to get your hair done? What in the world do they do—charge by the strand?"

"No. I have my hair fused in. I wanted to add some length and fullness."

"Oh."

"I'm telling you now that I'm not giving up my hair. I want long hair and this is the only way I can get it."

"Macy, you can't afford to have something like this. Buy yourself a wig."

She opened her mouth in dismay. "I don't want it to look fake,

LaRue. That's *why* I spend so much money having it bonded to my own hair. I don't want anyone to *know* that I have a weave."

"What about braids?"

"Everybody knows that braids aren't your real hair. LaRue, you're not hearing me. I want people to believe that this hair on my head is what I was born with. I'm not going to negotiate on the hair. This is a must-have. Even more than food."

"You're crazy."

"I'm not crazy. I just need my hair."

"Macy, you have more going for you than the hair on your head. Surely you know that, don't you?"

"I know that, LaRue. Having long hair just works for me. I don't want to give it up."

Patterson

Patterson unlocked the door and entered the apartment. She found LaRue sitting at the dining room table and Macy pouting.

"What's going on?" she questioned.

Macy looked to LaRue with a strange expression.

"We were going over the bills," LaRue answered. "Macy and I were just talking about making some changes. We need to cut back on some expenses. Like maid service for starters."

"Oh, I agree. We can clean the apartment ourselves."

"I was just explaining to Macy that each of us will have to pull our weight around here. Right?"

Macy could only nod.

"Are we still going out tonight?" Patterson inquired. "I've been looking forward to it all week."

LaRue shrugged. "That's up to Macy."

"I . . . I'm a little broke this week, Patterson. I thought I had more money, but as it turns out, I don't."

"If you'd like, I'd be more than happy to pay for us. That's what friends do for one another," Patterson said.

Macy shot a glance at LaRue.

"We promised Patterson," LaRue announced. "Tonight will be my treat. I'm paying for all of us."

"I can help, LaRue. You don't have to do this," Patterson said.

"You said it earlier—this is what friends do."

The phone in LaRue's room started to ring, interrupting their conversation.

"I'll be right back."

When LaRue returned, she was wearing a big grin on her face. "We're definitely going out tonight. I got the job with the charter school. I got another job offer, too. It was on my voice mail, but I hadn't heard it until now."

Patterson rushed over to embrace her. "I'm so happy for you. Congratulations."

Patterson

Saturday morning, Patterson crawled out of bed after only three hours of sleep. Last night had been interesting. Impromptu was a nice club, nicer than some of the ones she'd gone to in Atlanta. She still wasn't much of a dancer, but Patterson managed to have a good time. She'd even met a couple of nice-looking men.

Patterson gave out her telephone number and took theirs. She still hadn't heard from Miller, and she couldn't find the courage to be the aggressor.

LaRue definitely enjoyed herself and was tipsy by the time she left with Roger, which was two hours earlier than when Patterson and Macy left.

Patterson wasn't sure LaRue had even come home until Macy, being nosy, peeked into her room.

LaRue was there, already in bed and sound asleep.

Patterson jumped in the shower to speed up the process of waking up. She dressed in a pair of shorts and a tank top and pulled her hair into a ponytail. After brushing her teeth, Patterson left the bathroom.

Today was their designated cleaning day, so she decided to start in the kitchen. She went through the refrigerator, throwing out outdated items and leftovers.

By the time she was ready to mop the kitchen floor, LaRue was up and moving about. She began cleaning the living room.

"I had fun last night," Patterson stated while mopping.

"I did, too," LaRue replied. "That was a nice club."

"I wonder what time Macy's gonna come alive."

"Oh, she's up already," LaRue announced. "I heard her moving about in her room."

"Wow. She really is making changes. I didn't think she was really serious." Patterson smiled. "This is so wonderful."

She heard her telephone ring, but decided to let it switch over to voice mail. Whoever it was, she could call them back. Patterson was sure it wasn't the one man she wanted to hear from.

Chapter 19

Macy

She screamed.
She'd already broken two nails in her pitiful attempt at dusting. "This is not working!" she yelled.

Patterson and LaRue came running into the room.

"What's wrong, Macy?"

Her eyes flashed with outrage. "*What do you think?* I broke two nails." She pulled off the rubber gloves and held up her hand for them to see. "Look at this."

"That's all?" LaRue questioned. "Gurl, you haven't seen nothing yet. We still got to clean the rest of the apartment."

"NO!" Macy shouted. "Okay, this is where I draw the line. I'm not cleaning the bathroom. *No.*"

LaRue's eyes issued a gentle but firm warning. "You have to clean your bathroom, Macy. Nobody else is going to do it for you. I know I'm not."

"LaRue, I'll cut you a deal on the rent if you'll clean it," Macy's throat ached with defeat. "I can't do it. *I can't.*"

"You can do it, Macy. *And you will.*" LaRue's tone encouraged no argument.

"I hate my life. . . ." With a moan of distress, Macy turned away.

Quickly losing patience, LaRue snapped, "Gurl, you need to stop being such a drama queen."

Her hands on her hips, Macy glared at her. "I am not being a 'drama queen,' as you put it. I'm just not used to doing this . . . this stuff. We've always had maids."

"It's called housework. Some call it chores."

Folding her arms across her chest, Macy rolled her eyes and muttered a string of curses under her breath. "You make me sick, LaRue," she fumed. "I don't give a flip what you call it. I'm not interested in doing it. That's why I hired a maid in the first place."

"Then get a job, Macy. When you can pay for a maid, you can get one." LaRue handed her the broom. "But until then, we are going to have to do the work ourselves. By the way, you owe me a quarter for cussing."

Pulling a five-dollar bill out of her pocket, Macy handed it over to LaRue. "I can't stand you, LaRue Arnette-Hawkins. You might as well keep the change, because I'll owe it to you by the time this day is over."

"Aw, honey . . . you're hurting my feelings." Shaking her head, LaRue chuckled. "Girl, I've got to get back to work. We have a lot to do."

Macy took several deep breaths before summoning up enough strength to finish the bathroom.

She called LaRue everything in the book she could think of as she swept back and forth, the sound of the broom swishing against the ceramic tile floor.

Patterson walked into her bathroom. "Macy, you look like you're trying to kill something."

"*I am,*" she answered. "LaRue."

Patterson burst into laughter. "It'll be okay."

"Don't you people get it?" she yelled. "I don't want to be okay with this. This is not what I'm about, Patterson. I actually enjoy having someone wait on me hand and foot. I don't think it makes me a bad person."

"Nobody is saying that, Macy."

Her eyes filled with tears of frustration. "Then why can't I have a maid?"

"Because apparently you can't afford to pay for one. They don't work for free, Macy."

"I know."

Patterson eyed her roommate. "You're really having a hard time with this, huh?"

Macy didn't want anyone pitying her. She picked up the rubber gloves and put them back on. With her chin lifted, she stated, "I can do this. I've never let anything beat me, and I'm not going to start now." She glanced over at Patterson. "Shouldn't you be doing your share? We've got to clean this whole apartment."

Patterson gave her a mock salute. "Yes, ma'am. See you in a bit."

"Whatever . . ." Macy grumbled.

Two hours later, the apartment was spotless.

Macy was in her room, too weary to do anything other than lie on her chaise. She'd managed to take a shower and dress in a pair of sweatpants and a sports bra. Her hair was pulled up in a ponytail and her face was free of any make-up.

She closed her eyes.

A soft knock on her door startled her.

"Come in," she called out to her visitor.

"Were you sleeping?" LaRue inquired as she entered the room, followed by Patterson.

"Just about," Macy mumbled.

Patterson and LaRue exchanged looks.

"What are you two up to?"

"We were thinking that after all the hard work we've done," Patterson began, "we should reward ourselves. You worked so hard. . . ."

"We'd like to treat you to an afternoon of pampering," LaRue finished for Patterson. "I think we all can use it."

Macy sat up. "Are you serious?"

Patterson smiled and nodded. "You can get your nails done, a pedicure—whatever."

"Can I get a facial, too? I really need a facial. And my eyebrows—they look terrible."

Laughing, LaRue nodded. "You can have whatever you want. Well, let me change that. *Within reason.* Patterson and I are on a budget."

Macy was suddenly suspicious. "Why are you doing this for me?"

"Because we know this isn't easy for you, Macy. We just wanted to show our appreciation for your being such a good sport about it."

"I've never met any women like you two."

"That's okay. We've never met anyone like you either," Patterson responded.

"I need to get dressed." Macy rushed to her feet. "But it'll only take me five minutes."

LaRue

She smiled as she watched Patterson's excitement over getting her first facial. Even Macy appeared to be enjoying herself, despite all her weariness. LaRue knew that she was touched by their thoughtfulness.

After their pampering session, Macy took them to get something to eat and insisted on paying, despite LaRue's resistance.

"Just let me do this. You two treated me to the spa. I want to pay for our dinner. Believe me it's not going to come up near what you two spent. I can afford to pay for our meals. I have some money left on one of my credit cards. I *want* to do this."

LaRue gave a reluctant nod. "Okay. Let's go."

On Sunday morning, she woke up to find Macy up and getting dressed.

"I'm going to church with Patterson," she announced. "It's been a while so I figured I'd put in an appearance. I think you should go with us."

LaRue shook her head. "Not interested."

Macy spun around slowly. "What do you think about this outfit? Is it okay for church?"

Nodding, LaRue answered, "You look great."

Patterson walked out of her bedroom. "Good morning, ladies."

"Morning," they responded in unison.

"Macy, I'm surprised to see you up and dressed. You must be meeting someone."

"No. I'm going to church with you. I just told LaRue she needed to go with us."

Patterson's gaze met LaRue's. "Are you gon' come with us?"

"I told Macy I wasn't interested. If I need some religion, I can get it right off the television."

"Well, I'll see you when we get back."

"I might be out. Roger and I are gonna hang today."

Grabbing her purse, Macy said, "Remind me later this evening to show you ladies something. I've been playing around with a couple of ideas in my head."

"You have some new designs?" Patterson asked. She flicked a piece of lint off her shoulder.

Macy nodded as they neared the door. "I've been working on them for a couple of weeks now. I want to know what you and LaRue think. Tell me the truth now."

"Oh, we will," LaRue assured her. "You don't have to worry about that. Especially since you've never met a thought you didn't share."

She waved at them as they walked out of the apartment.

Alone, LaRue turned on the television and prepared a quick breakfast. Her father's face was the first thing she saw.

"James 4:14 says, '*For what is your life? It is even a vapour, that appeareth for a little time, and then vanisheth away.*' The late President Kennedy never dreamed on Friday morning, November 22, 1963, as he ate breakfast during the peak of his life, that by two o'clock that afternoon, he would be in eternity. Life is short—even if it is not cut off as was President Kennedy's. Thousands of people showed up for work on Tuesday morning, September 11, at the World Trade Center and the Pentagon with absolutely no clue what would await them that day. They didn't even have time to pray. Often when death comes, it comes suddenly. . . ."

LaRue picked up the remote to change the channel, but couldn't. It was as if an invisible force prevented her from turning from the station where her father stood, looking regal in his robe, surrounded by thousands of church members.

"Life without God is empty because knowledge brings no peace. . . ."

She had the strangest feeling that her father was talking to her. It was as if he knew she would be listening to him.

"Life without God is empty because pleasure, wealth, and works bring no lasting satisfaction. . . . Bring God into your life and obey Him—because your life is being recorded and will be revealed."

LaRue shuddered.

Patterson

Two days later, Macy rushed into the room, saying, "There's a model cover search next weekend. I think we should do it."

"What agency?" Patterson inquired.

"It's not for an agency. This is a real paying job. They are looking for models with nice figures and dancers for body painting."

"For what?"

"Body painting. It actually goes beyond that. It's a combination of art, dance, movement, and runway modeling," Macy explained.

Patterson shook her head. "I doan know 'bout that. I doan think I can do sumptin' like that. Doan you have to be naked?"

"I guess so. I don't have a problem showing off this gorgeous figure of mine."

Folding her arms across her breasts, Patterson uttered, "Well, I do. I doan think LaRue will go for sumptin' like that either."

"Go for what?"

Macy glanced over her shoulder. "I was just telling Patterson about a paying modeling job."

"Really? What is it?"

"You have to walk around naked on a runway," Patterson answered. "Body art or sumptin' . . . Macy can tell you 'bout it."

"The show is visually stunning, LaRue. One has to see it or be part of it to experience it. These types of shows take place in a number of venues in New York and other states. I attended the one once. They're casting the show on Friday at seven P.M. at the Gershwin Hotel."

"What do we have to bring to the casting?" LaRue questioned.

Patterson gasped. "You really considerin' this?"

"It's a paying job. It'll look good on my resume."

"You have to bring a photo or comp card. LaRue, you really need to consider having some comp cards done—those pictures of yours are played out. Oh, and you need to bring heels and a bikini."

"I can't believe you're really gon' do this."

"Patterson, I might not even get the job. Gurl, you can't be shy when it comes to being a model. You got to get over all that."

Shaking her head in dismay, Patterson stated, "Maybe this is not for me."

"Patterson, you will have art covering your body. It's not like you're going to be walking around stark naked. There's nothing nasty about the female body or art."

"I know what you sayin', Macy. I just can't do it."

"You're right," Macy uttered. "Maybe modeling really isn't for you."

Macy

She smiled when Patterson walked into the dressing room. "So, what did you think?"

"It was a nice show. I enjoyed myself."

LaRue strode over to where they were standing. "This was so much fun. I had a good time." She wrapped an arm around Patterson. "Gurl, you shoulda joined us. I was nervous at first, but then I just let the music take over."

Patterson smiled. "I'm glad y'all had fun."

"So what are we doing when we leave here?" LaRue asked. "Roger wants to take us out for a late dinner."

"All of us?" Macy inquired. She sat down and began taking the pins out of her hair.

"That's what he said. Y'all wanna go?"

Patterson nodded. "Yeah. I'm starving. That little food they had heh didn't do nothin' for me."

Macy glanced at them from over her shoulder. "Frederick's here so I'm going to probably spend some time with him."

"Okay. Well, let me hurry up and get dressed. Patterson, we'll have dinner with Roger."

"Maybe I should go home. I doan wanna be a third wheel."

"You won't be," LaRue assured her. "We're just friends."

Macy brushed her hair and touched up her make-up. She got up and removed her robe to change into the navy blue and white pant-suit she wore to the hotel.

She rushed out of the dressing room, fully expecting to find Frederick waiting for her. Macy glanced around. He was nowhere to be found.

"Where . . ." Macy reached into her Kate Spade handbag and pulled out her cell phone. She scrolled to Frederick's name in the directory and selected it. Even though she'd told him to lose her number, he still called every once in a while. They'd made up long enough for her to invite him to the show.

He answered on the second ring.

"Great show tonight."

"Where are you?" Macy didn't hide the anger in her voice.

There was a slight pause before he answered. "I had to meet a friend."

"You couldn't tell me that you were leaving? I thought we were friends, Frederick."

"Sweetheart, I'll make it up to you. I'm sorry."

"I hate you," she snarled into the phone.

"I said—"

Macy clicked off her phone. Cussing under her breath, she stalked off.

Chapter 20

LaRue

The second day of August marked the first day of work for the staff at the Frederick Douglass Charter School. LaRue was happy to finally be back in the workforce. She'd enjoyed her time off, but was ready to get back to having a full-time job.

She spent the rest of her Sunday afternoon going through her closet and planning her wardrobe for tomorrow and the rest of the week. She would be meeting her students and wanted to make a good first impression.

When she was done, LaRue sat down on the edge of her bed and opened her Day-Timer. She was jotting notes when Patterson knocked on her slightly ajar door.

"Come on in."

"Macy and I were thinking about taking a stroll around Central Park. Want to join us?"

"I'm gonna pass this time. I want to make sure I have everything ready for work."

"You're really excited about working at the charter school, aren't you?"

"I am," LaRue confessed. "I taught school for a little while after I graduated from college. It was on the elementary level, though. I think I'm going to like working with ninth-grade students much better."

That night she went to bed early so that she would be fully rested.

The next morning, LaRue took a taxi to West Forty-third Street.

Part of her duties as a counselor included conducting group sessions on career planning and development, crisis intervention, and referrals.

LaRue was excited about this new direction in her career. She was able to find another use for her master's degree in counseling. She played around with the idea of eventually pursuing her doctorate.

Deep down, her heart still yearned for modeling. LaRue considered trying out for some of the local fashion shows.

A beautiful bouquet of flowers awaited LaRue in her office. They were from Macy and Patterson. She smiled as she read the note.

"You're very popular," a woman said as she walked into the office carrying another floral arrangement. "These just arrived."

LaRue relieved her of the flowers. "Wow. I'm feeling pretty special right now." She sniffed and inhaled the scent of one of the carnations. "They smell so good."

She was extremely excited about her new job and looked forward to meeting the students. LaRue hoped to do some good during her time at the school.

Patterson

She stared at the piece of paper in her hand. Miller Baisden's handwriting jumped out at her. She'd had his number since June, but had done nothing with it, even though Miller stayed on her mind from the moment she met him. She still hadn't heard from him either. *Maybe he's forgotten all about me, or he could've lost the number.*

Each time she'd picked up the phone to call him, Patterson chickened out.

Her mother had always advised her to let men make the first move. She constantly cautioned against being the aggressor. "But he asked me to give him a call. It's not like I went after him or asked for the phone number. He came over to me . . ."

Patterson decided to take a chance. She picked up the telephone and dialed.

Just as Patterson was about to hang up, Miller answered. "Hello."

"Hey, this is Patterson. I met you—"

"I remember you. I was beginning to think I'd never hear from you. I would've called you, but I lost your phone number. I kept hoping I would hear from you."

"I'm sorry. I'm . . . I'm not used to making the first move like this."

"You have a strong Southern accent. Where are you from?"

"A small town in Georgia. You probably never even heard of it. I know I sound real country."

He laughed. "I like the way you talk. It's cute."

Patterson broke into a wide grin. "I like your accent, too."

Her door had been left slightly ajar, and twice LaRue stuck her head inside. When she saw Patterson on the phone, she left.

They talked for almost two hours. Patterson emerged from her room after the call and found LaRue sitting in the den watching television.

"I figured you were gonna be on that phone for the rest of the night. I know your ear is sore."

Joining her on the sofa, Patterson giggled. "I finally called Miller."

"I thought you were gonna let him make the first move."

"He lost my phone number. I'm glad I called him, LaRue. He's so funny. I really liked talking to him."

"Really? I never would've guessed."

More giggles erupted from Patterson. "Miller seems like a nice person. I think we're going to have fun getting to know each other."

"So he asked you out, then?"

Nodding, Patterson answered, "We're going out on Friday night. Can you believe it? I actually have a real date."

"Good for you. I guess going to the movies is out."

"Oh, dear," Patterson mumbled. "LaRue, I'm so sorry. I forgot all about our plans."

"Gurl, don't worry about it. You go out and have fun with Miller. We can always go to the movies."

A look of tired sadness passed over LaRue's face. "Are you sure you don't mind? I know you really wanted to see this movie. Maybe Macy will go with you."

"It's fine. If I feel like going on Friday, I will. I'm not afraid to go out by myself."

Although LaRue kept saying she was okay with the change in plans,

Patterson didn't believe her. "I feel so bad. Maybe I should call Miller back and reschedule. We can go out on Saturday."

"Don't change your plans for me," LaRue stated. "If I don't go on Friday and you still want to join me, we can go on Saturday."

"It's a date. Let's just plan to see the movie on Saturday, LaRue."

"All right by me."

Patterson embraced her. "Thanks so much for being so understanding." She continued to observe LaRue. Her roommate seemed okay, but Patterson couldn't shake the feeling that something was wrong.

LaRue

LaRue wished fervently that she could talk Patterson into staying home. It wasn't that she didn't want to see her happy, she just didn't think Miller could be trusted. She was pretty sure the man was up to no good where Patterson was concerned.

From the moment Miller laid eyes on Patterson, LaRue recognized the look of pure lust.

A stab of guilt lay buried in her chest that she hadn't been more vocal, but then again, LaRue had no proof of what she was accusing Miller of. She knew absolutely nothing about the man, and she didn't want to upset Patterson unnecessarily.

All I can do is pray, she decided.

LaRue closed her eyes. "Dear Lord, I know it's been a while since I've come to you, but this is not for me. You let me down when it came to Tom, but I'm giving you another chance. I ask that you please wrap your arms of protection around your child Patterson. She is so sweet and so innocent. Please open her eyes so that she will see this Miller Baisden for what he really is. I pray this in your name. Amen."

When she was done, LaRue felt somewhat better. She picked up the photo album covered in satin and ribbon that laid on top of the nightstand. Her eyes teared up even before she opened it. Glued on the pages were memories that had once been happy—the happiest of her life—but were now so painful. Her heart broke when Tom died, and she feared it could never be repaired. That constant ache would never end—she was sure of it.

LaRue ran her fingers across one of her wedding photos. "I miss you so much, sweetheart."

Her father called her an hour later, surprising her.

"You were on my mind, LaRue. God dropped in my spirit that I should call you."

"I don't know why," she murmured.

"It's not good to hang on to all this anger."

"I want to," she interjected quickly. "Dad, I just can't get over Tom's or Janine's death. I just can't dismiss it. Sorry."

"No one is asking you to do that. LaRue, why don't you move back home for a while. I know you're not working . . ."

"I have a job, Dad. And I was in a fashion show not too long ago. It was fun." LaRue dared not tell him that the only thing she modeled was body art.

"Is that what you're calling your job? This modeling?"

"Not yet," LaRue responded. "I don't know why you're so against modeling. It's something I really want to do, and I'm not gonna give up on it. I was ready to—until you called. You just made me realize just how badly I want it."

"God has a purpose for your life and it's not modeling."

"You don't know that," LaRue argued.

There was dead silence on the other end.

"You still there?"

"I'll let you speak to your mother, LaRue. Maybe she can talk some sense into you."

"I'm not changing my mind, Dad. If I can find somebody to take me on, I'm going to be a model."

The next morning, LaRue enrolled in a modeling class sponsored by a local agency.

Chapter 21

Macy

"You're not going to wear that dress on your date, are you?" Macy couldn't believe her eyes.

Patterson looked like she'd been thrown into a strawberry patch. She'd never seen such an ugly dress; sleeveless, the knee-length garment was covered with a strawberry pattern against a green background. "Where in the world did you find that?"

Patterson glanced down. "What's wrong with it?"

"There's nothing wrong with what you're wearing," LaRue quickly assured her. "Leave her alone, Macy. Patterson looks fine."

"Yeah . . . for going to church, maybe. This is a date. Not Sunday school."

Patterson turned to LaRue to unzip her dress. "Could you unzip me please? I'm changing."

Macy headed to her bedroom, saying, "I have something hanging in my closet that will be perfect for you. We're about the same size, so it should fit you."

On a mission, Macy strode out of the room, leaving both Patterson and LaRue stunned by the sudden show of generosity.

"Wow. I can't believe I heard her right. Macy's actually thinking of someone else. Humph."

Patterson gave LaRue a slight nudge in the arm. "Be nice . . ."

Macy bounced back into the bedroom carrying a slinky black dress draped across her arm. "This is going to look so good on you. . . ."

Taking the dress, Patterson held it against her body. She stared at her reflection in the full-length mirror. "Oh, Macy, this is gorgeous." She turned around. "You sure you don't mind my borrowing it for tonight?"

"You can have it. I made it, but it doesn't look that great on me. My boobs are much bigger than yours, and the dress looks too tight across the top."

"I'd be more than happy to pay you for it."

Macy shook her head. "You don't have to do that. It's yours, Patterson. Wear it and have a wonderful time tonight."

Patterson squealed and wrapped her arms around Macy. "Thank you. Thank you."

Wearing a tight smile, Macy backed out of the embrace. She wasn't used to all the hugging Patterson and LaRue liked to do.

Macy was a little envious of Patterson going out on a date—even LaRue was seeing someone. *Why can't I find someone? I'm beautiful— heck, I look better than the both of them. Why does my life suck so badly? All I want is a career, a man, and lots of money. I just want the lifestyle I've been accustomed to all my life.*

She heard Patterson and LaRue laughing. Macy screwed up her face in a frown and pouted.

Patterson

"You look beautiful," Miller murmured when Patterson opened the front door.

"Thank you." She stepped aside to let him enter the apartment.

His large hand took her face and held it gently. "I hope I didn't keep you waiting too long. I got caught in some traffic on the way here."

Patterson broke into a short laugh. "I can imagine. There's always traffic in this city."

"I like your laughter. You are so cute."

Carried away by Miller's gaze, Patterson failed to notice when Macy and LaRue walked into the living room.

Miller gave her a soft tap on the arm. "We have visitors."

Patterson glanced over her shoulder. "Oh, these are my room-mates." She took Miller by the hand and led him over to where they were standing.

Patterson introduced Miller to Macy. "You already met LaRue."

He nodded and put on his best smile. "You were with Patterson at the restaurant."

"*I was.*"

Patterson was a little taken aback by the cool tone of LaRue's voice. "Good seeing you again."

"You, too."

Again her response carried a chill.

Miller took Patterson by the hand. "We'd better get going if we want to keep our reservations."

"Have a good time tonight," Macy said.

"We will," Miller responded. His eyes traveled to LaRue. "Good seeing you again. Don't worry. I'm gonna take real good care of your girl here."

Patterson could tell just by looking at LaRue that she didn't like him. She made a mental note to talk to her when she returned home after their date. She couldn't understand why LaRue was acting that way.

LaRue

When they were alone, Macy turned around to face LaRue, with her hands folded across her chest. "You were sort of rude. What's your problem with Miller?"

She saw no reason to lie to Macy. "He's up to no good."

"LaRue, how can you say that? You don't know anything about the man. You've only seen him one time."

"I feel it in my spirit, Macy."

"Well, that certainly says a lot, considering you and God are not on speaking terms."

"I'm serious. Macy, I trust my instincts. They've never led me astray. There's something that just doesn't ring true with Miller."

Macy sighed. "Well, I like him. I think he and Patterson will make a nice couple."

"He's nice looking—I don't deny that—but Macy, being handsome doesn't exactly make you a nice guy. I believe that Patterson is going to get hurt if she continues seeing Miller. You don't want that, do you?"

"Of course not. I do think that we have to let her make her own mistakes. LaRue, Patterson is a grown woman. Don't forget that."

"We're supposed to be her friends. Friends look out for one another, don't you agree?"

"Yes, I do. But LaRue, we can't just interfere in Patterson's life. We can't disrespect her like that."

"Wouldn't you want to know if someone was trying to hurt you?"

"If you had some proof that Miller was out to hurt Patterson, I would agree."

"Why don't we just agree to disagree on this subject?" LaRue suggested. "I'm not gonna get up in her business, but I'm not gonna pretend he's God's gift to Patterson either. I'm sorry, but I won't do it."

Patterson

Miller dropped her off safely at home, pausing long enough to leave a kiss on her lips. "I hope you'll let me take you to this new play opening tomorrow night."

"What time should I be ready?" she whispered against his lips.

"I'll pick you up at seven."

There was no light from under LaRue's door, so Patterson assumed she'd already gone to bed. She was a little bit disappointed, as she wanted to share how her night went.

She set on her dresser the bouquet of roses that Miller had waiting for her at the restaurant.

Half an hour later, Patterson lay in the drowsy warmth of her bed, reliving her time with Miller.

The flowers had been a nice touch, but when a quartet came over to serenade her, that had been her undoing. Patterson's eyes grew wet at the memory.

Miller couldn't seem to keep his eyes off her, which pleased her. Patterson had never felt so much affection coming from anyone. She and Vincent had grown up together, so maybe that's why their entire relationship paled in comparison to this one date.

She was so lost in her own reveries that the soft rap on her bedroom door startled her.

LaRue stuck her head inside. "It's just me. Didn't mean to scare you, but I just wanted to check to see if you'd made it home okay."

Patterson sat up in bed.

"Don't get up."

"I had a nice time tonight. Miller was a perfect gentleman."

Smiling, LaRue stated, "I'm glad. We'll talk in the morning. Good night."

"Wait, doan leave, LaRue. I need to ask you sumptin'."

"What is it?"

"Why doan you like Miller?"

LaRue walked over and sat down on the edge of Patterson's bed. "It's something about him that doesn't sit right with me. I can't really explain it."

"He was real nice to me tonight."

"It was your first date, Patterson. Look, I'm not telling you not to see this guy—I know how much you really like him. I just want you to be careful. Okay?"

Patterson smiled. "I will."

LaRue stood up. "I'll see you in the morning."

"Good night." Patterson plumped up her pillows and lay down.

Miller was her last waking thought before she drifted into sleep.

The next day, she went to work in a cheerful mood.

Five minutes after twelve, Jason walked over to the cosmetics counter where Patterson was working. "Ready for lunch?"

She nodded. "I'm starved."

They went to their favorite spot, a little café across the street from the store. Patterson ordered a grilled chicken Caesar salad while Jason had a turkey sandwich.

"So have you found a church home yet?" he asked.

Patterson shook her head no. "I've visited a couple of churches, but I doan think I've found *the* church yet."

"I'd love to have you visit mine. Bring your roommates with you."

"I'd like that." Patterson gave him a smile. "Thank you for the invitation, Jason. We'd love to come."

She opened her purse and pulled out a piece of paper. "Would you write down the information for me?"

Jason did as she asked. "Think you'll be coming Sunday? Reason I ask is because I want to make sure I'm not singing in the choir or something."

"I have your number, so I'll give you a call."

He drank some of his soda, then picked up a French fry. "Have you met many people since coming to the Big Apple?"

"Not really," Patterson answered. I actually went on my first date last Friday night."

"So you've found a boyfriend already? I'm not surprised. You're a very beautiful woman."

She broke into a wide, open smile. "Jason, thanks for the ego booster. I appreciate it, but I have to tell you the truth. I doan have a boyfriend. I did meet someone that I like a lot. Maybe in time he will be my boyfriend, but not right now. It's still too soon."

He nodded and dropped his gaze.

To Patterson, he looked troubled. "You all right, Jason?"

"I'm fine." Jason turned his attention to his sandwich.

"When's your birthday?" Patterson questioned.

"May tenth."

"No way," she exclaimed. "Jason, that's my birthday."

He pushed his glasses back into place. "You serious?"

"Yeah. We share the same birthday. Isn't that incredible? What time were you born?"

Jason laughed.

"Really. What time?"

He pushed his glasses up the bridge of his nose. "Let's see . . . I think my mom said I was born at one twenty-five in the afternoon."

"You're older than me, but only by five minutes."

"You're not serious?"

Grinning, Patterson nodded. "I am. Jason, I'll bring my birth certificate to work with me, if you want to see it."

"Well, that makes me your elder. You know I have to look out for you now."

"What if it'd turned out that I was the one older?"

"I'd hate to have to listen to you." Jason raised his eyes heavenward. "There definitely is a God . . ."

"Very funny," Patterson uttered. "You are so funny."

Jason checked his watch. "We'd better head back."

Patterson stayed busy until it was time for her to clock out. She stopped over in the formal dress department before leaving the store. She needed something to wear for her date with Miller.

Chapter 22

LaRue

LaRue closed her novel. The hour was getting late and Patterson was still not home. She had been out with Miller for the last three nights. *It's a good thing Patterson is working 1 P.M. to close tomorrow at the store. She's not gonna be able to keep this up—going out on the town every single night.*

She had a date with Roger, but had come home two hours earlier. She had to get up early to be at the school for a meeting.

Although Patterson constantly sang Miller's praises, LaRue continued to feel unrest in her spirit where he was concerned.

"Please be safe, Patterson," she whispered. "I don't like that Miller Baisden. There's something about him I just don't trust."

Just then she heard the front door opening. LaRue climbed out of bed and rushed to her door. She opened it just as Patterson came walking by.

Patterson put a hand to her mouth and whispered, "I'm sorry. I didn't mean to wake you. I was trying to be quiet as a mouse."

"You didn't wake me," LaRue assured her. "I was getting worried about you and couldn't sleep. You know we roomies have to look out for each other." She stepped aside to let Patterson into her room. "You have a good time tonight?"

Grinning, Patterson nodded. "As usual, Miller was a perfect gentleman. We had dinner and then he just took me around New York. He even took me on a carriage ride around Central Park and gave me these."

Patterson held up a small bouquet mixed with red roses and baby's breath. "It was very romantic."

LaRue held her tongue as she turned her lips upward into a smile. "I'm glad you're home safe, so I'll see you in the morning."

"Thanks for caring, LaRue." Patterson gave her a hug. "You get some sleep, 'cause you got to get up early." She opened the door and left the room quietly.

"Lord, please let Patterson see the true Miller Baisden before it's too late," LaRue whispered sleepily.

Her eyes were closed before she hit the pillow.

Patterson

Miller's kiss still sang through her veins.

Patterson couldn't deny that even she was shocked at her own eager response to the touch of his lips on hers. She'd been kissed before, but never experienced the spirals of ecstasy that ran through her body now—not even with Vincent.

Miller's slow, drugging kisses made Patterson feel like a giddy high school girl. Humming a soft melody, she pulled the covers back on her bed.

She was blissfully happy.

Although she'd only know Miller for a short time, she was experiencing emotions like none she'd ever felt before. Patterson was too smart to believe she was falling in love.

It was much too soon.

But I do like him, though. I like him a lot.

Miller was everything she liked in a man. He was nice looking, wore clothes that complemented his body, had a wonderful sense of humor, and always had a smile. His bubbly personality matched her own.

"Lord, please let Miller be everything that I believe him to be," Patterson prayed. "I love LaRue to death, but I doan wont her to be right about this. Please doan let her be right."

LaRue

LaRue could've slept for another couple of hours. She was bone tired after staying up until two-thirty in the morning waiting for Patterson to come home.

Sluggishly, she pushed herself out of bed and padded barefoot to the hall bathroom that she shared with Patterson. LaRue had to be at work by eight A.M. This gave her ample time to get ready without rushing.

In the shower, LaRue scrubbed her body to an awakened state. She felt revived afterwards, enough to read her morning devotion and prepare for work.

An hour later, LaRue left for the subway.

Once she arrived at the school and after getting settled in her office, she began her day. She truly enjoyed working with the students.

By noon, LaRue felt like she could barely keep her eyes open. She pushed away from her desk and got up. She stretched, hoping to wake up.

"Lord, help me make it through this day. I'm so tired."

LaRue yawned.

"Late night?" the secretary asked.

"In a way," LaRue responded. "Is Reuben Greenwood here?"

The woman nodded and handed her a file. "Want me to send him in?"

"Could you give me a minute? I want to look over his reports from the last school."

LaRue decided that her days of waiting up for Patterson were over. Like Macy said, she was a grown woman.

She could handle herself. Patterson was smart. Eventually, she'd see Miller for the snake he truly was.

When she arrived home hours later, LaRue found a message on her voice mail from Roger. She called him back.

"It's me."

"I know you've been taking modeling classes, and so I mentioned you to a friend of mine. He's in need of some models for an upcoming fashion show. It's a fund-raiser."

LaRue was touched by Roger's thoughtfulness. "Really?"

"I think you'd be perfect for the show. If you're interested, I'd like to set up a meeting between the two of you. We could have dinner."

"When did you have in mind?"

"Is tonight too early?" Roger asked.

"No, of course not," she responded.

LaRue navigated over to her closet, scanning to find something to wear for her dinner meeting. A wave of excitement flowed through her.

She talked with Roger for a few minutes more, then hung up to get ready for her evening.

LaRue couldn't believe it. She was actually getting a chance to model. She couldn't wait to tell Macy and Patterson. She made a mental note to see if there was room to include them. It would really be nice if the three of them could be in the show together.

Macy

Macy couldn't wait to hear how Patterson's latest date with Miller went. She pounded questions at her as soon she strolled through the door shortly after six-thirty P.M. "So how did it go? You and Miller have a good time last night? You two are sure seeing a lot of each other."

Patterson sat her purse down on the sofa table. "Yeah. We had a great time. He took me on a ride around Central Park and bought me some flowers. He's really a great guy."

"He's nice looking," Macy complimented. "You found yourself a real catch, Patterson. What does he do for a living?"

"He's a real estate attorney. He works for Kauffman, Myers, Davis, and Simms."

"Really? That's impressive." Macy nodded her approval. "If things work out, you're going to be financially stable. That's good."

Patterson shook her head. "Oh, I'm not even thinking that far ahead. I just met Miller. We still have to see if we're even interested in pursuing a relationship."

"You two look so good together. I have a feeling that your relationship is going to move pretty quickly between you two. I'm usually never wrong about things like this, Patterson."

"I'ma just take it one day at a time. Ain't gon' be no hanky panky going on. I'm saving myself for my husband."

Macy was amazed by her determination to remain celibate. "Patterson, how do you do it?"

"Do what?"

"Miller is fine. . . . I'm sure he's going to want to have sex. You are going to get those feelings, too. How are you going to be strong enough to turn him down?"

"It's never been easy, Macy. I'm not immune by no means. I just keep in mind what the Bible says. In Genesis, the scriptures say that Adam *knew* Eve. He had sex with her. Well, sexual intimacy gives you full knowledge about the person you are sleeping with. My pastor back home says all the time that what we do intimately with our bodies affects the spiritual states of our souls."

Macy broke into a short laugh. "Goodness. You make it sound as if we're infected with something."

"It is a contamination in a sense. When you have sex outside of marriage, it separates you from the Lord."

"It's not easy to stop having sex. At least it isn't for me."

"It's not easy to be celibate either," Patterson confessed. "Take it from me. I have to be so careful what I watch, read, and listen to. I pray every night for God to keep and preserve me so that I won't fall."

"I guess it's working."

Patterson held up a hand towards heaven. "Praise God. I certainly can't take credit for it. Being single, saved, and in a city like New York—it's a daily struggle. Back home on the farm, it was a little bit easier for me." She gave a small laugh. "There weren't too many men around that weren't related to me."

"I have a feeling Miller is going to be a big challenge for you. He's gorgeous."

Smiling, Patterson said, "I'll just keep praying for God to keep me."

The telephone in Patterson's room rang.

"That's probably Miller," she said as she raced off.

"That man is going to be your undoing if you're not careful," Macy predicted. "Maybe LaRue is right to be worrying about you."

"Did I just hear my name?" LaRue asked.

Macy did a double-take. "Where are you going? Another date with Roger?"

"I'm having dinner with Roger and a friend of his. I think his name is Victor something . . . I can't remember," LaRue announced. "And guess what? This friend is looking for models."

"Really, LaRue?" Patterson asked as she strode back into the room.

LaRue nodded. "He's putting together a fashion show for charity and needs models."

Macy waved her hand in dismissal. "Oh no, I'm not interested. I've done enough of *those* types of events to last me a lifetime. I only did the body art because I'd always wanted to try it. Besides, with my luck, my parents would be there."

"You don't know anything about this event, Macy. How can you just dismiss it like that? It sounds like a pretty big event from what Roger told me."

"Well, I'm interested," Patterson stated.

"You'd be interested in modeling at a dog show," Macy uttered. "Girls, you really need to be a little more selective. You—"

LaRue cut her off by saying, "*You need to shut up, Macy.* Don't be trying to rain on our parade. If you not interested—if it's so beneath you—then don't do it. But don't act like you're so much better than we are. From where I'm standing, you're still looking to be picked up by an agency just like me and Patterson."

Macy flung her hair about her shoulders. "Fine. Don't listen to me, then. Go out there and find out for yourselves."

"We intend to do just that," LaRue shot back.

Macy stalked out of the kitchen and to her bedroom, slamming the door. She rushed into her bathroom and closed the door. Putting her hand to her mouth, she burst into tears.

"Why do I have to suffer so?" she demanded. "Why can't I be picked up by some big modeling agency? My life sucks. . . ."

When her tears stopped, Macy pulled herself together and washed her face.

She stood in front of the mirror for the next half hour, scrutinizing her appearance. "There's nothing wrong with me," she whispered. "I have beautiful skin, a nice figure, and I photograph well, so what's the problem? Why haven't I been picked up already?"

She sighed softly. "Why doesn't anything good ever happen to me?"

Chapter 23

LaRue

She sat at her desk, going over notes taken from her last appointment. LaRue had been meeting with students all week to help them develop a personalized academic plan.

She had an hour free before seeing her next student, so LaRue decided to grab a bite to eat. She pushed away from her desk and got up.

After posting the "Out for Lunch" sign on her door, LaRue left the building. She grabbed a sandwich and ran some errands. Her mother was flying in tonight for the fashion show, and LaRue was looking forward to seeing her.

She hoped that after seeing her on the runway, her mother would have a different impression altogether of modeling. She'd also planned visits to museums and other tourist attractions, including a visit to Ellis Island to tour the Statue of Liberty.

When her lunch hour ended, LaRue returned to work, working diligently, pausing every now and then to check the time. Her mother's plane was arriving at five thirty-five. Patterson and Macy had both offered to go with her to LaGuardia Airport, but LaRue turned them down.

Patterson had insisted on cooking dinner for them and would not take no for an answer.

Three hours later, LaRue was in a taxi and on her way to the airport. She was meeting her mom in the baggage claim area.

Macy

Macy was reading a magazine in the living room when Patterson arrived home.

"Is LaRue's room ready?"

She nodded. "Yeah."

Patterson laid down her purse on the sofa table. "Have you decided if you're gon' come to the fashion show? LaRue and I wont you to come. You can sit with Mrs. Arnette."

"I guess I'll go and support you and LaRue. If my parents are there, I'm not talking to them."

"Macy, I know it's not my business, but doan you think you should make peace with them?"

"No, I don't. They are the ones who ruined things between us—not me, Patterson. Right now, I don't have any parents as far as I'm concerned."

"You're supposed to honor your parents."

"Whatever," Macy muttered.

Patterson changed the subject. "Did you get the flowers?"

Macy dropped her magazine. "No . . . I forgot." She jumped to her feet. "I'll be right back, Patterson. I need to run out for a minute." She cursed. "I can't believe I forgot the flowers."

Checking her watch, Patterson stated, "There's still time."

"I'll be right back." Macy ran out of the apartment and headed to the elevators.

Austin approached as she waited.

"Girlfriend, you look stunning as always," he greeted.

"What are you up to, Austin?"

"Looking for a good man. You know how it is. . . ."

Macy laughed.

"How are things between you and the two divas you have living with you?"

"Okay," she responded. "I think we're getting along well."

The elevator doors opened and they both got in.

Macy eyed her reflection as Austin lamented about his current lover. She nodded every now and then to give the illusion that she was listening to him. Truth be told, she could not care less.

Patterson

"Hurry up, Macy. LaRue and her mama will be here shortly."

"I'm almost done," Macy yelled from within LaRue's bedroom. She arranged the fresh flowers in a glass vase and sat it on the dresser. She picked up her shears and strode out to the kitchen where Patterson was cooking.

"What did you make for dinner?"

"Salmon. You know LaRue don't eat red meat, so I figured her mama don't either."

"It smells wonderful." Macy peeked into the oven. "I love those yeast rolls. They are so good. I can only have one, though. Don't let me get anymore. My trainer is already frustrated with me, because I'm supposed to be on a no-carb diet."

"I can make you something else, Macy. If you'd like."

"No, don't go to any trouble. I'll be fine."

"Have you checked Emerald's site lately to see if they've posted call-backs?"

"I checked a few days ago, but our names weren't on the list." Patterson gave Macy a wry smile. "I guess it's just not meant for me to be a model."

"I saw in the newspaper that TM Models, Inc. is holding an open call. Do you want to go?"

"Are they a good agency?"

"Real good," Macy replied. "They're not as big as Emerald, but they can hold their own. Bette Crosby is one of their models and so is Elyse Martaan."

"Really? Bette is on this month's cover of *Glamour.* I think she is so pretty."

"I'm going to attend the open call. It's on Saturday."

"Tomorrow?"

Macy shook her head no. "Next weekend."

They heard the locks click on the front door. LaRue and her mother entered the apartment.

Patterson and Macy walked out of the kitchen.

LaRue made the introductions. "Mama, these are my roommates. This is Macy and this is Patterson."

"Hello, Mrs. Arnette," Macy greeted. "Welcome to our home."

"Thank you for letting me visit my baby. LaRue told me that this is your apartment. I really appreciate how you've opened your home to two strangers."

"They're great roommates. We have fun together."

Patterson embraced Ruby Arnette. "I've heard so much about you. I feel like I know you already."

Grinning, the woman responded, "I feel the same way." Ruby gave Macy a big hug. "Lord, you such a pretty girl. Just beautiful." She reached over and took Patterson by the hand. "You a real beauty, too. All three of you. I know that doorman downstairs always got a smile when he see the three of you."

Patterson and Macy giggled.

"Something sure smells delicious in the kitchen." Ruby moved through the house as if she owned the place.

Peeking into the oven, she turned around and nodded approvingly. "LaRue must have told you how much I love salmon. You two are such a dear."

"Now I have to let you ladies know. I'm Mom and you all don't have to worry about spoiling me. I don't need no special attention. For this week, anyway, just treat me like the fourth roommate. Is that okay with you all?"

LaRue was amused over the way her mother had effectively and smoothly walked into the apartment and taken over without offending Patterson and Macy. That was Ruby Arnette's way. It's one of the qualities she loved about her mother.

Macy

She hung up the phone smiling.

Frederick was in town for a few days on business. He was pleading for some of her time. Macy had been tempted to see him, because it had been a while since she'd been intimate with a man. Right now she was feeling very lonely and vulnerable.

Alone in her room, Macy continued to replay the conversation she'd had with Patterson on the subject of sex. Since the little country mouse had moved in, there were moments when she felt so guilty just thinking about having sex.

"Why did Patterson and LaRue have to come into my life? I was doing just fine . . . without them. . . ." She frowned. "Patterson with her goody-two-shoes self . . ."

In that instance, Macy raised her eyes heavenward. "Did you do this, God? Did you send them into my life?"

Tears filled her eyes and rolled down her cheek. Macy wasn't even sure why she was crying. She just felt like doing so. "What is going on with me?"

Macy washed her face and changed into a pair of sweats.

She brushed past Patterson in the hallway. "I'm going to the fitness center. I'll be back in an hour."

"Have a good workout."

She stayed on the treadmill until she found herself dizzy and nauseated. *I shouldn't have worked out so soon after dinner. That's why I feel like this.*

LaRue was practically overflowing with happiness to have her mother visiting. Ruby Arnette was nothing like Macy originally envisioned. She was outspoken, but warm and loving—very nurturing. Although she would never tell her, LaRue was a lot like her mother.

Macy considered her own mother selfish, cool, and judgmental. She was often more critical than complimentary, and she looked down on those less fortunate. *It didn't take her long to give up on her own daughter,* Macy thought bitterly. *I've been banished from my own life.*

Chapter 24

LaRue

Saturday morning, LaRue and her mother were up early. She helped Ruby make homemade buttermilk pancakes, fresh fruit, and turkey sausages.

This time it was Patterson who was sleeping in after a late night out with Miller. When she finally emerged from her bedroom, it was ten-thirty in the morning.

Patterson came into the kitchen, greeting Ruby and LaRue. "I can't believe I slept so late."

"That's what happens when you stay out late like that," LaRue said.

Patterson grinned sheepishly. "I was out with Miller."

"I know. You and Mr. Baisden have been seeing a lot of each other." LaRue handed her a plate of food.

Patterson joined Ruby at the breakfast table. "We're going out again tonight after the fashion show. He's taking me to some reception for this actor. I think his name is William Michaels."

"You running with the big dawgs, I see." Ruby downed the last of her orange juice. "Humph. That William Michaels is right up there with Denzel Washington. He's a good little actor. It's a shame they have to do all that cussing."

Patterson poured buttered-pecan syrup over her pancakes. "I've seen him in a couple of movies. This does seem to be his year."

"Good morning," Macy greeted as she joined them in the kitchen.

"Morning, baby," Ruby responded. She stared at Macy. "You must've had contacts in last night. Your eyes looked lighter than that yesterday."

"Yes, I wear contacts," Macy confirmed.

"You got some pretty eyes without them. If you don't need contacts, leave them out. I'd hate to see you mess up your eyes in the name of vanity. I've seen it happen."

"Yes, ma'am." Macy fixed a plate of assorted fruit and carried it over to the table where the others were sitting. "I try to be careful with the contacts."

"Baby, you're beautiful," Ruby complimented. "Be happy with what God gave you. I tell that to LaRue all the time. She used to be ashamed of her height."

"That's enough, Mom," LaRue quickly interjected. "We don't need to do any more sharing."

Everyone laughed.

"Patterson, you should put some cucumbers over your eyes," Ruby suggested. "It'll shrink the bags under them. If you gonna be socializing with people like that William Michaels . . . you want to look your best."

Macy practically choked on her cranberry juice. "Wha—who are you going out with?"

"Miller's taking me to a reception for that actor William Michaels."

"He's in town?"

Puzzled, Patterson asked, "Who?"

"William," Macy stated. "Is he in town?"

"You know him?" Ruby inquired.

Macy nodded. "He's my ex-boyfriend. We broke up right before I met LaRue and Patterson."

No one spoke for a moment.

Tossing her hair across her shoulders, Macy pasted a smile on her face. "It's okay. I'm over him. William doesn't mean a thing to me."

She gulped the rest of her juice down and finished her food in silence.

After cleaning up the kitchen, LaRue and Ruby showered and dressed for their day of sightseeing before the fashion show.

LaRue had arranged to take her mother on a double-decker bus tour that would take them all over the city and included a ferry ticket to the Statue of Liberty and Ellis Island. They had to be home by four o'clock so that LaRue could get ready for the evening.

She'd invited both Macy and Patterson to join them, but her roommates declined, citing that LaRue should have this time with her mother alone.

Patterson

Patterson enjoyed watching the way LaRue and her mother interacted with each other. It was a tender reminder of what she was missing with her own mom. She made a mental note to call her mother later.

"I'm taking Mom to see the Statue of Liberty," LaRue announced. "You sure you don't want to come with us? You keep saying you want to go back to get more pictures. We can grab something to eat while we're out. After lunch you can come back home if you want."

"I don't wont to intrude on y'all's time. I'm kind of tired anyway. I really need to get some rest."

"You're sure? You know we'd love to have you join us."

"Y'all go and have fun. I think I'm just gonna lay down for a bit and take a nap."

After they left, Patterson found herself alone in the apartment. She lay down across her bed to watch television, but soon fell asleep.

The ringing of the telephone woke her from her nap.

Patterson answered her phone on the second ring. "Hello?"

"Hi, beautiful. You stayed on my mind all day today. I can't wait to see you strutting your stuff on that runway."

Grinning, Patterson greeted, "Hey, Miller."

"Did you miss me?"

She laughed. "I thought about you once or twice today."

"Are you excited about tonight? Not everybody gets to be on stage like a superstar and then party with celebrities afterward."

"I'm looking forward to it. But I have to get home early tonight, Miller. I've been staying out way too late. It's catching up with me."

"You're not working tomorrow. You can sleep all day if you want, Patterson."

"I'm going to church tomorrow, and I don't want to be so tired I can't concentrate on the sermon."

"You'll probably see some ministers at the party tonight."

Patterson wasn't sure what Miller was trying to hint at. "It's not gon' be a problem with me leaving the party early, is it?"

"No, it's not gon' be a problem," he said, mimicking her.

She wasn't amused. "Please doan do that, Miller. Don't mock the way I talk."

"Lighten up, sweetheart."

"I'm sorry. I'm tired and more than a little cranky. I need to get off this phone, Miller. I need a nap. I want to look my best for the fashion show."

"Okay, sweetheart. I'll see you later."

Patterson hung up and fell back against the pillows.

She was soon fast asleep.

LaRue

After the fashion show, LaRue sought out her mother. The stern expression on Ruby's face told her that her mother was not pleased with what she'd seen. Her shoulders dropped and she released a soft sigh in resignation.

"What didn't you like about it, Mom?"

"You were practically naked, LaRue."

"I had on a body stocking. I wasn't naked."

"I thought you were gonna be modeling real clothes—not this skimpy stuff."

LaRue tried to hide her anger. "It's just a show, Mom. Why do you have to be so negative?"

Ruby shook her head. "I don't understand, LaRue. This is not what God called you to do. You know that just as well as I do."

LaRue glanced over her shoulder, then back at her mother. "We'll talk about this later. Here comes Roger."

She painted on a smile and pretended all was well.

Before she left, LaRue was approached by Victor.

"I have another fashion show coming up in a month. I would love to have you participate. You're wonderful on the runway. In fact, I'd like to make you a permanent part of my troupe."

LaRue stole a peek at her mother. Ruby was clearly not pleased, but kept silent. She turned her attention back to Victor. "I would love to be a part of your show. Thanks."

Victor stopped a passing waiter and picked up two champagne flutes. He gave one to LaRue. "Here's to our future. . . ."

She tapped her glass with his. LaRue took a sip, then glanced over at her mother. She smiled and tilted her head in defiance.

Ruby shook her head in sadness.

LaRue turned away, unable to bear the look of disappointment on her mother's face.

Roger took them out for a late dinner.

Ruby was polite but, for the most part, she was silent.

"Why are you so quiet, Mom?" LaRue asked when Roger excused himself from the table to make a quick phone call.

"I just don't know what to say. I'm at a loss."

"This is my life."

Ruby gazed at her daughter. "Hon, I know that. Believe me, I do. I'm not trying to tell you what to do."

"Yes, you are, Mom. You and Dad don't approve of my moving to New York or that I want to model. Well, I live in the Big Apple now and I do want to model. I loved being out there on the runway. It was fun."

Ruby nodded. "You were always strong-willed. All we can do is sit back and wait. You belong to God and you will not escape Him—no matter how much you try to run. He will draw you near to Him."

LaRue didn't respond. She rubbed her arms to ward off the chill she suddenly felt in her body.

Chapter 25

Patterson

"I promise not to keep you up too late," Miller stated when they got into the car. "Okay? Or would you rather not go to the party?"

Patterson was exhausted and was hoping to get out of partying. "Would you mind terribly if we didn't go? I'm really tired and not in the mood to be around any more people." She hoped she hadn't offended Miller, but she really just wanted to go home and get comfortable.

"What would you like to do then?"

"Why don't we go back to the apartment, Miller? I can change into something more comfortable and we can watch a movie or something."

"Are your roommates out for the evening?"

"Macy planned to go out with some friends after the fashion show, and LaRue will be out with her mother. We'll have the place alone for a couple of hours at least."

"I see. I guess you have everything all planned out."

Patterson eyed him, noting the way he seemed to be leering at her. "I'm just talkin' 'bout us hangin' out, Miller. Nothin' more."

"No problem."

Patterson changed into a pair of shorts and a halter top as soon as she got home. She left her long hair flowing freely around her face.

She sank down on the sofa beside Miller.

He kissed her on the cheek and looked her over seductively. "You look so beautiful."

"You doan look too bad yourself. Thanks for being so understanding about my wonting to stay home tonight."

Miller's gaze dropped from her eyes to her shoulders to her breasts.

Feeling self-conscious, Patterson folded her arms across her chest. "I guess we need to pick out a movie."

"You don't have to do that. I brought up one of the ones that I keep in the car. We can watch it in your room."

"There's nobody home. We can watch it in here."

"You sure you don't want to watch television in your room?"

She shook her head. "No, this i-is fine. I doan have a television in my room. I plan on buying one, though."

The smoldering flame she saw in his eyes startled her. Patterson tried to throttle the dizzying current racing through her body.

"Lord, give me strength," she whispered.

Miller strode over to the entertainment unit to put in the video before joining her on the sofa.

Patterson tried to keep a respectable distance. However, Miller wanted her closer and pulled her into his embrace.

"You don't have to be afraid of me, baby."

"I'm not." Patterson found herself extremely conscious of Miller's virile appeal and felt powerless to resist. She was grateful that the movie was getting ready to start. *Lord knows I need the distraction.*

Her mouth dropped open in shock at the scene unfolding on television.

Patterson turned to Miller. "What type of movie is this?"

He kissed her on the lips. "What do you think?"

"Miller, th-this is p-porn," she sputtered. "I doan watch stuff like this."

Patterson put a hand to her face. "I can't believe you brought this over heh." She reached for the remote control and cut off the video.

Miller gave her an innocent look. "Baby, I didn't mean nothing by it. I just thought we'd get a kick out of watching something like this together. I have some friends who do it all the time, and so I thought we'd try it."

"I'm not mad at you, Miller. I just doan like movies like this." Pressing a hand to her heart, she said, "My goodness. You doan need to be watching stuff like this either."

"Have you ever seen one?"

"No," Patterson admitted.

"Then how can you put down something you haven't seen first-hand?"

Patterson shrugged. "I guess you have a point."

She cast a glance his way. "Do you watch these a lot, Miller?"

"I told you I didn't. I just thought we could share this together." He shook his head. "Don't go trippin', because it's no big deal."

Patterson felt bad for hurting his feelings. She sought to find a way to compromise without sounding so self-righteous. "Miller, I'ma give it a try. But we're turning it off if it gets to be too much. Agreed?"

He grinned. "Whatever you say, baby."

Miller reached over and turned off the light as Patterson started the video.

LaRue

Darkness greeted LaRue and Ruby as they entered the apartment. Out of the corner of her eye, she caught sight of two shadowy forms scuffling around in the living room.

Ruby turned on a nearby lamp. "Why is it so dark in here?"

Patterson, her hair mussed and her shirt untidy, looked as if she'd been caught with her hand in the cookie jar, while Miller looked as cocky as ever.

Trying to comb her hair with her fingers, Patterson gave them a weak greeting. "I didn't expect to see y'all home so early."

"We see," Ruby responded with a laugh. She strode over to where they were sitting and introduced herself. "And you are?" she asked Miller. "I saw you at the fashion show, but we didn't get a chance to be introduced."

"Miller Baisden. It's nice to meet you."

He didn't stay a good ten minutes after LaRue and her mother came home.

Embarrassed to the hilt, Patterson bade them good night and rushed off to her room.

"I don't care for Mr. Baisden," Ruby announced as she took a seat on the sofa.

LaRue joined her. "I don't either. I keep telling Patterson to be careful."

"If she don't, she gonna find herself with a belly full of baby and that man nowhere to be found. *Mark my words.*"

"I'm hoping that doesn't happen, Mom. Patterson is a sweet person. I don't want to see her life get messed up like that."

"They both grown so there's not much you can do."

"Let's see what's on television. . . ." LaRue murmured as she reached for the remote. "I'm not gonna spend the rest of my evening worrying about grown folk."

Ruby gasped. "Oh, dear Lord. . . ."

LaRue pressed the remote, trying to remove the writhing bodies off the forty-two-inch screen. "The batteries just died."

Patterson

Patterson sat on the edge of her bed, wanting desperately to forget what happened. "I didn't do anything," she whispered. "Miller and I were just kissing."

She couldn't fool even herself. If LaRue and Ruby had not walked in when they did, Patterson would've given in to Miller. She knew better than to watch something so erotic. . . .

Realization dawned on Patterson. The tape was still in the VCR.

Horrified that LaRue and Ruby might see it, she rushed out of her room.

It was too late.

"I'm so sorry. That's Miller's tape. Oh, I'm so embarrassed." Patterson pressed her hands to her face.

Ruby went over to embrace her. "Honey, it's okay. You don't have to be ashamed. You are a red-blooded woman. We've all been through what you're going through. You just have to stay strong and stay in the Word, Patterson." She gestured for LaRue. "Hon, come over here and let's pray for her right now."

They formed a circle and held hands as Ruby began to pray.

"Father God, please forgive your child Patterson for the sinful images in her mind. Lord, we commit her thoughts to you. We surrender the burden of holiness to you, and ask that you will strengthen her now to direct her thoughts in righteousness. Father, help Patterson to not dwell on any image or memory that will cause her to sin. Please wash her mind with the blood of Jesus Christ. Please remove every depiction of sin from her memory and strengthen her to continue walking in obedience and faithfulness to you. Please give her the strength and endurance to walk to victory, no matter how long it takes. We invite your Holy Spirit to fill her afresh now and restart the renewal process of her body, mind, and spirit in Jesus Christ. Thank you, Father, and may we glorify you in everything that we do from this point forward. In Jesus' name I pray. Amen."

Patterson was crying when Ruby finished her prayer. She embraced both LaRue and Ruby. "Thank you so much." Patterson accepted the napkin LaRue offered and blew her nose. "I feel so stupid. Things just kind of got out of hand."

A lone tear rolled down her cheek. "I just wanted to stay home tonight. That's all."

"I'll make you some tea. Why don't you go on and get ready for bed?"

"I didn't do anything, LaRue. We were just kissing." Patterson paused. "Why did you come home so early? I thought y'all would be out for at least another hour."

"It was dropped in my spirit to come back to the apartment," Ruby stated. "I told LaRue that we needed to get back here. God was looking out for you, the way I see it."

"Yes, He was," Patterson murmured softly. "I guess I definitely needed watching."

"Don't be too hard on yourself, Patterson. You're human."

Patterson gave Ruby a grateful smile.

When she went back to her bedroom, Patterson fell to her knees in prayer and repentance. She knew better, but still she hadn't wanted to disappoint Miller.

"I really like him, Lord. He makes me weak whenever I'm around him. Help me to be stronger. I doan wont to lose Miller. Please help him to understand and respect my wishes, Lord. . . . Help me. . . ."

Chapter 26

Patterson

The cosmetics department at Macy's was empty now, which gave Patterson time to consider what almost happened between her and Miller while she displayed new lipstick colors on the counter. Still too embarrassed to speak to Miller, Patterson decided to avoid his calls.

He'd called four or five times over the past couple of days and left messages on her voice mail. On one message he asked about the video he'd left over by mistake.

LaRue hadn't been convinced it had been a mistake. She believed that Miller left the tape on purpose in the hopes that Patterson would view it privately.

Patterson didn't quite know what to believe.

When she was not busy at the counter, Patterson played the conversation she needed to have with Miller over and over in her mind.

The phone rang.

"Chanel counter. This is Patterson speaking. How may I help you?"

"Hello, beautiful."

"Miller. How are you?" Patterson wasn't quite ready to talk to him, because she wasn't sure what she wanted to say. Out the corner of her eye, she spied a man staring at her.

"Patterson?" he prompted. "You there?"

"I'm here. Miller, can I call you when I get home? I'm kind of busy right now."

"I feel like you're avoiding me."

She gave a nervous laugh. "I'm not. I've just been real busy. I'll give you a call later, okay?"

"I'll be waiting for your call. Oh, I need to get my friend's video-tape back. He and his girl want it." Miller chuckled. "Guess they really are missing it."

"I've got to go. Bye." Patterson hung up before Miller could say another word. She couldn't deny that she was still a little upset with him for bringing over the video in the first place.

The man had been watching her for almost fifteen minutes.

Patterson was beginning to feel uneasy. Almost, as if he sensed her panic, he approached the counter.

"May I help you?"

He smiled. "Hi. My name is Philippe and I was wondering if you'd done any modeling."

The man pulled out a business card. "I'm with TM Models, Inc."

The tension Patterson initially felt went away. She gave him a big smile. "Your agency just had an open call. I wonted to go but I was scheduled to work."

"Are you a model?"

"I really wont to be one. I have a portfolio and I've done some modeling in local fashion shows back home. I'm from Three Oak, Georgia."

Philippe's smile grew bigger. "I've never heard of it."

"Most people haven't. It's 'bout twenty miles outside of Atlanta."

"I'd like to schedule a test shoot for you. When is your day off?"

"I'm off tomorrow."

Philippe made arrangements with Patterson before taking his leave.

"Thank you, Jesus," she murmured. Glancing down at her watch, Patterson wished she were going home soon, but she still had four hours to go.

Today was Jason's day off, so there was no one special around to share her news. She would just have to wait until she went home.

During a quiet moment at the counter, Patterson sent up a quick prayer of thanks.

Macy

The hair on Macy's neck stood up at the shrill sound of someone calling her name. She turned away from her mirror and rushed out of her bedroom. "What's wrong, Patterson? They can probably hear you next do—"

Macy ran smack into LaRue, who rushed out of her room, too, and asked, "What's wrong?"

"I don't know," Macy responded breathlessly.

"I'm so sorry . . . I . . ." Patterson stated as soon as they burst into the living room. She was grinning from ear to ear. "I didn't mean to scare y'all. I'm just so excited. I've got some wonderful news. You're not gon' believe it. You—"

"Slow down, Patterson," LaRue advised. "Now tell us what's going on."

"What's happened?" Macy questioned. "Did something happen to one of your parents?"

Patterson shook her head no. "Oh, no. It's nothing like that. I met Philippe Mannington at the store today. He's with TM Models, Inc. Mr. Mannington wonts me to come in tomorrow for a test shoot. Can you believe it?" She placed a hand to her chest. "Oh, thank the Lord."

Macy couldn't believe she'd heard right. "What did you say?" She'd just attended the open call the agency hosted. She hadn't heard a peep from them, but Patterson was approached by the great man himself at the Chanel counter.

"Congratulations, girl. I'm so happy for you." LaRue wrapped her arms around Patterson, giving her a big hug.

"I can't believe this," Macy snapped in anger. "Why do they hold open calls in the first place if they're going to pick up women right off the dang streets? This is so crazy."

"What's so crazy about it?" LaRue demanded. "*They wanted Patterson.* Several models have been discovered that way."

"Macy, they haven't finished the callbacks, I'm sure. You're going to hear from TM, too. I believe that."

"I don't need some hick from Tree Trunk, Georgia, to pacify me. I know how beautiful I am. I don't need your pity. Nobody needs to pity me."

Patterson cleared her throat noisily before saying, "I doan pity you, Macy, and I'm really getting tired of you snapping my head off. If you back a dog into a corner, he'll bite. You might just wont to take that as a warning, missy. Doan make me lose Jesus, 'cause you'll be real sorry. I'm tired of being yo' whipping horse."

Macy's mouth dropped open. She turned to LaRue, who merely shrugged.

"I don't know why people are always telling tall skinny girls that they should become models," Macy continued to complain. "It takes much more than that."

"I suppose you think you have what it takes?"

Macy's gaze met LaRue's. "Yeah, I do. My look is more commercial than yours or Patterson's. You look stunning, but you're way too old. Patterson doesn't have anything special about her either. She's just a country girl."

"Excuse me?" Patterson interjected. Her eyes flashing anger, she took a menacing step toward Macy with her hands balled into fists. "You might just wont to take that back."

Macy took a step backward. "I don't mean anything bad by it, Patterson. I'm just saying I look like more of a model than you do."

"Like I said, modeling is not all I'm about," LaRue stated flatly. "I'm enjoying my job."

"It's a good thing, too," Macy agreed. " 'Cause something like this could devastate you."

"Yeah, I can see what it's doing to you."

"I'm okay," Macy lied. Deep down, she was fuming. *How could Patterson be so dang lucky?* Obviously, this was just not the place she should be. They didn't know quality when confronted with it. "I've been to several agencies. Emerald Model Management and TM Models, Inc., is definitely not the only game in town."

"They are two of the biggest modeling agencies here in New York."

Macy didn't hide her irritation. "Yes, I know."

"Let's not fight," Patterson advised. "I really don't want this to come between us or our friendship. We've all become so close. I know we can get past this."

"F-Friendship?" Macy sputtered. "Girl, we're not friends—just roommates. Actually, you two are roommates and I'm the landlord." She regretted the words as soon as they came out of her mouth, but her wounded pride wouldn't let her retract them.

"All right, Macy . . ." LaRue warned. "You don't want to go there with us. We're here because you need us, don't you forget it."

"Whatever," she muttered.

Macy turned on her heels and stormed off to the sanctity of her bedroom. Inside, she grabbed her purse and keys, then left the apartment.

She needed some air. No, what she needed was to do some serious shopping to make herself feel better. Macy headed to Bloomingdale's.

Loaded down with the newest items in the Dolce & Gabbana collection, Macy made her way to the nearest cashier.

Her mood darkened when the woman turned to her, saying, "I'm sorry, but your card has been declined. Do you have another form of payment?"

Embarrassed, Macy pulled out another card. "Here, try this one."

"That one has been declined also."

Macy was about to pull another card out of her wallet but the expression on the cashier's face changed her mind. "Just forget it. I don't want them anymore." Even as she said the words, her eyes lingered on the cheetah-print dress lying on the counter. It was marked down from four hundred ninety-five dollars to one hundred sixty-nine dollars. She really wanted that dress.

Holding her head high, Macy walked as fast as she could out of the store. She'd never felt so humiliated.

She left the store and headed straight to her favorite bar.

Two hours later, Macy poured out of a taxicab with the help of the doorman.

LaRue and Patterson showed up a few minutes later, adding to her embarrassment. They waited near the door for her to join them.

"Are you okay, Macy?" Patterson inquired.

"No." She tried to walk past them without assistance, but tripped on the carpet and fell to the floor in a drunken heap.

LaRue opened her mouth to speak, but Patterson touched her arm and shook her head to silence her.

Without saying a word, they helped her get up and assisted Macy to the elevator.

In the apartment, Patterson and LaRue made themselves comfortable in the den after leaving Macy in the safety of her bedroom.

The next morning, she was still angry over her credit cards being denied. The memory of the night before was still etched in her mind. Macy felt guilty over the way she treated her roommates.

They were in the kitchen having breakfast when Macy left her room. She walked over to the glass breakfast table and sat down.

"I'm sorry about last night. I owe you both an apology. I didn't mean what I said to you."

LaRue apparently wasn't going to let it go with just an apology. Macy would've been shocked if she had. "What about the drinking? I thought you'd quit."

"I did. Things just went from bad to worse last night. I was depressed and so I went to Bloomingdale's to do some shopping. The Dolce & Gabbana collection was on sale."

"I thought you didn't buy on sale," LaRue interjected.

"I buy what I want, when I want it. Now let me finish my story. I went to pay for my selections and got humiliated. That little minimum-wage cashier actually had the nerve to take my credit card and cut it up."

"I'm so sorry," Patterson murmured.

Macy gritted her teeth. "I could kill my father for putting me through this hell."

"Gurl, when are you going to take some responsibility for what happens?" LaRue questioned. "This is not your father's fault—not all of it anyway. You don't manage money well."

A shadow of annoyance crossed her face. "You don't have to keep throwing that up to me."

"I'm not trying to throw anything anywhere. Macy, you're a grown woman, or trying to be anyway. It's time for you to take responsibility."

"I already have parents, LaRue. I don't need any more."

"Then quit acting like a child," she retorted. "Grow up, Macy. I know this is the last thing you want to hear, but I'm gonna say it anyway. You need to get off that high horse of yours and get a J-O-B."

"LaRue's right," Patterson contributed. "Working and earning your own money gives you a sense of freedom, Macy. You've said many times that you want to be free of your parents. Well, this is one way for you to do it. You have to stop being so dependent on their financial help."

"What help? They haven't helped me in a while."

"Prove to them that you doan need their help then," Patterson challenged. "Show your parents that you can survive on your own."

"Humph," LaRue uttered. "Prove it to yourself."

Macy rolled her eyes heavenward. "I've never held down a job. Nobody is going to give me employment with no experience. I don't even have my college degree."

She pushed away from the table. "I'll figure out something. I always do."

Deep down, Macy was scared.

LaRue

"That gurl got a lot to learn, I'm here to tell you." She shook her head in dismay. "Macy needs to get a job."

"But what can she do, LaRue? You heard her—she doan really have no experience doing nothing. Back home, she couldn't even get a job tending the cows. They might let her get the eggs out of the chicken coop."

LaRue burst into laughter. "That's too bad."

"We're going to have to keep praying for her. If Macy's not careful, she's gon' end up an alcoholic, and we don't want that."

"No, we don't. But all we can do is talk to her. We can't make Macy do a thing."

"Why not?" Patterson wanted to know. "Why can't we?"

LaRue considered her words. "Hmmmm. You know . . . Patterson, you may be on to something."

She leaned forward and whispered her plan to Patterson.

Chapter 27

Patterson

The month of October burst onto the scene, bringing brisk weather on its heels.

Patterson began her day as usual by singing in the shower. This morning she'd gotten up early just to prepare a nice breakfast for the three of them.

After Macy went to bed, she and LaRue decided that they would not only pray for Macy, but also step in and help her find a job.

After she got dressed, Patterson headed to the kitchen while LaRue entered Macy's bedroom. She heard a string of profanity coming from the room and burst into laughter. If she wasn't careful, Macy would soon owe LaRue her first paycheck.

When breakfast was ready, Patterson called out to LaRue and Macy.

"Gurl, it smells good up in here." LaRue took the plate of turkey sausages Patterson held out to her. "I'm starving."

"I can't believe you drug me out of bed this early," Macy grumbled. She put her hands to her face. "I'm tired and I don't feel well. There's no way I can go out there looking for a job like this." Peering into a nearby mirror, she added, "I look like hell."

"It's amazing how she can always find a mirror," LaRue teased.

"We've been living here for a couple of months now and I've never noticed that mirror near the door until now." She glanced around the room. "Hmmm. There's a lot of mirrors in this apartment."

Patterson chuckled. "C'mon you two. Eat up. We all got to get out of here shortly. I've got an early morning meeting." She placed a newspaper in front of Macy. "I went downstairs and got this for you."

Macy gave her a puzzled look. "What am I supposed to do with this?"

"Find a job," LaRue announced. "You *do* know how to look through the classifieds, don't you?"

"Yeah. I do." Macy settled back against her chair with her hands folded across her chest, pouting. "This is so ridiculous."

LaRue reached for a muffin and placed it on Macy's plate. "Eat. You're going to need your strength for pounding the pavement." She took another and placed it on her own. "Patterson, you something else in the kitchen, gurl. I can't believe you made pancakes, scrambled eggs, sausage, biscuits, and gravy. I'm gonna need to walk the twenty blocks to work this morning."

Patterson burst into laughter. She glanced over at Macy, who looked like she was about to burst into tears at any moment.

She opened her mouth to say something comforting, but changed her mind. Patterson didn't want to get her feelings hurt.

Macy

By the end of the day, Macy felt like crying.

She'd already been turned down by four companies. One lady practically laughed in her face before suggesting she take up a trade or something. Macy had no skills whatsoever. She knew nothing about computers other than to turn them on and send e-mail. When she was in college, she usually paid someone to type her assignments whenever she felt inclined to complete one. "I can't type. . . ." she mumbled.

Her mind traveled back to the memory of the very last interview of the morning. The person conducting the interview tested Macy on the PBX phone system and the results were disastrous. "I can't even answer a frigging phone. The only thing I can do is shop. . . ."

A thought entered Macy's mind. "I can shop. Yes. That's it. The answer to my problems. I can be a personal shopper."

Patterson

"Have you spoken to Miller yet?"

She glanced up at LaRue. "He called the store yesterday. I was supposed to call him back last night."

LaRue leaned against the living room wall for support. "You can't avoid him forever, Patterson."

"I know. I just feel so bad. I feel guilty."

LaRue opened her mouth to speak, but Patterson stopped her. "I know I shouldn't, but I do. I know better. I walked right into that situation with my eyes open."

Surveying her face, LaRue questioned, "Are you sure nothing happened?"

"We just kissed. I mean Miller touched me in certain places." She could feel the heat rising to her face. She was so embarrassed just talking about this with LaRue. Patterson placed a hand to her mouth.

LaRue grinned. "Gurl, don't be so embarrassed. Those are just normal feelings. You just got to keep them under control."

"I'm tryin'. Lord knows I am."

"I think you need to decide what you're gonna do with Miller. If you don't plan on seeing him again, then you need to tell him."

"I need to talk to him. He needs to know the boundaries."

LaRue nodded. "I agree. Why don't you go on and give him a call?"

Patterson sighed in resignation. "I guess I can't keep hiding forever, huh?"

"Nope. At least this way you can see if you two are on the same page."

She agreed with LaRue, but deep down Patterson worried that she could lose Miller, and she wasn't ready for that.

"Are you worried that you're gonna lose him?"

Patterson felt like LaRue could read her thoughts. "I don't want to have to stop seeing him. I like him a lot." She released a heavy sigh. "This is so hard. Why does it have to be so hard? God gave us all these feelings and emotions that betray us at a moment's notice. This is so hard trying to do the right thing."

"You take it one day at a time, Patterson. You sometimes have to slow down and take a step back. It's a part of life."

Patterson nodded. "I guess I shouldn't complain. I'm glad to be able to get up each day. I'm glad to be alive."

"Yeah," LaRue murmured. "Me, too."

Patterson headed to her bedroom. "I'll be back. I have a phone call I need to make."

She returned to the living room twenty minutes later, saying, "La-Rue, I invited Miller to have dinner with me. I figure I'd do this in person."

Laying down the magazine she was reading, LaRue asked, "You sure about this?"

"Not really, but I think it's best. At least we're gon' be in a public place." Patterson pushed away a stray curl. "Say a prayer for me, please."

LaRue nodded. "Will do. You be careful."

Chewing on her bottom lip, Patterson turned on her heels. She needed to take a shower.

She was meeting Miller within the hour.

"I was glad to get your phone call," he said as soon as Patterson arrived at the restaurant forty-five minutes later. "I thought maybe you didn't want to see me anymore."

"I told you that I've been busy, Miller." Patterson handed him the videotape in a gift bag. "Please make sure you take this with you."

"Did you watch it?"

Patterson frowned. "No. I told you I doan watch mess like that." She wondered if perhaps LaRue had been right about Miller.

"It's just a movie, baby. You don't have to twist your face up like that."

"Miller, we need to talk."

They were led to their table.

Patterson waited for him to take a seat before saying, "Things really got out of hand the other night."

"I don't agree," Miller responded. "I think things were moving pretty smoothly." He took Patterson's hand in his. "I'm crazy about you, baby. I have a feeling that you feel the same way about me."

Patterson was annoyed at the transparency of her feelings.

"Am I wrong?"

She shook her head. "But—"

Miller hushed her by leaning over and kissing her. His demanding lips caressed hers.

Patterson could feel warmth spreading through her body, the sparks of desire igniting. She reluctantly pulled away from him. Her eyes traveled the room, trying to see if anyone was paying attention to them. She was thankful they had been seated in a booth in a dimly lit area.

Putting a hand to her lips, she murmured, "I guess you proved your point, Miller."

"We belong together. You know it and so do I." His lips recaptured hers, more demanding this time.

Patterson succumbed to the forceful domination of Miller's lips. She wound her arms inside his jacket and around his back.

Miller's hands explored the hollows of her back and felt her tremble beneath his touch.

"I can't fight it anymore. I love you, Patterson," he whispered in her ear. Although she was trying to fight it, Miller knew it wouldn't be long before he had her right where he wanted her.

A waiter arrived with water glasses. He pulled out a pad to take their order.

When he walked away, Miller asked, "What's got you wearing such a pretty smile? I hope this has something to do with me."

"I have some great news to tell you. TM Models, Inc., arranged a test shoot for me. I'm meeting with them on Monday to evaluate the results. Philippe said that if they feel that my look is marketable, they are going to put my first composite card together with photos from the test shoot. This will be my calling card to present to potential clients."

Miller took a sip of his wine. "You sound very excited."

"Yeah. I'm so excited. This is what I've wontned for so long. All of my life actually."

When their meals arrived, Miller dove into his food with relish.

Patterson eyed him for a moment, then turned her attention to her meal.

He surprised her by reaching over and taking her hand. "I'm proud of you, Patterson."

She squeezed his hand. "Thanks. I really appreciate it."

Patterson knew she needed to have a much deeper conversation with Miller, but sitting here with him like this—she just couldn't do it. She was afraid he would leave her.

Right now her feelings for Miller outweighed what she knew was the right thing to do.

Chapter 28

Macy

"Call the *New York Times* and schedule a press conference," Macy shouted when she burst into the apartment.

"Why?" LaRue and Patterson asked in unison.

"I have a job," Macy announced.

She danced around the room. "Macy Baldwin has a regular nine-to-five, so to speak. Doesn't pay much—in fact the salary is downright insulting, but it is a paycheck."

"Congratulations," Patterson murmured. "This is wonderful news."

"What are you gonna be doing?" LaRue questioned.

"I'm going to be a personal shopper for Stanwyck's Department Store."

"This is cause for celebration. Gurl, we need to break out the champagne. Macy's a working gurl now."

She stopped dancing long enough to say, "We don't have any."

Laughing, LaRue shook her head. "I was only kidding, Macy. About the champagne anyway. We should do something special, though. Why don't we go out to dinner?"

"I think that's a great idea," Patterson stated. "Macy, I'm treating you. You pick the restaurant."

"You know where I want to go. It's one of my favorite restaurants in all of New York."

LaRue asked, "So how soon can you be ready?"

Macy looked at LaRue. "What's wrong with what I've got on?"

"Nothing. I didn't know if you wanted to change or something."

"I'm going to freshen up a bit, but no, I'm not going to change. This is one of my favorite suits, and I look wonderful in it."

"Yes, you do." LaRue chuckled. "Gurl, you something else."

Macy bounced off to her room. Today, she felt like she'd conquered the world by getting this job.

She refused to think about the fact that she would be assisting some of her mother's snooty friends. Macy focused instead on the fact that she'd be bringing in a paycheck and getting a fifty-percent discount on clothing.

"I can do this," she whispered. "At least until I can do better."

LaRue was still doing fashion shows with Victor, and Patterson had gone on a couple of assignments. Macy had even volunteered to be in Victor's upcoming fashion show for the Heart Foundation.

She still couldn't understand why she hadn't been picked up by any of the agencies she'd gone to. *What is it they don't like about me?* she wondered.

LaRue

LaRue headed to the front door with her duffle bag. She glanced over at the clock and sighed.

"Macy, I don't want to be late. You need to hurry up."

They had to be at the Gallery at the Gershwin Hotel within the hour for the fashion show.

Macy rushed out of her bedroom with one shoe on and the other dangling from her hand. "Don't leave me. I'm ready. I knew I should've packed my bag last night, but I thought I'd have time to do it this morning. But then I went to church with Patterson."

"How was it?"

"Okay," Macy responded. "Next Sunday we're going to visit another church. The guy that works with Patterson invited us. You should go with us."

"Now I know I got to be dreaming," LaRue uttered. "You're inviting me to church. . . . I don't believe it."

Macy made a face. "Very funny. . . ."

LaRue opened the door. "Let's go."

While they waited on the elevator, she considered Macy's invitation. Maybe it was time for her to return to the church. She was tired of running. No matter how much she wanted to hate God, she couldn't. She still loved him and knew without a doubt that He still loved her.

I'm still mad with you, God. I just want you to know that. I didn't want to lose the two people in the world I cared the most about. A small part of her believed that He had allowed her to suffer those losses so that she could make room for Patterson and Macy. Before Tom and Janine died, LaRue had no room in her heart for anyone else. They were her world.

An image of Roger formed in her mind. They were still going out and, although he wanted to take their relationship to the next level, LaRue wasn't interested. She'd even gone as far as to be intimate with him, but left feeling empty.

LaRue knew she would never love Roger—not in the way he wanted. They could only be good friends.

Macy

On Sunday, Macy and Patterson were shocked when a dressed LaRue walked out of her bedroom.

It took a moment for Patterson to speak. She cleared her throat and said, "Let's go. We doan wont to be late."

Macy stole a peek at LaRue while they were waiting for the elevator. She chewed on her bottom lip and fingered the necklace she was wearing.

Macy noticed that LaRue didn't say much during the taxi ride to the church in Harlem. She wondered why she looked so uneasy, but didn't ask.

Jason was standing outside Mission Baptist when they pulled up. After Patterson made the introductions, he embraced each of them and escorted them inside.

Macy had a feeling that Jason was infatuated with Patterson. She smiled when he caught her watching him. He wasn't much on looks, she had to admit, but he was a real nice young man. She hoped Patterson realized the jewel she had in Jason. She'd been alone long enough to know that she'd been looking for the wrong qualities in a man. Macy decided it was time to take a step back and just work on her own life.

It was time to grow up.

LaRue

LaRue looked up toward the front of the church and her heart lurched madly. The man standing in the pulpit caught her attention.

He was a tall portly man with a handsome face and dark curly hair. LaRue had never reacted so strongly to a man before. Not even Tom or Roger had evoked such strong emotions.

She closed her eyes to shut out any awareness of the Reverend Clyde Whitcomb.

When he spoke, his voice was like a caress.

"This morning our text is taken from the fifth chapter of First Thessalonians, eighteenth verse. '*Give thanks in all circumstances; for this is the will of God in Christ Jesus for you. . . .*' Today we will learn three things. One is that the habit of being thankful must be learned. You know, church, our natural reaction to disappointment is to complain and be depressed. God desires that we take inventory of the things for which we can be thankful."

"Amen," Patterson whispered.

"The second is the wisdom of developing the habit of being thankful. Listen to me, church. The habit of giving thanks will produce joy."

Reverend Clyde Whitcomb pulled a gold-colored handkerchief from the pocket of his dark suit and wiped his forehead. "Our thankfulness brings joy to the heart of our Father God. Our thankfulness brings joy to the hearts of those around us. Our habit of giving thanks brings joy to ourselves as we recognize the thing for which we can rejoice. . . ."

LaRue began nodding her head vigorously.

"The final point I want to make is that we have to develop the habit of being thankful. . . ."

When the service ended, Jason took them to meet Reverend Whitcomb. LaRue held out her hand to shake his. When their hands touched, she nearly jumped as a spark ignited deep in her belly.

Stunned by her reaction to the pastor, LaRue politely excused herself and walked away.

What in the world is wrong with me? She wondered wildly. Her heart was beating a rapid pace and she felt a little lightheaded. *Am I dying?*

LaRue waited outside for Macy and Patterson. There was no way she could face Reverend Whitcomb after making such a fool of herself.

"I wondered where you'd disappeared to," Macy commented when she strolled out of the church. "What happened?"

"Nothing. I just needed some fresh air."

Jason and Patterson walked outside, joining them.

"I had a nice time," LaRue began. "Jason, thank you for inviting me."

"I hope you'll come back. All of you."

She eyed Jason discreetly, quietly observing him. LaRue could tell that he had feelings for Patterson. They actually made an attractive couple, she decided.

LaRue prayed that Patterson would open her eyes before she missed out on the jewel that was right in front of her face.

Patterson

Patterson couldn't be sure, but she thought she detected something in the handsome pastor's eyes when he gazed at LaRue. She wondered if that was why LaRue suddenly decided to leave.

"Did you like the service, Macy?" Jason inquired, bringing Patterson out of her musings.

"Actually, I did. Reverend Whitcomb held my interest. I have to keep from falling asleep at that other church Patterson took me to. We should come back here from now on."

Jason chuckled. "We'd love to have you come back."

"I'll be back for sure," Macy promised. "I like this church."

"Will wonders never cease," LaRue mumbled under her breath.

Macy shot an amused look her way. "I heard that."

After having lunch with Jason, the three women went home. They spent the rest of the day relaxing.

The next morning, Patterson got up early and went to the fitness center to work out. She was dressed and out of the house by seven-thirty, because she had an early photo shoot.

After a day of make-up, several hairstyle changes, and posing for a cranky photographer, Patterson bounced into the apartment excitedly.

"Hey, y'all. I got some great news!"

There was no one in sight. Patterson went from room to room of the apartment looking for her roommates.

A few minutes later, LaRue entered the apartment, with Macy following closely behind.

Patterson returned to the living room, panting, "I . . . I was just looking for y'all." She put a hand to her chest. "I'm sorry. I'm just so excited."

"What's going on?"

"Philippe said that there are a whole range of possibilities for me. Editorial and catalog shoots, advertising, and television commercials." Patterson let out a squeal of joy. "Can you believe it? I'm a model. A real fashion model."

"Well if I were you, I wouldn't go leaving that Chanel cosmetics counter just yet," Macy advised.

Patterson refused to allow Macy's catty remarks to dampen her enthusiasm. She hoped what she had to say next would encourage her. "I overheard Philippe talking about needing new faces for a commercial print ad. They are looking for women twenty-five years old and older. Isn't that great news?"

"Not for me," Macy stated. "I'm only twenty-four. I look like I'm twenty, so it wouldn't work for me. You should definitely go for it, LaRue. You certainly look older than I do."

LaRue looked at Macy in amazement. "Gurl, just when I think you are getting yourself together, you come around and prove me wrong. You still the witch you always was."

"I agree with Macy, this time, LaRue. I think you should do it, too," Patterson interjected. "I don't mean about you looking older, though."

"I don't know. . . ."

Patterson embraced LaRue. "I have a good feeling about this. I think you should at least give it a shot. They're holding an open call this weekend. The ad will be in the paper tomorrow."

"You really think I should do this?"

Patterson nodded. "I do."

"So do I," Macy contributed. "It may be your only chance to do some print modeling. I'm sure you don't want to miss out on that."

"For the record, Macy, I am very happy being a counselor and doing runway modeling. I don't need to be some supermodel. Especially if it's gonna turn me into someone like you."

LaRue turned on her heels and stormed off to her bedroom.

"Now look at what you've gone and done, Macy," Patterson snapped in anger. "Why can't you just be happy for other people sometimes? Do you always have to be so mean?"

Chapter 29

Macy

Macy eyed Patterson in amazement. She couldn't believe she'd just said those horrible things to her.

But Patterson wasn't backing down. "You know, I'ma tell you just what I think of you. I know you're full of yo'self, Miss Thang, but you need to really look into all these fancy mirrors you got hanging on the wall. You ain't all that beautiful with your nasty ol' attitude."

Macy had heard enough. Placing her hands on her hips, she demanded, "What did you say? Girl, you don't know who you're talking to."

"Oh, I know all right. You think you so much prettier than us, and you think you better than me and LaRue—only you ain't foolin' nobody but yo'self. Ever wonder why you haven't been chosen by a modeling agency? It's 'cause they can see the ugliness inside you. Why doan you try being happy for somebody else? Maybe things will change for you."

"Just shut up, Patterson."

"Macy, if I didn't care for you, I wouldn't say these things. Somebody got to tell you the truth. You hateful."

"I am blunt and you and LaRue can't seem to handle the truth."

"Then let me lay some truth on you. You can't stand it that LaRue and me have been able to achieve some of our dreams while you haven't. Right?"

Patterson hit it right on the head, but Macy wasn't about to confirm or deny. "I'm not going to dignify that with a response. You and LaRue are just too sensitive for me." She turned. "I'm getting a headache, so if you'll excuse me. I need to take some Tylenol."

"What you need is some Jesus in your life."

Macy smiled. "I'll keep that in mind. Thank you."

She walked away.

She took some medicine and lay down on the bed. Tears ran down the side of her face. Macy couldn't get Patterson's harsh words out of her brain.

She was right. Macy would never tell her so, but Patterson had been correct in all her assumptions.

She got up twenty minutes later and walked out of her room. She stood outside LaRue's bedroom for a few minutes before knocking.

"Can I come in, please?" Macy asked as she stuck her head inside.

"I'm not in the mood for drama."

"No drama." Macy walked all the way into the room. "Just a much-needed apology. LaRue, I'm very sorry for the things I said. I hope you know I didn't really mean them."

"Yes, you did, Macy. You meant them."

Macy dropped down on the edge of LaRue's bed. "Okay, I meant them, but not quite the way they came out. Even to me they sounded mean."

"They were mean-spirited."

"LaRue, they really weren't. I don't know why I do things like that. I speak my mind—Lord knows it's gotten me into a lot of trouble." Macy stared down at her hands. "LaRue, I like you a lot and your friendship means more to me than you can ever imagine. I'm going to work on my attitude, I promise. You've been wonderful to me—it's time I return the favor."

"Macy, we're not in any competition with each other. Just remember that, okay?"

"Friends?"

LaRue nodded. "If you want to have friends, you have to learn how to be a friend."

"I understand." Macy rose up. "Come on out of this room. Let's do something fun tonight."

Together they left the room in search of Patterson.

"Are we all right?" She wanted to know.

Macy and LaRue glanced at one another. "Yeah," they answered in unison.

Grinning, Patterson hugged them both. "I'm so happy we're all friends again. I don't like fighting and arguing."

"Humph," Macy grumbled. "You sure do it well to not like it."

LaRue burst into laughter. "I heard Patterson telling you off."

"She did a pretty good job of it." Macy gave Patterson a playful jab. "I didn't know you had it in you, girl."

"I doan like showing that side of me, but you really ruffled my feathers."

Her comment brought on another round of laughter.

Patterson

Patterson made sure she went to bed early because of the early morning photo shoot that had been scheduled for her.

She woke up feeling refreshed and rested.

After getting dressed, she applied base makeup as instructed and was soon on her way.

Upon her arrival, Patterson was introduced to the photographer she would be working with. After exchanging a few pleasantries, he went over the game plan. Then it was time for her to change clothes.

Patterson was whisked away almost immediately by a make-up artist and hair stylist.

"So this is just your third time, huh?" the make-up artist inquired.

"Yeah. I'm still real nervous, too."

"Just have fun with it, girl. You're going to do just fine."

It was time.

Patterson prayed, asking God to relieve her body of the tension. She didn't want to blow this chance that she'd been given.

Once the camera started clicking with music playing in the background, Patterson was in her element. By the time of the first break, she felt like a pro.

The make-up artist whisked her away a second time to repair her look, while the photographer made last-minute lighting and set adjustments.

The art director came over to compliment Patterson while they waited to shoot the next series of photos.

The photographer walked over to check on her, while his assistant double-checked the equipment. "You might want to use this time to recharge."

"Okay," she murmured.

When the shoot ended, the assistant worked quickly, cleaning up, and packing.

After changing back into her clothes, Patterson stood around with the photographer asking questions about modeling.

"You were very good. It's hard to believe you're a freshman," he stated. "I like your professionalism."

Patterson grinned at his compliment and murmured, "Thank you. I had a great time. This was so exciting."

He laughed. "I hope the next time I see you, you'll feel the same way."

"I'm sure I will."

"You really are a novice."

She decided to change the subject. "When will the pictures be ready? I'd like to sit down with you and hear what you have to say about them."

"You sure you want to do that? I can be brutal."

"It's the only way I'm gon' learn to be a better model."

Patterson couldn't wait to get home. She was dying to tell Macy and LaRue about the photo shoot.

The front door opened, startling Patterson. She turned around. "Oh, Macy, you scared me. I thought you were already home."

"I went out to dinner with a couple of cousins who were visiting. Thank God, they are leaving tomorrow morning. They were getting on my nerves." Macy bent to remove her Stuart Weitzman shoes. "These babies cost a lot of money, but they hurt so much."

She walked barefoot over to the club chair in the living room and sat down. Rubbing her foot, Macy mumbled, "The things we do for attention."

Patterson nodded in understanding. "How is the job coming along?"

"Ugh." Macy waved her hand in dismissal. "Let's not talk about that. Let's talk about you, Miss Model. How did it go?"

"It was so much fun. I had a great time, Macy. I love it."

"That's going to get old real soon. But then, you're still brand new at this."

Patterson sank down on the sofa. "Why does everybody keep saying that? If modeling is so horrible, then why do so many people want to do it?"

"Patterson, the first thing you're going to have to do is stop looking at everything through those rose-colored glasses of yours. It's not always glamorous."

"Macy, I know that. I just spent eight hours in a studio. Before I could even make it home, Philippe called to tell me that I have two go-sees and another booking for a catalog tomorrow."

Macy smiled. "Wow. Good for you, Patterson. I'm thrilled for you." She changed the subject. "How are things going with Miller?"

Patterson dropped her gaze. "Okay, I guess."

"Just okay?"

Patterson pretended to be interested in the stack of mail lying on the sofa table. "I think we need to slow down a bit."

"If things go any slower, you two will be in your eighties before you get engaged."

"Macy, I want to get to know Miller."

"I thought that's what you were doing. Isn't that what dating is all about?"

"The truth is that Miller wants to take things up a notch. He's acting kind of strange."

"In what way?" Macy prompted.

"He's not real happy about my modeling and he won't tell me why."

The door to LaRue's room opened. "I thought I heard voices out here. I wasn't sure who was talking, so I thought I'd better be prepared." She showed them the baseball bat she carried in her hand.

"What do you plan to do with that?" Macy questioned.

"Fight for the right to be safe. What do you think I'm gonna do with it?"

"Humph. That's not going to do much against someone carrying a gun."

"So, Miss High-and-Mighty, what kind of plan do you have, in the event something happens?"

Without missing a beat, Macy announced, "I have a gun. I see no point in half-stepping. I'm a good shot, too."

Patterson's mouth dropped open in shock. "Macy!"

"I would only use it when forced to do so. I'm also a black belt in karate."

"I'm planning on enrolling in a self-defense class myself," LaRue announced. "Patterson, you should join me."

"I will. I've taken a small beginners' class in Atlanta, but that was a few years ago."

While giving a full recount of her day, Patterson joined LaRue in the kitchen and raided the refrigerator.

"I made some cookies when I came home from work," LaRue announced.

"I hope you made your chocolate peanut butter cookies. I love them," Macy confessed to LaRue. "You have to show me how to make them one day."

"For what?" LaRue asked as she held out a plate toward Macy. "It's not like you're going to ever really bake them. I'm not into wasting my breath."

"You wrong for that, LaRue." Macy laughed as she reached for another one.

LaRue

Roger wanted to have a talk with her.

LaRue had a feeling she knew what it was about. He wanted to have a real relationship with her.

She met him at his favorite restaurant. They were seated almost immediately.

After the waitress took their orders, Roger reached over and took her by the hand. "I'm glad you were able to meet me tonight."

"You said it was important," LaRue reminded him.

"LaRue, I hope you know that I've come to care for you a great deal."

"I care about you, too," she quickly interjected.

"I'm falling in love with you," Roger announced.

His words silenced LaRue. She fully expected him to complain about the lack of intimacy in their relationship. Since the one night she allowed him to make love to her, Roger had been asking for sex.

"Did you hear me?"

"Are you saying this to get me back into bed?"

"No. LaRue, I mean it. I love you."

She gazed into his eyes, looking for a glimmer of something that would show he was lying. All she saw was the truth.

LaRue dropped her eyes to the tablecloth. "Roger, I care a lot for you. But I have to be honest." She looked up at him. "I love you as a friend. A good friend. I'm sorry if I ever led you on."

"I guess I'm not surprised. Ever since the night we made love, you seemed to be backing away. I wasn't sure why."

"I realized as soon as it happened that I'd made a mistake, Roger. I shared a very special part of myself with you, and I realized that I was just trying to make the pain go away for just a little while. I was lonely." LaRue reached over and took his hand. "I made myself believe you were feeling the same way."

"I'm ready to move on with my life. My fiancée is gone and she won't be back. Tom won't be back either."

LaRue nodded. "I know. Roger, I'm not the woman for you. You're not the man for me either. I do hope that we can remain friends, though. I want to have you in my life."

"Maybe in time, LaRue. I'm not sure I can handle just being friends right now."

"I understand."

LaRue's eyes filled with unshed tears. She hadn't wanted to hurt Roger. "I'm so sorry. You're a wonderful man."

They ate their dinner with little conversation.

She was grateful when the evening ended and she was on her way home.

Before she climbed in bed, LaRue fell to her knees and prayed that God would bless Roger with the woman he deserved.

Chapter 30

Macy

From where Macy stood in the suits department, she spotted her mother across the aisle shopping in the St. John department.

As stealthily as she could, Macy turned on her heels to go back the other way, hoping to escape.

Rhetta spotted her and called out her name.

Macy froze.

Groaning, she slowed her walking, pausing long enough to let her mother catch up. "This is just great," she uttered in a low whisper.

"Macy, what are you doing here?"

"I'm shopping," she responded as drily as she could. "Why else would I be here, Mother?"

"Of course," Rhetta stated with a short laugh. "It's just that when I first approached, it looked as if you were working here."

"I *am* working here, Mother. This is where I work."

Rhetta's mouth dropped open in shock. "Since when?"

"I've been here for a few months."

Her mother glanced around to see if anybody was standing nearby. Lowering her voice to a harsh whisper, she asked, "Macy, why did you come to Stanwyck's?"

"It was the only company that would give me a job. Neither Macy's nor Bloomingdale's would."

"So you're a salesclerk?" Rhetta said it as if she had a bad taste in her mouth.

"I'm a personal shopper, Mother. Not a salesclerk."

"I don't see that there's much difference, dear."

"Whatever . . ."

"Must you take that attitude with me, Macy? What is wrong with me wanting the best for you?" Rhetta kept glancing around to see if they were within earshot of anyone.

"Nothing. What infuriates me, Mother is this: You and Father put me in this predicament and now you want to judge me. I am doing the best I can." Macy glanced down at her watch. "I have an appointment with a client. I'll talk to you later, Mother."

She walked away without waiting for a response.

"Oh, my Lord, the Sheffields are here," Macy groaned. They were absolutely the last people she wanted to see. She'd just had to deal with her mother and now Prudence and Charla Sheffield. It went from bad to worse.

There was no escaping them, so she pasted on a smile when the women spotted her.

"Macy, honey, is that you?" Prudence Sheffield inquired. Her beady eyes zoomed in on the tag Macy wore. "My dear, are you working here?"

"Yes, I am. What can I do for you?"

Prudence pressed her bejeweled fingers to the expensive blouse draped across her flat chest. "Why, I'm in shock. What must you be thinking? Do your parents know about this?"

Hearing what sounded like a snicker, Macy sent a sharp look Charla's way before responding, "Mrs. Sheffield, I'm an adult. I'm working here because . . . because I want to do so."

"You sure have changed," Charla commented with a smirk. "I never thought I'd see this day. Not you."

"Some of us actually have responsibilities, Charla. We don't live off our parents' money."

"Humph." Charla walked away and pretended to admire a designer gown hanging on a nearby rack.

"It's nice seeing you. I'm afraid I have to get back to work. My clients are waiting." Macy excused herself. She never liked Prudence nor her stuck-up daughter. Charla had been after Frederick for years.

Macy took several calming breaths and tried to salvage the rest of her day.

Patterson

"LaRue, do you think I should give Miller a call? I haven't heard from him in a week."

"I wouldn't," LaRue responded. "But then, I'm not the best person to ask."

"Why would you say that?"

"I just let a really nice guy walk out of my life."

Patterson was stunned. "Roger? You two aren't seeing each other anymore? When did this happen?"

"A couple of days ago. Roger told me that he loved me." She raised her eyes to meet Patterson's gaze. "I don't feel the same way about him. He's a good man—I just don't love him."

"I'm so sorry, LaRue."

She shrugged. "I had to be honest with Roger. I owed him that much. I still want to be his friend, but he wants to put some distance between us. I guess I can understand that. I'm just afraid I'm gonna lose his friendship."

"Maybe you could grow to love him?"

LaRue shook her head. "No. He and I can only be friends. I'm sure about that. He's not the man for me."

"How do you know?" Patterson asked. "I mean, I know that I care a great deal for Miller, but how will I know if he's the one for me?"

"Pray about it. That's the best advice I can give you."

"Did you pray about your relationship with Roger?"

"No," LaRue admitted. "I knew from the very beginning that Roger was just someone to fill the loneliness I was feeling."

"I never did have that talk with Miller. LaRue, every time I see him, my heart just goes crazy. I'm fallin' in love with him. I can feel it. The thought of losin' him is just too much to bear."

LaRue leaned forward, saying, "Patterson, you need to find out if you and Miller are on the same page, honey. If you don't, it may lead to unnecessary heartbreak."

Nodding, Patterson agreed. "You're right. I'm just a big chicken. I'm not ready to lose him."

"Just know that you're going into this with your eyes wide open. Just so you realize that this relationship may not go the way you want it. . . ."

Patterson smiled. "I know. I can handle it. I think the worst of it is that Miller wants to get me into bed and well . . . I've had lots of practice saying no. He's no different."

LaRue

LaRue was surprised when Roger appeared during her dinner with Victor. She greeted him with a hug. "It's good to see you."

"I missed you something awful," he admitted. "When Victor mentioned he would be having dinner with you, I invited myself. I hope you don't mind."

"I'm glad to see you."

"LaRue was just telling me that the troupe should be more involved in the community—outside of modeling—for the fund-raisers," Victor announced.

"I think she has a point," Roger stated with a smile.

"It could be something as simple as participating in Relay 4 Life or clothing drives for Goodwill. We could even offer to read to children at some of the local libraries."

"I think LaRue's suggestion should really be considered."

Victor nodded. "Actually, I hate I didn't come up with it."

Over lunch, they discussed more of LaRue's ideas.

LaRue could feel Roger's gaze on her, but pretended not to notice. She couldn't allow herself to get caught up in his web. She had a feeling he was still hoping to change her mind. Although it brought her sadness, LaRue knew she would never love Roger the way he deserved.

Chapter 31

Macy

"Hello, Frederick. What are you doing here?" Macy was surprised to see him. She hadn't known he was coming to New York. She stepped aside so that he could enter the apartment.

"I came to see you. Why else would I be here?" Frederick reached for her. "I've missed you."

Macy moved out of his reach. "I thought I told you to lose my number."

"I don't like this distance between us, Macy. I don't know what happened."

"We stopped being lovers," she blurted out. "Maybe somewhere along the line, we stopped being friends as well."

He gave her a tender look. "I hope not. About being friends, I mean. I miss talking to you."

"We didn't do much talking, Frederick. We spent most of our time in bed."

"I miss that, too. I won't lie." He walked over to the sofa and took a seat.

"I'm never going there again with you." Macy followed him into the living room.

He motioned for her to take a seat beside him.

She sat down and ran a hand through her hair. "I'm not sure we can be friends, Frederick."

"I know that we are no longer lovers, Macy. I want you to know that no matter what, I will always care about you."

Macy didn't respond. She concentrated on ignoring Frederick's deep, sultry voice and the way he made her feel.

His voice cut into her thoughts. "So what have you been doing?"

"Working."

"What did you say?"

Macy gave him a sidelong glance. "I have a job, Frederick. I work. I have a J-O-B."

"You?"

"Why are you acting so surprised?"

"We're talking about you, Macy. You'd rather sell yourself to some rich man."

"How dare you!" she fumed. "I can't believe you just said that to me."

"Why not?" Frederick asked. "Macy, you know it's true. You've been after me for months now. I'm sure it's not my charming personality that makes me so attractive, but rather my very large inheritance."

Rising to her feet, Macy uttered, "Frederick, please." She glared at him. "Who do you think you are, talking to me like this? You have no right. You're just mad that I've stopped sleeping with you. That's what this is really about."

Shrugging, Frederick responded, "I'm just being honest. Speaking of which, there is something that I need to tell you."

"What? You're getting married?" Macy was joking, but something in Frederick's expression made her ask, "*Are you?*"

"I'm seriously considering it. I haven't asked her yet."

Macy assumed immediately that he was referring to her. Softening her tone, she responded, "So when do you plan on asking her?"

"Tonight."

Macy's heart stopped. *He's about to propose to me. Thank—*

Frederick cut off her thoughts by saying, "I'm going there once I leave here."

"E-Excuse m-me," she uttered, almost choking on the words.

"I'm going to ask Charla Sheffield to marry me."

No wonder the cow was shopping for lingerie earlier.

Macy turned her back to him, blinking rapidly to keep her tears from rolling down her cheeks.

"Macy?" Frederick prompted from behind.

She quickly wiped at her eyes. Pasting on a smile, she turned to face him. "Huh? Oh, congratulations. I hope you and Charla will be very happy."

He was staring at her. "You okay?"

"She's the reason you've been coming to New York so often." It wasn't a question.

"I admit it. You were seeing William, and so Charla and I started seeing each other. I never expected it to be anything serious. You see, Charla knew about you. We . . ."

Frederick was grinning like he'd won an Olympic gold medal.

"We fell in love."

"*Cute story,*" she managed. "Your grandkids will love it."

Macy strode over to the fireplace, turning her back on Frederick. "Have a good life, Frederick."

"Macy . . ." He wrapped his arms around her.

She walked away from him. "Just leave, please. I just need to be alone."

"Honey . . ."

"NO. Please leave, Frederick. NOW." Macy refused to face him. She didn't want to give him the pleasure of seeing her cry.

"I don't want to lose your friendship."

"I can't think about that right now, Frederick."

He stood there a moment watching her. When Macy strode over to the window and stared out, he released a long sigh. Finally, he said, "Good-bye, Macy."

It was only after she heard the front door open and close, that she responded, "Good-bye, Frederick."

Macy tried to console herself with the truth that she didn't really love Frederick, but her pride had taken a deep hit, because he'd chosen to marry her worst enemy.

LaRue

"Miss Hawkins, how are you?"

The voice seemed to come out of nowhere.

Turning around, LaRue found herself face to face with Reverend Whitcomb. "I'm fine. And you?" She wasn't surprised to see him. She'd stopped at a Harlem bookstore that was located two blocks away from the church.

"Doing good. It's a pleasure to see you. I've had you on my mind."

LaRue wasn't sure how to respond, so she remained quiet.

"I wanted to speak with you on Sunday before you left, but you disappeared on me before I could get a chance to do so."

"What did you need?"

"Nothing," he responded. "I wanted to invite you to have dinner with me sometime."

LaRue was flattered. "Pastor . . ."

"I'm a single man, if that's what you're worried about."

The tension leaving her body, she laughed to hide her nervousness.

"I guess I should have asked if you're in a relationship with someone."

"I'm not," LaRue responded. "Not anymore anyway. I lost my husband a little over a year ago."

Clyde Whitcomb broke into a sympathetic smile. "I'm sorry to hear that."

"If you have a few minutes, why don't we have some coffee?" LaRue gestured toward the small area designated as a café.

They found a table and sat down.

"I'm glad you and your friends are still visiting the church. It's a blessing to have you worship with us."

"We're enjoying ourselves, pastor."

"Please call me Clyde."

LaRue awarded him a smile. "All right then." She chose her next words carefully. "Clyde, since his death, I haven't dated or even had any desire to date. I loved him very much, and for a long time I was very angry over losing him."

"You're angry with God?"

"Yeah, I am," LaRue confessed. "I'm trying to work through my anger, though, and your sermons have helped me with that."

"I'm glad to hear that."

"It's just that Tom and I were so in love. . . ."

"You don't believe that you can love like that again," Clyde finished for her.

"Exactly. I just wanted to be honest with you." LaRue hoped Clyde couldn't hear how loud her heart was thumping just sitting there talking to him. He stirred her emotions in a way no other man ever had—not even Tom.

"Thanks for your honesty. However, you never answered my question. Can I call on you for dinner, a play—something fun and exciting?"

LaRue chuckled. "Sure." She wrote her phone number down on a napkin and handed it to him.

Smiling, Clyde finished off his coffee.

LaRue was enjoying herself as they talked. He was funny, intelligent, and very handsome. She felt like a giddy schoolgirl, laughing at everything he said—even when he wasn't trying to be funny.

Macy

Macy, dressed in her bathrobe and no make-up, sat at the breakfast table eating ice cream.

LaRue did a double-take when she walked into the kitchen. "I can't believe my eyes. *You're eating ice cream.*"

"Apparently," Macy responded drily. "How on earth did you figure it out?"

"Ookaay." LaRue pulled out a chair and sat down next to Macy. "What's got you in such a raggedy mood, gurl? C'mon, talk to me."

"I told you about Frederick, right?" When LaRue nodded, she continued, "Well, he stopped by here right before you came home and announced he's getting married. To my worst enemy, no less."

"Macy, you also told me that you didn't love Frederick."

"I know, but it still bothers me. I hate the fact that while my life is so miserable and unhappy, that witch is marrying one of the richest men in the world. I'm shallow, I admit it."

"Have you ever been in love, Macy. Really in love?"

"Yeah, but he got married, too. He's a designer and he's living in London now. When his wife died, he became a recluse."

"Do you have any contact with him?"

Macy shook her head. "What's the point? I don't know what's wrong with me, LaRue. I'm beautiful. I pay large sums of money for this weave. I buy contacts so that men will think I'm exotic-looking. I'm not celibate. What the heck am I doing wrong?"

"Try being yourself, Macy. Let people see the real you."

"Like that's going to do anything," she uttered.

"It can't hurt," LaRue pointed out. "What do you have to lose?"

Macy thought it over. "I don't really know." She was afraid, but wouldn't admit it. "I'm not sure who I am anymore."

Patterson

"What are y'all doing in here?" Patterson asked when she arrived home.

"Talking about just how miserable our lives have become," Macy responded. "My Frederick is marrying my worst enemy. LaRue dumped Roger and now the good Pastor Whitcomb is sniffing after her." She paused for a second. "Actually, my life is the one that sucks. LaRue is a man magnet—only she's not interested in them. Me . . . well, nobody wants me. Not anybody with money anyway."

"I might as well toss in my woes, then." Patterson joined them at the breakfast table. "I haven't heard from Miller in a while. I've called him twice and he keeps telling me that he's working on some big project. He's been traveling a lot, too—at least that's what he's telling me."

"Don't believe him," Macy uttered. "Men suck. . . ."

"They're not all bad," LaRue countered.

"That's because nobody is dumping you." Macy flung her hair about her shoulders. "Maybe I should try some green contacts or something." She pressed a hand to her stomach. "Am I getting fat? What's wrong with me?"

"Macy, you're beautiful." Patterson reached over and took her hand. "You are one of the most beautiful women I've ever met."

Waving her hand in dismissal, Macy muttered, "Girl, you from Tree Trunk—you haven't seen many women, period."

Irritation flashed in Patterson's eyes. "For the last time—I am from Three Oak and we had women in the town. Plenty of them."

"Whatever . . ."

"Macy, you probably don't have no man because you so mean," Patterson stated. "Try changin' your attitude. Stop lookin' at a man's checkbook balance and love him for him. Maybe then you'll find yo'self a good one."

"Sure. And be poor. That's just what I need, huh?"

"I told you what you need to do, Macy," LaRue interjected. "You need to show a man the real you. Not this well-made-up version. No man is gonna believe that you're sincere if you don't allow him to really get to know you."

Macy rose to her feet. "I'm so glad to have Oprah and Dear Abby as roommates. Don't know what I'd do without you. Now why don't you fix yourselves while I go in my room and delight myself with a real pity party. See you later. If I need more advice, I'll call you."

When Macy shut the door to her room, Patterson whispered, "She really needs to work on her temper."

"She does," LaRue agreed. "But not only that, Macy needs to learn how to be happy with herself. She's trying to fit into this image that she perceives she should be."

"I guess life is full of lessons. Once you get them all, you die."

"Amen. . . ."

Chapter 32

Macy

Macy was in a bad mood.

She carried an armload of clothing to one of the dressing rooms. "Miss Rutherford, here are the dresses I told you about on the telephone."

"Thanks so much, dear."

Another woman peeked out of her dressing room. "Could you bring me a size four, please?"

Macy wanted to tell her that she was only helping her client, Millie Rutherford, but doubted it would matter. She hated the way the customers treated her—like she was nothing special. Macy hated her job.

An hour later, Millie left a very happy woman. In the meantime, Macy was left with the purchases. She carried them to the shipping department, where they would be boxed and delivered to the Rutherford estate.

When Macy returned to her office, she received a request via phone to select the perfect black dress for an upcoming black-tie event.

"Oh, I hate this job," she muttered to herself. Macy pushed away from her desk. "I can't take much more of this. I can't. Dear Lord, please help me."

Macy left her office in search of the perfect black dress. She strode over to the couture department. Her eyes landed on a rack of four gowns. She fingered the first one, loving the feel of the soft silken fabric.

Standing near Macy were two women close enough for her to hear what they were saying.

"I saw Sable yesterday and she had little Bethany with her. That little angel looks just like her mother. Such a shame what happened."

"Indeed. River has held up well in light of his loss. He's a good father to Bethany. He's looking for a nanny now. He'd called to see which agency my daughter uses."

"Right after poor Whitney died, River lost himself in his work. Sable was so worried that he couldn't handle being around his daughter—because she reminded him so much of his wife."

"He's a strong man."

"Handsome, too. I think I'll have Sable introduce him to my niece, Vivian. I think she'd be good for him and she loves children."

Macy pretended to be busy while eavesdropping on their conversation. River Littleton needed a nanny. River was the designer behind R. L. International and Whitney Rivers Couture. She wasn't just a huge fan of his designs, but Macy adored the man himself. She had been devastated when River announced he was marrying Whitney. Macy even refused initially to attend the wedding, but her parents forced her to go.

After the death of his wife, River had taken his daughter and moved to London. Macy had no idea he'd returned to the states until now. A plan formed in her mind, bringing a smile to her lips.

She left work early and instead of heading home, Macy took a taxi to Second Avenue, where River Littleton lived. It hadn't occurred to her until she arrived that he might not be home.

She paid the taxi driver and got out, running up the steps of the newly constructed condominium residence.

"Lord, please let him remember me," she prayed as she rode the elevator to his floor.

"What am I doing here?" Macy whispered before knocking. She really couldn't expect River to take one look at her and fall madly and deeply in love. But if he had any sense at all, he would. They were made for each other.

Macy was momentarily taken aback when River Littleton opened the door. She'd expected him to have someone else—perhaps a housekeeper—to perform such tasks.

"Yes?"

"River. Hi. I met you last year at the Heart Foundation Ball, remember?" He was still as handsome as she remembered.

He gave a polite nod. "Your face is familiar, but you'll have to forgive me—I'm terrible with names."

"I'm Macy Baldwin. You know my parents, Maynard and Rhetta."

"That's right." River opened the door wider to let her enter. "Come on in. You must be here for the check."

Confused, she inquired, "What check?"

"Your mother called me last week asking for a donation. I meant to ma—"

Macy interrupted him. "Oh, no, I'm not here for that." She quickly added, "I can take it to Mother for you, but I'm here for another reason."

"And that would be . . ." River prompted.

"I overheard Mrs. Worthington talking today at Stanwyck's, and she mentioned that you were looking to hire someone to watch your little girl."

"She's right. I am looking for a nanny. Do you know one?"

"Actually I do."

River picked up a pad and pen. "Can you give me her name and number?"

"You're looking at her. Me."

River's expression changed to one of surprise. "You want to be Bethany's nanny? Why?"

"I need a job. I don't really have any experience in anything, but I love children and—"

"I'm sorry, Macy," River responded quickly. "I'm just not sure this would work out."

A little girl ran into the room.

"Daddy, let's make cookies, please. . . ."

He gave her an indulgent smile. "In a minute, sweetie. Right now we have some company. Say hello to Miss Macy Baldwin."

Bethany did as she was told. "I've been to your store. I've been to Macy's. Grandma takes me there all the time. You sure have a lot of pretty things in there."

Macy laughed. "It's not my store, Bethany. I was named after the department store because I was born there. My mother was shopping and went into labor. They couldn't get her to the hospital in time."

"Wow," Bethany murmured.

"I like your name, too."

"My mom named me after her sister. My aunt died before I was born, so I never got to meet her." Bethany pointed to a photo on the piano. "That's a picture of her right there. I look like her. Everybody says so."

She glanced over at the picture. "You sure do. You are as pretty as she was." Macy glanced over at River to see if he was paying attention. She hoped that he would change his mind once he saw how well the two of them interacted.

Bethany took Macy by the hand and led her around the room, showing her pictures, identifying each subject.

River silently observed her every move. Macy moved around the room, following Bethany while discreetly studying the décor.

A vase of fresh flowers cast a subtle floral scent about the room that had been decorated by someone with eclectic tastes. There was a tasteful blend of the more traditional styles with contemporary colors.

Bethany took Macy's hand. "Do you want to see my room? Daddy just bought me some new furniture. It's pretty."

Macy looked to River for permission. When he gave a reluctant nod, she said, "Sure. I love furniture."

In Bethany's room, Macy found that River had chosen the most beautiful hand-painted furnishings. The bedroom had been decorated in a lavender and sage color scheme.

"It's perfect for a cute little girl like you. I love your room, Bethany."

"I love it, too. I think Mommy is even smiling in heaven." Bethany ran her hand along the soft-looking lavender and white comforter. "This is her favorite color."

Macy embraced the little girl. "I bet she's so very proud of you. Knowing Whitney, she's definitely smiling all over heaven."

Bethany's eyes grew large. "You knew my mom?"

Macy nodded. "I met her when she and your dad got married. I was at their wedding."

They left Bethany's room.

"Will you tell me about my mom?"

"Sure. I'll tell you everything I know. It's not a whole lot, I'm afraid."

River met them as they were descending the stairs.

He sent Bethany off to the kitchen in search of cookies, while he and Macy talked.

"My daughter seems to have taken a liking to you."

"I like her as well. River, I really want this job."

"Why *this* job?" He assessed her from head to toe. "I would never figure you for wanting this job. You look like you've stepped out of a fashion magazine."

Macy couldn't tell him that she hoped to marry him one day—that it was all she'd ever dreamed about. "Because I have no real experience doing anything other than babysitting my cousin's children from time to time. I'm currently working at Stanwyk's as a personal shopper. To be honest, *I hate it.*"

River sent her a look of disbelief. "You hate shopping?"

"For other people, I do." Macy broke into a short laugh. "I never would've believed this of myself."

"What about Baldwin Pharmaceuticals? Why don't you ask your father for a job?"

"I don't want to work for him," she answered thickly. "Being a receptionist definitely doesn't interest me."

Bethany ran into the room. "Macy, can you be my nanny?"

Macy raised her eyes to find River watching her.

"Daddy, I want Macy to watch me. Please, Daddy?"

"Bethany, I want you to know something," Macy stated. "We can be friends, you know. If it's okay with your dad, I'll come by sometime and visit you. Would you like that?"

The little girl glanced up at her father.

"Macy, if you really want the job. It's yours."

She smiled and embraced Bethany. "Thank you, River. You won't regret it."

LaRue

"Why are you looking so happy?" LaRue inquired when Macy bounced into the apartment. "What did you do?"

"I got a new job."

"Congratulations."

"Yeah. Congratulations, Macy," Patterson echoed from the kitchen. "I didn't know you were looking for something else."

"I couldn't take those old snobby women another day. They were truly getting on my last nerve."

"Snobby . . ." LaRue burst into laughter. "I can't believe you said that. You of all people. . . ."

"Whatever," Macy huffed.

"Congrats, gurl. You deserve it."

"What are you going to be doing?" Patterson asked. "Is it something similar to what you were doing at Stanwyck's?"

Macy shook her head no. "I'm going to be working for the renowned and incredible designer River Littleton."

LaRue and Patterson looked at one another.

"Surely, you've heard of his labels, Whitney Rivers Couture and R. L. International? River's one of the top designers in the world."

"I've heard of R. L. International," Patterson responded. "Can't afford the collection, though."

LaRue answered, "I've heard of him. His clothes are beautiful. My dad owned a couple of suits from his men's collection. So you're going to be his assistant?"

She gave a slight nod. "Something like that."

LaRue eyed Macy. "What do you mean by that?"

"I'm going to help him with his daughter, Bethany. You've got to see her—she's adorable."

"Are you going to be her babysitter?"

"Her nanny," Macy corrected.

Before she could respond, Patterson interjected, "Why are you being a nanny when you've got all these wonderful designs? Did you tell him about your wonting to be a designer?"

"No. Actually, my reason for working for River has nothing to do with my designs."

"You want the man," LaRue accused.

"I've been in love with him for years," Macy confessed. "He's part of the reason I became interested in fashion design in the first place. When he married Whitney Carver, it nearly broke my heart."

"So where's his wife now?"

"Patterson, she died in the terrorists attacks on September 11."

"Oh, my goodness. I had no idea."

Macy could feel LaRue's eyes on her and asked, "What is going through that mind of yours?"

"I was just wondering what River Littleton believes."

"What are you talking about, LaRue?"

"Does he really believe that you only want to be the nanny?"

Shrugging, Macy answered, "He hired me, LaRue. I'm not going to give him any reason to doubt me. He'll see how wonderful Bethany and I get along. River will eventually see that I can be an asset to him. He and I will make a great team. He'll see that and, within six months, I plan to have him eating out of my hands."

LaRue turned to flick off some microscopic dust on the end table's polished surface. "I knew there was more to this sudden desire than to become a nanny."

"I love kids," Macy stated truthfully.

"I know. You've always got your face stuck in somebody's stroller, and you're always playing with children."

"LaRue, I really love this man. I had given up hope when he moved to London after Whitney's death. Now that he's back, I'm going after what I want. Since I'll never be a designer, I might as well marry one."

Patterson

When she heard Miller's voice on the other end of the phone, Patterson's heart flipped.

"Hey . . . I didn't know if I was gonna get to talk to you before I left," she said.

"So you going to the Bahamas?"

"Yeah. I've never been, so I'm really excited."

"I wish I could join you. I haven't been back to Nassau in a few years. I went there for my ho—"

"Huh?" Patterson asked.

Miller cleared his throat. "I was saying I went there for my homeboy's wedding. I was the best man."

Patterson didn't know anyone who'd gotten married on an exotic island. "Wow, I bet you had a nice time."

"I did," Miller confirmed. "I really wish I could take a couple of days off and meet you in Nassau."

"Miller, I really need to talk to you. Do you think you could come by the apartment tonight?"

"Can't we talk on the phone?" he asked after a moment of silence.

"No, I think we should do this in person."

"What? You don't want to see me anymore?"

"That's not it, Miller. It's not that at all." Patterson chewed on her bottom lip, hoping he wouldn't press the issue. She knew she couldn't put off this discussion any longer.

"I can't make it tonight, baby. I'm sorry. Look, why don't you call me when you get back. We'll talk then. Okay?"

Patterson nodded. "Sure," she mumbled. "If we have to wait, then we'll talk when I get back from Nassau."

"Baby, I gotta go. Have a safe trip and I'll see you when you come home."

Miller was gone before she could utter a word.

Patterson told herself not to take it personally. She told herself that he was just very busy and she'd caught him in the middle of something.

As much as she tried to believe otherwise, Patterson felt like something was terribly wrong.

Chapter 33

LaRue

Patterson had been gone for three days. LaRue was happy for Patterson, but missed her dearly.

She got up early Sunday morning, made breakfast, and got dressed for church.

She walked past Macy's door and debated whether to knock. Macy stopped attending church a few weeks ago, although LaRue didn't know why. She knew she'd been out the night before with Frederick and suspected Macy was trying to use sex to sabotage his relationship with his fiancée.

She gave into her spirit and rapped lightly. "Macy, why don't you come to church with me? Reverend Whitcomb is preaching this Sunday. I know how much you like him." LaRue couldn't deny she liked him, too.

Looking exhausted, Macy ambled over to the bedroom door, throwing it open. "I do, but I think I'm just going to relax this morning. I didn't sleep well last night."

"I guess not. You were out pretty late."

Macy gave her a sharp look. "I don't need you checking up on me."

"I'm not checking up on you, Macy, but I am gonna warn you to be careful. You playing with fire."

Macy remained silent.

After a moment, she said, "I think I've changed my mind. Just give me fifteen minutes and I can be ready."

LaRue looked skeptical, prompting Macy to add, "Really, I can. Just give me fifteen minutes."

"If you're not ready, I'm walking out the door."

"Since when did you and God become so close? Or is it the good Pastor Whitcomb that's got you beating down the doors of the church?"

"Go get dressed, Macy."

"I guess you and God are back on speaking terms, huh?" Macy uttered.

"We're getting there."

LaRue walked back into her room to finish getting ready for church. She sat down on her bed. "Lord, please forgive me," she whispered. "I've been such a fool and I ask for your forgiveness. I need you in my life. . . ."

Macy

Her head jerked to attention when she heard Reverend Whitcomb mention the topic of his sermon.

"Church, I've heard a lot about answered prayer over the past week and a half . . . but at the same time . . . Ever since I entered the ministry, I have heard many people say, 'I don't think God answers my prayers' . . . or 'I prayed for this and it didn't happen . . . therefore, I am mad at God.'"

Macy listened intently. She could certainly relate to everything he was saying. She'd been praying most of her life to be a designer. She wanted God to change her father's mind, but felt like He'd ignored her.

She glanced over at LaRue.

"Yeah, he's talking about me this morning," she whispered.

"About the both of us."

"Let's take a look at James, chapter 4, verses 1 to 3. Hmmm . . . When you ask, you do not receive, because you ask with wrong motives, that you may spend what you get on your pleasures." Reverend Whitcomb paused to let his words sink in.

Macy couldn't find the scripture in her Bible. LaRue reached over and assisted her.

"When we have prayed for something and we have not received it . . . were we asking for something with the wrong motives? Did we ask for something, simply to gratify our lusts? Let's look at Psalm 66, verses 16 to 20. The Psalmist tells us that if he or she had cherished or clung to sin in his or her heart, the Lord would not have listened and heard the Psalmist's voice in prayer. We're starting to see a pattern here, are we not? Sin obstructs prayer. Our own selfish desires obstruct prayer."

His words fell upon Macy like a heavy cloak.

Forgive me, Father God, the words came from her heart. She could feel her eyes water and blinked rapidly.

"The good news is that our God is the God of love who loves sacrificially. God has a plan for our lives and that plan is a good plan. It is a plan for us to call on His name and be saved by grace through faith in Jesus Christ . . . so that we can begin the Christian journey . . . and start the process of being changed more and more into the image of Christ. And there is no greater plan in all the earth. There is no other plan that is filled with so much unselfish, unspoiled, pure, and holy love for each and every one of us . . . and God is not going to do anything to keep us from, or get in the way of, our ability to accept His offer of free salvation by making Jesus Christ the Lord of our lives."

LaRue reached over and took Macy's hand. With her free hand, Macy wiped away her tears.

"Before I sit down, church, I want to leave you with this. There is one prayer that we can know for sure . . . without a doubt, God will answer. If we come to God, honestly asking Him to forgive us of our sins, honestly repenting and turning away from our sins, honestly giving our lives to Him . . . honestly calling on the name of Jesus Christ . . . thanking Him for paying the penalty of our sins through His death on the Cross, and asking Him to give us eternal Life . . . which saves us from eternal hell and damnation . . . we will, without a doubt, be saved. That prayer will never go unanswered."

Before the service, when Reverend Whitcomb had opened the doors of the church, Macy had shocked not only LaRue, but herself as well by walking up to the front. Now, before the reverend could say another word, Macy whispered, "I want to be saved. I want eternal life with Jesus."

Reverend Witcomb heard her, then smiled and said, "Welcome home, daughter of the King."

On the way home, LaRue kept saying over and over, "I can't believe you joined the church. I can't believe it. You didn't even want to come this morning. Gurl, God is so good. He's worthy to be praised."

Frowning, Macy asked, "You're not going to start shouting in this cab, are you?"

LaRue gave a short laugh. "I'm so happy for you, Macy. This is the best decision you could've made for your life."

Macy glanced out the window of the taxi. "I think so, too. Maybe now my life will finally have some order." She glanced over at LaRue. "I just want peace of mind. I want some good things to happen for me."

"They already are. Look at you. You're working for that designer."

"*As his nanny.*"

"Why don't you show him some of your designs?" LaRue suggested.

"Because I'm not into getting my feelings hurt. They aren't any good."

"Macy, you designed the outfit you're wearing. Look how many compliments you received today at church. People are always asking you where you shop."

"I'm an amateur, LaRue. I'm not close to being a designer. Have you seen his stuff? River is magnificent."

"Then why not take some classes? It's what you really want to do."

Macy shrugged in resignation. "There's no point."

"Don't you think—"

She cut LaRue off by saying, "I don't really want to discuss it, okay?"

"Okay. But it's a shame to let such wonderful talent go to waste. When God gives you a talent, you should use it."

"Are you using the talent God gave you, LaRue?"

Macy was too caught up in her own thoughts to notice that LaRue didn't respond to her question. There was no way she would embarrass herself by showing her drawings to a man like River.

She had a better chance getting him to marry her.

LaRue

LaRue had dinner with Clyde Whitcomb.

"When you said you would meet me at the restaurant, I wasn't sure you'd actually show up."

She smiled. "I wouldn't do something like that. I'm pretty much straightforward, Reverend . . . I mean, Clyde."

"You look stunning. Red is a nice color for you."

"Thank you." LaRue took a sip of her water.

"So, are you a model as well?"

She nodded. "Just runway. I'm with a modeling troupe here in New York, and I take some classes."

"I'd love to see you on stage one day."

"Well, I do have a fashion show coming up in a couple of weeks. I would love to have you attend."

"I'll be there. Just tell me when and where."

Over dinner they lapsed into a conversation about the modeling industry.

"My parents aren't happy about what I'm doing. I hate that there's this distance between us, but right now, this is something I want to do."

"I couldn't believe it when you said your father is Larry Arnette. I'm a big fan of his."

LaRue smiled. "He is a man who definitely loves the Lord. When Tom died and I walked away from the church, my father cried. He did everything he could to get me to see that Tom was in a better place, and that God had healed him by taking him to heaven. I guess I was just too selfish to see it that way. I wanted Tom here with me."

Clyde nodded in understanding.

"When I moved here," LaRue said, "I started drinking—something I hadn't done since I was sixteen years old. But you know what? It just made me sick. I couldn't enjoy it. Finally, I just gave it up."

"Losing someone is hard."

LaRue agreed. "I guess I just couldn't quite figure out how to move on with my life."

"How are things going for you now?"

"Better. It's still hard to digest that I won't see Tom again. That he's no longer a part of my life, but I'm managing." LaRue's gaze met Clyde's. "I'm looking forward to seeing him in heaven."

"That's a healthy attitude, LaRue."

"I'm trying."

"That's all you can do. Just take it one day at a time."

"I always say that. It's hard to take your own advice." She picked up her fork. "I'm really glad we're having dinner. I look forward to getting to know you." LaRue wanted to reassure Clyde and put him at ease that she was ready to move forward with her life.

That evening when she went to bed, LaRue had a dream.

She and Clyde were dressed in robes and standing amidst the clouds. He took her hand and held it in his.

Sleeping, LaRue turned to her left side, a tiny smile tugging at her lips.

In the dream, Clyde was still holding on to LaRue's hand, but then prepared to hand it over. She and Clyde were standing before Jesus.

LaRue felt a warmth like none she'd ever known when Clyde placed her hand in Jesus' hand.

With a start, LaRue bolted upright in bed.

Patterson

She was thoroughly enjoying her first swimwear photo shoot on the elegant and extremely beautiful Nassau Island in the Bahamas. She knew from the moment she stepped off the plane and heard the Bahamian music drifting through the airport that this was going to be her most incredible modeling experience ever.

The island breezes and the sparkling waters of the Bahamas, combined with the glamour of the swimsuits, the hair, and the makeup, made Patterson feel beautiful.

For this photo shoot, Lyndon Swimwear set up the location camp on a very private, exclusive island, and, to Patterson, it was perfect. Beautiful stone walls, lava rocks, and water were everywhere, making the island the most beautiful place she had ever seen.

The routine for her swimwear shoot wasn't too different for Patterson. They got up early every morning to do hair and make-up in the hotel. Then they hopped into a boat that took them on a smooth ride as the sun began to rise.

The crystal-blue water was so clear you could see straight to the bottom, and the ride to the secret, private island was extraordinary.

The only regret was that she couldn't share this with LaRue and Macy. Or even Miller. Her parents would've loved coming to this island.

I wonder if Hawaii is anything like this.

On day one, Patterson went through a fitting. There were over five hundred different bikinis to try on for the editors of the catalog. Assistants took Polaroids of every look, and then the editors decided what she would wear in her photo shoots.

Patterson couldn't get over how much work actually went into choosing merchandise for a catalog.

Today they were photographing her in a new line of bikinis. Patterson had never worn one before, but fell in love with the way the tops fit her body. After lots of fittings, the stylists would choose the perfect bikinis for her and then test her with the right hair and make-up for the perfect shot.

When she got a break, Patterson called her mother.

"Hey, Mama. You ain't never gon' believe where I am right now."

"Where are you?"

"I'm in Nassau—in the Bahamas. Can you believe it?"

"Chile, what you doin' way down there?"

"I'm on a modelin' assignment. They just took a bunch of Polaroids of me. When I saw at the pictures, I got this real strange feeling lookin' at myself. It's like I can't really believe that person is me. I just doan see myself like that at all." Patterson lapsed into a discussion of all she'd done while on the island.

"Sounds like you havin' a good time."

"Mama, I am. This photo shoot has just been a dream. It's been absolutely wonderful. The people are really nice, too."

Patterson heard someone call her name. "Mama, I gotta go now. I'll call you later. I love you."

She hung up.

Patterson went back to work. In the beginning, she was a little uncomfortable wearing some of the skimpy swimwear, but kept focused on the fact that this was just a job.

She worked past her nervousness to bring out the feeling that the bikini gave her during the photo shoot. She accomplished this by the certain way that she looked into the camera, and by the way she positioned her body.

She intended to make the most of her budding modeling career.

Chapter 34

LaRue

"**R**everend Whitcomb is a real handsome man," Macy observed. "I think you two make a great couple."

LaRue dismissed Macy's comments with a wave of her hand. "I don't know about all that. He's just being nice and friendly. We've gone out twice so far, but it's just two friends enjoying each other's company. There's nothing romantic going on."

"I don't believe that for one minute. The good pastor is courting you," Macy insisted. "Reverend Whitcomb likes you a lot."

LaRue gave her a confused look. "How do you know this?"

"I can tell by the way he looks at you. I think you like him, too."

"Like I said. He's a nice man." LaRue's tone was noncommittal. "I really enjoy his teaching."

"And?" Macy prompted.

"And nothing. He's a nice man. There's nothing more to it."

Macy regarded LaRue from where she was sitting in the living room. "You're not the least bit attracted to him?"

LaRue could no longer deny her feelings. "I'm not gonna lie to you, Macy. I like him a lot. He was initially the reason I started going back to church in the first place. But now I realize it was more than that." She chuckled. "God knew exactly what it would take to bring me back to the fold."

"You think God brought you two together?"

"I do. I don't think it was a love match, though."

"Then why else would He do it?" Macy asked. "If not for love?"

"Because He wanted Clyde to bring me back to Him."

Macy was skeptical. "You really believe that?"

LaRue nodded. "I had a dream not too long ago. It was strange at first, but now I have a better understanding of it." She looked over at Macy. "Clyde and I were standing before Jesus. At first, it looked like we were about to be married. But then Clyde took my hand and placed it in Jesus' hand. I woke up after that."

"So, what's the problem? Maybe you two were getting married and Jesus was blessing it. I hope you're not planning to push him away."

"I'm not trying to push him away, Macy. I'm just taking some things slow. If I let myself get carried away, I could get hurt."

"I think I'd feel like I was tricked."

"I did initially," LaRue confessed. "But I know deep in my heart that God is not like that. See, I know Him through and through. I guess He just knew what I needed."

"A man?"

LaRue shook her head. "Hope. He knew that I needed to see the light at the end of the tunnel."

"I can understand that."

While LaRue did her laundry, Macy sat in one corner of her sofa and began sketching on a drawing pad, humming softly as she drew.

She was concentrating so heavily that she didn't hear LaRue's approach from behind.

"You really have a gift, Macy."

She looked up. "I can see it in my mind so clearly, but putting it on paper . . . it's just not really coming together." Macy released a frustrated sigh. "I have so much to learn. I can't do this."

"I've never known you to walk away from a fight."

"LaRue, I can't do this." Macy propelled herself off the sofa and headed to her room. "This is just a dream for me. A dream that won't ever come true."

"Just put it aside for a while, then go back to it," LaRue suggested.

"I think I will. I'm going to lie down and take a nap."

"I might be doing the same." LaRue pressed a hand to the side of her face. "I'm getting a bit of a headache myself. I don't need that right now. I'm meeting Roger and Victor for dinner later."

"Roger still hanging around you?"

"He's been seeing someone. Roger's moving on with his life. We're just friends."

Macy eyed LaRue. "So, it doesn't bother you?"

Shaking her head, she answered, "No. I'm really happy for him. He deserves to be with a woman who loves him as much as he loves her."

"You're a good woman, LaRue. I'm not that nice."

"Is that why you're trying your best to ruin Frederick's relationship with Charla?"

Macy gave her an innocent look. "I'm not doing anything like that. I swear."

Folding her arms across her chest, LaRue, with a point-blank stare, said, "I don't believe you."

"I don't want Frederick."

"And you don't want Charla to have him either."

Macy uttered a curse. "You think you know everything, don't you?"

"I do. And you owe me a quarter."

Patterson

An exhausted Patterson practically had to drag herself through the front door of her apartment. She sat her luggage in the hallway outside her bedroom.

She was so glad to be home. All Patterson wanted for the moment was a nice hot shower and the warmth of her bed.

The apartment was empty. For the first time ever, Patterson reveled in having the place to herself for a few hours.

Patterson felt better after her shower. She pulled down the covers and climbed into bed. She fell asleep almost instantly.

Somewhere hidden in the fog of her brain, Patterson heard a persistent ringing. In her dreamy state, she spun around slowly, trying to locate the source.

Patterson opened her eyes.

She'd been dreaming. Patterson shifted her position in bed and closed her eyes.

The ringing started again.

She debated whether or not to answer the phone. Patterson recognized Miller's cellular number, and picked up.

"Hello . . ."

"When did you get back into town?"

She stole a peek at the clock. "Almost three hours ago."

"Why didn't you call me?"

"Miller, I was tired. I came home and got into bed. I woke up when you called." Patterson rearranged her pillows with her free hand. She sat up, her back against the headboard. "I called you last night, but kept getting your voice mail."

"What do you have on?"

"My pajamas. Why?"

"Can I come over?"

Patterson ran her fingers through her hair. "I d-don't think that'll be a good idea. I'm exhausted and I just want to get some sleep."

"Are you home alone? I thought you wanted to talk to me."

"I still do," Patterson replied. "Can we do it tomorrow?"

"I can't spend a couple of hours with my lady?" His tone had become guarded.

Patterson struggled to keep the irritation out of her voice. "Fine. Why don't you meet me at my place?"

"I'll be there in half an hour."

"Miller, can you at least give me an hour, please? I am about to fall on my face—I'm so tired."

"Sorry. I just can't wait to see you."

"I just need an hour."

She hung up.

Patterson set the alarm and closed her eyes.

Six-thirty rolled around.

Patterson got up and showered. She slipped on a pair of shorts and a T-shirt. She sat in the living room, expecting Miller to show up at any moment. Patterson was more than ready to get this conversation over with. She had to find a way to make him understand her feelings regarding sex.

LaRue walked into the apartment.

Patterson got up and greeted her with a hug. "Hey. I missed you."

"When did you have time to miss me? Hanging out on the beach and living the glamorous life of a supermodel."

"Working hard is more like it. I was so tired, LaRue." Patterson stole a peek at the clock. "Miller's on his way over here. I need to have a long talk with him."

LaRue gave an understanding nod. "I'll stay in my room while he's here."

"You don't have to do that. I can talk to him in my room."

"It's not a good idea, Patterson. Especially with the . . . eh . . . the tension between you two. . . ."

"You're probably right. I—"

The sound of the doorbell ringing cut her off.

"That's probably Miller," LaRue announced. "I'll make myself a sandwich and get out of the way."

Patterson walked over to the door, opening it wide to admit Miller.

He greeted her with a long kiss.

She pulled away in embarrassment. Although LaRue was busy in the kitchen, Patterson had a feeling she hadn't missed the kiss.

"LaRue's in the kitchen," she whispered.

Miller waved at LaRue, who greeted him in a nonchalant manner.

He assessed her from head to toe. "I really missed you. You look good, though."

"I missed you, too. I did a lot of thinking while I was away."

"About me?"

"About us." Patterson decided to wait until LaRue went to her bedroom before she continued.

As soon as she heard her door close, she stated, "Miller, I want to talk about slowing down our relationship. I think we've been moving a little too fast."

"Baby, I act on pure emotion. I'm sorry if you think I'm rushing things. I'm crazy about you, girl."

"Miller, I'm practicing celibacy. I care a great deal for you as well, but as far as having sex with you—it's not going to happen."

"How are we supposed to just rein in our emotions, Patterson?"

"I'm a Christian. Having sex before marriage is wrong."

Miller burst into laughter. "Then all the Christians I know are going to hell."

"That has nothing to do with me."

He reached over and took her hand in his. "Sex is normal, Patterson."

"It was designed for people who are married, Miller. The Bible is very clear on this."

"Tell me something. Say you wait until marriage and then you find out that you two are not compatible sexually. What are you going to do?"

"I . . . I don't know. I can't believe tha—"

Miller interrupted her. "Wouldn't you prefer to be with someone who excites you and gives you pleasure?"

"Yeah, but . . ."

"Are you willing to take that risk, Patterson? God has too many other important things to deal with than your sex life. Why do you think He gives you choices? If He wanted to control every aspect of our lives, He wouldn't give us freedom of choice."

Miller leaned over and kissed her.

Patterson couldn't think clearly when his kisses conjured such trembling sensations through her body. She tried to pull away, but he tightened his hold on her. She moaned against his lips.

"You can't tell me that what you're feeling is wrong. What we have between us is not wrong, Patterson. We belong together and you know it."

"I doan know what's right anymore." Patterson ran her fingers across her lips. They were still tender from his ardent kisses. "God help me, I just doan know. I've never felt this way before."

"That should tell you something."

"It does, Miller," she admitted. "I'm just not sure what."

"Go with your feeling, baby."

Patterson closed her eyes and prayed. *Keep me strong, Lord,* she whispered in her heart.

LaRue

LaRue was on a mission.

She opened the refrigerator looking for something to eat. She heard a knock on the front door and went to answer it, saying, "Patterson, I didn't expect—"

"Who are you? Where's Macy?"

LaRue stared down at the woman standing at the door. "Macy's on her way home. She should be here shortly."

"Are you the housekeeper?" the woman inquired.

"I'm not," LaRue responded. "I live here. I'm Macy's roommate."

"Excuse me?"

"Macy and I are roommates. We have another roommate, too. Her name is Patterson."

"Macy is my daughter. She doesn't have any roommates."

"Mother, what are you doing here?" Macy exclaimed as she came through the door.

"I came by to see how you were doing. We hadn't heard from you in a while." Rhetta glanced over her shoulder. "Where did you find this person?" She whispered loud enough for LaRue to hear.

Clearing her throat noisily, LaRue said, "I'll leave you two alone."

Macy

She turned on her mother. "How dare you come in my apartment being rude like this. LaRue is my roommate, Mother. I have two roommates now."

"Macy, I really don't think this is a good idea." She glanced over her shoulder before continuing. "Do you even know these people? And for how long? This is no way to get back at your father and me. I just—"

Macy cut her off. "This is not about you. I'm not trying to get back at you or Father. I didn't want to lose my apartment. You two disowned me, remember?"

"We did no such thing," Rhetta shot back. "We were simply trying to help you become more responsible."

"That's what I'm doing, Mother. Learning to be more responsible."

"By letting strangers move into your apartment?"

"I had no choice. I had to find a way to pay the rent. It's not like you are still contributing or anything."

"Contributing," Rhetta repeated. "We were carrying the load for you, Macy. Your father and I paid all of your bills."

"I'm well aware of that. Besides, things have changed now. You and Father aren't helping me at all. Mind you, I'm liking it this way. I'm really on my own."

"I'm sorry you're still very angry about this, but it really is best this way, Macy. I must admit that while I'm not crazy about the idea of you having people like this LaRue staying in the apartment, I am glad to see that you're trying to act responsibly."

"I have a new job by the way," Macy announced.

Rhetta looked surprised. "Really? What are you doing?"

"I'm working for River Littleton."

"As his executive assistant? He's a wonderful man. I really like him. It's a shame about Whitney, though—losing her in the 9-11 tragedy . . ." Rhetta released a soft sigh. "Such a shame. I don't know why he allowed her to continue working in the first place. She certainly didn't need to."

Macy delighted in telling her, "I'm his nanny, Mother. I look out for his daughter Bethany."

Rhetta looked ashen. "You can't be serious."

"I am. I have no skills. There isn't much out there I can do."

"River Littleton's parents and I are good friends, Macy. We've known their family for years. How can you do this to me? I don't understand why he would hire you. Did you tell him you were our daughter?"

"He knows. I was the one who mailed the check to you for the Heart Foundation. He gave it to me when I applied for the job."

"How could you do this to me, Macy?" Rhetta asked a second time.

"I'm not doing anything to you, Mother. This is the best job I could get for now."

"I'll talk to your father. He'll find you something else to do at the company. I'll not have you embarrass us in front of our friends."

"I don't want Father to do anything for me. He's the one who started this turn of events. I'm fine where I am. As for embarrassing you . . . Mother, this has nothing to do with you and Father, so why should you be ashamed? Unless you're feeling guilty about something."

"I have no reason to feel guilty," Rhetta snapped.

"Then don't worry about what I'm doing. I want to pay my bills and will do whatever is necessary."

"I can see that. I'll just have a talk with River—make him understand that you are simply acting out."

Macy gasped in anger. "*Acting out?* Mother, I am not a child. You will do no such thing. River hired me and I intend to work for him." She walked briskly to the door and opened it. "I've got a lot to do. If you're done, I need to go take a shower and change. I'm going out to dinner with my roommates."

Rhetta eyed her daughter. "Rudeness isn't attractive, Macy." Picking up her purse, she added, "I'm sure you'll be hearing from your father. He's going to want to have a word with you."

"He knows how to reach me," Macy shot back. "I'm not going any-where."

Rhetta made her way to the front door. "We'll be in touch."

She left without so much as a backward glance.

"You can come on out now, LaRue," Macy called out. "Mother's gone."

LaRue walked out of her room. "You okay?"

Nodding, Macy responded, "I am. I think for the first time in a long while, I'm doing fine."

"Your mother didn't seem to like the idea of you having room-mates."

"She was only worried about how her friends would feel if they found out."

"Why would they care?"

"Because they're snobby. Mother doesn't want her friends to know that her daughter is nothing but a nanny for some rich guy. That would mortify her."

"How do you feel about it?"

"I love being with Bethany. She's a great kid."

"But how do you feel about being a nanny?"

Macy was quiet for a moment. Then she said, "LaRue, I never ever dreamed I'd be someone's nanny. I always thought I'd be the one hir-ing a nanny."

"It's honest work."

"I know and I like it. I really do. It's just that I'm a little embar-rassed by it as well."

"Macy, you should never be ashamed of anything you do."

"Maybe ashamed is too strong of a word. I'm just not real comfort-able with it yet."

"Then why don't you talk to River about a job with his company? You can learn the business."

"I've been so busy trying to get the man to fall in love with me, I've never thought of that."

"I know you don't believe it, but you *are* good at what you do."

"LaRue, you think so, but you're not a designer. River would take one look at my work and laugh me out of the building. Besides, I love that man. I don't want to mix business with my personal life. I'm willing to forget my own dreams for River. He's a wonderful person, a great father. I think it's a nice trade-off."

"Macy, don't sell yourself short. I don't know if you're aware of it, but you're becoming everything you despise about your mother. Think about it."

Chapter 35

LaRue

"Yes, I'm still doing fashion shows, Mom. I told you that I wasn't giving that up." LaRue itched to hang up the phone, but would never disrespect her mother like that.

"Does that preacher know what you do?"

"Yes, he does. He doesn't have a problem with it. Just you and Dad have issues."

"I can't believe he will allow you to continue doing stuff like that if he gets serious and wants to marry you."

"Mom, we are only going out every now and then—we're not dating, if that's what you're thinking."

"You told me that you like this man a lot."

"I do. But he may just want to be my friend."

"If you don't stop sashaying your half-dressed body across the stage, he's gonna keep you a friend."

LaRue groaned inwardly. "Mom, I need to go. I'll give you a call later on in the week. Tell Dad I said hello."

"Why won't you reach out to your father, LaRue? You always call when you know he's not home. This isn't fair to him."

"I don't want to fight with him."

"Then don't. Try talking to him," Ruby suggested. "He misses you so much, LaRue."

"I miss him, too. But Mom, I'm not gonna change my mind. I'm loving my life right now. It's been a long time since I was able to say that."

"I understand what you're saying. I just don't agree with it."

"Mom, it's not about you. This is my life and I intend to live it my way. Okay?"

LaRue hung up a few minutes later, feeling better than she had in a long time. But her heart was heavy when she thought of Clyde Whitcomb. She cared more about him than she would ever admit.

Macy

Standing in the hallway outside River's office, Macy pulled on the short skirt she was wearing. She wanted him to get a good look at her physical attributes, but she didn't want to make it blatantly obvious that she was trying to seduce him.

She pushed her conversation with LaRue right out of her mind. Macy vowed she was nothing like her mother.

River had decided to work from home, much to Macy's delight. She pranced around him like a butterfly, hoping he would strike up a conversation with her.

He continued working on his computer as if she didn't exist.

Initially, Macy thought River was simply pretending not to notice her, but when he didn't bother to acknowledge her at all, she changed her mind.

She avoided him for the rest of the day. Macy wasn't about to make a fool of herself. She'd been working for River now for almost two weeks. The only time she really saw him was right before he left for the office, or when he was coming home for the evening. He would either leave instructions for her, or inquire about Bethany's behavior, her homework, or recreational activities. It was obvious to Macy that River loved his daughter and was concerned about her well-being.

When Bethany arrived home from school, Macy was thrilled to see her. She'd had enough of folding the little girl's laundry. Thank goodness her housekeeping duties were light.

Macy prepared a sandwich and a glass of milk for Bethany. For herself, she decided to make a salad.

River joined them in the kitchen.

"Would you like a sandwich?" she asked. Macy was about to get up from the table.

River waved her back down. "I can do it. Don't worry about me." He made himself a sandwich and sat down with them at the table.

Macy watched in silence as father and daughter conversed. Her heart melted at the sound of his deep laughter. He was such a good father.

She helped the little girl with her homework.

"I'm taking Bethany to dinner tonight, so you're free to leave, Macy," River announced afterward.

"I'll see you tomorrow then."

He shook his head in the negative. "I won't be in until late. My mother will actually come by to relieve you tomorrow."

"I don't mind staying a little longer. Bethany and I will have a wonderful time together, won't we?"

"You're sure you don't mind? I probably won't be in until after midnight."

"That's fine," Macy grinned. "I'm your nanny. Use me."

He laughed. "Thank you, Macy."

"You're welcome."

"I'll have my driver take you home."

Gesturing toward the other room, Macy responded, "I'll get my things."

"Oh, before you go, I wanted to let you know that your mother called me this afternoon."

Macy felt like going through the floor—she was so humiliated. "She didn't."

"She wanted to inform me that you were over-qualified for the job as my nanny. She was concerned that you were wasting your time here."

"River, please ignore my mother. She's crazy."

"She's concerned, Macy. I know how you were raised. In the lap of luxury. I was brought up pretty much the same way. But to me, it gives you a false sense of security. Now, mind you, I like nice things—expensive toys, being able to travel when and where I want to go—I'm not complaining. I want to give all those things to Bethany, but I also want her to be grounded."

"You think I'm a pampered princess, don't you?"

River's smile made her weak in the knees. "I know you are. I also know that you're trying to prove something to your parents."

"Are you going to fire me?"

He shook his head no. "You're a grown woman."

River escorted Macy to the door. "Is that what you loved about Whitney? The fact that she was grounded—that she believed in working for whatever she wanted?"

"That was a major part of it."

Macy nodded in understanding. "Good night."

On the drive to her apartment, she vowed, "I'm going to marry you, River Littleton."

Two days later, Macy decided to try a different approach. She wanted to prove to River that she was nothing like the pampered princess he assumed she was.

"What are you doing?" Bethany questioned.

"I'm trying to clean the bathroom." Macy glanced around the room and sighed. "I hate cleaning."

"Nana says that you should wear gloves to keep your hands soft when cleaning."

"Is Nana your mother's mom?"

Bethany nodded. "Well, your Nana is absolutely right. Only your daddy doesn't seem to have any on hand."

"He doesn't use them."

"He should hire a maid," Macy mumbled.

"Huh?"

"Nothing, sweetie. Don't mind me. I'm just having a nervous break-down." She wiped her face with both hands.

Bethany sat down beside her. "I can help you, Macy. Nana and I clean the bathrooms sometimes. It's fun."

She looked at the little girl as if she'd lost her mind. "You think cleaning the bathroom is fun? Honey, we've got to get you out more."

Bethany giggled. "I like it. Nana and I like to clean, so we do it all the time. I even go to Nana's house and clean up. We always have a good time—me and Nana."

"I wish your Nana was here now. I could sure use her help."

"I can call her," Bethany offered.

"No, sweetie. You don't have to do that." *The first thing I intend to do as Mrs. River Littleton is hire a maid.*

Patterson

Patterson walked out of her building arm in arm with Miller. She slowed her pace when she spied the stretch limo waiting at the curb.

Her heart fluttered wildly in her breast. "Is this for us?"

Miller kissed her cheek. "Only the best for you, sweetheart." His voice was low and smooth.

As they neared the car, the driver got out and presented Patterson with a bouquet of red roses.

"What's going on? Why all this special treatment?"

"I want to make this night special for us."

Patterson gazed into his eyes, and tried to gauge his intentions. She wasn't sure if this was part of his seduction.

"I hope you heard everything I said to you," she said.

Miller wore a look of innocence.

Her defenses began to subside; Patterson relaxed and settled back against the heated leather. She peered out of the window. "Where are we going?"

"Just sit back and relax."

He seemed very pleased with himself. "Miller, why are you being so secretive?"

"It's all good," he murmured.

Fifteen minutes later, Patterson was escorted into the Helmsley Hotel on East Forty-second Street where Miller had reserved the Presidential Suite. The two-bedroom suite featured an elegantly appointed living room with breathtaking views of New York City.

The suite had been transformed into a romantic fantasy. Flowers and scented candles were everywhere. In the center of the room, a table had been dressed and set up for two. There was even champagne and chocolates.

"It's beautiful up here," Patterson murmured as she strolled around the room.

"We're having roast duckling with Grand Marnier sauce."

She glanced over her shoulder. "You're trying to seduce me."

Miller gave her a sexy grin. "Is it working?"

Patterson moved toward him. "Let's eat. I'm starving." She didn't miss the warning bells going off in her head. Her heart cautioned her to be on guard.

"Why are you so quiet?"

She looked up. "I was just thinking about the conversation we had. I meant what I said, Miller."

"I know that," he replied without inflection.

"Then why did you bring me here?"

"To have dinner. Patterson, I wanted to be alone with you."

"Why didn't we just go back to your place?" she asked softly, her eyes narrowing.

"Because my place isn't as nice." Miller laid down his fork. "Why the interrogation, Patterson? If you're uncomfortable, we can leave."

"I don't mean to sound ungrateful. I just wont to make sure we're on the same page, that's all."

"I wanted to bring you someplace nice, Patterson. If I could've closed down a restaurant for the evening, I would've done that. I don't have that kind of money." Miller got up from the table and walked over to the sofa. He picked up a small gift and brought it over to her. "I just wanted this night to be really special."

Tears filled Patterson's eyes when she opened her present. "It's stunning."

"Let me put it on you." Miller's voice was like silken oak.

Patterson allowed Miller to clasp the diamond tennis bracelet around her wrist, as tears of joy rolled down her cheeks.

"I love it." Taking Miller's face in her hands, she pulled him closer, studying the lean light-skinned face. "I love you," Patterson whispered.

"I love you, too. You are the best thing to ever happen to me, Patterson."

She waited until her quickened pulse had quieted before she spoke. "Our dinner's getting cold. We should eat." It was too easy to get lost in the way Miller looked at her.

Macy

Macy took her time getting to the restaurant where she was scheduled to meet her parents for dinner. They had already been seated by the time she arrived.

The mâitre d' led her over to where they were sitting.

"Why did you want to see me?" Her question held a note of impatience.

Maynard gestured for Macy to sit down. "Your mother tells me you've acquired a couple of roommates."

She detected a hint of censure in his tone and didn't make a move. Macy had a feeling she would not be staying long. "Yes, I have."

"What do you know about these two women?"

"They pay their bills on time. They are great cooks and they go to church." Macy paused a second before saying, "And they're my friends. What else do I need to know?"

"Where did you meet them?"

"At an open call. What does it matter?" She stood with both hands on her hips. "This has nothing to do with you and Mother." Macy clenched her mouth tighter.

"Macy, lower your voice," Maynard stated. He glanced around the restaurant to see if anyone was paying attention. "Sit down. People are staring."

The corner of his mouth twisted with exasperation. "Please, take a seat."

This time Macy did as she was told.

"Order anything you like."

"I'm not hungry, Father."

They stared at each other across a sudden ringing silence.

Rhetta finally spoke up. "I've found you an apartment. One you can afford. It's not as big, but I'm sure you'll love it. It's not too far from us."

Macy smiled smoothly, betraying nothing of her annoyance. "I don't need another apartment. *I already have one.*" She made a move to get up. "I don't need this. . . ."

"Hear us out, Macy," her father implored.

The waitress arrived to take their drink orders.

After the waitress left, Macy said, "I'm not selling my apartment just because you don't like the idea of my having roommates."

The waitress returned with their drinks, and after setting them on the table, she took their meal selections.

"I'd like the veal," Rhetta stated.

Macy ordered a spinach salad. Her father gave his order last.

When they were alone, her mother said, "Macy, a nanny is along the same lines as being a maid. We didn't raise you to be a maid or a nanny."

"What's wrong with being a nanny, Mother? It's an honest living. A job shouldn't define who you are as a person. If it did, I guess one might consider you a bum."

"Excuse me?"

"You don't have a job—you've never held a job. All you do is live off of Father. See, when you say it that way, it sounds disgusting, doesn't it? You need to stop looking down your nose at other people."

"Macy, don't be rude to your mother."

"It's the truth."

"Why shouldn't I want more for my daughter?" Rhetta questioned.

"This is not about what you want, Mother. And, speaking of which, I really don't appreciate your going behind my back and calling River. It didn't work by the way. He considers me an adult."

"I didn't go behind your back. I told you I would be calling to talk some sense into the man."

From lowered lids, Macy shot a commanding look at Rhetta. "Stay out of my business, Mother."

Rhetta's smile did not indicate compliance.

"I mean it. Stay out of my affairs. You and Father want me to make it on my own. Leave me alone then." Macy pushed away from the table. "I've lost what little appetite I had."

"Macy . . ."

She kept walking. There was no point in trying to talk to her parents. They wouldn't listen.

Chapter 36

LaRue

She had just gone to bed when Patterson knocked on her door. She stuck her head inside. "Were you sleeping?"

LaRue shook her head. "No, I was just about to, though. Is something wrong?"

"Can we talk for a little while? I could really use some advice."

She saw the troubled expression on Patterson's face. "Sure. Come in."

She moved over to allow Patterson to sit beside her. "Okay, what's going on with Miller?"

Patterson regarded LaRue with amusement. "How did you know this had to do with him?"

Her smile curved in tenderness. "I'm a woman, Patterson." LaRue pointed to the gleaming tennis bracelet. "Very nice."

"Miller gave it to me last night." Patterson fingered the bracelet and announced, "LaRue, I'm falling in love with him."

Patterson's confession troubled her. LaRue decided not to counsel her friend. This was not the time, but she prayed Patterson would find out the truth about Miller. "How does he feel?"

"He told me that he loved me, too. This is the first time he's ever said it. LaRue, he made me feel so special tonight. Miller booked the Presidential Suite for us. So that we could have an evening alone."

"Did you . . ."

Patterson shook her head. "No. Nothing happened between us. I'm sure he wanted it to, but I made it clear from the beginning that we weren't going there."

LaRue was relieved. "Let me ask you something. Do you know if Miller is a Christian?"

"We've never really talked about his relationship with Christ."

"Don't you think you should?"

"I know you're right, LaRue. It's just that when we're together . . . well, the subject just doesn't ever come up."

"I understand. I really do." LaRue couldn't hold her tongue. "Patterson, you're gonna have to be careful around that man. I don't want to see you get hurt."

"Miller has been very sweet to me, LaRue. Girl, he's everything I ever dreamed about. I have a feeling that he's my Mr. Right. So stop worrying, Mama Hen. I hate to see you fretting so much."

Sighing in resignation, LaRue responded, "Well, for your sake, I hope you're right. I know men like him, Patterson," she said with quiet emphasis. "I've been burned by people like Miller. They prey on your innocence."

"I thought Tom was the only love in your life."

"He was my only love." She gave Patterson a wry smile. "I wasn't always saved. Tom and I broke up for about two years when I was in high school. I started seeing this other guy and I got pregnant. My baby was stillborn."

"How old were you?"

"Sixteen."

"What happened to the guy? Was he there for you?"

LaRue shook her head. "He disappeared before I could tell him that I was pregnant. The one person I thought would turn his back on me . . . didn't. Tom was so hurt when he found out that I was pregnant, but he stuck by me from the beginning to the end. I think that's when I fell in love with him."

"I don't think Miller's like that at all. He's been totally honest with me."

"How can you be so sure? Patterson, you can tell me it's none of my business, but I have to ask. Has he been trying to get you into bed, telling you that it's an expression of his love for you."

"Yeah, but then every boyfriend I've ever had tried to do that."

"Just be careful, Patterson."

"I will," she promised. Getting up off the bed, Patterson said, "I'm gonna let you go to sleep now. Thanks for listening."

She made her way to the door. "Good night, LaRue."

LaRue relived the pain she went through all those years ago. Losing her virginity in the backseat of a car, followed by her becoming pregnant, had been stressful.

It still amazed her how Tom stuck by her side during that time. Although she felt bad that Tom had not been her first, LaRue knew he never held it against her.

There were days LaRue felt she couldn't go on. It was only the love and support of her parents that kept her from suffering a nervous breakdown. She was too young. LaRue had not been mature enough to handle her growing sexuality and impending motherhood. It was after that, that she gave her life to the Lord.

Now, years later, LaRue wondered if she would ever have another child. Although she hadn't been ready for motherhood, she loved her baby son and grieved for him still.

A hot tear slid down her cheek.

Patterson

She understood it now.

Patterson had often wondered at the reason behind the sadness in LaRue's eyes. She'd assumed it was mostly due to losing her husband, but Patterson always felt that it ran much deeper.

Her heart felt heavy at stirring up LaRue's painful past. Now she understood fully why Miller bothered her roommate so much.

Miller's not like that, though. He would never do something like that to me. He loves me. A smile tugged at her lips. *Miller loves me.*

But even with that belief, Patterson couldn't shake the uneasy feeling that threatened her peace of mind.

Macy

"The way to a man's heart is through his stomach."

Macy could still hear her grandmother saying those words to her—during one of those summer-long visits to Boston. She loved her grandparents a lot but hated spending her vacations in their modest little house, while her parents were off to Europe or some exotic island. Her father had offered many times to buy them another house, but they refused. It was a matter of pride, he told her.

It wasn't until she was fifteen that they allowed her to travel with them for part of the summer. The other part was spent with her grandparents.

Her grandmother loved to cook and often tried to teach Macy, but she wasn't interested.

"Grandmother, I don't need to learn how to cook. I'm going to be like my mother and hire someone like Martha to cook for me."

Her grandmother had chuckled before replying, "Honey, that's fine if you want to hire someone, but it may be wise to learn nonetheless. Your mother may not cook, but she does know how. That's how she got my Maynard to marry her."

Macy had been floored by that news. She couldn't ever recall seeing her mother doing anything else in the kitchen, other than supervising the planning of menus. When she'd asked her mother about it, her mother admitted to knowing how to cook, but insisted, "I don't believe in doing anything I can pay someone else to do."

From that day on, that response had become Macy's motto as well. Until now.

Macy knew that River considered her another shallow rich brat, and she wanted to change his opinion of her. She'd tried everything to get him interested in her, but nothing worked so far. This was a last resort.

She got up off the chaise and strode out of her room. Macy found Patterson in LaRue's bedroom. They were sitting on her bed eating potato chips and talking.

Knocking softly on the open door, she asked, "Can I come in?"

"Sure," LaRue answered. "Anytime the door's open, just walk on in."

Macy took a deep breath and said, "I have a favor to ask of you two."

"What is it?" Patterson questioned between bites.

"I want to learn how to cook."

LaRue almost choked on her sandwich. "What did you say?"

"You heard me. I want to learn how to cook. I want to make a special dinner for River and Bethany."

"Why?" LaRue wanted to know. "Did you tell River that you knew how to cook?"

"No . . . well, I kind of said that I could cook a little. He hasn't asked me to do it, he just gave me a look that clearly indicated he didn't believe me. I want to prove him wrong."

"But Macy, you can't cook. River's right."

"I know that, Patterson. He doesn't know it, and I don't want him to. Are you going to help me or not?"

Patterson glanced over at LaRue who responded, "I don't mind. When do you want to start?"

Satisfied, Macy grinned. "Can we start right away? I don't have a lot of time to waste. I want to make this dinner soon."

"Soon? Why are you in such a hurry?"

"No special reason, LaRue. I'm just real excited about this and ready to get started. That's all."

"The first thing you have to do is get some paper and a pen," Patterson stated. "So you can take notes."

"I don't need to take notes. I've got a memory like an elephant."

"It's a lot to remember."

"Patterson, I'm not going to let you discourage me. Now come on and let's get started."

"What are you planning to cook?"

"I don't know. I hadn't really thought about it."

"You need to plan your menu," LaRue interjected. "We may have to run out to the store."

"Oh," Macy mumbled. "Okay. How about fried chicken, some buttermilk biscuits, macaroni and cheese . . . what else should I have?"

"What about some mixed vegetables?"

"That sounds good. And I think I'll just have some rolls instead of the biscuits. They might be too country for River. No offense intended, Patterson."

"None taken."

"Do we have any chicken in the refrigerator?" Macy asked.

"No. You need to make a shopping list." LaRue climbed off the bed. "When do you plan on cooking this dinner?"

"Monday. But I want to practice cooking it here first. You guys in the mood for some Southern fried chicken?"

"Let me make sure I'm understanding this. You want to practice cooking this meal on us before you cook it again on Monday." When Macy nodded, LaRue continued, "Why not cook your meal here on Sunday and just take it over to the Littleton house with you?"

"Because he won't believe I cooked it by myself. I want him to see the evidence in the kitchen."

Laughing, LaRue shook her head. "Gurlfriend, you something else."

"This is very important to me."

"I know. We sure haven't been able to get you into the kitchen for anything other than eating."

"I do the dishes."

"You put them into the dishwasher. Yes, we know, Macy."

"LaRue, will you stop giving me such a hard time? I really like River and it's important that I try and change his opinion of me."

"Are you in love with this guy?" Patterson inquired.

"I've loved River for as long as I can remember. He's a wonderful man." Macy smiled. "So, you see? You have to help me. I won't ask for anything else."

"Before we take this any further—"

"Aww, LaRue," Macy interrupted. "Come on."

"No. I just want to make sure you care for this man and are not just after his bank account. I won't help you if you're just trying to take advantage of him."

"Macy wouldn't do that," Patterson defended. "She's not that kind of person."

"Get real. She tried to take advantage of us. The only reason she let us move in here was because she needed help paying her bills. If her parents hadn't cut off her money, we wouldn't be here."

"She didn't mislead us about that, LaRue. Macy told us the truth."

"Fine. Whatever."

"LaRue, you're right. I wasn't exactly forthright in the very beginning, and I admit that I initially planned to evict you if my parents had changed their minds. Since then I've gotten to know you and Patterson and I have no regrets. I like having you two as roommates. I really do."

"We like being here, Macy. Don't we, LaRue?"

"Yeah."

"As for River, it's him that I want. Not his money. I love Bethany as if she were my own daughter. I would never do anything that could potentially hurt her. She doesn't deserve that."

"So will you help me with the cooking?"

LaRue nodded. "You still need pen and paper to make the shopping list."

Macy surprised them both by hugging each of them.

Patterson

Macy held out a strange-looking object. "This is called a what?"

Patterson burst into laughter. "It's a whisk."

"How is the lesson going?" LaRue asked as she entered the kitchen.

"It's gon' be okay," Patterson responded. "Macy's doin' fine. She's just really nervous."

"I want this dinner to be perfect, that's all."

"You can't go wrong with honey-barbecue chicken. It's easier than having you fry chicken."

"Making the baked beans wasn't hard at all. Just some sugar and barbecue sauce. I can remember that with no problem."

"Macy, I really think you should write some of this stuff down. You're not gon' remember the measurements—"

"I have a photographic memory."

"Since when?" LaRue asked.

"Must you be so negative?"

"I'm not being negative, Macy. Just realistic."

"If you're not here to help, then go watch some television or something."

"I said I would help and I will." LaRue rolled up her sleeves and washed her hands in the kitchen sink.

Chapter 37

LaRue

"Macy, for your first time, you did a fantastic job. This chicken is delicious."

"Wow, coming from you, LaRue, that's a huge compliment."

Patterson wiped her mouth with her napkin. "I had fun today, cookin' with you and LaRue."

Macy laughed. "Patterson, only you can find true enjoyment in cooking with your roomies."

"I'm serious. It reminded me of how my mother and grandmother would get together in the kitchen on Saturdays to cook Sunday dinner."

Macy gave her a puzzled look. "They cooked *Sunday* dinner on Saturday?"

"Yeah. The Bible speaks of Sunday being the Lord's Day. A day of rest. Well, my family took it seriously. They would cook on Saturday and after church on Sunday we'd come home and just heat everythin' up."

Patterson picked up her knife and began slicing off a piece of chicken. "I liked those times we spent in the kitchen. They would let me cut up the potatoes for the potato salad, or I'd clean and cut up the greens. We'd be in there laughin' and talkin' 'bout everything.

When I turned twelve, Nana and Mama let me do all the bakin'. We always had dessert on Sunday, so I would always try to make something different."

"That's why you're such a good baker." LaRue took a sip of her tea.

"I love makin' cakes and cookies. Pies are okay, but I don't like making them as much."

Macy glanced up from her plate. "It sounds like you have some wonderful memories."

"I do. When Nana died, it took a while before Mama and me could cook a complete meal without burstin' into tears."

"Your grandmother lived with you?" Macy asked between bites of food.

Patterson nodded. "Nana lived with us even before I was born. Daddy told me that when Mama was carrying me, his parents' house burned down, killing my granddaddy. He moved Nana in with us. She stayed until her death one month after I graduated from college."

"Are your maternal grandparents still alive, Macy?"

She shook her head no. "My grandfather died when I was five or six. My grandmother died when I was in high school. I didn't see much of her. She was in a nursing home." Macy stared at her water glass. "I wanted to see her, but Mother said it depressed her going to places like that. I asked her once if she'd consider bringing grandmother to live with us. She said no."

"Did she tell you why?" LaRue asked.

"She said that she'd done her job by providing her mother with the best care money could provide."

They were silent for a moment. Macy continued.

"I listen to you and Patterson talk about your childhoods. It sometimes amazes me how happy you two were. I grew up surrounded by luxury—everything money could buy. Don't get me wrong, I was happy. But . . . I don't know. I just feel like our lives were so different. I grew up in the church like the two of you. I grew up with two parents who say they love each other. The only real difference I see is that my family has more money."

"Maybe the real difference is that you talk about being a Christian as if it's a fashion statement. It's not that you're a bad person or anything, and I'm not saying that."

"What *are* you saying?"

"I think that true happiness can only be found in God. When you have a relationship with the Lord, it shows. You know how people talk about lovers glowing . . . well, this is the same thing. You glow when you love God and live life according to His word."

"I love God," Macy insisted. "I do."

"I don't think that's what LaRue is saying, Macy. She's not saying you don't love God."

"Look, I know that I haven't lived the life of a saint. But my heart is good. I give to charities and I go to church."

"Being a Christian is more than that, Macy," LaRue stated.

"Then what am I doing wrong?"

"I wouldn't say you're doing anything wrong." LaRue paused a second before continuing. "I guess being Christian means that you've realized that you are a sinner, first of all. In the story of the prodigal son, the scripture says that he *came to himself* and decided to go back to his father and offer himself as a hired servant. When he left home, he left with a *give me* attitude and when he returned to his father, he came back with a *make me* attitude."

"What LaRue is saying is that a true Christian is willing to repent or willing to accept that he has failed, and the only way he can get out of the fallen state that he is in is through Christ Jesus. A Christian admits that God's Word is right."

"Patterson's right. A Christian knows that he is a sinner and that God loved him so much that He gave the world His only begotten Son. My father used to say that a Christian knows there is a God. A lost man may think there is a God, but only a Christian knows God."

Macy nodded in understanding. "I want to be better. I think my life would be so much better if I had God. I want peace—it's something that has eluded me for a while now." Her voice broke.

When Patterson realized that Macy was crying, she got up and walked around the table to embrace her. "God loves you, Macy. You know that, doan you?"

"I know. It's just that sometimes I wonder if I'm praying right or saying the right things to Him. I don't know how to go to Him."

"You talk to Him the same way you are talking to us."

"LaRue, how do I know if I'm really saved?"

"If you've asked him to come into your heart, and you have received him as Lord, and you intend to allow him to be the controlling center of your life from here on, I can tell you on the authority of the Word of God, that you have been saved, Macy. God has already begun the new life that will change you from the inside out, and you will never again be the same person."

Patterson clapped her hands with glee. "I think we should say a prayer."

LaRue got up and came around the table to join them. They stood in a circle holding hands.

"Our Father, we give grateful thanks for these clear words from Paul. We know how he himself struggled and sought to establish his own righteousness, and tried hard, Lord, to be acceptable before you in his own strength, and he, too, failed, until there came that wonderful day on the Damascus road when he met Jesus and he was changed into a new creature in Christ. We lift your child Macy up this evening. She has opened her heart to Jesus, made him Lord in her life, realized that He was the one who had died for her and made possible the blessings of the glory of God in her life. Lord, we thank you for bringin' us together. Now we pray that we may serve you together. We thank you in Jesus' name. Amen."

When Patterson opened her eyes, tears rolled down her cheeks. She wiped them away with the back of her hand. "This is such a blessing. You and LaRue are blessings to me. I want you to know that."

"Enough of the waterworks," LaRue complained. "I don't want to start crying, too."

Macy reached out and embraced LaRue. She hugged Patterson next. Wiping her face with her napkin, she said, "Thank you for being in my life. I don't know what I'd do without you."

That evening when Patterson went to bed, she was happy. She believed that she and her roommates had been brought together for what happened earlier. She was thrilled for Macy and vowed to do her part in nurturing her as she began her new life in Christ. She made a mental note to purchase a nice study Bible for Macy.

"Might as well get one for myself, too," Patterson murmured sleepily.

Macy

"My parents have invited us over for Thanksgiving dinner," Macy announced when she got off the phone. "Please say you'll go with me. I don't want to deal with them by myself."

"They're not that bad, are they?"

"Patterson, my mother gets on my nerves. She doesn't really mean to—she just does. Our relationship is different from the one you have with your mother. We're not close at all. Sometimes I think we just tolerate each other."

"Have you tried to talk to her, Macy?"

"There's no talking to her. Mother doesn't want to hear anything I have to say. I have to run it by my father first. It's like she doesn't have a mind of her own. I can ask her for something, and she'll tell me to speak to Father."

The telephone rang.

Macy answered. When she hung up, she said, "Miller's on his way up."

"Hmmm. I wonder what he's doing here," Patterson murmured. "I wasn't expecting him. How do I look?"

Macy eyed her from head to toe. "You look fine."

LaRue remained silent, but Macy could tell that she wasn't thrilled about Miller's surprise visit.

"I'm going to redo my hair," Patterson said as she rushed out of the room.

"He must care about her, LaRue. Miller's still coming around and nothing's happened between them."

"Men like him don't give up that easily."

"I've known a few dogs myself and usually when they find out that they won't be getting any, they do a disappearing act afterward."

"They also disappear after getting what they want."

"LaRue, come on," Macy began. "Have a little more faith."

"Okay. I have faith that Patterson is going to come to her senses *soon.*" It was her fervent prayer. LaRue couldn't shake the feeling, no matter how hard she tried, that Patterson was going to be hurt.

It was none of her business, as Macy constantly reminded her, but try as she might, LaRue just couldn't find much to like about Miller. She was very careful to keep her feelings private. There was no point in upsetting Patterson.

"Patterson will be fine," Macy reassured her. "I have a good feeling about her and Miller."

"I wish I did."

The sound of the doorbell ringing put an end to their conversation.

"I'll get that," Macy stated as she left the kitchen.

Sighing in resignation, LaRue sought out the comfort of her bedroom. She decided to work on a couple of reports while Miller was visiting with Patterson.

Hopefully he won't be here long. I don't want to be locked up in my room all day. LaRue didn't want to see him. She couldn't stand the smug expression he always wore.

Patterson

Miller was seated in the living room when Patterson walked in.

"Hey you," she greeted. "This is a nice surprise. I didn't expect to see you today."

He stood up and presented her with flowers. "These are for you, beautiful." Embracing her, Miller kissed her.

"The flowers are beautiful, Miller. Thank you so much." She inhaled the fragrant scent of the mixed bouquet.

Patterson took the flowers to the kitchen and placed them in a vase. She left them for the time being on the kitchen counter.

Miller was seated again on the sofa. She joined him there.

"I've never gotten so many flowers. Thank you for being so thoughtful."

"I know how much you love them." He reached out and took her hand in his. "The reason I stopped by is because I have an idea. Why don't we go away this weekend? I know the perfect place for us." Miller kissed her gently on the lips. "Someplace very romantic."

"It sounds nice, Miller, but I can't go."

"Why not? If you're worried about the sleeping arrangements, you don't have to be. I'll get a two-bedroom suite. Just like the one we had at the Helmsley Hotel."

"Miller, I want to tell you something." Patterson took a deep breath. "I'm a virgin. But it's more than that. When I gave my life to Christ at the age of twelve, I made a promise to abstain from sex until marriage. I mean to honor that vow."

"I see."

"You do understand, don't you?"

"What I understand is that I love you very much and I want to spend the rest of my life with you, Patterson. What I need you to understand is that I can't even consider marrying you until I know that we're compatible in every way."

"Compatible in every way? What exactly does that mean?"

"I think you know. Honey, I have to know that we can please each other sexually. I'm sure you wouldn't want to be with someone who doesn't turn you on."

"I don't think that's a problem we'll have, Miller."

"Not that part, but we don't know about the other. Me, I have to know what I'm getting."

"I trust that if we wait and do this the right way, God will honor that and make us compatible."

"I don't share that kind of faith. Sorry."

Patterson drew a deep breath before asking the one question she should've asked a long time ago. "Are you a Christian, Miller?"

"Yeah, I am."

"But you don't want to honor God's Word?"

"Patterson, let's be real. We are human and prone to mistakes. God knew this. He knows that we are going to fall."

"So we should do this willingly?"

"You're going to sit here and tell me that you've never done anything wrong, Patterson?"

She shook her head. "I'm not saying that."

"That's what it sounds like to me. I'm just being honest. I have needs and there are times I act on them. I'm not a ho or anything. I'm a one-woman man."

"Miller, I love you deeply. I just want to wait. I hope you can handle that."

He kissed her again. "I love you so much, Patterson. I don't know if I can hold out. I just want you so much. A love like ours—how can making love be wrong?"

"I don't know."

"It's not wrong, baby. It's not. You know how I know?"

"How?"

"*Because you're the one for me, Patterson.* I know I want you in my life forever."

Is he going to propose? Patterson stirred uneasily.

Miller's steady gaze bore into her in silent expectation.

The idea of marriage to Miller sent her spirits soaring.

"What are you thinking about, baby?"

"Miller, are you talking about marriage?"

He nodded. "I can see marriage and children in my future. Soon."

His words wrapped around her like a warm blanket.

"Baby, there's only one thing standing between us. You know what that is."

Patterson nodded. "Sex."

"Making love," Miller corrected. "I don't believe in divorce. That's why I *have* to know that we are compatible in that way."

It made sense to Patterson, but deep down her heart kept telling her to stay strong.

"I've got to get back to work." Miller stood up. "Think about everything I've said and give me a call, okay?"

"Wait." Patterson rose to her full height. "This weekend . . . is it just about getting me into bed?"

"No. I told you we could have separate bedrooms. Baby, I'm not saying we have to make love this particular weekend. I'm just letting you know that before I can even ask you to be my wife, I have to know that we're a perfect fit." Miller gave her a tender smile. "I hope I'm not putting pressure on you. I don't mean to. I'm just being honest. You have to have honesty in a relationship."

"I agree." Patterson escorted Miller to the door. "I'll go. Make the arrangements, but get a two-bedroom suite."

He pulled her into his embrace. "I love you."

"I love you, too," she whispered against his lips.

With Miller gone, Patterson stood at one of the oversized windows, admiring the stunning skyline. Her heart sang with delight over the knowledge that Miller wanted to marry her. Only one thing kept that dream from coming true.

She stole a glance over her shoulder when LaRue entered the room.

"It's beautiful out there," she murmured when LaRue joined her at the window.

"It sure is."

"Miller asked me to go away with him for a weekend."

LaRue glanced over at her. "What did you tell him?"

"That I'd go."

"Oh."

They stood staring out the window in silence.

LaRue finally turned and strode to the kitchen. She began pulling pots out in preparation to cook.

Macy walked out of her room. She glanced around. "Where's Miller?"

"He left. He had to get back to work."

"On a Saturday?"

Patterson nodded. "He travels quite a bit, so he usually works at least one Saturday a month."

Macy stole a peek into the kitchen. "What's up with LaRue?" she whispered. "She's so quiet."

"I think she's upset with me."

"Why?"

Patterson gestured for Macy to follow her to her bedroom. Once there, she told her, "Miller wants me to go away with him for one weekend."

"That's wonderful, right?"

"I think so."

"Are you planning to go?"

Patterson nodded. "He's getting a two-bedroom suite for us. I've already made it clear that we won't be having sex."

"It's your business—whatever you do. You don't have to justify your actions to anyone. You're grown."

"I don't want LaRue thinking bad of me."

"She won't. LaRue is a woman. She's been there. She understands what it's like to be in love. Patterson, take it from me. You have to grab hold of any piece of happiness you can get. Life is way too short."

LaRue

While Macy and Patterson chattered during dinner, LaRue pretended to be interested in the food on her plate.

She kept telling herself that she had no right to be upset—that Patterson's going away with Miller had nothing to do with her. That it was none of her business. That she shouldn't take it personally.

"Why so quiet, LaRue?" Macy asked.

"Just got a lot on my mind."

"I hope you're not mad with me."

LaRue eyed Patterson. "I'm not mad with you. I won't lie and say that I'm thrilled either. I just hope you know what you're doing."

"Nothing sexual is gon' happen. I've already made that clear to Miller."

Smiling, LaRue said, "Well, I hope you have a wonderful time."

Later that evening, Macy stole into LaRue's bedroom. "You did good, girl. Don't worry. Patterson's a smart girl. And she's strong. We'll just keep her lifted in prayer, okay?"

Chapter 38

Macy

Bethany peered over the kitchen countertop. "What are you doing to that chicken? It looks kind of funny."

Children are so honest. Putting on a smile, Macy said, "Bethany, honey, why don't you go watch some television."

"I want to help you cook. Why can't I help?"

"Because . . . because I'm not sure I know what I'm doing, sweetheart."

"Do you even know how to cook?"

"I've had a few lessons."

"You sure you don't need my help?"

"I think I'd better handle this on my own. Thanks for being such a sweetie and offering to help. I really appreciate it." Macy reached for the telephone. She tried to reach Patterson first at home, then by cellular. She muttered a curse and hung up without leaving a message.

Macy tried LaRue at the school. When she got voice mail, Macy hung up. "I'm on my own."

She should have written down the ingredients, she decided. But it had seemed so simple at the time. Macy didn't count on forgetting, or having to estimate the measurements.

When River arrived home an hour later, Bethany met him at the door. Macy could hear them talking and laughing.

He stuck his head inside the kitchen. "Bethany tells me you've cooked us a wonderful dinner."

"I hope you like it."

"I'm sure we will. I'm going to wash up, and I'll be down in a second."

Surveying the food, Macy felt like crying.

The rolls were rock hard, the barbecue chicken was funny-looking, and the macaroni was burned in spots. The meal was ruined.

She blinked rapidly to keep the tears from rolling down her cheeks.

Bethany rushed into the room. She eyed Macy for a moment. "What's wrong? Why do you look so sad?"

"Dinner is ruined," she murmured.

Bethany glanced over at the food. "It doesn't look that bad, Macy. It smells okay."

She smiled at the little girl. "You are such a sweetie. Come here. . . ." Macy bent over to embrace Bethany. "I love you so much."

"I love you, too." Bethany wiped away Macy's tears. "Don't let Daddy see you crying. It'll make him sad."

"I won't." She went into the powder room and repaired her make-up.

Over dinner, Macy watched River's face for signs of disappointment when he saw the pitiful display of foods. Only the broccoli seemed appealing, even to her.

He surprised her by spooning up some of the macaroni. River placed a sample of each entrée on both his and Bethany's plates.

Macy stopped him. "You know what? Let's not put ourselves through this. How about pizza?"

Bethany cheered.

"Pizza it is," Macy announced with a laugh. Rising up, she said, "I'll call and order it now."

Later that evening, River pulled Macy to the side. "I appreciate what you tried to do tonight."

"It was horrible. I really wanted to make you a nice dinner."

"There will be other opportunities. And for future reference, I keep the cookbooks in here. I remember my first attempts at cooking. Now *they* were horrific."

"But you're a wonderful cook, River."

"It's taken lots of practice, I assure you."

"You're so good at everything you do. I wish I could be like that."

River met her gaze. "You're very good at what you do, Macy. Very good."

Macy wanted to ask him to elaborate, but Bethany came bouncing into the room, wanting her to read a bedtime story.

"Macy's getting ready to go home, sweetie. Why don't you let me read you the story?"

"No, I want Macy," Bethany whined.

Macy gave River a smile, then took Bethany by the hand. "Just one, okay?"

River's gaze followed her up the stairs.

Patterson and LaRue were waiting for Macy when she arrived home.

As soon as she walked into the apartment, they battered her with questions.

"How did your dinner go?"

"Did you do what I told you to do?" LaRue questioned. "Did—"

Macy held up her hand to stop them. "Hold up. One at a time, please. First, Patterson, you were right—I should've written every-thing down. Things didn't go very well. I messed up everything."

"What happened?"

Macy told them how the evening went. They were laughing by the end of her story.

"It actually ended better than I thought. River showed me where he kept his cookbooks. He even told me his cooking horror stories." Smil-ing, Macy added, "It was nice. I felt like we really bonded tonight."

Patterson

Miller and Patterson drove two hours upstate to the Catskill Moun-tains.

"I heard one of the partners talking about this place," Miller said as they pulled onto a rustic forty-acre estate. "According to him, they have the best hiking trails in the Catskills Forest Preserve. There are golf courses, open and covered tennis courts, riding stables, biking trails. If you like skiing and skating—"

"I've never done any of those things, except ridin' horses. I can do that."

"What types of things do you like to do?"

"I enjoy swimming. I love the beach."

"I reserved Cedar Cottage for us. It has two bedrooms, a Jacuzzi, and a barbecue in the back."

"It sounds wonderful." Patterson was caught up in his enthusiasm. "I'm excited about this weekend."

Located across a spectacular footbridge, across the river from the main house, sat Cedar Cottage. Inside, the villa boasted two bedrooms, cooking facilities, and tableware. There were flowers and candles everywhere.

"You did this, didn't you?" Patterson asked Miller.

"Guilty."

Patterson walked through the villa, surveying everything. There was an apple orchard in the back, a nice-sized deck, and the barbecue pit.

"This is so nice."

Miller came up from behind and wrapped his arms around her. "I'm glad you like it." He turned her around so that Patterson was facing him. "I'm glad you came with me. We needed to get away from the city."

"We've been going out for a few months now. Why is it that I've never been to your place, Miller?"

"Why are you asking me this now?"

"I guess I've always wondered why I've never been to your apartment." Comprehension dawned. "Miller, do you live with your mother?"

He gave her a tiny smile. "Actually, my mother has been living with me. She's been sick and was afraid to go back to her house. She's going home soon, though."

"That's very sweet of you." The shadows around her heart disappeared.

"As soon as she leaves, I'll bring you to the apartment."

Patterson released a soft sigh of relief. She couldn't wait to tell LaRue that she'd been wrong in assuming that Miller could be married.

After getting settled, she and Miller took a walk around the property. The air was cold, but Patterson didn't mind. The heat radiating from the explosive currents running through her body kept her warm.

When they returned to the cottage, Patterson made herself comfortable in one of the chairs near the window in the living room. She reveled in the rustic beauty of her surroundings. "What are we doing for dinner?"

"I'm cooking," Miller announced.

Patterson was impressed. "Really? Boy, you sure are full of surprises. I doan think a man has ever cooked dinner fer me."

He moved to stand beside her chair, placing his hand on her shoulders. "I don't do this for everybody, so you're pretty special to me, baby."

Miller's touch sent an involuntary chill through her. Patterson glanced up at him. "You're pretty special to me, too."

"Why don't you take a nice, long hot bath while I cook?" he suggested. "I intend on pampering you this weekend."

"You're so good to me, Miller."

Without a word, he swept her, weightless, into his arms. Patterson wrapped her arms around Miller. She buried her face against his throat to hide her tears—tears of happiness.

Miller lifted her face so that he could kiss her.

Patterson kissed him back with a hunger that belied her outward calm.

His tongue traced the soft fullness of her lips. Raising his lips from hers, Miller gazed into her eyes. "I want to make you mine forever, Patterson."

In her mind, Patterson believed Miller was referring to marriage.

After a delicious dinner, they settled back to enjoy the rest of their evening. Miller turned on the television, but neither one of them was really paying attention. They were too wrapped up in each other.

When Miller's hand traveled from Patterson's throat to her shoulder toward her breast, she stiffened.

"Just go with it, baby," he murmured against her lips. "We can't be perfect people, even if we tried. Just enjoy this moment. . . ."

Instinctively, Patterson's body arched toward him.

Macy

Macy caught River going through the family photo album.

He looked up to find her watching him. River gave her a sad smile.

She sat down beside him.

"Whitney was very beautiful." Macy played with the hem of her sweater. "I have a little confession to make. I was so jealous of her."

River looked surprised. "Really? Why?"

"Because she seemed to have everything. Beauty, a job she loved . . ." Macy wasn't ready to share her feelings for him. "Right after she had Bethany, I can remember thinking about how quickly she'd lost all her weight from the pregnancy. Whitney just seemed so good at everything and I hated it."

River smiled. "She was like a mad woman once the doctor gave her the okay to exercise."

"I understand totally. I'd be that same way."

River met her gaze. "Yes, I believe you would."

"I know how much you must miss her."

"I miss her a lot. So does Bethany. Not a day goes by that we don't think of her." Shaking his head sadly, River added, "She died much too soon."

"All those people did."

He nodded in agreement. "I remember trying to get Whitney to stay home that morning. I can't tell you why, but I know I just didn't want her going in to the office that day. Whitney worked from home two days a week, but this particular week, she'd gone in every day."

"Did you have a feeling of danger?"

River shrugged. "Not really. Well, I felt like something wasn't right, but it wasn't anything like a sense of impending doom."

"I'm so sorry, River."

He nodded. "I am, too. I feel bad because I couldn't save my wife. The only peace I have about that day is that I was given a chance to say good-bye to her—and that Jesus was with her. She wasn't alone."

"You spoke to her?"

"Yeah. She called me from her office to tell me what was going on. Her main concern was that I get home to Bethany. She told me she loved me and asked me to make sure our daughter knew how she felt." River's voice broke. "W-when Whitney told me to give Bethany the letter she'd written to her on the day she was born, I knew I would never see my wife again."

"Oh, River. . . ."

"She told me that she wasn't afraid because she could feel the warmth of Jesus' arms wrapped around her."

"I don't understand how God could let September 11 happen. I'll never understand, River. I lost two friends that day and I'm very angry about it. One of my roommates lost her husband not too long ago and she was very angry. She'd prayed and prayed for God to heal him, but He didn't. Don't you feel the least bit of anger toward Him? I still feel like He let us down when all those people died."

"It saddens me when people die, but I have to hold on to the Word. Revelation 14:13 says, '*Blessed are the dead that die in the Lord.*' If a person that we have known for a long time dies believing in the Lord Jesus Christ, we have a reason to celebrate that death, because that person has been passed from death into everlasting life in heaven. Corinthians 5:8 tells us that '*to be absent from the body is to be present with Lord.*' I believe Whitney is with Jesus."

"My father always says that death for the Christian is nothing but an open door that leads to everlasting life."

River nodded in agreement. "There are scriptures in the Bible that give us assurance that if we die believing in the Lord Jesus Christ, we shall have everlasting life."

Macy smiled. "I know that one. John 3:16. '*For God so loved the world that He gave his only begotten Son, that whosoever believeth in Him should not perish, but shall have everlasting life.*' "

"We have to hold on to our beliefs, Macy. No matter what happens. That's what faith is all about."

"I know. I'm working on it, River. But it's a whole lot easier said than done."

He agreed.

Macy stood up. "I'd better get home. My roommate and I are going out." She felt the need to add, "We're going to see a play."

"Have a good evening. Luke's in the car waiting for you."

"River, I can take a taxi. . . ."

"Luke will see that you get home safe. As a matter of fact, why don't you and your roommate have him drive you to the theater? My treat."

"Thank you, River." Macy was touched by his generosity.

Chapter 39

Patterson

Miller dropped her off in front of her building as soon as they returned to the city. He said, "I'm sorry for running off like this, but I've got to get home to check on my mother."

Patterson nodded. "Please give her my best. I'm hoping you'll take me to meet her soon."

He kissed her chastely on the cheek. "I will."

There was something different about Miller, Patterson noted. He'd been quiet during the two-hour drive home. She was different, too.

Patterson was no longer a virgin.

She had hoped that Miller would propose marriage before the weekend ended, as if that would justify the sin she'd committed.

Disappointed, she climbed out of the SUV and entered the building. Once she was inside the elevator, she whispered, "Lord, I'm so sorry. I was weak. I know it was wrong, but I couldn't help myself." With tears in her eyes, she pleaded, "Please, forgive me."

She found LaRue home alone when she walked into the apartment.

"Where's Macy?" Patterson inquired.

"She went over to her parents' house. She's got some family in town."

"Oh." Patterson walked across the room and set her overnight bag outside her bedroom. She came back into the living room. "How was your weekend?"

LaRue glanced up from her novel. "Good. Yours?"

She gave LaRue a tiny smile. "Good. We had a great time."

"I'm happy for you, Patterson." LaRue returned to her reading.

"I think I'm gon' take a nap. I'm kinda tired."

"Okay," LaRue mumbled without looking up.

Inside her room, Patterson fell to the floor in a heap. She put a hand to her mouth to hide her sobbing.

LaRue

Patterson kept to herself most of the week after her trip. When Macy tried to pry details of the weekend out of her, Patterson abruptly shut down.

Although she didn't say anything, LaRue hadn't failed to notice the changes in Patterson. She suspected the reason behind those changes had to do with the fact that Patterson had lost her virginity.

She never said as much, but LaRue was pretty sure that's what happened.

LaRue also noticed that Miller hadn't come around, and she assumed he hadn't called either.

When Patterson refused to attend church with them on Sunday morning, LaRue was convinced she'd been right all along.

After church, Clyde approached her, wanting to take her out.

"I'd love to go, but I think that we should reschedule. Patterson really needs a friend right now. I should go home."

Clyde looked concerned. "Is she all right?"

"I don't know. I just don't know."

"If there's anything I can do, please let me know. Tell Patterson, I'm here if she needs spiritual counseling."

Smiling, LaRue nodded. "I will."

Clyde escorted her outside the church. "Why don't you and Macy let me take you all home?"

She smiled and nodded. "Fine by me."

A few minutes later, they were on their way.

Macy's cell phone started to ring. She answered it.

When she hung up, Macy announced, "I'm taking Bethany to the circus later on. River was supposed to take her, but he has to leave for Los Angeles tonight and will be gone for a couple of days. I'm going to be staying at his house while he's gone."

Patterson was still in her pajamas, which shocked both Macy and LaRue.

"There's something going on with her," Macy whispered. She walked over to Patterson and inquired, "Honey, are you okay?"

"I . . . I don't feel that well."

LaRue could tell that Patterson had been crying. Her eyes were puffy and red.

"Patterson, why don't you go back to bed and lie down. Have you eaten?" When she shook her head no, LaRue continued, "I'll make you some tea and a sandwich."

When Macy left for River's house a few hours later, LaRue went to check on Patterson.

She could hear her sobbing. Taking a deep breath, LaRue exhaled slowly. She knocked on the door before walking inside.

Patterson wiped her face with the back of her hand.

LaRue picked up a box of tissue off the dresser and carried it over to the bed. She sat down beside Patterson. Wrapping an arm around her, she said, "This, too, shall pass."

Patterson began sobbing harder. LaRue held her until the tears came to an end.

"God loves you and He forgives you."

"I kn-knew better, LaRue. How could I be so weak?"

"You were a woman in love. You made the wrong choice. Now you've got to forgive yourself."

"I feel so stupid. I've called Miller so many times, and he hasn't called me back." Patterson reached for a tissue to blow her nose. "You were right about him, LaRue."

"I didn't want to be right."

"I know that. I just wanted so much for this relationship to be perfect. I guess after Vincent, I wanted desperately to find a man who wanted me. Who really loved me."

"I just wanted you to consider some things. One is that if Miller were a Christian, would he push you to go against God's Word? The

other is that staying in God's Word is the only way to fight temptation."

"You're right. I admit that once I got involved with Miller, I didn't
get into the Word as much. I was more focused on him."

"Patterson, did you use protection?"

She nodded.

"Thank God for that."

"Maybe I'm jumping to conclusions, LaRue. Maybe Miller is out of
town and that's why he hasn't called me back."

"Patterson, let's really look at the big picture. Miller has a cell
phone. It travels with him. He has never given you his home number.
Do you even know where he lives?"

"Miller's mother is living with him right now. She's sick, so that's
why he hasn't taken me over there."

"Who stays with her when he's traveling? Who stayed with her while
you two were away? Better yet, why can't you call over there if it's really his mother who is living with him?"

"I don't know. . . ."

Patterson was getting upset again, so LaRue said, "Just think about
everything we've talked about. Look at what you know about him."

"Miller said that he saw marriage and a family in his future. I thought
he was talking about us."

"More like he was just talking to get you right where he wanted you."

"He awakened sumpthin' in me, LaRue. I have always dreamed of
my weddin' night since I was sixteen years old. That weekend was
nothin' like the way I dreamed."

LaRue gave an understanding nod. "That's why we have to be so
careful what we feed into our spirits. Sex is such an incredible blessing from God. It represents something so wonderful about who we
are, but it was meant for the context of a marriage relationship. When
sex escapes those boundaries and makes its way into other aspects of
our lives and into other relationships, all of a sudden it becomes a
raging inferno that will destroy us."

"That's what hurts me so much. I gave my virginity to a man who
didn't love me. It was a blessing and I didn't treat it with the respect,
and the honor, and the care that I should have. I can't just be mad at
Miller. This is my fault, too."

"Would you like for me to pray with you?"

Patterson nodded.

Together they bowed their heads.

LaRue began, "Father, we thank you for your Word. We thank you that it deals with all the issues that we face, even issues like sex. Where our culture would say that you have nothing to say, in reality you, Heavenly Father, have the last word. Your Word tells us who we are in relationship with you, and that we have been united with you by faith. We pray that you'd help us to understand sex and that we would see it as an expression of the union that you've given us, and that we would treat it with dignity and respect."

"We pray that you would help us resist the temptation," Patterson interjected. "And the desires that are so strong within us at times—because of how central this is to who we are in your image. We pray that you would help us to stand against that. In Jesus' name we pray."

"Amen," they said in unison.

Patterson opened her eyes and smiled her first real smile in a week.

"It's gonna be okay," LaRue assured her.

"I don't know if I'll ever feel clean again."

"You will. I promise you."

Macy

Macy found Patterson in her bedroom packing. She was scheduled to leave for Chicago in a few hours.

"How long will you be gone this time?"

"Two days, but from Chicago I have to go to Los Angeles. I won't be home until Saturday morning."

Macy sat down on the edge of Patterson's bed. "I've been thinking about studying the Bible. I know that you and LaRue study together sometimes. I'd like to join you two the next time you all get together."

"Macy, we'd love it. This is going to be so much fun."

"I wouldn't exactly call it fun, Patterson."

"But it is. The Bible is interesting. Really, it is. It's not just instructions to live by. It's history and so much more."

"I like history."

"When I get back Saturday, we can sit down and discuss when we want to conduct our studies."

"Well, I'm ready. I've purchased highlighters, I have the brand new study Bible you gave me, and a special notebook."

Patterson looked at Macy in amazement. "You actually sound excited."

"I am. I'm on a mission. I want to know more about this incredible God we serve."

Chapter 40

LaRue

LaRue admired her reflection. The black dress Macy designed for her was stunning. She knew Clyde would like it as well. He had an eye for fashion, which LaRue found surprising at first. He enjoyed attending fashion shows and shopping. For a man his size, he was a well-dressed man. Most of his suits had been custom-designed.

Clyde was fun-loving, was a wonderful writer, and enjoyed going to concerts. Tonight they were going to see Donnie McClurkin, Yolanda Adams, and Mary Mary. LaRue loved music, so this was right down her alley.

Macy was in the living room, going through her study Bible like a child with a new toy. She seemed mesmerized. LaRue was delighted to see her roommate getting into the Word.

When Patterson returned, they would sit down and choose a night to study together. She was looking forward to it.

"Clyde's here," Macy announced.

LaRue assessed herself one final time before leaving her room.

She found Clyde sitting in the living room discussing the book of Matthew with Macy. She just stood there watching them in silence.

Clyde looked up and smiled. "You look beautiful. That dress is exquisite."

LaRue knew, at that very moment, she loved the good Reverend Clyde Whitcomb. She didn't know how or when it happened, as she had long accepted the fact that they were never meant to be a couple.

She had accepted the fact that she and Clyde would only be friends.

Macy

While LaRue and Patterson oohed and aahed, Macy sat with her back pressed against the leather seat in the back of the limo. She remained silent during the five-mile drive from the East Hampton Airport.

Nervous energy settled in the bottom of her stomach as they began the half-mile wooded drive to the main house.

Macy loved going to the Hamptons. She loved this house more than their home in New York City. The lawn, the beautiful gardens that bloomed in bright colors during the summer, and the shimmering ponds seemed worlds apart from the sterile feel of the four-story Romanesque Revival that she grew up in.

Patterson was in awe. "Macy, this house is incredible. This is where you grew up?"

"Some of the time. My parents also have the place in the city on West 162nd Street."

The chauffer got out and opened the door to let them out.

LaRue was the first to step outside, followed by Patterson, then Macy. They waited for her to lead them to the front door.

A woman wearing a crisp black and white maid's uniform opened the door. She gave Macy a tiny smile and said, "Happy Thanksgiving, Miss Baldwin."

"Same to you," she responded. "Louisa, these are my . . ." Macy glanced over at Patterson and LaRue. "These are my friends. This is Patterson and this is LaRue."

"Happy Thanksgiving," she repeated.

They followed Louisa into the foyer, where they removed their coats and scarves. The housekeeper took them, handling them as if they were precious jewels.

"When I was little, I was afraid to venture downstairs when it got dark. There are about thirty rooms in this house."

"I can see why. I'm grown and I'd be a little nervous now." Patterson's eyes bounced around the room. "You could fit my entire house in this room heh."

LaRue pointed at the gleaming ebony piano. "I love that Baby Grand, gurl. That's nice." She shot a look at Macy. "Do you play?"

"Just a little. My mother is the one who plays."

"This is such a beautiful place," Patterson complimented again.

"You should see it during the summer. The gardens are gorgeous. The grass is so green." Macy smiled. "It's picture perfect." *Just like my family*, she added silently. *We only look like the perfect family. Now you'll see the ugly truth before this day is over.*

Maynard and Rhetta Baldwin entered the room that boasted twenty-four-foot-high ceilings, clerestory windows, and antique oak floors.

"Happy Thanksgiving," Maynard greeted. "Welcome to our home."

"Thank you for invitin' us to share Thanksgiving dinner with y'all."

"It's our pleasure, Patterson." Rhetta glanced over at her daughter and smiled. "Macy tells us that you all are getting along rather well."

"Yes, ma'am. In the beginnin' it was kind of awkward—you know, with us being from different cities, lifestyles, and all. But it's worked out nicely. I really enjoy havin' LaRue and Macy as roommates. We're like a family."

"I agree," LaRue interjected.

"So do I," Macy threw in. "We're now having Bible study together once a week. We're calling it our 'girls' night out'. We don't make any plans on that day, and after our study, we do something fun together."

Surprise registered for a split second in Rhetta's eyes. "Really? Well, that sounds nice."

Maynard gave an approving nod. "You girls have had a wonderful influence on Macy. She's changed a lot."

Noting the look of hurt in Macy's eyes, LaRue replied, "It wasn't us, Mr. Baldwin. Macy wanted to make some changes in her life. She's never been the type of person to hide her faults—not even from herself. She didn't like the person she was becoming, and so she decided to make some changes."

A twinge of sadness ripped through Macy. "Father, I know that you're very disappointed in me and you have every right to be. I messed up, but all that's going to change. I'm a much better person now. Eventually you'll see that."

She gestured for LaRue and Patterson to have a seat.

"Macy, honey . . ."

"It's okay, Father." Macy picked up her glass of iced tea and said, "Today is Thanksgiving. Let's just enjoy the holiday, shall we?"

Her parents had Louisa bring in a round of drinks while they waited for dinner to be served.

"Macy, dear, that dress is stunning. Where ever did you find it?"

"I made it," she announced quietly. Macy hoped this would not escalate into something bigger.

"You've very talented."

"We keep telling her that," Patterson threw in. "I think she should be a designer. You should see some of her designs. She's—"

LaRue nudged her. "Drop it," she whispered.

"Macy needs to do something worthwhile. Like obtain a college degree." Maynard signaled Louisa to bring him another glass of wine. "She needs to forget this foolishness."

"I'm right here, Father. Stop talking about me as if I weren't in the room. You're no longer paying my bills, so I don't see where you have any right to comment on anything that I do."

He bristled at her. "Don't sass me. I won't have it."

Macy rose to her feet. "This was a bad idea. I knew we shouldn't have come."

Rhetta jumped up to stop her daughter from leaving, but Maynard grabbed her by the hand. She sat back down.

LaRue spoke up. "Mr. Baldwin, I certainly understand that you want the best for your daughter. But I feel you have to allow Macy to determine what is best for her."

"She doesn't know what's best for her. She's spoiled, selfish and—"

"Human, therefore prone to making mistakes," LaRue finished for him. "Macy's also creative, has a strong eye for fashion and color, caring, and is under the assumption that she's failed her parents because her dream is not theirs."

Macy was stunned. Her father actually seemed to be listening.

"Mr. Baldwin, your daughter really does have a gift," Patterson stated. "This dress that I'm wearing is also one of her designs. I believe that it's when you do what you have a passion to do, that you are truly successful."

"Did you set out to own a pharmaceutical company?" LaRue inquired.

Maynard cleared his throat. "I was a heart surgeon."

"Then you designed a line of cardiac heart markers," Rhetta interjected. "Baldwin Pharmaceuticals was born. I remember how upset I was when you announced that you were leaving the hospital for this venture. I was angry because I was afraid you'd fail. I didn't want to leave my comfort zone."

Macy had never known this about her mother. She was stunned.

"It's the same way I'm sure you're feeling about Macy." LaRue gave Maynard and Rhetta a reassuring smile. "Sometimes you just have to trust that all will be fine. Macy's smart and incredibly talented. She needs your support."

Louisa entered the room. "Dinner is served."

Macy took a deep breath before following her parents into the formal dining room. In a short time, LaRue said all she'd been trying to say to her parents for years.

LaRue

They were each given a bedroom with its own private bath. LaRue had never been surrounded by such luxury. The French doors in her room led to a covered porch with a view of the boathouse and the pond. The lawn and trees were covered in snow, creating the illusion of a winter wonderland.

Patterson's room was across the hall from hers and featured a sitting area with a built-in bookcase stocked with books written by African American authors. Both bedrooms came complete with fireplaces.

From Macy's room, LaRue could view the pool, a waterfall, and the poolhouse area. They had been given a complete tour of the house, including Rhetta's greenhouse. LaRue was impressed with the complete layout of the "Baldwin Compound," as Macy referred to her home.

"You didn't have to do that," Macy said as she walked into LaRue's bedroom later that evening. "I don't need anyone to defend me."

Laying the book she'd been reading aside, LaRue responded. "I didn't say it to defend you, Macy. I only spoke the truth."

"Oh."

"Look, I don't know what's going on between you and your parents. It's not my business. I told you once before that if God places something in my spirit, I'm gonna say it. That's what I did."

"LaRue, I've always known what I wanted to do. I want to design clothes. I want my own collection. My parents—you heard them. They think it's a waste of time. I've always felt like I had to choose between what I love and who I love."

"You feel like you can't have both?"

"I can't. My parents won't love me unless I do exactly what they want. Their love comes with strings attached."

"I'm sure that's not true."

"Sadly, it is, LaRue." Macy turned and walked toward the door. "Good night, LaRue."

"Macy, wait."

She paused at the door.

"Don't give up on your dreams. Never give up on what you have a fire and passion to do. Your parents will see the light. Eventually."

Patterson

Two days after their return from the Hamptons, Patterson had dinner with Jason.

"How was your holiday?" she asked. "Were your parents surprised to see you?"

"They were. We had a great time. I'm glad I decided to go home for Thanksgiving. I got to see some of my friends and two cousins I hadn't seen in a while."

"We had a good time, too. We went to the Hamptons."

"I thought you and LaRue were going to have dinner with Macy and her parents." Jason straightened his glasses.

"We did. They have another house in the Hamptons. They are so rich, Jason. That house had to be about fifteen or twenty thousand square feet. They had a boathouse, a greenhouse, pool house, and a whole 'nother house just for guests. That one had five bedrooms and four baths. The main house had sumpthin' like twelve bedrooms and seventeen bathrooms. Can you imagine?" Patterson continued on.

"The house had a movie theater. It was like going to the movies— you know, set up just like a small theater. Only this is for free. They have a gym and a real nice wine cellar, a tennis court, a ballroom, and two kitchens. The house is so huge, Jason."

He laughed. "Sounds like it." Jason took a bite of his food. "I know you and Miller broke up, but have you heard anything from him?"

She suddenly felt sick to her stomach. Patterson shook her head no. "He wasn't the man I thought he was."

She broke into a tiny smile. "Let's change the subject, please."

"I'm sorry."

"No, Jason. I'm okay with it. I just doan want to spend the evening talkin' about my bad choices in men. I'd like to move on with my life. Live and learn. . . ."

He nodded. "Live and learn. . . ."

"I'm glad we came out tonight. Both Macy and LaRue are busy tonight. I didn't want to be home alone."

"How's the modeling coming along? I don't see you much since you left the store."

Talking about her modeling career was the only thing that could bring a smile to her lips these days. "It's a lot of fun. Hard work also. I never realized it was so hard. I like it, though. I—" Patterson stopped short when her eyes landed on a couple coming their way. Her hands started to tremble.

"What's wrong?" Jason inquired.

Leaning forward, she whispered, "That's Miller coming this way. He sure didn't waste any time finding someone else," she muttered. Her eyes traveled to the woman's distorted belly. "Dear Lord . . ." Patterson dropped her eyes as they walked by.

"She's pregnant," Jason stated in a loud whisper. "He's been lying to you, Patterson."

"I know." Her eyes grew wet, and Patterson swallowed hard. "I've been so stupid. I can't believe this. I should have listened to LaRue. She said he was up to no good."

"I'm sorry, Patterson."

"It's not your fault. I was the stupid one. I can't blame anyone for this mess." She stole a glance over where Miller was sitting. At that moment, their eyes met, but he acted as if he had never seen her before.

"Do you want to leave?"

Patterson shook her head no. "I can handle this. If we leave, he'll think that he's won in some way. I refuse to give him that satisfaction."

"He's a jerk," Jason muttered. "I don't understand men like him."

Patterson stole a peek at the woman. "I doan either. Whoever she is—she's stunning." She could feel herself becoming angry. "I doan know why'd he talk to me in the first place."

"I think you know the answer to that question."

"Yeah. I guess I do," she responded thickly. Patterson's appetite suddenly vanished. "I'm not hungry anymore." Folding her arms across her chest, she uttered, "What I feel like doing is walkin' right over there and tellin' him off. I don't cotton to being treated like this. It's bad enough that I . . ." her voice died.

Before Jason could respond, they heard a commotion. Looking over her shoulder, Patterson saw Miller in a state of panic.

"I need help," he began to yell. "My wife just went into labor."

Patterson swallowed hard. "What did Miller just say?"

Jason gave her a sympathetic look. "He's married. He just called the woman his wife."

A knifelike pain ripped through her heart. "I've got to get out of here."

Jason signaled for the check. With all the excitement at Miller's table, they had to wait a few minutes.

Patterson met Miller's gaze for a moment. He gave her as much attention as he'd given any other stranger. He remained focused on his wife.

"I'm glad I'm goin' home for Christmas. I need to see my mama. I miss her and Daddy so much." Patterson took a deep breath and then exhaled slowly. "Jason, I've been thinkin' 'bout stayin' in Georgia."

"Why? Because of what happened?"

"That's a big part of it."

"I don't want you to leave, Patterson. I want you to stay here in New York. With me."

"I'll stay in touch, Jason. I wouldn't leave and just forget 'bout you. I'm not like that."

Jason paid the check and they left without a backward glance.

Patterson wasn't in a talkative mood, so Jason didn't press her for conversation.

She thanked him for seeing her home, then went upstairs.

Her roommates were in LaRue's room doing their nails when she arrived.

Macy glanced up when she entered the bedroom. "Patterson, what's wrong with you? You look like you've seen a ghost."

She sank down on the edge of the bed. "I need to tell you and Macy sumpthin'."

LaRue stood up. "Wait. Let me make you some tea. Matter of fact, I'll make some for all of us. Just from the way you sound, I think we're gonna need it."

The trio headed to the kitchen. Macy and Patterson took seats while LaRue heated up a kettle of water.

"While Jason and I were having dinner, y'all will never guess who walked into the restaurant."

"Who was it?" Macy questioned.

"Miller—and he wasn't alone." Patterson accepted the cup of hot tea from LaRue. "He's married. But not only is he married—his wife is pregnant. So pregnant that she went into labor while they were eating dinner."

Macy's mouth dropped open in her surprise. "*You're kidding?*"

"Her water broke right there in the restaurant. I'd never seen him look so scared."

"Why?" LaRue asked. "Was it because he was afraid you would say something?"

"No, I think he was worried about his wife." Patterson gave a little laugh. "Can you imagine that? Miller concerned for someone other than himself."

Macy reached over and patted her hand. "Patterson, I'm so sorry."

She gave a slight shrug. "Not only did I lose my virginity, but I lost it to a married man whose wife is pregnant...." her voice died. Patterson glanced over at LaRue. "He is the worst kind of jerk. I wish I could just hog-tie him to a car and drive his cheatin' butt all over New York."

Shaking her head in disgust, LaRue uttered, "I feel sorry for his wife. I wonder if she has any idea what type of man she married."

"I should have listened to you, LaRue. Me and my hard head. Mama always said a hard head makes a soft behind. I feel so stupid."

"But at least you know the truth now," Macy contributed.

"It just doesn't make me feel any better. I feel worse." Patterson got up. "I'm going to bed. I'm tired."

She went to her room. Patterson undressed in the dark and climbed into bed, where she cried until no more tears would come.

Chapter 41

Macy

Patterson and LaRue departed for the airport just hours before, leaving Macy alone for the Christmas holidays.

In the beginning she was thrilled with the idea of having her apartment back to herself, but now the place seemed so empty—and lonely.

Macy stared down at the doll in her hands. She stuck it in a gift bag, taking special care to decorate it with tissue and ribbons. Every now and then she would check the clock. Macy was leaving soon to have dinner with Bethany and River. She enjoyed spending time with them and looked forward to the evening.

Armed with gifts for River and Bethany, Macy took the elevator downstairs. River was sending his driver to pick her up.

The driver immediately jumped out of the car when she walked out of the building. He took her packages and set them on the seat beside her. They were soon on their way, and Macy surprised him when she handed him an envelope. "Merry Christmas, Luke," she said.

"Merry Christmas to you, Miss Baldwin, and thank you. Enjoy your evening."

She rewarded him a smile. "I intend to do just that."

Macy could hear the Christmas music even before River opened the door.

He looked so handsome standing there in his black suit. She wanted to reach out and embrace him, but such a bold move would place a wedge between them. The more she got to know River, the more she realized that he didn't care much for overly aggressive women.

"You look nice, Macy. I really like your dress. Who is the designer?"

"I . . . I made it myself," she managed through tight lips.

"You sew extremely well. Did you make this from a pattern?"

"No. I bought a pattern but altered it . . . a lot."

"I didn't know you could sew."

"You probably thought I lived in haute couture. Well, I would if I could afford it, but since I can't, I have to make my own."

He laughed. "I guess that's how I got started. I started with clothing for men. It was actually Whitney who suggested that I design a line of women's clothing."

Bethany came down the stairs wearing a beautiful red velvet dress. "Macy," she squealed in delight. "I'm so glad you're here."

Macy bent to give Bethany a hug. "You look like a beautiful angel."

They sat down to open their gifts.

She watched River's face as she opened his gift. He collected artwork by African American artists. Macy sold some stock that had been given to her from her grandparents to purchase a painting by Clementine Hunter.

"Macy, I don't know if I can accept this. This is *The Funeral on Cane River*. It must have cost you a fortune."

"I want you to have it, River. You have two of her other paintings and I saw this at an auction. . . . it's my gift to you." She gave him a bright smile. "Merry Christmas."

"Thank you."

"Open your present, Macy," Bethany encouraged.

She did as she was told. "Oh, my Lord. . . ."

"I saw you looking at the sketch. You were the inspiration for this dress, so I want you to have it."

"It's beautiful," Macy murmured as she fingered the silky folds. "I love it." Her eyes found River's. "So I inspired you?"

He laughed and nodded. "Guilty."

Macy sensed, at that moment, her relationship with him change.

When it was time for dinner, River confessed, "I have to be honest. I didn't cook dinner. I had everything catered."

"Daddy burned the ham," Bethany announced.

"Thanks, sweetie," River muttered while Macy tried to hide her laughter.

Three hours later, a smiling Macy returned home. She'd just climbed into bed when the telephone rang.

"Hello . . ."

"Macy, its LaRue and I've got Patterson on the telephone. We're on three-way."

"Merry Christmas," they said in unison.

She laughed. "Merry Christmas, roomies. I can't believe I'm actually saying this, but I miss you all."

"I miss y'all too."

LaRue laughed. "Same here. Macy, we called so that we could open our presents together. *Patterson's idea.*"

"I believe it." Macy swung her feet out of bed. "Wait, let me run and get my gifts." She ran into the living room and pulled the presents from beneath the Christmas tree. "Okay."

Macy's eyes grew wet. "A gift certificate for maid service. Thank you, LaRue. "

"You've earned it, girlfriend."

They heard Patterson gasp.

"I love it," she screamed. "Thank you, Macy. I can't believe you actually bought me a Louis Vuitton duffle bag."

"Well it looks so much better than what you've been carrying around. You're a big time model now."

Macy could hear the tears in LaRue's voice. "Thank you, Macy."

"I knew you wanted a Coach purse, but knew you would never buy it for yourself. I for one believe that we should do little things to pamper ourselves."

"But this is too much, Macy. I don't want to put a damper on things, but where did you get the money?"

"I had some stock and I sold it. I wanted to do something nice for the people I care about and so, I did."

They shed more tears as they opened the rest of their gifts.

"We love you, Macy," Patterson expressed.

"I love you and LaRue, too. Please hurry home."

Patterson

"Don't forget to tell your mama I said hello . . . okay, bye . . ." Patterson hung up her telephone.

"Sounds like you made yourself some good friends."

She turned to face her mother. "I did, Mama. LaRue and Macy are like sisters to me. We had some rough times in the beginning, but all that's changed."

Lema hugged her daughter. "I'm real happy fer you. As much as I miss you, I know leavin' heh was the best thing fer you."

"I miss being home sometimes," Patterson confessed. "Things can get so complicated at times. . . ." her voice died. "Look at me, I'm just rattling on and on. I'm supposed to be helping you cook dinner for tomorrow."

She reached for a mixing bowl. "I need to get started on the potatoes."

"Baby, is there something botherin' you?"

Patterson couldn't look at her mother. "No ma'am. I'm fine." She turned around and pretended to look through one of the cabinets. "Where do you keep the cayenne pepper?"

"Where I always keep it. Right on the spice rack."

Patterson made a short nervous laugh. "How could I forget that?"

Her mother didn't push for any more questions.

They cooked until well after midnight. Patterson was exhausted by the time she crawled in her bed.

Miller entered her thoughts, but Patterson fought to forget him. But the nightmare only got worse.

Just when she'd thought she could move forward and get past the guilt, she'd found out he was a married man. A married man with a baby on the way.

Guilt poured from every pore on her body. It had become very clear that he'd been playing her all along. "I knew better. So how did this happen?" She whispered in the darkness.

LaRue

LaRue returned to New York four days after Christmas. She wanted to bring in the New Year in New York with Clyde.

Macy gave her a recap of the time spent with Bethany and River. After Christmas, he'd taken her and Bethany skiing for a couple of days.

"It sounds like you and Mr. Littleton are getting closer," LaRue stated.

"It's more like we're getting along. I don't think he's interested in a relationship with me outside of friendship."

"How do you know?"

"He's still very much in love with his dead wife. He just wants a nanny for Bethany, and I'm okay with that."

"Liar."

"Okay, so I'm not okay, but I have no other choice. I'm not going to make a fool of myself over this man."

"Have you told River that you're interested in him?"

"LaRue, are you listening to me?" Macy exclaimed in irritation. "Didn't you just hear me say I'm not about to make a fool of myself?"

"I'm just saying I think you should be honest with the man. I have a feeling he's very interested in you. I'd put money on it—if I were a betting woman."

"LaRue, I think you need to concentrate on your own relationship. I hear wedding bells in your future. You ready for that?"

"Wedding bells. Macy, what are you talking about?"

"Reverend Whitcomb is in love and I know you feel the same way, too."

"Yes, I love Clyde," LaRue admitted. She gave a short laugh. "I've never said it out loud before."

Macy gasped in surprise. "Not even to him?"

"No. I'm not gonna tell him."

"Why not?"

"Because I don't think we have a future together." LaRue gave her a wry smile. "I'm just trying to enjoy the time I have with him."

Macy shook her head in confusion. "I really think that you're taking that dream much too seriously, LaRue. You love that man."

"I've loved and lost before, Macy. Only this time I'm prepared to love Clyde for as long as I can. When our season ends, I'll go on with my life. This is the way it has to be."

Later that evening, Clyde pulled LaRue into his office.

"The service was nice. You really preached tonight."

Clyde smiled. "So you were listening," he teased.

She gave him a playful pinch. "Of course I was listening. Although if you wanted to tell me something, you could've just pulled me to the side. You didn't have to do it in front of the entire church." LaRue broke in a small laugh. "I thought you cared for me—calling me out like that."

Clyde took her by the hand. "I do care for you, LaRue. I care a whole lot. I prayed for someone like you. I asked God for almost seven years to send this special woman to me. When you walked into my church, I knew it was you, LaRue."

His words brought her tears.

"Honey, I know that this new year will bring a lot of changes. I know that you care for me, LaRue, but I can't help but feel that you are holding back. Is it because of Tom?"

LaRue took a seat on the couch in Clyde's office. "No, it's not Tom." She told him about the dream she had.

"So you think that we're not supposed to be together?"

She nodded. "Don't you?"

Clyde shook his head. "I know that I know what I know—God has ordained that you are to be my wife, LaRue. I knew it the moment I saw you walk through the doors of my church. Search your heart and seek God. I trust he'll show you the truth."

All the angst she'd felt in her heart concerning Clyde suddenly vanished. LaRue felt like jumping for joy. As much as she'd tried to keep from loving him, it was to no avail. LaRue had fallen madly in love with him.

Macy

The next morning, River pulled Macy into his office. "Are you free to meet me for lunch today?"

"Sure. I don't have to pick Bethany up from school until two."

They arranged a time to meet.

Macy didn't know what to take from her conversation with River. Was he going to dismiss her? She wondered.

She shook her head no. That couldn't possibly be it.

She couldn't concentrate because River stayed on her mind. Macy played every scenario in her mind. There was a part of her that wondered if by some small chance her dream was about to come true. She loved River, but never considered that he would love her in return. It just didn't seem possible.

Macy met River at the restaurant.

He pulled out a chair for her to sit in.

River got straight to the point. "Macy, the reason I asked you to meet me is because I thought we should talk."

"I gathered as much. Have I done something wrong?"

River shook his head. "Since you've come to look after Bethany, I haven't seen my little girl so happy in a long time. You really made a difference in her life. Mine, too."

"Yours?"

He nodded. "I never thought I'd feel this way ever again. When Whitney died, I just figured I'd live out the rest of my life alone. But now . . . now things have changed."

Macy had to pinch herself to see if she were dreaming.

"Why are you so quiet?"

"I'm just waiting to hear what you have to say."

River gave her one of his devastating smiles. "Macy, what is it that you want to do with your life? I'm sure you don't intend to be a nanny forever."

"My dream has always been to be like you," Macy confessed. "I've always wanted to be a fashion designer."

River was surprised. "Really? I had no idea."

"My father never wanted me to study fashion, so I didn't. That's why I haven't graduated from college. Nothing holds my interest. I know what I want to do—I want to be a designer."

"Do you have any designs?"

"I have a bunch at home in my apartment. I made this dress I have on."

He peered at her intently. "Very nice. You do the beading yourself?"

"I did."

"Macy, I'd like to see some of your designs."

She smiled. "You don't have to do that, River. That's not why I approached you."

River settled back in the booth. "So why did you approach me? I know it wasn't because you had this sudden desire to be my nanny."

"No, it wasn't," Macy confessed. "I was interested in you."

River reached over and took Macy's hand. "I would like to know if you're still interested in me."

In her shock, she removed her hand from his grasp. "How . . . how did you kn-know?"

"I'm not blind. You made your intentions known early on. You know with all the little looks and the short skirts . . ."

Embarrassed, Macy took a sip of her tea. "Was I that obvious?"

"Very."

She averted her eyes, too humiliated to face him. "I feel so foolish."

"You shouldn't feel that way. I liked the attention. I was flattered."

Macy's gaze met his. "I've had a crush on you since I was seventeen. I was so angry when you married Whitney. My heart was broken."

"Is that why you were so rude to me on my wedding day?"

She nodded.

"I thought you were just being a snob. I thought you were a spoiled brat. I vowed then that none of my children would grow up to be like that."

"I'm sorry, River. I was a brat and I truly apologize."

"Macy, I'd like to see where our relationship will take us. I like you . . . I like you a lot. So does Bethany."

"Are you saying that you want to date me?"

"Yes, I am. We have a new year coming—a new beginning. I want it to be a new beginning for all of us."

The next day, Macy handed over a stack of her drawings to River. "I just want to warn you. They aren't very good."

She stood there silently while River scrutinized her work. Macy chewed on her bottom lip as she awaited the verdict.

After a while, River looked up. "These are quite good, Macy. You have a gift."

"You don't have to say that."

"I mean it. Macy, you're very talented. I especially love your collection of wedding dresses."

"River, you really mean it? I love designing bridal gowns."

He nodded.

"I've been thinking of going back to college. Only this time I want to take fashion design. I don't think it'll take me long to finish my degree."

"That's good to hear because I have a proposition for you. I would like to give you an internship with my company. Our interns obtain hands-on experience in all areas of the business, including design, fabric and color selection, marketing, shipping, and inventory control. You have sewing experience, so that's a plus. Are you interested?"

"Yes," she replied excitedly. Macy suddenly grew serious. "But what about Bethany?"

"You can still pick her up after school. Just work at the company during her school hours. Or if you prefer, I can hire another nanny."

Macy shook her head. "It's too soon for that. I'll plan my classes around her school hours."

Deep down, Macy wanted to jump for joy. She couldn't believe her dream was finally coming true.

That evening, she made a special trip to see her parents.

"I have an announcement," Macy yelled as she rushed through the doors of her parents' house.

Rhetta was instantly at her side. "What is it, dear? Are you getting married?"

Macy's smile disappeared. "No, it's not that."

"Then what is it?" her father wanted to know. "You're not in any trouble, are you? Because if you—"

"I've decided to go back to school," Macy interjected.

"What do you plan to study this time around?"

"Fashion design. I'm doing what I've wanted to do from the very beginning."

Maynard cast a look in his wife's direction. "Surely, you can't be serious. A fashion designer."

"It's what I want to do, Father. I love fashion design and sewing. River is giving me an internship with R. L. International."

Rhetta went to sit down on one of the wing chairs. "Thank God you're giving up that nanny job," she uttered.

"I didn't say that, Mother. I'm going to continue being Bethany's nanny."

Rhetta paled.

"How are you going to pay for school?" Maynard wanted to know.

"I'm going to sell the rest of my stock."

"You don't have to do that. We—"

"No, Father. I want to do this my way. R. L. International has a tuition assistance program. I plan to take advantage of that to help me. I've already enrolled."

"So you're serious about this?" Rhetta asked.

Macy met her mother's gaze. "Yes, I am. I'm very serious."

After a moment of tense silence, Maynard nodded. "If this is what you wanted to do, why didn't you?"

"Because I knew you wouldn't approve, Father. I . . . I was trying to please you and Mother."

Rhetta got up and took her husband's hand in hers. "We want you to know that if this is truly what you want to do—we will support you. We're very proud of who you've become, Macy. Aren't we, dear?"

Maynard smiled at her. "We are proud of you."

Macy raised her eyes heavenward. *Thank you, God.*

It had to be God. There was no other explanation.

Chapter 42

Patterson

Jason called her on Christmas morning and again on New Year's Eve.

"I wanted to wish you a happy new year, Patterson. I want you to know that I'm really missing you."

"I miss you, too, Jason."

"You are coming back to New York, right?"

Patterson didn't answer right away.

"Please tell me that you're coming back."

"I don't know."

"I don't want you to leave New York. And I know deep down you don't want to go. Patterson, you love living here and your career is taking off. Mostly, I don't want you to leave because I'm in love with you."

She could hardly believe she'd heard him correctly. "What did you just say, Jason?"

"I said that I love you. From the first time I laid eyes on you."

Patterson glanced around to see if her parents were within earshot. Keeping her voice down, she said, "I'm sorry. I need to make sure I heard you correctly. Did you just tell me that y-you're in love . . . you love me?"

Jason nodded to himself. "I know you don't feel the same way right now—especially because of what Miller did to you—but I'm willing to give it time. I'm not the best-looking man around, and I don't have all those muscles you women like, but I want you to know that I am a good man. I love God and I'm a hard worker. I want a wife and a family. Patterson, if you give me this chance, I'll be good to you. I will treat you like a queen."

"I think you look just fine, Jason, and you have been a wonderful friend to me."

"But you want to leave it at that. I understand."

She could hear the sadness in his voice. "That's not at all what I'm saying. Jason, I care a great deal for you. But before we go any further, I have to ask you something. I know that you are a Christian, but I need you to understand that I made a big mistake with Miller. I don't want to go through that again."

"Look, why don't you take some time to think about us while you're home. When you come back to New York, we can sit down and talk. Okay?"

"Sure."

They talked for a few minutes more before hanging up.

Patterson sat in the tiny living room with her parents to watch the merging of one year to the next. Her mind wasn't on the television—it was on the conversation she'd had with Jason.

It's funny the way things turn out, she mused. *All this time I kept pinning my hopes on the charismatic and good-looking Miller Baisden, when the entire time, a man who truly loved me, unselfishly stayed in the background, patiently waiting for just one tiny sign that I returned his feelings.*

Now she felt like more a heel. Talk about being blind. How could she not see what was happening? Jason was a good man. He was one of her best friends. He was very supportive of her modeling career—unlike Miller.

How can I go to him now? I've given away the only real gift I . . . Patterson closed her eyes and began to pray as the clock struck midnight.

LaRue

It was soon February and Valentine's Day was fast approaching. January had marked new beginnings for all of them. Jason and Pat-

terson were dating. So were Macy and River. She was now working at
R. L. International and preparing to start her classes in the spring.

For the past couple of dates, she and Clyde were considering marriage. He'd all but let her know that they would become officially engaged on Valentine's Day. LaRue assumed Clyde wanted to do the whole
get-down-on-your-knee-and-propose thing. He was old-fashioned that
way. It was one of the qualities she loved about him.

LaRue loved the fact that Clyde was a man who truly loved God. He
didn't just teach the Word—he was a man who lived it, too. Tonight,
they were having dinner because he wanted to share his vision with
her.

She was glad when the work day was over. LaRue rushed home to
take a nap before her date with Clyde.

A couple of hours later, LaRue felt refreshed. She showered and
dressed in a navy blue pantsuit. After pinning her braids into a neat
bun at the nape of her neck, she carefully applied her make-up.

As usual, Clyde was prompt in picking her up and took her to a
restaurant nearby.

When they were seated, he took her hand in his. "I am very excited
about what I'm sharing with you," he began. "God gave me this vision
long before I met you. I didn't want to say anything to you about it
until I was sure."

LaRue gave him a puzzled look. "Sure about what, Clyde?"

"About us. See, you fit heavily into this plan."

She could feel the hair on her neck stand up. "What is this plan you
keep talking about?'

"Ministry. We have a ministry together. As a couple."

LaRue shook her head. "I don't think so. You're wrong, Clyde.
You're wrong."

"Honey, what is it?"

"I haven't been called to preach. I don't know why God's not listening to me. I—"

Clyde surveyed her face. "Listen to me, LaRue. Let me finish. . . ."

She shook her head no. "I can't do it. I don't want to do it." LaRue
wiped a tear from her eye.

"Will you please let me explain?"

LaRue finally nodded.

"I was talking about you starting a woman-to-woman mentoring ministry program. You have such a heart for counseling—I believe the call on your heart is for this—not getting up in a pulpit."

LaRue now felt embarrassed by her actions. "Is this the vision that you had?"

Clyde nodded. "I want to start one for the men, and I think as my first lady, you should coordinate the mentoring ministry for the women."

The more Clyde shared with LaRue the details of what he had in mind, the more excited she became about the project.

"I would love to do this." Her mind recalled the prophecy over her life all those years ago. This is what He was talking about. Deep down, LaRue knew it like she knew the back of her own hand.

LaRue shared some of her own ideas while they ate dinner.

Clyde nodded. "See, that's what I'm talking about. Honey, we're going to make a great team. We have a lot of the same vision."

"It's important that our vision is in line with scripture. We can't forget that."

"You're right about that."

Right after dessert, Clyde reached into his pocket and pulled out a tiny velvet box.

LaRue's eyebrows raised in surprise.

"Honey, I want to make our union permanent. I hope and pray that you will do me the honor of being my wife."

"Yes, I will be your wife."

Clyde had never been much for romantic declarations. She hadn't either. Smiling, LaRue allowed him to place the emerald-cut diamond solitaire on the ring finger of her left hand.

She admired her engagement ring. "It's beautiful."

Clyde glanced around before saying in a low voice. "Now, I'm not wanting a real long engagement, LaRue. I'm . . . I'm ready to be a husband."

She laughed. "Oh, Clyde . . ."

"Honey, I'm serious. I'd marry you tonight."

"Why don't we just do it one Sunday after church?" LaRue suggested. "I've already had the big wedding. I'd rather put the money toward something else."

"You're sure about this, LaRue? I don't want to take away your dreams."

"I'm sure. I don't want a wedding. We can have a nice reception and invite everybody. For now, I just want close friends and family. If you'll give me two weeks, I'd appreciate it."

Clyde nodded. "I can do that."

LaRue held out her hand to admire her ring again. "Just wait until I tell Patterson and Macy."

Patterson

"I won, Jason," Patterson screamed. She laughed when she looked up at his face. "What's wrong, Jason? I told you that I knew how to play Scrabble."

LaRue burst through the door with Clyde following in her wake. "Okay, where's Macy?"

"Right behind you." Macy removed her coat and hung it in a nearby closet. "I kept calling your name outside, but you looked like you were on a mission. What's up?"

Patterson surveyed LaRue's face, then slid down to her left hand. She didn't miss the gleaming diamond. A grin spread across her face. "Oh, my goodness. . . ." She put her hand to her mouth.

Macy looked from one roommate to the other. "What in the world is going on?"

LaRue held up her left hand. "Clyde and I are getting married," she announced.

Patterson jumped up from the sofa and ran over to LaRue, hugging her for dear life.

Macy rushed over and joined the hugfest.

Jason walked over to Clyde, saying, "Congratulations, Pastor. I'm real happy for you."

They watched the women, laughing, crying, and talking—all at the same time.

Macy made coffee for everyone as they sat in the living room talking about wedding plans.

"You're not going to have a wedding?" Macy questioned.

LaRue shook her head. "I don't want one. All I need is a small simple ceremony with our friends and family present."

"I'm going to make your wedding dress," Macy volunteered.

"I'd like that."

"Where's River?" LaRue inquired.

"He's out of town. Bethany's with her grandmother tonight. They're going shopping tomorrow."

Patterson reached over and took Jason's hand. She sent up a prayer of thanks for being blessed with such a wonderful and loving man. She cared deeply for him and hoped that they would be as fortunate as Clyde and LaRue. She still wanted to get married and have a family. This time she would do it the right way.

Chapter 43

Patterson

"LaRue's wedding dress is gorgeous, Macy. You did a wonderful job." Patterson tossed a couple of peanuts in her mouth. She pushed the bowl away. "Take those away from me."

Macy began to shake her head. "I don't know how you do it. You eat anything you want and you don't gain a pound."

"Neither do you, Macy," LaRue intoned. "I'm the one who has to worry about her weight."

Patterson consulted her notes. "Did you pick up your lingerie for your wedding night?"

LaRue nodded. "Gurlfriend, that was the first thing I bought."

The three women laughed.

"I hope you got something sexy."

"I did. Macy, now I've been married before. I'm not some little old spinster woman who's getting married for the first time. Humph. I got everything I need to get my groove on."

"Mmmmm . . ." Macy put a hand to her mouth and giggled. "Look at you, Miss Thang."

Patterson lay back on LaRue's bed with her hands behind her head. "I wont a wedding night," she sighed.

"You'll have one. Just be patient."

She glanced over at LaRue. "Are you nervous?"

"It's been a while, but no, I'm not nervous. I love Clyde and it feels right between us."

Sitting up, Patterson asked, "How do you know when it's right?"

LaRue straightened the scarf covering her upswept hairstyle. "My dad used to tell me that when choosing Mr. Right, I had to ask myself one question: If I were to take this man home to Jesus, would He approve of him?" She thought about the dream she had when she and Clyde were standing before Jesus and smiled. "Would Jesus say this is the man I have chosen for you? When in doubt, just ask the Lord."

"I like that," Macy stated.

"I do, too." Patterson reached for the peanuts, but Macy pushed them out of her reach. "All right, Miss Model. No more for you."

"Just one, please?"

Shaking her head, Macy responded, "You said that the last two times."

"LaRue, are you still gonna model?" Patterson inquired. "I mean, you're gon' be a first lady?"

"Yeah. I love modeling. Clyde and I talked about it and he's okay with it—but he doesn't want me wearing really skimpy designs. I spoke with Victor and he's agreed to keep me in more conservative clothing."

"No more modeling body art for you. . . ." Macy contributed.

LaRue stifled a yawn. "No . . . no more of that. It was a one-time deal anyway."

Patterson got up off the bed yawning. She stretched and said, "We'd better let you get some sleep."

"Don't leave. You and Macy stay in here."

Frowning, Macy shook her head. "Girl, we can't sleep in here. The bed is way too small. Come to my room. We can hang out in there. At least if we fall asleep, we won't be all cuddled up."

Carrying pillows and snacks, the trio made their way to Macy's room.

They talked and laughed with each other until well after one in the morning.

LaRue was the first to fall asleep, followed by Patterson.

Macy eyed them a moment before she lay down, pulling the covers to her chin. LaRue had already moved most of her things to Clyde's house. She was saddened by the thought of LaRue's moving out.

After tonight, it would just be her and Patterson.

Macy

Macy glanced down at her class schedule. Her first class was Sketching for Communication, followed by a class in color and design. She would also be taking introductory classes to fashion business and textiles.

She strolled into River's office and handed him her schedule. "I'm so excited. I still can't believe this is actually happening to me."

Macy dropped down onto one of the visitor's chairs facing his desk.

"I like seeing you so happy," River observed.

"I like being this happy."

"How are the newlyweds?"

"Doing great. I spoke to LaRue earlier. Now you want to talk about being happy—she's floating."

"Clyde is a good man. I like his preaching and the church." River laid down his pencil and put away his drawing. "You ready to go?"

Rising to her feet, Macy nodded. "Before I forget, Bethany wants to spend the night with her grandmother. I told them you'd call to let them know if it was okay. Patterson and Jason will be meeting us at the restaurant."

Looping her arm through his, Macy added, "By the way, thanks for choosing Patterson as the featured model for the showing. She's perfect for the finale."

River nodded. "I agree."

They left the building and headed out to the waiting car.

As far as Macy was concerned, her life was perfect.

Patterson

The first week in April, Patterson left for Las Vegas.

She spent five hours in front of the camera during the location shoot. This particular art director was not only a perfectionist, but also a major jerk.

He kept yelling and spewing profanities at everyone. One model had actually done what Patterson was seriously considering—she walked off the set without looking back.

She was elated to return to the solitude of her hotel suite. Patterson wanted nothing more than to curl up with a good book. She'd brought her Bible with her to catch up on her weekly studies with Macy and LaRue.

Even though LaRue no longer lived with them, they still continued to meet on a weekly basis to have Bible study and their girls' night out. Patterson would miss being with them this time around because of her bookings.

After her shower, Patterson pulled her hair up into a ponytail and threw on a pair of sweats.

The knock on her door startled her.

Patterson got up from the desk, muttering, "Who is knocking on my door? I told them I didn't want to be bothered . . ."

She opened her door wide, prepared to give her uninvited visitor a piece of her mind. Her expression changed to one of pure happiness.

"Jason, what are you doing here?" she asked, throwing her arms around him.

"I came to see you. I've been thinking about this a lot. I want you to be my wife."

She pulled him all the way into the room. "I love you, Jason. More than anything."

"Then marry me," he implored her.

"Jason . . ."

"Marry me now. Right here in Vegas. We can get married in a number of places. They have chapels all over the place."

"After everything that happened between Miller and me, you still want to marry me? We had sex, Jason. I lost my virginity to him."

"You made a mistake, Patterson. None of us is perfect."

The forgiving expression on Jason's face was so genuine, Patterson's heart exploded with love for him. "I love you so much."

"Then be my wife. I can't live without you, Patterson. I want you in my life."

Patterson kissed him. "Okay, Jason. Let's get married. Right here. Right now."

Macy

"You two standing there grinning like Cheshire cats," LaRue accused Macy and Patterson as she strolled into the apartment. "What's going on?"

She glanced over at Macy, who responded, "They asked me to give you a call. They haven't told me anything."

Both pairs of eyes traveled down to Patterson's ring finger.

LaRue broke into a knowing grin. "I bet they got engaged."

"You're half right, Macy." Patterson held up a legal-looking document. "Jason and I got married two days ago. In Las Vegas." She opened up her shirt to reveal a wedding ring hanging on her necklace.

"I thought you were going there on assignment."

"I did."

"I followed her there because I wasn't going to take no for an answer." Jason said. "I wanted this woman for my wife."

LaRue chuckled. "Well, you certainly have her now."

Nodding, Jason grinned. "She's mine and I couldn't be happier. Patterson is the love of my life."

"Oh, enough already," Macy complained. "I'm happy for you, but try to keep from gushing all over the floor. Hey, wait a minute. . . . I've lost both my roommates."

"I'm going to pay rent for the next two months—"

Macy shook her head. "You don't have to do that, Patterson. I can manage."

"No, it's only right," Patterson insisted. "I'm moving out without much notice, so this is only fair. Now my mind's made up, so don't argue with me."

A look passed between Macy and LaRue.

"Humph. The girl gets married and now she thinks she grown."

"Just look at her, LaRue. She could light up the whole apartment with that grin on her face."

"Stop teasing me."

"Seriously, Patterson. Where are you and Jason going to live?"

"His apartment, I guess. We have to find a bigger place, though."

"They have some apartments available in this building. Maybe you two should check them out."

"We will. I love living here."

"If you need a bigger place temporarily, you guys can stay here with me."

"That's so sweet of you, but we'll manage in Jason's apartment until we get ours. Hopefully, we'll be able to find something within the week."

Chapter 44

Macy

"Tomorrow's the big day," River murmured. "These last two years flew by pretty quickly."

Macy turned to face him. "I was just thinking about that same thing. It's been a long time coming. My parents are thrilled."

"What about you? You should be happy."

Macy settled back in his arms. "I am. I'm finally getting my college degree. It's not what Father really wanted, but this is for me. A bachelor's degree in fine arts with a concentration in fashion design. I've made a decision, River. I'm not just going to stop here. I'm getting my master's as well."

"I'm proud of you, Macy."

"I'm proud of me, too. I wasn't sure I'd ever see my graduation day. I'm not sure I even had plans to ever really finish school. I've grown up some."

"Yes, you have," he murmured. River reached inside his pocket. "Macy, there's something I want to ask you."

"What is it?" Even as she asked the question, her heart started to beat faster. "Is something wrong?"

"No, baby. There's nothing wrong." River took a deep breath. Gazing into her eyes, he declared, "I love you, Macy, and I want you to be my wife." River pulled out a tiny box from his jacket. "Will you marry me?"

Macy could barely contain her joy. "I can't believe it. You want to marry me. Oh, River, it's all I've dreamed about. This is happening sooner that I ever expected."

"I take it your response means yes."

"Definitely. Yes, I will marry you, River Littleton. I've waited for this moment all of my life."

Patterson

Patterson held the camera up to her eye and quickly snapped a photo of Macy, River, and Bethany. "You can put this in your album and after you get married, it'll be your first family photo."

"We're going to cherish it always." Macy wrapped an arm around Bethany. "Aren't we, little girl?"

"Snap another one. I want one for my photo album, too."

Macy reached for River. "Your daughter wants us to take another picture."

Patterson snapped a second photograph.

When they finished, LaRue strode over to embrace Macy. "You did it. Gurl, I'm so proud of you."

Macy wrapped her arms around LaRue. "Thank you so much for saying that. I owe it all to the two of you. You know that, don't you? I don't think I would've gotten this far without you and Patterson. The apartment just isn't the same without the two of you. At least Patterson lives in the building."

"We're going to still have our girls' night out aren't we?" Patterson asked. "I don't want to give those up."

"We won't have to," Macy answered.

"I'll be there," LaRue responded. "That's our time to hang out." Patting her belly, she added, "I'll even have Daddy babysit this little one on those nights."

Patterson was relieved. "Good. I don't plan to miss our special evenings together. I really enjoy girls' night out."

"Except when you're off on some modeling assignment," LaRue stated with a grin. "Macy, did you see our girl on the cover of *Essence*? She's a big-time model now."

Patterson grinned. "I don't know about all that. Things are going well, though. I feel very blessed."

Macy's eyes traveled to River. "I know what you mean. God has given me so much favor. He's given me a wonderful family and an opportunity to straighten out my life. What a tremendous blessing."

"God definitely brought us together. I believe that," LaRue stated. "We never would've found each other otherwise. Three different women. The drama queen, the country mouse, and well . . . me. We weren't friends and we weren't enemies. We were frenemies."

"You're right about that," Macy agreed. "I didn't want anything to do with women or roommates, but I've learned a lot from you two. We went from frenemies to friends. I may have missed out on some wonderful relationships in the past because of my attitude. Thanks for caring enough to be honest with me—even when it hurt. I really a-appreciate i-it."

"Now I know you're not going to start c-crying . . ." LaRue blinked away her own tears. "Don't you start, too . . ." she warned Patterson.

"We've had some wonderful times together. I was so scared that I wouldn't make friends easily when I left Three Oak. But I found two best friends . . . and all in the same day. I will never forget our time together—the ups and downs. I'll cherish all of it."

"We are too mushy for words," LaRue declared. "We're standing here acting like we're never gonna see each other again."

Macy wiped away a tear. "I just never realized how much I'm going to miss you and Patterson. It hadn't hit me until now. But you're right, LaRue. We are still going to spend a lot of time together. First of all, we've got my wedding to plan and, of course, you ladies are my bridesmaids. Mother's going to want me to include some of my cousins, so I want you and Patterson to be my matrons of honor."

"We'd love it," they shouted in unison.

Patterson

LaRue tapped Macy on the arm. "Your future husband is trying to get your attention."

"I'll be right back."

Macy took off to join River and Bethany.

Clyde pulled LaRue away to meet someone, leaving Patterson standing alone.

Jason walked over to join her. "You okay, sweetheart?"

She cleared her throat. Looking into her husband's eyes, Patterson confessed, "I really miss my girls. I miss living with them. Macy and LaRue are my best friends. Don't get me wrong—I love living with you. It's just that we bonded."

"You're still going to see them. You all just won't be living together."

"I know. We just . . . I guess we became a family while sharing the apartment. It was right, you know. We were each on our own personal spiritual journey and, through our friendship, we found what we were looking for. Actually, I think we found more than what we ever expected."

"You share a special relationship. This much is clear. Honey, I don't want you to think that what you have with your girlfriends is over. This is just the beginning. We're going to have some good times together. All of us. While you were in Italy, River decided to join the church. So, you see, we'll all gonna be in the same church."

"Nobody told me."

"Maybe Macy wanted to surprise you. With the wedding now, I guess she forgot to mention it. Speaking of surprises, I have one for you."

Grinning, Patterson eyed her husband. "What wonderful something did you do now?"

"I'm taking us to Hawaii. But the real surprise is that we're bringing your parents along."

Patterson squealed with delight. "Jason, I love you so much. My parents have always wanted to go to Hawaii."

"I remembered you telling me that. We're going to Oahu first and then on to Maui. Two weeks of recreation and relaxation."

"We'll be doing the recreational part and my parents will do the relaxation."

LaRue

LaRue watched Patterson from across the lawn. A smile tugged at her lips as she noticed a tender moment shared by Patterson and Jason. She was thrilled that they'd found each other.

She was also very happy for Macy. She was finally doing what she wanted to do with her life, and she had the man of her dreams as a bonus. Most importantly, she'd found her way back to Jesus. Initially, LaRue wondered if Macy would grow bored with the idea of being a Christian, but she was still seeking God. Macy had surprised them all.

LaRue felt her eyes water as she thought of the three of them in that apartment. Each of them from different walks of life, found not only each other, but had also discovered themselves.

She'd never realized that she was filled with a rebellious spirit until the night Clyde shared his vision and proposed. God couldn't fully unfold His plan for her because she kept running. LaRue was in search of a choice that appealed to her flesh and not what she'd been called to do. She was ashamed of those actions now and asked for forgiveness.

Lifting her head to the heavens, LaRue offered up a prayer. "Lord, show me clearly what you want me to do with the gifts you have given me. Grant me the strength that I need to answer your call with courage and love. Make me a generous person so that others may experience your love through me. Help me always to look to you as the One who will show me the way to live my life. I pray this prayer for women everywhere. Saved, single, and just trying to live for you. In Jesus' name I pray. Amen."

SAVED IN THE CITY

JACQUELIN THOMAS

ABOUT THIS GUIDE

The questions and discussion topics that follow are intended to
enhance your group's reading of SAVED IN THE CITY by
Jacquelin Thomas. We hope the novel provided an enjoyable read
for all your members.

DISCUSSION QUESTIONS

1. Patterson Haney was spiritual from the beginning but when it came to Miller Baisden, she discovered that simply believing in God was not enough when it came to temptations of the flesh. What steps should Patterson have taken to keep her virginity in tact?

2. Do you believe that Patterson's lifestyle in a small town in Georgia made her naïve to Miller's seduction? Do you agree that it could have happened regardless of where she grew up?

3. When God called her, LaRue Arnette Hawkins had a rebellious spirit because she was angry over losing her husband and best friend; she also didn't want to be a pastor. Once she allowed herself to listen to God, LaRue was able to discern His will for her life, which was coordinating the women's mentoring ministry program. Have you ever found yourself in that position? If so, what did you do?

4. Macy Baldwin believed that attending church, making generous donations, and being a good person was enough to gain her entrance into heaven. In what ways does Macy learn that she cannot earn God's forgiveness through works and what it means to be a Christian?

5. Patterson really wanted to be friends with Macy. Why do you think it was so important to her? What do you think of the way Macy responded to Patterson and LaRue? How would you have responded to her?

6. LaRue's parents weren't very supportive of her decision to model. Do you think she was modeling as a way to rebel against them? What was her true calling? What made LaRue change her mind about embracing God's call on her heart?

7. What are your thoughts on Macy's relationship with River? Do you think she truly loved him or was she after his money? Why or why not?

8. Should LaRue have tried harder to get Patterson to see what type of man Miller was? What more could she have done?

9. What effect, if any, did Patterson have on her roommates? What effect, if any, did LaRue have on Patterson and Macy? What about Macy? How did she affect her roommates? Describe their relationships with one another.

10. What prompted Macy to question her spiritual walk? When do you think she became serious about getting closer to the Lord?

11. How did Patterson feel as a Christian when she not only allowed herself to be seduced by Miller, but also when she discovered he was a married man with a baby on the way?

12. Do you believe that Reverend Whitcomb helped LaRue find her true calling? In what way?

13. Describe Macy's relationship with her parents. By the end of the story, do you believe they were on the track to becoming closer? Do you agree with the way they handled Macy in the beginning? Why or why not?

14. Patterson came to New York with big dreams. In what ways did she accomplish those dreams?

15. LaRue came to New York to escape God's call on her heart. What did she find in the Big Apple instead?

16. Macy was intent on finding a rich husband and getting even with her parents. What, if anything, happened to change her focus?